PRIMAL VENGEANCE

DAVID FRAMEL

DAVID FRAMEL'S
PRIMAL VENGEANCE

Winter 2008

Published by
BisonHurricane Publications
Houston, Texas

First Edition paperback 2008

ISBN 978-0-578-00440-2

www.davidframelbooks.com

For Mom and Dad

We must, however, acknowledge, as it seems to me,
that man with all his noble qualities...still bears in his bodily frame
the indelible stamp of his lowly origin.

- Charles Darwin

All human beings...are commingled out of good and evil.

- Robert Louis Stephenson
from *The Strange Case of Dr. Jekyll and Mr. Hyde*

People's lives – their real lives, as opposed to their simple physical
existences – begin at different times.

- Stephen King
from *The Dark Half*

Chapter 1

Considering his options, Sonny felt he had made the right decision. Getting beaten up in a bar over some drunken woman was not his idea of a perfect evening, and besides, he could surely come up with another potential companion before the night ended. It was still early, eleven-thirty, and Sonny Melton had just avoided a situation in which he too frequently found himself.

A social drinker, but far from social, Sonny spent most Friday and Saturday nights hopping from one bar to the next in and around Topeka, a drink constantly in hand, in the hopes of finding a woman with whom to end the evening. When flattery didn't work, the allure of wealth had had its advantages.

His intentions never extended beyond the single night; he had no interest in a relationship. He was on safari, and conquest was his objective. It was a game really, a personal challenge he relished every weekend. The world had always been his playground, full of toys and gadgets to occupy his lonely existence, but early in life, Sonny had discovered that having everything material failed to fill an empty hole in his chest.

Genuinely friendless and a loner since birth (his socialite parents had seen to that), he had taken that hollow pain and filled it with primeval anger and hostility, the only emotion familiar to him in a sterile, loveless childhood. What cast him to the outskirts of human interaction only fueled his fire for revenge on a cold, hateful world. He sought gratification and redemption at the expense of others--family included-- and grew to cast himself in the role of the vengeful victim, seeking to punish women especially, who, like his mother, had always met his desires with cold, calculated denials.

Finding a target among the weaker of the species, using liquor and an ever-replenished roll of Franklins, Sonny would bait, bed, and abandon his conquests and feel an ultimate superiority that lasted him through the dreaded weekdays. Keeping his lifestyle now meant paying the price at his old man's corporate offices, but Sonny was determined to maintain opulence now while ensuring his future to be full of the same. The world was a desolate wasteland for him, a place where he found no comfort, and to survive within its oppressive borders he had to act as the aggressor, ever vigilant should heartache and disappointment thunder at his emotional door. Money guaranteed his ability to stay afloat in the sea of lonesomeness while finding entertainment and a purpose in life through extravagance and female deception.

Maybe I had one too many tonight, he reflected, swerving his car onto Old U.S. 75 in quest of another drinking establishment. She had seemed an easy catch when he had first seen her propped precariously at the bar. Sonny had always found it easier to pick on a woman separate from the herd, and if their emotional stature projected fragility, so much the better.

She had accepted the drink he offered, made enough conversation to show what Sonny interpreted as interest, and then gone stone crazy.

Yelling, accusing, pushing from the bar, she awkwardly spilled to the floor along with her drink in a drunken heap. What she had done as she struggled to regain her dignity, slurring obscenities through tears of anger and probably embarrassment, was place Sonny in a difficult spot. Her tirade and rough landing had not gone unnoticed.

Sonny considered helping her up, half bending to provide a semblance of effort and concern, completely out of character, but her flailing arms and accusations made him start thinking better of it. Her purse had scattered on the dirty floor, displaying its contents like the proverbial yard sale, and she randomly grabbed objects in a vain attempt to gather her property.

"Som' bitch," she slurred through tears. "Not some slut you can talk to like that. My stuff…"

There was obviously something wrong long before Sonny had interrupted her alcohol-soaked musings, but he was definitely the subject at hand for now.

"Bastard…leave me 'lone. Get away from me."

"The hell with this," he mumbled in frustration, and much louder, "Bitch."

As he made his way for the exit, thinking things had never gotten this out of hand and could only get better, he was roughly grabbed at the shoulder and spun on his heels.

"Say, boy, where do you think you're goin'?"

Sonny had completed this involuntary turn with a look of shock and mild irritation, but as he bent his head backward to view his inquisitor, a giant under a battered cowboy hat, he fought back his initial response.

A country bar was not an uncommon hunting ground for Sonny; he had often ventured outside the city limits in search of reward. He could take out the trash anywhere, and dress the part as well, trading his sports coat and Bruno Maglis for jeans and Dockers. What he often failed to consider, though, was his inability to blend into an environment he knew nothing about. The people of trailer parks and gun racks were as unique to their lifestyles as Sonny was to his elevated status on the social pecking order. Mix a chivalric responsibility to an economic equal with a fifth of Jack Daniels and an outsider soon discovers the inner workings of the underprivileged. In one way Sonny shared a commonality with these people – they both sought to feel better about themselves and their miserable lives at the sake of others.

"Uh...I'm leaving. Bar's dead," Sonny managed with a self-preserving twist on his previous verbal desires.

"I think you're the one that's dead, boy. Whadju do to Paula?"

Sonny only understood when his giant assailant glanced to the girl in disarray only now gathering herself up, holding to the bar railing for support. What had he done to her? He laughed nervously to himself. She hadn't needed his help to look the pathetic fool.

"I bought the lady a drink. That's it," said Sonny.

"Well, listen up, city boy. You and me's goin' to step outside here to talk about how to treat a lady."

Hence Sonny's options. One, follow Mammoth outside and take his chances, or two, and this was the logical choice he had made, forget *stepping* outside. *Run* outside.

Mammoth had a few friends-of-shared-interest beginning to flank him, equally as chiseled from a mountain and yearning to expend some pent-up frustration to demonstrate superiority in one aspect of their pitiful lives.

And off Sonny had gone, slamming out the front doors with ferocity, realizing if he faltered anywhere along the way, he was dead man. Or at least brutally separated from countless teeth and consciousness. A man discovers a lot about himself when confronted with a life-or-death situation, and Sonny had found out much. He was ultimately a coward with a yellow streak a mile long, but the sense of survival had been strong. *Maybe survival of the fittest should include survival of the scaredest*, Sonny thought as he recalled bursting into the cool evening and racing across the gravel parking lot.

Sprinting toward his car, Sonny realized his pursuers were far behind, only now exploding through the bar's entrance. He imagined them standing dumbfounded only briefly, looking at each other with loss, trying to fathom a *man* turning tail and running like a child.

Sonny fumbled for his keys as he approached his cherry red '78 Porsche 911 Turbo, one of Daddy's latest means to drown his guilt in a material bath drawn time and again for his forgotten son. If Daddy were only here now to get him out of another predicament. Before reaching his car, Sonny realized that even with this much lead-time over Mammoth and Co., everything had to fall into place. The key had to go into the door immediately; the engine had to turn over without hesitation.

Luckily, everything had performed as needed – well, almost. He had avoided personal injury, though the Porsche had suffered the consequences of his abrupt exit from the Town's End Bar parking lot. As Sonny pulled out, concern over Mammoth putting a foot through his passenger door window had caused him to be a little heavy on the accelerator. Gravel spewed from the tires, which failed to gain traction. The German import swerved, caught momentarily, then careened into the back bumper of a pick-up, sending what Sonny envisioned as a deep streak along the right rear side of his previously immaculate car.

But he was away, and to Sonny the appearance of his car was minor compared to his concern for the appearance of his face. He laid on the gas for a good ten miles, getting off and on the highway, allowing the high-dollar engineering to carry him far and away from the threat of pursuit. He never left Shawnee County, effectively remaining south of Topeka and home, while trying to zero in on another possible playing field. The highway seemed rather empty for a Friday night as he throttled down before an s-curve. *Damn county, damn state, is dead. Period*, he thought. Sonny would be glad to get out someday (the lure of the east and west coasts' opportunities occupied most of his weekly eight to four office time), but the fascination and promise his father's money held for him would keep him around, at least until the old man died.

Coming out of the turn, the Porsche's headlights fell on an establishment that presented promise while the car simultaneously gave in to the damage of which Sonny was not aware. The car lurched hard to the right, and Sonny fought to keep it on the asphalt.

"What the…?"

He could hear the repetitious thud of a blown tire on the pavement, and he immediately eased up to a coast while bringing Daddy's present to the shoulder and a stop. Roughly fifty yards from the entrance to what a neon sign proclaimed as *Trigger's*, Sonny opened his door and circled the car to survey the problem.

"No, no, no," he cursed, hands on hips while he struggled for an answer to his most present of problems on what was effectively a finished night on the hunt.

He looked up and down the highway and heard the faint chaos of music and conversation coming from the rustic property ahead. Sonny had tried many things in his comfortable life that were usually reserved for household servants or the frequent blue-collar visitors to their estate. At a young age, he had sought human contact from these sordid few who, though busy in their endeavors, were at least *around* and seemed to find some time to answer his inquiries.

Over time he would simply sit watching them in silence, recognizing their frustration with his questions, while they performed their manual tasks with a precision he observed with keen interest. Cooking, gardening, repairing a clogged sink – he had tried them all after attending many sessions with the hired help, practicing his own brand of manual labor on his own, which was quite often, in and around the big property. One thing he had never witnessed first-hand, though, was how to change a tire. Whether he even had the necessary equipment to extract the damaged rear tire and replace was uncertain.

Checking the trunk in the relatively pitch black, he did find a small emergency tire, but the lack of light kept him from locating the necessary jack and other tools required to do the job.

"Man."

A final glance both north and south on the highway prolonged the inevitable – he would have to get somebody out to fix it. It was late, but he felt confident a tow truck was a call away. He had his cell phone, but information could only give him a number for specific names. There was no one he could call, no friend to retrieve him in his hour of need, as he had purposefully assured himself free of more than the most casual of acquaintances. He would have to go to the bar for information or at the least, a phonebook. Locking up the Porsche but forgetting to turn on the hazard lights, Sonny was confident, though a little apprehensive; it would be safe on the side of the highway until he returned. The thought of a night-traveling semi swallowing it whole as it came out of the ribbon of highway haunted him, but he feared pushing it to the bar would be difficult and could further complicate his situation and the car's condition.

Sonny trudged up the shoulder to the bar, feeling the night begin to chill his skin. To both sides of the highway stood a thick deciduous forest, the heavy oak and hickory having already lost their leaves in response to the season. The bare branches interlaced and spiraled into a clear sky dotted with starlight. The only sounds reverberated from the lively establishment that was his objective. His shoes shuffled on the bare asphalt concrete, their echoes bouncing off the enclosed stretch of transport and mingling with that of the patrons. From his right came a low, guttural noise--not a growl, more of a grunt. Sonny snapped his attention to the dark columns of forest, only briefly slowing his stride, which he quickly resumed. *Coyote...whitetail deer maybe.* They were common in the northeastern half of the state, along with a variety of other wildlife. Kansas was known for its vast prairies, but there was sufficient precipitation in the east to support natural woodlands, home to many species of wildlife, including the owner of the vocalization he had heard. Hands in pockets, head down, Sonny quickened his pace. He wasn't scared, just uncomfortable. After tonight's activities, it was no wonder he was a little jumpy.

The singular sound failed to repeat itself as Sonny left the highway's breakdown lane and encountered a parking lot filled with roughly three-dozen weather-beaten vehicles. A sign at the front of the lot proclaimed *Live Musi ! Ladies Drink F ee!* as it flickered with sporadic electrical assistance. The emanations he had heard from the road were as he suspected, an upbeat rock-a-billy tune with varying degrees of laughter and whoops of appreciation, overlying a steady stream of clinking bottles and droned conversation. Sonny felt relief as he weaved through the herd of duallies, four-by-fours, and the occasional mid-size rust bucket and aimed for the front door.

The familiar smells of hops, smoke, and cheap cologne hit Sonny with welcome ferocity, and patrons near the door gave him the accompanying cursory glance as he stopped and noted his surroundings. Pretty typical really. A long heavy bar dominated the entire left side of the place--its twenty odd stools completely filled as two comfortable tenders pulled drafts, keyed bottle tops, and mixed the rare fruit and liquor. The other half was home to a short riser elevating the live music as advertised. An array of tables and chairs clogged the middle of the room, allowing for a minute dance floor where a few couples two-stepped in drunken glee. A single pool table claimed the far end of the place. The look was complete, and one Sonny had seen in many variations. There was a constant theme, though, whether it was an out of the way hole like this or the classiest of cocktail bars – those participating were escaping five days of drudgery, being micromanaged and overly evaluated. No one judged your skills here. No one questioned your intentions, goals, or choices. It was an escape, a withdrawal, which was exactly why Sonny found himself in rooms like this all over the county. That, and the opportunity to humiliate a woman, of course.

Sonny headed to the nearest end of the long drink station, thinking he might seek some liquid assistance before inquiring about a tow service. An older, hardened bartender approached him.

"Sir?"

"Bourbon and Coke no ice," Sonny blurted in rhythmic response.

The old man deftly went about his business.

"A little information if you could." Sonny hoped he could avoid a long phonebook search by using a little local knowledge.

The bartender looked up from Sonny's glass, the handheld Coke dispenser completing its carbonated delivery. "Three-fifty. What else for you?"

Sonny reached for his money clip and relieved it of a five. "Keep it. I was wondering if you knew of a wrecker or tow guy that could help me out. My car's on the side of the road a few yards back with a flat tire. I'm not real familiar with the area, so I didn't know."

"Virgil's can help you. Number's on the board at the door." He pocketed the five and turned his attention to beckoning customers.

"Uh, thanks," Sonny offered as he turned to the entrance, spying a rather sizable corkboard littered with various business cards and flyers. Drink in hand, he retraced his steps and began scouring the advertiser for Virgil's. If he had needed a used car, roommate, washer and dryer, dozen eggs, or insurance, he had come to the right place. After a few seconds of searching, he spied a tow truck on a worn business card, a greasy thumbprint on its edge.

Virgil's Auto Body and Wrecker. 24-Hour Service. 785-555-1408.

Sonny reached for his cell phone and punched in the number, stepping outside to muffle the bar noise. After three rings, a voice on the other end demanded, "Virgil's. What's your problem?"

Taken back by the gruff nature in which Virgil or whoever handled the customer relations portion of the business, Sonny responded, "Yes, I have a flat tire out on 75 just south of a bar called Trigger's. I need someone to replace it."

"Flat tire. Trigger's. Okay." The man on the other end was slow, almost methodical in his conduct. "Do you have a spare?"

"Well, I'm not really sure. It's a new car, and I can't see what's in the trunk. I would think so." Sonny felt like an incompetent ass, somewhat emasculated for not knowing more about his car and what was probably a simple process.

Virgil's representative muttered, "Uh, huh…okay, fifty dollars to come out and change the tire. Twenty-five more if I have to tow it in here."

The cost of a service, with all the allure money held for Sonny, never bothered him. It was why you sought to possess it. To use it for things. The more you had, the more you could use it for.

"Fine. It's a red Porsche on the shoulder. You can't miss it. I'll be here at the bar watching for you."

"Probably be thirty minutes, Mr...."

"Melton. Sonny Melton. Good. Thank you."

He turned back to the door, confident he could finish this and another drink before the pride of Virgil's Auto Body arrived.

Twenty minutes later Sonny, warmed by the sweet brown liquid dispensed at Trigger's, walked out to the Porsche to await his savior. The night continued to cool, and Sonny could discern his breath in the evening air. Luckily, there was no wind, so a few minutes in the elements shouldn't be bad. Reaching his car, he realized turning on his emergency lights might have been a wise idea. The semis he dreaded would have valued the warning, as would have his father has he discovered his boy's new toy was a twisted piece of medal in a ditch in rural Kansas, a far cry from its roots on the Autobahn traveling at a blistering pace. He opened the driver's door and fumbled for the hazards, turning them on the same instant an eighteen-wheel nightmare plunged out of the darkness. Sonny jumped in the car completely, grabbing the door and pulling it shut as the semi-trailer truck thundered by, almost sucking the little German sports car down the highway with it.

"Judas Priest."

His father's corporate world had taught him the value of the long-hauler, their ability to keep commercial and industrial companies in business, their cost and dependability far exceeding that of rail or air, but Sonny still thought them the scourge of the American highway. They labored in traffic, keeping important people like Sonny behind schedule, and once at speed, they were hurtling rockets of mass destruction, far too heavy to come to an immediate stop.

Debating whether to remain in the car or stand outside (the former proving to be much more agreeable as he warmed to the car's interior), Sonny felt a compulsion to open the trunk as well, in case Virgie boy mistook his Porsche for one of countless red German imports to be on the side of the road in Backwater, Kansas. To be safe, he exited the car and unlocked the trunk.

From the density of the trees came the low grunting noise again. Sonny froze. It was stronger this time…and closer. His mind rifled through the possibilities of animal that could possess that vocal call – raccoon? Wild pig? Bear? *For God's sake, it wasn't a bear. He'd heard of deer, coyotes, foxes, and the rare bobcat. Even buffalo. The area was full of birds. This didn't sound like any of those.*

Again, the sound…deep…pushed air through a strong throat. It sounded big. Menacing.

Sonny's heart skipped, and then lodged somewhere high in his throat.

He put his keys back in his pocket and stood perfectly still, steering his body and auditory focus to the forest of trees before him, trying to fix his eyes on any movement in the vast nothingness of dark.

Nothing.

He shifted his weight.

Still nothing.

The air left his nose in intermittent streams of white smoke. The forest remained silent.

He gave it another minute, a solitary figure transfixed by sound on a lonely stretch of road. But there were no more sounds issuing from the dense trees, and dropping his hands in his pockets, Sonny turned to seek warmth in his car.

The impact was quick and devastating, a blow that crushed his sternum and sent Sonny twelve feet backward, where he landed hard on his back. The pain was agonizing, and in that brief instant, he thought he had been hit by one of the very trucks he had cursed earlier. But other than the moan that struggled to release itself from his mouth, the only sound he heard was someone walking briskly toward him, no truck engine, and no brakes to signal an accident.

Whoever he heard was upon him, raining blows, pulling tearing, slashing at his body. Sonny suffered in fear and confusion, unable to fight back or cry for help. And now his attacker was grabbing his neck and lifting him off the ground, where he hung struggling to breath. His mind was dazed; his eyes swam in tears of pain. His limbs flailed sporadically, finding purchase with nothing. He was airborne again, tumbling head over heels to the rough asphalt near his car. The collision with the road sent flares of piercing agony through his body.

He tried to yell, but the air that had flowed freely from him just moments ago now found entrance difficult. Blood ran from his mouth and scalp, quickly pooling at his head.

His assailant was on him again, his crushing grip sending rivers of pain through Sonny's decimated body that jerked with involuntary reaction. Through the blood and tears, he could only see a shape, dark and Herculean, surrounded in a red heat of Sonny's agony. His chest felt cavernous as he fought to breath, and he was unable to offer any resistance.

There was no end to the destruction taking place on and within Sonny's body. His clothes clung blood-soaked and shredded to broken limbs and ruined torso.

Somewhere deep in Sonny's fading awareness he could now hear the low grunts issuing forth from the woods again, but now here, above him, from his assaulter. They grew in volume and length, and soon resembled rage.

He was nearing unconsciousness, a place free of the searing pain that ravaged his now deformed frame, and he welcomed it. Steel fingers enveloped his throat and he was free of the ground once more; his body hung limply like a puppet awaiting its master's strings.

Sonny's passion was nearing its end.

Following a final primitive shriek, his neck was snapped effortlessly. Mercifully.

The drone of drunken camaraderie continued to flow from the bar.

Chapter 2

The death of Sonny Melton drew little attention on the evening news, an afterthought running on the heels of word that China was expecting more unrest from hostile youth factions and the crash of yet another commercial airliner, this one a Boeing DC-10 going down in a residential section of New Hampshire. Melton's death was reported along with the daily menu of tragedies and worldly evils befitting sensationalized news. A local man found dead. The reason it had gained coverage at all, though, was not because of the nature of the crime (the media was unaware of the circumstances) but due to the economic and political power and notoriety of the Melton name.

Residents of Shawnee County wholly, and Kansans in the eastern half of the state for the most part, knew of T.W. Melton and his vast empire of holdings. With corporate offices in Topeka, a short 40-minute drive from Kansas City, Melton was able to wield heavy influence in a state capitol rich in small town tradition. Melton Properties held interest in roughly sixty percent of Topeka alone, with investments as far west as Salina and south to Wichita. Thomas William "Billy" Melton, self-made and self-glorified, the local boy made good, surveyed his kingdom from the twenty-second floor (his favorite number from football days at the college academy) of the Melton Building, a tower of indulgence symbolizing Billy's rise to wealth and place in the heavens. His only child, Thomas W. "Sonny" Melton Jr., had been in and out of trouble with authorities since an early age. Topekans with their ears to the ground kept abreast of his exploits and Billy's subsequent rescues of his son for years, but recent talk had placed Sonny at the right hand of his father, apparently grooming him for succession to the throne.

The body had been discovered some fifteen miles southwest of Topeka just outside the town of Auburn, a small township of barely 1000. Made up of farmers, truck drivers, mechanics, and administrative support workers, Auburn thrived below every state average, including property values and educational levels of its residents. But survive it did, offering locals a simple life within distance of metropolitan opportunity. The population fluctuated with minimal gains, as some ventured to Topeka and the allure of the big city while others returned to the rural charm it held. Crime was unknown, with no murders, rapes, robberies, or assaults occurring in years. A few petty thefts had been the only matters of law and order for the Auburn Sheriff's Department in quite a while, so the discovery of Sonny Melton in Auburn's jurisdiction had signaled worry for many in the tight-knit community.

Sheriff Ran Price sat across from the portable television in his somewhat portable office in the sheriff's department.

"...reported the body of twenty-five year old Thomas Melton Jr. was found late this morning in a field three miles west of Auburn. Authorities have not released the cause of death nor have they revealed any information regarding police investigation of the matter. Melton was the son of Topeka developer T.W. Melton, who reported his son missing three days ago. KSTV spoke with..."

Price shifted his feet, positioned comfortably on his empty desk, and knocked back the rest of his coffee. Ran Price had been sheriff in Auburn for three years, and he had to laugh to himself often about the title affixed to the front of his name. With a staff of two deputies, one part-time, Price felt more like a child playing cops and robbers with neighborhood friends then he did a real police officer. But that was his position, and he had taken the job as a last ditch effort to remain in law enforcement, a seemingly impossible task after Los Angeles.

The small town setting was pleasant enough, the pay reasonable considering the little he had to do in this law-abiding environment, but it had done nothing to curve his appetite, his desire to *work--to do real police work.* His need to interrogate, stake out, and bust were the things being a policeman were built around. In Auburn he was lucky to have a disorderly conduct. Even traffic tickets were minimal.

The call regarding the Melton discovery had shocked him at first--him, a veteran of one of the most crime-riddled cities in America. Death had been his constant companion in LA, delivering him a daily dose of investigation and detective work. An event of this magnitude should have charged his drained battery; death bringing forth life. But he had been out of the game too long. It was another time, and another Ran Price. To some degree he feared the impending inquiry; it signaled the opening of old wounds. Auburn had been good for Price for two reasons: he was still a police officer, but more importantly, he was free of the human carnage that fifteen years of work on the LA homicide unit had exposed him to. Here he saw compassion and basic respect. Blood in a truck bed was that of a ten-point buck, not a Latino gang member's. A crying little girl was distraught over her missing puppy, not because her mother's boyfriend had shot the only parent she had ever known right before her eyes. The Grim Reaper in his black-hooded gown limited his visits in the Midwest to elder men with lung cancer or retired librarians in their sleep. There was no bloodshed here.

Until Sonny Melton.

That old familiar adrenaline was beginning to coarse through Ran's veins.

When the news ended, Ran gathered his thoughts and turned his attention back to the ever-growing file on the Melton case. The phone rang as he reached to turn off the television.

""Hello, Sheriff's Office. Sheriff Price speaking."

"Shouldn't you be out checking for tire marks or something? What do they pay you for?"

It was Glen Dobbs at the *Trib*. When Ran had taken the job in Auburn, Dobbs's paper, *The Topeka Tribune*, had run a piece on him--West Coast big shot detective takes on jaywalkers in rural plain's state type thing. It had been favorable and not taken any cheap shots. Ran liked Dobbs, though his time in LA had helped him to grow to hate Dobbs' profession. The California media was as lost as its government, in Ran's humble opinion--a detriment to the people and their well-being. He and the LA police force had had enough to contend with, and the politically-driven media and their twist on the news only magnified their mistakes. Glen Dobbs was an exception--impartial, fair, thorough--the kind of proper reporting Ran likened to police work.

"Yeah, I really do, but I just can't seem to put down this feature of yours on the plight of the Kansas prairie beetle. Riveting."

"And we tax payers don't pay you to be funny either, thank goodness. Do you have any new developments for me worth mentioning in the morning edition?"

Of the few civilians Ran would want to talk to about the Melton murder, it would be Glen Dobbs, but he couldn't go too deep in their findings just yet.

"Nothing new, Glen. We're still trying to piece some things together."

"Anything from the lab boys or the coroner?" Dobbs tried. He was hardnosed to an extent, but his friendship with Price kept him at bay. Dobbs knew Ran's job came with restrictions (for all the right reasons), but he was also aware that the Sheriff would give him whatever he could.

"Now you know I'm not going to get any of that until late tomorrow." That was true. Ran had confirmed with state investigators that lab information would take at least twenty-four hours minimum, and he knew autopsies were never rushed. Had Auburn the necessary tools in their own backyard, Dobbs could have more to his story, but things didn't operate that way in rural areas. Small town law enforcement turned to city or state police for assistance, who in turn put those problems on hold until their own questions were answered. The only reason Ran could expect timely results was the nature of the crime and the victim's family ties.

The delay did not bother Ran, though, who was familiar with the investigative process. He understood the reasoning because he had been a part of it, especially the patronizing of small town departments. Unjustly, metropolitan law enforcement often treated small police and sheriff's organizations like illiterate stepchildren. The assumption that they were unfamiliar with the system because of their size and location was ludicrous. It had allowed him to understand for himself the difference between ignorance and stupidity. Rural law was ignorant of various procedures and techniques because they were without the proper equipment and facilities. To think they were anything else was an act of stupidity.

"Off the record: how is your investigation going? Are things falling into place or is your big city prowess going to be called upon for a change?"

"Glen, you're going to have to be patient on this one. Things are sticky right now, and I don't want to issue statements that unnecessarily worry the good people of Auburn. Suffice it to say you need to trust me on this one. I'll get things to you as I can."

Dobbs mused, "Ran, you give me what you can *when* you can."

"Just tell your readers to stay tuned. We'll have something for them in good time."

"That type of writing doesn't make news or sell papers," Dobbs chuckled, "but I guess for now it will have to do."

"Glen," Ran said," thanks."

"Oh, Mr. LA detective is showing respect for the media. Now there's a story."

Hanging up the phone, Ran had not wanted to avoid the issue, but it was as far as he could go in the domain of the public's right to know. He had to be honest with himself and Dobbs; he had no answers and didn't know what happened-not really. There was more than what he had told Dobbs, but it was all circumstantial and sketchy.

In front of him remained open the reports he and Monk had compiled last night. Monk Collins was Ran's deputy and closest friend in town (in or out of town in truth), a place not known for its red carpet treatment of strangers, and especially from all places, California. None of the information had made sense then, and as Ran thumbed dejectedly through the notes, he saw it was still an enigma.

What had happened to Sonny Melton?

Ran had seen the physical results of that question, results that had caused most of his day's meal to try to back out the way it had gone in. He had seen crime scenes before that had sickened him, but this had been different. Maybe it was the town, the people, and the general atmosphere of Auburn. Melton's death didn't belong. It scarred the otherwise pleasant landscape that was this small community.

Whatever it was, it had horrified him. The image of the body still invaded his thoughts. It could easily have been a New York crime, a California crime. It was out of place. Maybe that was it. Things take on a darker significance when they are sudden, unexpected, or just don't fit into the normal patterns of daily life. Funny how the unpredictable human factor preferred order in a world that could be called nothing less than out of control.

Ran scanned the pages multiple times, but knew there were no knew clues, no bits of information he had overlooked.

He and Monk had arrived on the scene some twenty minutes after the call had come in about the body's discovery. A young couple, unable to give their hormones a rest in Ran's summation, had come upon the body in a moonlit field just west of Indian Hills Road near the Kansas Turnpike. At first they thought it was the remains of a deer, dumped after butchering. Local hunters rarely saw the harm in the dumping of a dead carcass, and more than once, Ran had had to assist farmers and ranchers in the area in the disposal of the gutted animals. The title of sheriff came with a variety of duties in Auburn, dead animal disposal among them. The teenagers soon recognized that deer don't wear shoes and had raced themselves to a phone to contact the authorities. Ran was off duty that night, but nevertheless was immediately called.

"Ran, we've got a problem."

"Monk? What time is it? What's the matter?"

Ran had been asleep, a state that had not come easily for him in the last few years. He was awake enough to register the alarm in Monk's voice and knew only something important would cause his deputy to make a call this late.

"A body was just found off Indian Hills by some kids. They sounded pretty shaken. I thought you'd want to check it out with me."

It never took Ran long to come fully awake--years of police work had conditioned him to shake off the remnants of sleep. This news bolted him upright in bed.

"Pick me up."

Ran's home was a modest two-bedroom on the south end of town, one he had rented sine his arrival. Never sure he could adjust to the slow pace of Auburn, he had balked repeatedly over the idea of buying a place. But now three years later, the rental felt comfortable, and he was remiss to let it go. They could save time if Monk got him on the way as he was relatively between the station and the location of the discovery.

Dressing hurriedly (repetition of this very instance had taught him to always have clothes at the ready), Ran mulled over the thought of a body being found in Auburn. It was unprecedented, at least during Ran's employment. Reasons and scenarios flooded his mind, and as he looked back now, his impulse, now seemingly the best bet, had been murder.

Monk pulled up to Ran's house in one of the three cruisers comprising the Auburn Sheriff's Department fleet. A second sat in the driveway, Ran's personal Ford Crown Vic, white with blue trim. The third member of the auto pool sat inoperable at Jayhawker Auto in Wakarusa, a terminal patient in need of retirement. The budget demanded it be patched up instead of replaced. As Ran got in the cruiser, he noticed Monk was anxious, a little edgy but under control.

"What do you think, Ran? A drifter maybe?"

"Let's not make any judgments until we've seen the body, if that is even what we have. Have you contacted the County Medical Examiner?"

"Not yet," Monk hesitated. "I wasn't sure what I needed to do other than call you. Hell, Ran, a dead body! What are we doing with a body out here?"

"Relax. You did the right thing. I don't want half the county over here until we are sure of what we have. Let's just get over there and assess the situation."

Ran often felt he was alone when working with the likes of Monk Collins, who had very little experience in police work. But his good nature, dependability, and eagerness to learn made Monk enjoyable to have around. Ran figured he could show Monk the ropes. Better to have a man under you whom you trained instead of one with bad habits picked up elsewhere.

"Where exactly on Indian Hills?" Ran queried his deputy.

"You know Luke Robertson, right? The kid from the high school. All-everything athlete?"

If you lived in Auburn without reading the paper or ever coming in contact with fellow residents, you might not know the name of Luke Robertson. Ran knew the boy, had even answered some of his questions about California colleges. The kid was a natural, a sure bet to land a scholarship somewhere.

"Well, he called the station around 12:15. Claimed he and Deirdre Alston were parked on the side of the rode, you know, parking, just south of the Dunham place, when they get this idea that they are going to walk through the field."

"What do you indigenous types call that around here? Sowing your oats?" Ran quipped.

"I'm not any type of Indian, Ran. And I don't think they are either. Luke may have a little Cherokee in him. His daddy used to say…."

Ran nodded his head, "So they went into the field and…?"

"And they saw this shape on the ground. Scared Deirdre. Luke got a closer look, and that's when he saw hands and a foot. He sounded out of breath. Must have run all the way back to the car."

"You know these kids pretty well, Monk. Could it be a prank? Could someone have thrown a mannequin out in the field to scare a hunter?" Ran was not totally convinced.

The deputy shook his head as Ran asked his questions.

"These are good kids, Ran. Solid families. And Luke wouldn't jeopardize his future on a prank." Monk sounded convinced. "Blood. He could see blood. No, it's a body for sure."

They were at the location of the reported discovery within five minutes. Ran had made hundreds of these same trips, at all hours of the night, and if his years of experience had taught him anything, you weren't always out to the site of some atrocity. Here, it was a new experience, and he couldn't dismiss this town as free from the evils that preyed upon the rest of the world. True, Auburn had flown below the radar for most of its existence. Residents were hard-working, God-fearing, and practiced tougher than tough love. Not that they enjoyed an absolutely pristine history. They liked a few cold ones on Friday nights, and Auburn had seen its share of scandal, as have all small towns, though minor in comparison. Vic Peck had embezzled from the First National, Irene Dunne had run off with some young stranger, leaving a husband and four kids behind, and Wally Rivers had lost his job with a Topeka construction company because he drank too much. A murder seemed out of place, but then again, for Ran it was a natural progression.

Monk brought the car to a halt in the gravel on the shoulder of the two-lane road. A young couple stood just ahead of them near a Dodge pick-up, arms around each other, blending in the relative dark of the night. Neither had a jacket, and the night chilled Ran's bones as it always did as he stepped from the cruiser. *Never get the California weather out of my bones*, he thought.

"Hello, Luke. Deirdre, is it? Are you kids all right?" Ran asked.

"Hey, Chief Price. Yes, were fine. Deirdre's just a little shaken." The boy was solid, all of six-four, and his massive frame smothered the tiny frame of his girlfriend.

"Well, let's see if we can't get you out of here just as quickly as possible."

One thing Ran had acquired from his surroundings during his time in Auburn was an ease in his dealings with the public. In LA everything was fast-paced, his charges always in a hurry. A laidback approach was the only thing conducive to productive relationships in Auburn; Ran had found that out early on. His supercharged mentality would be disliked and distrusted here.

As always, Ran allowed his deputy to handle transcription of witness information. Not only was it good training for him, but Ran hated the paperwork aspect of police work.

"After Deputy Collins takes your statements, he'll call your folks and let them know you are headed home." *Folks*. He certainly was making strides.

From somewhere deep in Luke's high school sweatshirt came a tiny voice.

"We don't have to go back out, do we?"

Ran understood her fear. "No, no, Deirdre. You can stay right here with Luke. Just answer the deputy's questions, and Luke, can you point the direction of the body you saw?"

Luke was quick to respond, pointing with his left arm while the right remained tightly wound around his diminutive companion.

"It's about a hundred yards straight out, just past the first tractor path."

Ran had brought the heavy-duty flashlight from the squad car, its metal casing already cooling to the night air. After verifying with Monk the procedure required, he stepped off the road into the shallow ditch that lead to the vast pasture. The barbed-wire fence enclosing the property was not newly strung but still offered a bit of resistance to Ran as he pushed down on the middle length of metal and swung first his right leg, body, then left leg through.

The ground, hard and unyielding, had obviously not been worked that spring. A few tufts of Indian paintbrush and scattered weed growth were the only visible evidence that the field was not totally empty. Why the kids had come out here was beyond his understanding, but he had been young once, and impulsivity was the name of the game as a teenager. Ran continued forward in a rounded, slightly zigzagging pattern, figuring a straight path into the remote area would have been difficult without a point of reference.

After what looked like a football field of distance between himself and the cruiser lights back on Indian Hills, Ran cast his flashlight beam in a three hundred and sixty degree survey of the area. Ridges of forgotten tilled soil mounded in simulation of a lying body, but as Ran focused on each potential rise in the terrain, nothing caught his eye.

Nothing.

Ran walked further, the light sweeping the earth in search of the object of Deirdre's mild shock. He turned south for a few yards and then back north. The mystery was not revealing itself. Auburn's sheriff stood puzzled, adjusting his holster with thumb and forefinger as he pondered his recourse. Resigned to have the boy lead him back out here at the expense of his girlfriend's ease, Ran took one last look straight ahead, advancing another twenty yards before turning to go.

There, some fifty more feet away, he saw it. Just a dark shadow breaking the steady horizon. He walked toward the spot, feeling for the first time since arriving at the location a sense of foreboding. The dark hump took on more definition as Ran got closer, but in the moonlight he felt even if he were right on top of it, he would have trouble deciphering anything clearly.

Ran stopped within a few feet of the form, surprisingly reluctant to shine his light on what lay before him. It wasn't a matter of fear; he had seen an undertaker's share of corpses. Ran knew that if his light exposed a body, one that was the object of an unnatural demise, then Auburn would no longer be a haven of sanctity. Death of this nature would be a profane visitor, unwelcome and unwanted. The town, its history, forever tainted.

A familiar odor began to invade his nostrils, and before the flashlight revealed Ran's suspicion, he knew a human body shared this piece of ground with him. Death hung determinedly in the still air, and what the night sky had failed to fully reveal, the Surefire LED presented in shark contrast.

After twenty years in law enforcement, homicide the majority of that, Auburn Sheriff Ran Price stood transfixed, staring at a sight he had never seen before. He put his hand to his face and drew it down to his chin. The need to look away was tremendous. The urge to scream stifled only by his hand over his mouth. There was no great detail, nothing ordered to the form, but of one thing he could be initially certain: it was a human body--originally.

Chapter 3

The aftermath was always the same for Caine: two solid days of complete exhaustion.

Closed up in the house, shutters drawn, lights out, he would collapse, unresponsive and lethargic. The first twenty-four hours were occupied fully by sleep, an empty, stark rest during which his body rarely changed position and his mind seemingly refused to entertain a memorable dreamscape. If he stirred, it was involuntary jerks and starts, his musculature tensing and calming through recovery, the tableau of his face intermittently altered with spasmodic ticks. For Caine it was an extreme anabolic state, as organs, nerves, and body processes rejuvenated at an alarming rate. Cells and tissues reconstructed themselves. His breathing slowed, blood pressure dropped, and metabolic rates eased. It was functionally a state of hibernation, but in this instance, he was not passing the time in stagnation. Growth hormone surged through the various systems, rebuilding the damage, renewing the expended. Uncharacteristic of an organism in dormancy, Caine did not enjoy the capability of arousal during this sleep-like period; a balance between rest and wakefulness was nonexistent. It was a dangerous time for him; exposed to potentially harmful situations, he was vulnerable and this Achilles heel could bring to a conclusion his unique essence. His only recourse had been to fashion his conventional life as a cocoon, impervious to society's frequent invasions.

The second day involved little activity, though it was semi-wakeful. During these spurts of consciousness, he began the nutritional process, recharging his batteries with massive amounts of proteins, carbohydrates, and gallons of water, and even then he was prone to sit, his muscles still weary from exertion. Caine had lived this reality for years, never sure when he would be overcome, but innately aware of the need to heal. His life had been effectively shaped around the rage. Careful planning and preparation allowed him to exist among others without jeopardizing his freedom. Over the years he had grown more and more tolerant of the transformation that afflicted him, though his comprehension of its evolution continued to elude him.

Day Three found him alert and still ravenously hungry. Replenishing would continue into the evening. He would shower and dress, moving his recently discarded clothes to a large burn barrel, and handle any business obligations that had arisen, all while inhaling red meat, raw vegetables, fruit, and sports drinks. It was a repetitious exercise he completed with only cursory regard; the time between episodes was shortening and his intimacy with recovery was only fortified as a result.

Caine grabbed the remote and flipped on the television, hoping to catch a bit of news that might spark some memory through bites of packaged deli meats and long draughts of fluids. Though a newspaper would more quickly give him immediate insight into his exploits, he had never subscribed to one in fear that a few days worth of thrown papers lying untouched on the driveway could raise suspicion, even in the rustic setting he had chosen to live, remote and private. The nearest home was a mile to his south, so here he could avoid the untimely visits of solicitors and the bothersome drop-ins of neighbors while still receiving all the creature comforts county services had to provide, especially phone lines, the life blood of his income. It was through these lines that Caine operated his computers, three to be exact, and his business. Remote computer repair was a thriving industry, the market place spilling over with amateur operators (usually residential) who couldn't solve the frequent problems that slowed or shutdown their systems. The obsession of the country (the world, for that matter) had become the computer--surfing the Internet, communicating long distance with family and friends at a cost far less than telephone companies could compete, or simply making grocery lists. The public had grown to need its computers, and remote repair was a timesaving, cost-effective deliverance from drop off or in-home servicing. Working out of his house, accessing computers all over North America, was a perfect scenario for Sebastian Caine, a comfortable living that ensured the concealment of his disparity. Here he could configure and assist, install new software, and solve all the glitches prone to the technology without being attached to the demands of regular hours and an expectant employer.

After a brief recap of the weather, national and local news followed. Caine never stopped marveling over man's fascination with death and destruction. He could count on the media to deliver the information he sought in a large part because the public liked to see that someone else had it worse, that it wasn't they that had died in a three-car pile up or been stabbed in a car-jacking. They could go back to their boring jobs, floundering in their unhappy, unexciting lives, living paycheck to paycheck, knowing it could be worse. A little gratification before putting their head on their pillow at night. Not that John Q. would ever, ever admit to relishing in others' misery. The contentment was an inward reflection that eased the soul, breathed life into the mundane, and offered a flicker of relief. For Caine the broadcasts were far more esoteric. In the news he sought answers, a piece of the puzzle he was destined to try to link after each occurrence, though was forever unable to put completely together. What the stories he related to did offer was a glimpse into the darkness where only single frames of memory had been stored for him. Ultimately, he could gather only a cloudy confabulation.

Heartache followed misery in the reports while Caine occupied himself with the computers, firing them up for perusal. When the brief synopsis about the death of Sonny Melton first passed the anchorman's lips, Caine perked up to the subject matter. The body had been discovered just last night near Auburn, a small town southwest of Topeka, and for Caine, a location closer to home than he had ever remembered. One thing he had relied on in the past was proximity--for whatever reason, he, unconsciously, or the rage in its subtle mastery of his *black period*, guaranteed himself a twenty-five mile buffer zone, a circle of both distance and deniability, a cushion of ignorance. By what means he acquired his locations was unknown to him; how he returned from them he had a faint idea, but one thing with which he had been able to satisfy his lack of knowledge was knowing that events that occurred following the advent of the rage were played out far from the world he had created here. He hoped this nearness would be a one-time thing or his relocation would be necessary. Though leaving was inevitable, finding a new dwelling that met all his needs was tiresome, and he had hardly made use of this latest domain. He would go if he had to, continue his nomadic subsistence, but it had been so recent since his last pilgrimage.

The Auburn sheriff was interviewed, though his closely-guarded answers did little to tell Caine whether the authorities were on to him. Their performances in the past had been fruitless, and he doubted that some one-horse town sheriff would be any better at finding the truth.

He turned his attention elsewhere once the news story evolved into a history of the victim's father and the son's role in the empire he was to inherit. Caine, desensitized by now to the human loss that resulted from the rage, could only concern himself with his survival. There was no more room for regret or empathy; he had cycled through all the emotions, all the while clinging desperately to sanity and secrecy. Having made it to the other side by relinquishing his own free will and allowing acceptance to replace denial, his life was once again balanced. It was what it was. By learning to live with who and what he had become, Caine soon considered that what he thought was an affliction was actually a superior trait. He was unique, a highly advanced product of humanity's future. Fighting the change had been only natural, but it was very clear to him now.

Caine was an absolute power.

Chapter 4

With little else to do until the medical examiner's report was completed, Ran left the office to give his mind a rest from the events which had taken place over the course of the last few days. Polly, the department's dispatcher, would just have to manage things alone, Monk was due in later, and surely the normal serenity the town was known for had returned to its place of prominence.

"If you have any problems, and make sure it's a real problem, I'll be at the house. Otherwise, just take a message and I'll get back to them," he instructed her as he passed her orderly workplace on the way to the door.

"Aye, aye, Sheriff. And shall I swab the deck, hoist the jib, ready the boom?"

Polly Sheridan was the model of efficiency, a fifty-something, twice-married ball of fire whom Ran depended on unconditionally, without necessarily letting on to the fact. The department had flourished under her rule prior to Ran's arrival, and he was certain it would continue to prosper long after he had retired his badge.

Her sarcasm was quick; her concern for those close to her quicker. He had been hesitant about taking the position in Auburn, had spent many lonely nights longing for the hustle and sights of LA, but friendships like Polly's had made the move bearable. Granted, he was still alone.

"You can swab all the booms or decks you want, just make sure Monk doesn't burn the place down until you leave."

Polly handled incoming calls from midday until early evening, crossing over into Monk's shift. A number of part-time deputies and dispatchers filled in during the interim, instructed to redirect all major crises to the sheriff. Ran was the only one who operated on a regular schedule, though his phone and service were accessible twenty-four hours a day. On days he had taken time off, driven into Topeka or simply taken care of obligations around the house, he had eventually succumbed to boredom and called in, verifying his presence wasn't needed. It never was, which made the late night call from Monk earlier so unique.

"Sheriff, what if Mr. Melton calls again?"

"Just tell Billy Melton to go to…to wait until he hears from me," Ran said rather forcefully, then regretted his abrupt response.

He had heard about all he wanted to hear from Billy Melton in regard to his department's lack of efficiency in handling his son's case. What else was he to do? The crime scene had been covered with a fine-toothed comb, potential witnesses questioned. There was simply nothing left to do until the body and lab results were processed. Given that information, Ran could then begin trying to piece together the events leading up to the boy's death in earnest. It wasn't that Ran lacked compassion for Melton's loss, but the man was acting as if his prominence and social standing afforded him some special treatment. That was just not going to be the case in Ran Price's department. By the book, as it had been in LA. It wasn't like he had a huge crime lab or a large staff to assign to the investigation. The state's investigative bureau was stretched thin, and Ran knew he couldn't expect their on-site assistance until all the information was in. He had done what he could for now; the crucial facts were yet to be added to the pot.

"Sorry, Pol. I would like some answers myself. Between Melton and Dobbs and every passer-by who watches enough CSI to fill a DVR, I am tired of the questions. They just don't understand these things take time."

Polly smiled, "I'll appease him and the rest. Now go on home and get some sleep. Waiting around this mausoleum is only going to make you pack your car and head west."

Ran had really grown to appreciate his chief dispatcher. "Thanks, Polly."

"Hey, part of my job description."

Ran stepped out into the clear evening, hands on hips, stretching his rigid back in the failing light. His patrol car sat in a small parking space at the side of the building. The township had no courthouse, and the brick structure he had just departed was the dilapidated home of two other public service departments, water and electric. His portion of the space allowed for a small office, an open reception area where Polly steered the ship along with two other desks, and jail space for three, though Auburn had never needed more than one at any given time.

Auburn's former mayor (a position held in rotation among its council members for terms of one year), a no-nonsense legacy of generations past, had let him know in no uncertain terms when he has taken the position of sheriff that the budget was tight. That could have meant anything, but to someone fresh from a stint in one of the country's largest cities, it was an understatement. Ran had tried unsuccessfully for years to update the equipment with which he had to work, but it had been to no avail. A couple computers and no access to federal crime records (the expense could not be justified) left him in the dark. The twist was that in a town where very little crime happened, the need for moving Auburn into the twenty-first century regarding law enforcement wasn't necessary, as he had been told time and again. Well, they sure could use some things now. Even something as simple as crime scene tape was missed in this investigation. He had had Monk hammer rebar and run florescent rope from Bailey's Hardware around the perimeter of the area where Melton had been found. The state medical examiner's expression upon seeing the makeshift barrier had sent waves of embarrassment through Ran's flushed face. Maybe he should let Billy Melton know that his investigation into his son's death was being hampered by his lack of proper investigative tools. He could then go bug the city councilors for a while.

The quiet of the evening did nothing to still Ran's thoughts as climbed into the cruiser and headed home. He knew living close to work would keep him there more than was really necessary, but he had come to Auburn with a willingness to fit in, to be a part of the town and its day-to-day activities. Had he still been in contact with any of the detectives who worked with him in the Operations–West Bureau, they would not have believed him. Ran Price, the father of introversion, the man who lived on a personal island of aloofness, making friends and attending town picnics? No sir, you have the wrong guy.

But it had been the case. Difficult at first, the understanding persistence of the people he worked with and the general openness of the community in general has made the transition an easy one. He felt at home, and had he been asked what the possibilities were of such a condition existing in his life, Ran would have provided a flat denial. Today, three years later, he genuinely cared about the town and its residents and in so doing, took his job that much more seriously. He would have slept in one of the oft-empty jail cells had it been realistic.

It explained Ran's unavoidable occupation with the Melton case. If there was the slightest possibility that the people of Auburn were in danger, that this was not just an isolated incident, well, Ran couldn't allow that. Waiting for answers had been as difficult for him as it had been for the likes of Billy Melton, so until all the information was in, Ran could only pass the time recounting what they did know.

The younger Melton's car had been found exactly where a southern county tow service had been dispatched, though its owner was neither at the vehicle or in the nearby bar where it was confirmed he had made his call of distress. The scene on the highway's shoulder and northbound lane was graphic to say the least, but no bodies had accompanied the blood-splattered carnage following an extensive search in a 500-yard radius. The Shawnee County Sheriff's Office, Kansas Highway Patrol, and the Kansas State Bureau of Investigation had all arrived within a few hours of the discovery, diverting traffic on U.S. 75 and beginning the arduous process of cataloguing the scene. First suspicions of a vehicular accident, possibly a speeding eighteen-wheeler having slammed into the Porsche's driver, were soon dismissed. Though semi drivers were known to fly along the highway with its blind turns and tree-lined embankments, there were obvious indications that some type of altercation had taken place. Even if a truck had slammed into an unsuspecting Melton as he stood hailing traffic on a dark stretch of road in the early hours of the weekend, the informative features of that kind of collision were missing. There was no lengthy blood smear from a body nestled among black tire marks made as a heavy truck came to an arduous stop. Even if the unfortunate victim had been hurled into the woods by impact and carried away as incriminating evidence, what authorities found did not support that or any other scenario involving man versus machine. No, it had been a much more intimate encounter, one that left law veterans commenting on the volume of fluid and the odd presentation the crime scene had offered. Forensics teams scoured the ground, car, and nearby woods in an effort to compile as much information as possible. Past experience had shown men like Ran Price that gang fights, domestic violence, even mob slayings, whether blood was spilled with flesh or weapon, provided telltale markers to give investigators some idea of what events had unfolded. Based on the various locations of organic matter, blood pools, and patterns of blood splatter, an unholy war had taken place. Samples were taken from dozens of areas to determine blood type and hopefully the number of victims/combatants involved. Everyone had agreed that the sheer volume would suggest at least three or more men had been injured in the conflagration, but only the lab could determine that. Of course it was possible that not everyone present had contributed from his or her life stream, but it was a safe bet that there were multiple donors. Among the reports Ran had obtained (his office had remained uninvolved until Auburn had laid claim to the deceased), technicians had estimated the blood spilled along the road, shoulder, and side of the car to have been roughly five quarts, the total amount in the human body. Death usually resulted when a person hemorrhaged less than half that amount. There was no one large pool at the crime scene, which would have argued for a single victim. Human material was thirty feet in every direction from the vehicle, and even it showed signs of proximity to traumatic wounds. Shreds of red stained clothing were removed from the concrete, the congealed blood acting like glue as the tattered remnants were peeled away. What appeared on preliminary inspection to be bits of human flesh were also collected, bagged, and numbered for laboratory analysis. There was little else to be found. Surprisingly, considering the devastation that had obviously taken place, there were no complete foot or fingerprints anywhere. What they did extract was partial at best with considerable smudging. Neither the dense woods to either side of the highway nor the parking lot of the bar proved to expose clues to what had occurred. Patrons of the drinking establishment had not seen or heard anything, though the bartender and owner had identified Sonny Melton as the man who had inquired about a tow truck. Melton's whereabouts prior to his flat tire had placed him at a few drinking establishments in and around the Topeka area. One such place had been witness to a minor altercation involving Melton and the honor of a drunken woman, though the young man had apparently fled the scene before locals had made a tin can of his German import. Stories and alibis verified, there was little else to go on except crime scene photos and reports until the final lab results were out, and little if any headway had been made on the case until the body had turned up in Ran's jurisdiction.

Disappointingly, the remains of Billy Melton's son provided more questions than answers.

Almost six miles from the baffling slaughter, the corpse was little more than a ragged pile of tissue and organs. Only two limbs were still attached, and the torso and head had sustained massive butchery. Ran didn't have to be a medical examiner to know the cause of death. The body that had once housed the mind, emotions, and spirit of Sonny Melton was a ravaged husk. The skull showed signs of deadly trauma; cavernous indentations exposed the gelatinous interior. The entire rib cage was crushed, the jagged bones pointing in numerous directions and revealing a depository of ruptured viscera and rent tissue. A single arm and leg had been violently extracted from their natural sockets, the sinew hanging worthless at the joint. It appeared that there was no skeletal structure to the mass lying discarded in a field for two teenagers to happen upon during a moment of youthful exuberance. The formerly sturdy structure, centuries of development in the making as it rose from the evolutionary chaos of cellular growth and took its place as the bipedal king of the jungle, was nothing more than a balled carcass of discarded skin, connective tissue, and contractile organs. Remarkably, Sonny's identification had stayed in his shredded pants, a steadfast testament to their owner. Dental records would positively identify the body later, though the possibility that a mortician could ready Sonny for a public viewing was as credible as the cause of death being attributed to natural causes. It was the young heir--everybody connected to the case had agreed.

Ran was unable to stand over the body for too long, having returned to the location where Monk was completing his interrogation of Luke and Deirdre, his face flush, his manner disconcerting.

"Did you find anything, Sheriff?" Monk had asked, looking up from his clipboard while the teens stood transfixed in the dame position of oneness Ran had left them in.

"I've got to get on the horn and call the medical examiner," Ran mumbled as he opened the door of the cruiser and fumbled for the radio microphone.

He leaned out of the car, his expression clearly serious. "Wrap it up and send those kids home. We need to get this area completely cordoned off."

Monk was a greenhorn when it came to police procedure, but he recognized the tone in the sheriff's voice and hurried the kids to their vehicle. Later, rejoining Ran, the deputy stood motionless and expectant.

"…No, the area is not yet secure. It's me and my deputy for God's sake. I need at least six men, and we're going to have to block Indian Hills north and south. The ME is en route but probably half an hour out." Ran looked frustrated. "Yes, and try to keep this on the QT for a change. We don't need the added media flood."

Monk remained stoic; his eyes told a different story, though, darting and wrapped with lines of worry.

Ran regained a partial calm. "Monk, I need your best effort on this one, now. Are you okay?"

"I'm fine, Ran. Fine. What do I do?" Monk asked in rapid response.

"All right, I'm going to need you to take the flares out of the trunk and drop them in both directions in intervals on the road. Then call the office and tell June to contact the KHP and get them out here to help with traffic. We shouldn't expect too much this morning, but I don't want any problems," Ran explained deliberately. "Meet me out in the field with the rebar and rope when you are done. I am going to begin some preliminary examination. We're by the book on this one, deputy. No mistakes."

As Monk hurriedly gathered his props from the trunk, Ran retrieved the flashlight and headed back to the body.

Hours later, Ran pulled into his driveway within minutes of leaving the office, stretching his back a final time in the chilly dusk before heading to the front door. The house was small but adequate for the single sheriff, a two-bedroom, single bath contemporary with beige siding and a short flight of steps leading to hunter green oak door. The interior of the home spoke volumes about its resident: uncluttered, stark, simple. Ran had only acquired what he needed, what he used. A country-style camel brown sofa dominated the far half of the living room that opened from a short foyer. A functional TV stand with swivel top stood at the front window, its modest screen sat cold and reflective. A used recliner shared an end table with the couch in audience. The wood-floored hallway skirted the carpeted living area and continued to a tiled kitchen which Ran rarely visited unless it was to grab a beer from the refrigerator or start a load of laundry in the utility room that connected off the back of the house. From the kitchen the hallway continued at ninety degrees to a master bedroom to the left. The tour was completed with the lone bathroom and finally a smaller second room to the right. Here Ran stored records and personal objects he couldn't bear to leave behind in his sudden departure from California.

He collapsed in the recliner, resolute to eat or watch television. For now, he just wanted to be, without input or stimulus. It was funny how the slow-paced job of Auburn sheriff had gone through a major transition in such a short period of time. A week ago Ran would have welcomed some social injustice, anything to energize his batteries. A robbery maybe, or even the destruction of public property would have broken the dulling effects of Auburn's existence. But now he looked for a free moment of escape. The case was fresh, barely two days old, and he was already seeking escape. *Maybe I just don't have the drive anymore,* he thought. *Maybe I left it all back there with me, back there with them.*

His eyes closed as his head lay propped toward the textured ceiling, his legs providing the slightest of rocking motions as the chair conformed comfortably to his familiar frame. He drifted there for a while, his mind fixing on nothing in particular, the soft sway of the chair catching the motorized rhythm of the fan that turned methodically above him, its steady wisps of air washing his body with cooling caresses. Since moving east he had missed the familiar touch of bay breezes and circulated air. The ceiling fan was his one link to the past's pleasures.

Ran soon caught himself dozing, and more often than not, he would recline the chair where he would remain all night instead of seeking the reclusion of his bed. When he started this time, though, his thoughts immediately returned to the Melton case, and in particular, the horrific sight that had confronted him a night earlier in the field. He rose wearily from the chair and headed to the kitchen where he knew he could find some liquid release.

The phone's shrill tone broke the calming silence.

"Sheriff Price."

"Sheriff. Monk. Were you asleep?"

Ran smiled. The deputy was always one question away from a good barking from the sheriff, but he somehow avoided asking it with his dogged determination to do the right thing.

"No, Monk, no news yet from the ME or forensics. How is everything there?"

Monk sighed, "Polly just left. Jean will be in later. Thought I would make my rounds early in case you need me to look into something."

Ran thought of a puppy eager to play fetch or roll over. "Business as usual tonight, Monk. Let's not forget why we are here. Our first responsibility is to Auburn and its people. We'll evaluate the ramifications of the autopsy and lab results when we get them. For now, steady as she goes."

"You bet, Sheriff. Sheriff?"

"Yeah, Monk."

"You need to get some rest."

Ran smiled again. *I got a feeling we are all going to be missing some sleep pretty soon.*

"I'll do that, Monk. Have a good evening."

Heading back to the recliner with his beer, Ran surfed through late night programs in the hopes of finding something distracting. It proved futile. It had been this way for him his entire career, and he wondered if he would ever be able to accept the inevitable. He lived the cases he was assigned. Lived them. Whether it was an innate empathy that drove him or simple obsession, he wasn't sure.

His division partners, to his chagrin, often referred to him as Rabid Randall, a moniker he despised for its childish presentation and because he hated his full name. Had never cared for it. His father called him Ran early on in an unintentional creation of a pet name that he clung to fiercely. He had always felt his tenacity was an asset to the job, and his steady climb from beat cop to special detective had been a testament to that. Law enforcement heads identified Ran Price as an up-and-comer, a future division commander, with a sterling record and stalwart reputation. When loosed upon a case, Price was like a badger, relentless in his digging, incessant in his pursuit of answers. Tireless yet purposeful. But unlike his burrowing relation, Price was a loner, a people person by profession only. He was private, preferring to work after hours when his associates had retired for the day. It was this indefatigable trait coupled with extroversion that made Ran Price the most respected yet misunderstood homicide detective in the LA precinct. Ultimately, it meant he was treated as a rogue, a pariah that was allowed within the parameters of normal society to perform his much needed functions. Outside the job, though, it meant Price was shunned, avoided, and left to his isolated personal life.

He found himself equally divorced from humanity in Auburn, though he had made great strides to dissolve the wall of detachment and rejoin society outside his profession. People like Glen Dobbs, Monk, and Polly made his remigration that much easier. For the first time in many years, Ran saw people as friends.

And so it was here, nestled in his favorite chair, the increasingly familiar sounds of rural Kansas muffled in the twilight, where Ran and his thoughts returned to the case before him. The stark, vibrant vision of the mangled body was ever-present, a specter that floated and teased, playing off his compulsion. *What could have done that?*

The medical examiner had finally joined him, along with a number of state and county officers, at the site of the discovery some two hours after his presence was requested. Short, red-haired, a chip on his shoulder better described as a boulder, Clifford Weyland carried a small black examiner's kit that hung pendulously from his pale, elfin hand. A pressed lab coat hung loosely from his meager frame.

"Sheriff Price, is it? Weyland. Medical examiner's office. What do we have?" Professional and authoritative, Weyland looked up at Ran, his arms remaining stiff at his sides. Only his head broke the contour of his anatomy.

Ran gestured toward the body, completely immune to the attempted intimidation and ready with his own brand of interaction, "Thank you for your prompt arrival, Mr. Weyland. To answer your question, I'd say we have an eviscerated, mutilated corpse, but I'll let your professional judgment decide."

Surveying the tightly strung florescent rope that encircled the scene, Weyland had expected Barney Fife to accompany the small town flair, but he was obviously mistaken.

"Forensics has already completed a preliminary sweep of the perimeter to ground zero. We are prepping to extend the search with first light. I'll leave you to your job," Ran fired off with seasoned assurance, leaving the ME speechless, his usually stern countenance flustered.

While Weyland was left to do his initiatory inspection prior to a much-needed autopsy, Ran joined Monk and Lieutenant Tony Sartin with the Shawnee County Sheriff's Department. Sartin had made Ran's indoctrination into Midwestern law enforcement a painless one, always ready to lend an ear and provide much need schooling when Ran was at a procedural loss.

"Well, gentlemen, the ME is finally on task. We can spread out here in a minute and see what information the remaining area may hold." He looked at Monk. "Have you coordinated the sweep with our reluctant neighbor here," glancing toward Tony with a playful nod of his head.

Monk responded in a military deliverance, "All logistical considerations have been outlined, Sheriff. We are only waiting for your word."

Ran bobbed his head in both impression and mild humor, again offering Tony a fleeting look. *Logistical? We're did he get that one?* The last thing Ran wanted to do was discourage Monk's efforts to make himself a quality deputy, so he always treated Monk with professional respect. Tony saw this endearing quality in his friend Ran Price and complied with his proficient handling of his deputy.

"Very good, deputy. Tony, I appreciate the efforts."

"No problem, Ran. Do you think we are about ready? Deputy Collins has positioned us for a one hundred yard peripheral pass of the grounds."

Ran turned to Monk, "Let's get started, Deputy. Disperse your men."

As Monk marched away to perform his charge, Ran and Tony stood in casual scrutiny.

"I really appreciate the compliance, Tony. Lord knows Monk is feeling important."

Though the body laid to rest within the township of Auburn, the county had jurisdiction and could have pulled rank. Sheriff Sartin was fully aware of Ran Price's background, even the events that had led to his dismissal out west, and had no reservations allowing him to handle the investigation in its infancy. Crimes of this nature, where foul play was evident, inevitably involved more than one department anyway. At this stage all that was required was careful, efficient processing, of which Price was most capable.

Sartin smiled, "Not a problem, Ran. We are at your service."

"What is your assessment?" Ran asked.

"The body was obviously dumped, but I am at a loss as to how it got here. I'm hoping sunlight and closer scrutiny give us more to go on. As of now, I haven't noticed a sign of the body being dragged or more than one set of footprints to indicate the crime occurred here." He shook his head. "From an initial point of view, odd. Very odd."

What Sartin was referring to were circumstances Ran had been brought up to speed on only in the last hour. The discovery of Sonny Melton's wallet in a cursory processing of the body without disruption of the crime scene had given some explanation to the bloodbath on U.S. 75. Point A had yielded all indications of a violent confrontation; the body, some six miles away, demonstrated in a very graphic style the aftermath of such an event. The puzzle piece that failed to fit early in their investigation was why and how a clearly dead Sonny Melton had completed his journey of death to Point B.

"I have to believe he was loaded in a vehicle and then driven here where he was carried and tossed. My confusion is why in the open? Leaving the body at the initial location would have been less risky. The killer or killers could have been seen here, even though it is a remote stretch of road," Ran pondered.

"And why such an assault? It looks like he went through a cotton gin. If I had come upon this on the highway," Sartin pointed toward the site where Clifford Weyland was probing and peeling back, "I would think he had been hit by a car or attacked by wild animals. Maybe someone dragged him all the way here behind their vehicle."

"We can backtrack a natural course to the highway both north and south, but I don't think we are going to find any indications of the body being dragged," Ran countered. "I think our best bet is cover the area, wait on the cause of death, and see if the murder book shows us anything after the two scenes come together. But I agree with you-odd."

The sweep under Monk's delegation revealed nothing of significance. The body had occupied its resting place far too long for beaten grass to expose footprints, though a few faint impressions were photographed with the risen sun in a spot of clear earth just feet from the remains.

Weyland's early assessment of the cause of death was blood loss due to trauma, a conclusion the most unqualified could have deduced.

So, Ran found himself in a familiar holding pattern, awaiting the medical research before he could begin his own investigation in earnest. Customary didn't make it any less desirable.

The beer bottle half empty on the end table, Ran fell into a fitful, dream-filled sleep.

Chapter 5

Ran was at his desk thumbing through faxes and checking phone messages, the early morning sun dropping intermittent rays through the office's yellowing window blinds, when he got a call from KBI lab technician Hunter Wilkins. The puzzling disposal of a body in Auburn believed to be that of Sonny Melton had provided Ran with immediate access to all information pertaining to the missing person's case. Without delay, he had put his name on the notification list for all completed lab analysis, and in the process had struck up a dialogue with one Hunter Wilkins. The state bureau's forensics department had completed its examination of samples obtained during the proceedings outside Trigger's, and Wilkins, intrigued with the town sheriff's determination and concern, had promised a personal delivery versus the standard electronic dispatching of findings.

"Hunter, I appreciate the call."

"Not a problem. I have a soft spot for the underdog. State and county will be getting it this afternoon, but I thought you might want a head start. It's only preliminary. The full report, complete toxicology and chemistry will not be issued for at least two more weeks," Wilkins said.

"Considering what little I have to go on now, anything is welcome."

"Well, I don't know. After you hear this, you may want to forget I called." Wilkins sounded perplexed. "I'm not sure how much of this is going to help you or make your job that much harder. To be honest, some of it doesn't even make sense."

Ran stared out the window, his suspicions coming to bear on the technician's words. From what he had learned about the scene found on the highway, coupled with his department's own gruesome revelation, the chances of a cut and dry outcome were iffy. "What is it?"

"Sheriff, I've been at this for twelve years now, and it's the first time I've seen data like this. Very confusing, almost unthinkable."

"Seems to go hand and hand with what we have thus far," Ran said.

"Leave out the statistical qualities of the report. I can get those from the electronic transcriptions. What are we looking at here?"

Wilkins continued, "Okay. Well, let's start with the blood samples. All the blood, and I mean each of the dozens of samples we collected, was O positive. One donor."

Ran challenged, "*One* donor? But from what I read and was told there was enough blood for half a dozen individuals."

"Yes, specialists estimated the amount to be somewhere near five quarts, along with other bodily fluids typically found in a major decimation of the human body."

"So you're telling me one guy painted that roadway? You were right, Hunter…confusing."

"Only the beginning, Sheriff. The remnants of organic matter also matched with the single donor. It explains the severe blood loss, but it opens up a whole new can of worms when you consider the manner in which the tissue was separated."

Ran was beginning to understand Wilkins's initial bewilderment.

The technician advanced, "We found no evidence of a cutting or slicing of the material. Microscopic detail shows the flesh was torn away from the body. Bitten and ripped away in some instances. It is doubtful a conventional weapon was used."

"Torn and bitten? Was it an animal?"

"That brings me to my next bit of confusion," Wilkins countered. "Within some of the samples collected we found saliva. The saliva was not consistent with the victim."

"So an animal of some type. A bear? Big cat maybe?"

"Chemical analysis shows it to be human."

Ran sat shocked. The horrendous acts of violence and depravity he had witnessed in LA came rushing back to greet him. Sociopathic and ritualistic brutalities beyond his understanding had crudely accented his profession in increasing numbers in the last few decades, exposing the primitive nature of man and his ever-growing propensity for evil. Ran shuddered at the memories; the ability to desensitize himself to it was a skill he never acquired. Though he had learned over the years to carry out the steps of police work with apparent indifference (the success of a case often depended on cold, calculating reason), his emotions registered a strong attachment to the pain inflicted on victims and their families. He spent many nights unable to capture sleep, his mind dancing with images of suffering and heartrending anguish. The war to keep Ran the investigator apart from Ran the compassionate human being was one he had constantly waged in the recesses of his soul, and the ultimate loss of a particular battle had left him jobless.

"So what are you telling me?" Ran said. "Somebody chewed this guy up and left crumbs on the highway?"

"Understand, not every sample indicated saliva. It appeared in only a few. But we did find trace elements of DNA in all the blood and tissue samples consistent with the saliva. Our best guess is through transudation."

"Trans what?"

"Transudation. The release of chemicals through the pores."

"So my assailant bit and sweat all over the victim?" Ran asked.

Wilkins laughed, "In so many words. But within the specimens we extracted from the blood and tissue of the victim, we found not only urea and salt, the basic components of perspiration, but unusually high levels of hormones."

"Hormones. That could have been from the glands of the victim. I mean, his body was apparently leaking all over the place," Ran said. This was getting unnerving.

"Again, the transudation was linked directly to this second person."

Wilkins was trying to patiently explain complex chemical and biological processes to Ran who, though he was familiar with standard lab results, was a lay person nonetheless. "Hormones are generated in the endocrine glands or within a group of endocrine cells and are then transported by the bloodstream to regulate various physiological processes. Humans have around twenty different hormones, originating from the thyroid, pancreas, even the brain. These somehow made their way from the bloodstream to the sweat glands where they were released. Our boy apparently is an avid sweater."

"I'll say."

"It's not completely unheard of,' Wilkins lectured. He was obviously enjoying the opportunity to enlighten someone on biological events he had made a life's work. "In humans we have a variety of circumstances, though rare, when the body extracts fluids uncommon to normal perspiration. With hematidrosis, it's what happened to Jesus in the Bible, high levels of stress can cause you to sweat blood. Since hormone production is glandular, it is not ridiculous to find some hormonal discharge in the sweat glands. The variance was the amount of hormone production and subsequent loss."

Ran hated to ask. "How much did you detect?"

"The majority of hormone we found was adrenal: steroid and

epinephrine. Taking into account that what we found was a small part of an evacuation of hormonal elements, and that discharge, if we put into evidence the normal processes of the human body, was also a smaller part of a bigger store."

"A part of a part of a whole."

"Exactly. After microscopic review and the crunching of numbers, we determined that within the sample, the smallest part of the whole, there was enough adrenal hormone to supply ten men."

Again, Ran was temporarily lost for words. He was no scientist, but he recognized a biological inconsistency when it jumped up and bit him in the ass. Everything Hunter had told him led his mind back to the mental picture he held of the atrocity that had lain in a pasture in rural Auburn, Kansas. The victim he described could easily be that mound of human matter. And what did it take to transform a man into a ravaged, twisted shell without machine or weapon? Well, it would take a dozen men, or ten.........or one?

"Sheriff? Sheriff?"

Ran jolted from his mind trip, "Yes, here, sorry. Wow. Tell me that's the worst of it."

"For the most part. We still have some work to do with some partial prints, but for now we are awaiting the autopsy report like I am sure you are. Hopefully we can tie our findings to your body, but according to some I've talked to, that's a foregone conclusion."

"We hate to speculate, but based on identification on the victim, the condition of the body, the preliminary estimate of time of death, yeah, we're pretty sure it's our missing person," said Ran.

"You should be getting a full report end of next week, Sheriff, followed by a final summation in conjunction with the autopsy. I hope this has given you something to go on."

"Hunter, I owe you big time. Thanks for all your help. If you learn anymore, let me know."

Ran fell back in his chair with a heavy sigh. *What in hell? Enough blood to account for six men was all from one victim. The body had been dissected manually, with teeth and hand. The perpetrator was by all accounts an animal, but human, with enough hormonal activity to support a football team for a full season.*

He needed a drink.

The medical examiner's report was delayed due to a backlog of cases stemming from a rather high demand in northeastern Kansas and surrounding areas, so Ran would have to wait longer than anticipated to receive the final pieces of what had escalated into a nightmare. The awareness of forensic technology was driving the heavy workload in investigative bureau labs and county medical examiner offices throughout the country. DNA evidence, autopsies, firearms testing – the shopping list for forensic study was ballooning as physical evidence grew in importance. The Topeka office was busting at its seams, and the two years of additional forensic training for a scientist was keeping qualified personnel at a minimum.

The one positive piece of news regarding the body's identity was provided early because of the departmental and political interest in the findings. State, county, and local authorities had a hand in the investigation, and naturally, Billy Melton was holding his sword of financial influence over the heads of lawmakers in Damoclian fashion. Dental records confirmed what Ran and most of the others attached to the case knew--the life journey of Sonny Melton had ended in a semi-remote field in Auburn, Kansas, the final chapter in a brutal saga that had begun at a startling criminal scene half a dozen miles away. Newspapers were still doggedly keeping public interest alive, reporting each detail as things progressed, not only filling their newsprint pages but also the minds of residents in the normally placid localities. As ground zero, Auburn was experiencing an extra dose of concern, and with it, Ran's usually tranquil setting was alive with queries, conjectures, and amateur explanations.

Busied with daily tasks but invariably returning to his growing Melton file, Ran actually thrived in the atmosphere. He couldn't say the same for his overcome staff. Even Polly Sheridan, the essence of calm, was feeling the weight of Auburn's unrest.

"No, sir, we have not considered the body was airlifted to the field. Yes, we will look into it. Thank you for the information." Polly ended the call without her usual professional air. Ran's smile only added to her frustration.

"You're actually enjoying this, aren't you?" she accused.

Ran chuckled, "When you find out where Amelia Earhart is, let me know."

Polly turned away in mock protest. "You'd be edgy too if you were having to deal with this. The whole town has gone mad. The last time I dealt with calls this outlandish was when some rumor spread that the government was rearming the missiles in underground silos in Kansas facilities. Took two weeks for that to die down."

"I'll tell you what," Ran offered. "Direct any calls involving UFO or Bigfoot involvement to me."

"Oh, you're such the comedian. You know, I'm feeling faint. I may need to go home for the day. Who knows, it may be the two-week flu. Pretty common here. You wouldn't know about it being new and all."

Ran raised his arms in surrender, a cleansing chuck in his voice. "Okay, okay. I submit to your divine powers, Your Eminence." He dropped his hands. "I know it's a bother, but hopefully, when we start making some progress on this, it should settle down."

Polly knew the score. Even though she had been a dispatcher for what amounted to Mayberry, North Carolina, for years, she realized the importance of every lead, every call. "But Sheriff, *airlifted?* Are they serious? The idea that the victim hopped there before collapsing was more believable."

"Actually, I did call Forbes Field and KC International to see if any unauthorized flights had been reported or observed by air traffic control. Nothing. Even had Monk bring up helicopter's when he was checking with Old Man Dunham about hearing or seeing anything unusual along Indian Hills."

Polly was looking at him in disbelief.

"There was no evidence of entry or exit. If you had seen the body, you would have thought it had been caught in a propeller and fell from the sky."

"Don't share," Polly grimaced. "I don't want to know."

Ran realized for the first time, maybe because of the situation, that behind that together exterior lurked a soft-hearted woman. For all her organizational prowess and motherly command of the office, Polly was volatile to the suffering of others. It endeared her to him that much more.

"Sorry, Polly."

"Instead of regaling me with your sharp wit and stomach-turning graphics, why don't you assure me that you have this under control. I want to be able to tell these people something. Sheriff, I have known most of these people for a long time. They look to me for answers. I want to be able to tell them something comforting," Polly said.

Ran said, "I know, Pol, I know. And I would like to give them something to help them sleep at night, but we are not any closer to figuring this out than we were before. I've doubled our patrols. Monk is out most of the night, putting more miles on his cruiser than I hate to know, giving a police presence that I hope will both soothe and discourage. Three separate departments are on it, labs are compiling information. It's all we can do for now. I'm counting on the medical examiner's report to shed some light as well."

Polly was unappeased. "How much longer on that?"

"Another week."

"A week?"

"They're working overtime, Pol," Ran said. "We're not the only people with a dead body."

"I know, I know," she said, "and I shouldn't be frustrated. I guess it's the *not* knowing. I grew up in Auburn; anything that happens here is public knowledge."

Ran walked back to his office, feeling a newfound sense of guilt that he couldn't comfort Polly. He had always lived the cases, suffered an empathic response to the fears and dreads issuing from the people most affected. He recognized Auburn's innocence, its criminal chastity, and wanted to wholly deliver it from evil. At the same time he was a realist and knew through hard-fought experience that in most cases, time was all that was needed. Time to reveal; time to consider; time to heal. There was another consideration to a murder like this – one steeped in mystery and ambiguity. Discovery often required further instances. The thought had been fighting to make its way to the front of his brain, and he had forcefully denied it consideration. But the detective in him would not be nullified.

What happened could happen again, and in order to solve the riddle, they may need it to happen again.

It was one quality of homicide investigation that disgusted him.

The late afternoon brought more calls for Polly, Monk's early arrival, and thundershowers that altered the landscape, the heavy droplets pounding Ran's office window with a steady rhythm he had grown to appreciate in the late spring. It reminded him a great deal of California with its seventy-five degree highs and fifty degree lows combined with the year's heavier rainfall. Ran was encouraged by the precipitation, believing the town, the whole state, needed a refreshing cleansing. Nature's resilience would dissolve the stains of man's sinfulness and wipe clear the signs of his greed, covetousness, and propensity for wrongdoing. Noah's flood, the deluge of Gilgamesh, the waters of Zeus, all set upon the earth to erase the wickedness of man and bring about a rebirth, a fresh start.

Ran figured this storm's faucet needed to be left on a long time.

Monk stood at the doorway, his uniform smartly pressed during this very visible period for Auburn law enforcement. "Sheriff, do you have a minute."

"Sure Monk, what's up?"

The deputy, having received access, settled into a chair across from Ran's desk. "I've been thinking," Monk started, "I mean, I know we have talked to everyone, gathered all the information available, but I just thought that there has got to more that we can do outside of driving up and down the street night and day."

Ran sighed, "You too, huh?"

Monk stared at his hat, the brim tracking steadily through his thumb and forefinger as he rotated it slowly. The deputy had willed a great deal of courage to address Ran about procedure, and in turn, the sheriff respected his fortitude. Questioning was the most important trait an officer could bring to the position. If anything, Ran was an excellent teacher who led through example, but more importantly, allowed his underlings to think through their objectives. It was a proven method of facilitation, and class was in session.

"And what would you have me, *you*, do at this point?" Ran asked.

Monk's eyes remained downward. With his confidence would come the added bonus of looking a man in the eye, representative of his conviction. *One thing at a time*, thought Ran.

Monk started, "Well, I understand why I am on the streets every night. Our visibility is vital to public safety and a deterrent to future incidents."

Good.

"Everything possible has been done with potential witnesses, evidence, and the crime scene."

Better.

Monk concluded, "But why are we limited to Auburn? Why aren't we looking at the highway site, trying to make connections with our information here?

Not bad...but risky.

"Deputy," Ran encouraged, "you are right on every point, except the inspection of the highway scene. It is not within our jurisdiction, and besides, we have been given all the information pertaining to the analysis done there. One thing you learn early on, Monk, is the territorial nature of law enforcement. It's not that we don't find cooperation from other agencies. We give and receive aid whenever it is needed. The site was thoroughly examined by state, county, and forensic units. Marching our happy butts over there would only suggest distrust and doubt in their investigative abilities. I haven't been here long enough to earn that kind of reputation."

The deputy nodded, "Yeah, I didn't think of it that way. It's just that I feel so useless right now. I always thought the first real crime we had here would be a whirlwind of police work. Instead I'm chugging through town with a stern look and no answers."

"I feel you, Monk. It's a helpless position to be in, but there really is nothing more to do until the autopsy is in or we get some leads handed to us."

"What about those guys at the bar…with the drunk woman. What more is there on those three?" Monk ventured.

Ran said, "Deputy Sartin told me that in addition to the report putting them in the same bar Melton fled between the times of his call to the tow service and the truck's arrival that the three were so drunk when questioned they wouldn't have had the ability to navigate out of the parking lot let alone over to Highway 75."

"Did he have enemies, people who could have done it to him? He's related to one of the more feared men in Kansas," Monk tried.

Ran allowed the interrogation only because it gave him the opportunity to sift through the facts yet again. "Sure he had enemies. I don't know a wealthy man or his spoiled offspring who doesn't exist without the jealousy and hatred of people he leaves in his wake," Ran said. "You read the Melton interview. The guy would have needed every hand in Auburn to count the people he has screwed over, and without the slightest regret. KSBI spoke with dozens of friends, business associates, and reputed rivals who suffered due to their involvement with or challenge to T.W. Melton. Everybody checked out, though some alluded to a satisfaction in learning of his suffering. We are as far as the investigation can carry us, Monk, so for now we just secure the home front and wait. Nothing more we can do."

"All right, Sheriff. I guess you're right. I was jumping the gun there."

Ran said, "Your evaluating the available information and seeking answers. It's natural police procedure, Monk, and I commend you for it. Things will start hopping soon enough."

Monk stood and headed to the door, then turned back to Ran, looking him square in the eye. "I remember you telling me one day that the folks out in California nicknamed you Badger because you were stubborn and how you hated that." He shrugged. "I thought that was what police work meant – never giving up. See you tomorrow, Sheriff. I'm going to get an early start."

Ran watched Monk don his hat and head for the front door, giving Polly a slight wave as he stepped into the dying sunlight. He leaned back in his chair and considered everything that had just transpired. His three years in Auburn had been rejuvenating, a chance to put the past behind him and start fresh. The accelerated world he had left had asked so much of him, his drive and perseverance, the skill to extract clues and discover facts while others waited for answers to come to them. The sleepless nights plodding over reports and testimony in sometimes vain but often rewarding outcomes. Auburn was the antithesis – deliberate and gradual, where Ran had abandoned his hell bent nature and reclaimed his sanity. There was no need for hard-nosed, dogged detection. The town and its people had never needed such big city grit.

Damn.

Chapter 6

Mitch Stanton shook his head in utter amazement. Why the old man had thought this waste of time was going to benefit the company, he could not fathom. Time wasn't something you bartered, hoping to gain productivity through an unproven endeavor, when future opportunity and growth was a power lunch away.

Of all people, he figured Kellogg would know that. But here they were for three days. *Three days!* Mitch regretted the lost advantages sacrificed so he and the others could attend a group awareness-training program in Backwater, America, in an effort to strengthen their people skills and develop a team concept. Well, if anybody needed to be released from this psychoanalytical dog and pony show, it was Stanton.

On the wraparound porch at the back of the main building, temporarily free from the constant dribble issued forth from their retreat leader, he pinched a small amount of white powder and let his nose deliver the euphoric package of vitality to his lethargic brain. Within seconds his nasal membranes absorbed the fine dust, and he knew from perpetual use that he was ten minutes away from making tonight's gathering bearable. He pinched his nostrils together rhythmically between thumb and forefinger, sniffing potential residue as he completed his own brand of personal enlightenment.

The night was clear; the moon cast its pitted face across the pristine lake that lay a hundred yards before him. Evergreens stood in faded silhouette along the lake's perimeter. From inside came the intermittent laughter of fellow analysts, their required escape from the world a welcome one. He smirked at their weakness and lazy natures. It wasn't that he didn't like some of his peers; most of them were bearable, a few even worthy of his rarely-offered respect. They just failed to see the bigger picture. Instead of putting job and performance first, they fumbled away what he considered missed chances in favor of family and amusement. Not that he didn't enjoy the finer things that hefty incomes made available. Mitch bathed in his success--dressed in it, drove in it, lived in it. There was no denying his career accomplishments, and it was important to him that people recognized that he was surrounded by achievement. What bothered him was the idle nature of those he accompanied in this bastardized version of EST. He was never compelled to leisure--saw no advantage to fruitless activity. If the action wasn't creating revenue, the expense of energy upon it was a futile release. He had fashioned his life around the singular pursuit of financial gain and subsequently adorned himself with the traditional symbols of success, refusing to introduce to the mix qualities, behaviors, or individuals that would jeopardize his vision. Even sleep his considered pyrrhic; its value exceeded by its loss. For Mitch, nothing was recreational, including the cocaine. A workaholic, he derived from the coke the energy necessary to manage his ever-running internal engine, and tonight, the power to conclude what for him had been days lost in trivial self-discovery. The Stanton mechanism was purring smoothly, its cylinders firing in perfect time, delivering unlimited performance and exceptional results. No need to overhaul this standard of engineering.

Mitch walked the entire length of the terrace, allowing the drug to wash over him and remove his anxiety. The break had come none too soon, as Mitch had squirmed in his seat wondering whether he could suffer another minute of the incessant babble, his colleagues appearing to enjoy the introspective role-playing that befit their too lackluster constitutions. The Kellogg Investment Group was a huge conglomerate that delved into all aspects of financial management and securities, including real estate, personal finance, trade, shares, and equity investing. Based in Kansas City, the group had holdings in multiple markets throughout the country and a few foreign locations, and was worth billions. A finance major with experience in stock trading and diversified investment, Stanton had found his calling under the tutelage of Samuel Kellogg, a self-made broker who had turned a few wise investments into the megastructure that was KIG. Kellogg's young apprentice had demonstrated a propensity for investment-specific technological progress, steering KIG capital into developing technologies that promise far-reaching dividends. Recognition of future progress in both equipment and structure guaranteed remarkable returns on KIG investment, and Stanton had a knack for identifying the potential market impact of new technology. It required a vast network of contacts, both economic and governmental, and though the legality of his procurement of information differed from one investment to the other, he had made himself and KIG a great deal of money. He would have thought his honored position at the right hand of Fortune 500's top-ten investor would have excluded him from the banal activities taking place that weekend at the Lake of the Forest just west of Kansas City, but he had been wrong.

"Mr. Kellogg. I really have more on my plate than can be set aside for a camping trip," he had complained.

"It's no camping trip, and I think it will do you good. A little mind and body overhaul is just what you need," said Kellogg.

"But I don't see...."

"The director of the program assured me that management would come away feeling fresh and alive. Invigorated, he said. The job will be here when you get back. Take some time. Relax. Who knows, you may learn something about yourself."

Take some time. Relax. Learn something. He couldn't relax wasting time, and all he had learned was group awareness seminars were a load of crap. In his professional estimation, a poor investment.

He gave his nose a final wipe to remove any conspicuous residue and reentered the brightly lit grand room.

"...but it didn't take him long to figure out which foot to use."

"Without the interest history, I had to pass."

The group had already gathered in their seats, little pockets of conversation well underway, while their discussion leader, John Franz himself, head of Franz Encounters, was looking over his mountain of notes.

"Stanton. We figured you made a beeline for the nearest hotel television and a market report."

It was Todd Mercer, head of real assets, taking one of his frequent jabs, though Mitch was just one of many targets. Stanton liked Mercer for his business sense and unrelenting pursuit of all things material; he hated his social ineptitude.

"Yeah, my car wouldn't start or I would be enjoying a thick steak and wondering whether you made it out of here alive," whispered Mitch.

"Just like you not to take the rest of us with you," said Mercer.

"Hey, you're an investor. You know it's every man for himself," said Mitch as he settled into his previous seat.

"All right, gentlemen, I believe we are all back, and we still have a lot of ground to cover, so if I could direct your attention to the screen, we will be returning to our discussion of self-assessment."

Mitch could think of literally a thousand other ways to throw away his weekend, but none of them seemed as fruitless as this. John Franz was attempting to teach twelve of some of the most highly successful businessmen in the Midwest how to make themselves better. It was ludicrous, and Mitch had hoped he could convince Kellogg that beating a dead dog was energy better spent. But upper management weekend getaways were the latest craze, not for the psychological well-being of employees, Mitch believed, but because top executives were grasping at any straw that could further secure their present and future financial status. The men seated before this laborious pundit were already highly motivated, fired up for the challenges that awaited them. They possessed the personal tools necessary to realize success, and that was a God-given talent to seek out and acquire the almighty dollar. A profitable yield on a calculated investment was the carrot that dangled within reach and would satisfy their hunger; teaching them how to appreciate the journey to the carrot was a foregone lesson. They had tasted the good life, knew what it took to achieve it, and were of the character that they could not accept life under any other conditions. So you stepped on some toes, took opportunity from the less informed, and failed to gauge the inner turmoil that could result. Forget the path; the reward, once savored in greedy satisfaction, was all Kellogg and his peers needed to keep offering their armies of moneymakers. Mitch longed for their noon dismissal tomorrow.

The Lake of the Forest Conference Center was a spacious 32-acre site nestled between Camp Theodore Nash, a Boy Scout retreat, and the lake itself. A private golf club was situated east of their location, dotted with homes occupied by residents seeking comfortable rural living within a stone's throw of the big city. The acreage they presently called home was occupied by a large main building that featured meeting rooms, a cafeteria, several leisure rooms housing everything from pool tables to quiet sitting areas, and a grand room with complete audio-visual capabilities, where they presently found themselves, and smaller, multi-unit bungalows that provided private bed and bath accommodations. Comfortable but too outdoors, pricey, Mitch could only imagine, and unproductive. He could see the sales managers at Lowe's gathering in droves for a weekend of pep talks and supervisory skills training. For financial wizards of their caliber--a money pit minus extravagance.

"It is these indirect channels of communication that are vital to complete feedback. And providing open-ended questions ensures you that your listener has understood the message to your satisfaction." Franz directed their attention to the screen where two-dimensional stick figures stood side-by-side, thick arrows pointing from one to the other in a circular representation of interpersonal exchange.

Mercer leaned over, "Are you getting this?"

"Come tomorrow, all I'm getting is out of here," said Mitch.

"What's wrong? Kellogg's boy not happy with Daddy's play date?"

Mitch had learned to stomach Mercer's subtle bullying. He actually tried to endear himself to people with his constant jabbing, though he usually turned them off in the process. Real asset investment required little in the area of personal contact; you could buy gold, for example, with the click of a computer mouse. He was an effective financier, but his social skills were terrible.

"Oh, come on. It hasn't been that bad. Just the guys, out in the wilderness, roughing it."

"Mercer, we're at a resort a few miles outside the city with running water and box lunches. It's hardly the wilderness," said Mitch.

Franz directed them to the screen again, explaining the group activity that would end their evening.

Mitch sighed with helplessness.

Back in his room later, Mitch lay wide awake on the bed, his eyes following the elongated shadows cast by the blades of the ceiling fan. He was unable to sleep, and the vehicles of release from his normal late night insomnia, the Internet or television, were unavailable to him. In an attempt to separate their location from others, the creators of the convention center boasted "a rustic experience free of the distractions of daily life." Kellogg had slid him the pamphlet across the mirrored surface of his rich mahogany desk, encouraging Mitch to embrace the weekend he had arranged for his management team. The brochure featured photos of comfortable rooms and large meeting spaces with intermittent frames of lakeshore and wooded trails. Granted, it was a tranquil setting, and the images had not done justice to the true beauty of the area, but Mitch was not Henry David Thoreau, and he had not come here because he was compelled. Unlike Thoreau, who had gone to the *woods because I wished to live deliberately, to front only the essential facts of life, and see if I could not learn what it had to teach, and not, when I came to die, discover that I had not live,* Mitch was here to fulfill a request, an order really, from his boss. Begrudgingly he had come, and the only positive he could embrace this late Saturday night was that he could return home tomorrow. Return to his familiar life, guided by the principle of work, not the preaching of some modern day Sigmund Freud.

After tossing and turning for thirty minutes, Mitch rose, still fully clothed, and stood at the patio door of his semi-private bungalow, the frustration washing over him in waves. It was late, well after midnight. Following their final exercise of futility and a flavorless meal in the center's cafeteria, the men had walked back to their rooms in silence. Some immediately went to their rooms to call wives and children on contraband cell phones (the attendees were instructed to leave phones, laptops, Blackberries, and any other links to the outside world behind), while others used the remainder of the night to read a book or play solitaire. Mitch, after exchanging a few barbs with Mercer in the common area of their bungalow, had retired to his room in the hopes of sleeping through the rest of the empty hours of obligation he owed the company. Whether it was the cocaine still active in his bloodstream or the sheer absurdity of his predicament, Mitch needed to find a way to pass some time before the scream that lingered just below his tongue made its escape.

Outside the heavy glass was a dark world of nothingness, a reflection of Mitch's inner sanctum. He stretched his arms over his head, yawned mightily, more out of boredom than exhaustion, and put his hand to the door's cool handle.

There was a knock at the door.

Wondering who else was lost in sleeplessness, Mitch paced to the other side of the room.

"Stanton. You in there? Come on, buddy, open up?"

Mercer.

"Hey, guy, thought you might want to share a little civilization with me," said Mercer, a satisfied grin on his face, his right arm cradling a twelve pack of beer.

"How did you manage that?" Mitch asked, standing aside to let Mercer pass. "Your suitcase?"

Mercer smiled, "Of course not, Stanton. Not worth hauling it out here when there is always someone willing to make a buck. That potbellied cook in the serving line? I offered him twenty bucks yesterday to pick it up for me." He handed Mitch a cold one. "Drink up. God knows we deserve it."

He really hated the guy, with his smug attitude and endless drabble. But on this night, Stanton could forgive the annoyance. Mercer dropped into the small room's only chair, a sigh of pleasure escaping his ample frame. Mitch figured the larger man for a schoolyard terror in his younger days, pushing around the smaller kids with visible satisfaction. What was still missing from Mercer's life was a devastating punch to the jaw, one so powerful that it would reach back twenty years and level that grade school bully, but Mitch wasn't the one to give it to him.

"You know what your problem is, Stanton? You're too tense, too wrapped up in the job to take advantage of the rewards," he said, tilting back his head and draining his can.

Mitch countered, "I acknowledge the rewards, but I also know what it takes to get them. Up here, being force-fed this garbage? Not a way to rewards as I see it." The beer was cold for sure. Mitch couldn't deny Mercer's ingenuity.

"Ah, just look at it as a paid vacation. No phones, no demands, no second-rate brokers wanting you to sample their wares. It's just fresh air and, hey, no screaming wives and kids," he said, snapping the top on another beer. "Oh, yeah, you don't have the pleasure of a home life. For that, sir, I envy you, and I toast you." Mercer's chin again lifted to the ceiling, his Adam's apple bobbing with each hearty swallow.

KIG's golden child began regretting the presence of the hulking Mercer in his room, but he saw no immediate way to bring the one-sided conversation to a conclusion. So he sipped his drink and let his guest ramble.

The exchange dragged on for another half-hour, Mercer offering his theories on everything from money markets to the price of gas and women's bipolar behavior, all the while drinking beer at an impressive rate. As Mitch was getting to the bottom of his second can, Mercer stood abruptly, announced that they were out of liquid sustenance, and made his way to the door.

His social habits were deplorable.

"Well, Stanton, I'm off. Thanks for drinking my beer," he laughed, the empty cardboard container hanging from his large hand. "Next time, you buy."

"Yeah, I guess I owe you one," Mitch said standing. "Thanks for stopping by."

"Sure, buddy. Glad you got to see me," he laughed again.

With that he was out the door, and Mitch was thankfully alone again, no more ready for sleep but closer to the end of his sentence.

The night continued to hold its allure for him as he returned to the dark setting that lay just beyond the sliding glass. He opened the door and stood at the threshold, his eyes surveying the black expanse while his ears registered the unfamiliar calls and rustles that issued from the near woods inhabitants. It was a windless evening as the trees stood in majestic silence. Stepping onto the short stoop, Mitch put his hands to hips and twisted side to side, allowing his spine and torso to free themselves of tension. They responded in uneven snaps and sharp jabs. Convinced now that brisk walk might further free him from edginess, he slid the door shut, determined his direction of late night exercise, and set out along the woods' perimeter. The moon and the facility's lighting provided the ambient glow he needed to traverse the grounds in relative ease.

With the brick enclosures to his left scattered her and there in an almost campground fashion, Mitch glided through the dampening grass, his steps fairly silent in contrast to the insectile and avarian concert that was unfolding in the dense woods to his right. Kansas nights, this far from the city, were an advertisement for simple living, though Mitch could never make this environment his home. Nature had its qualities, he realized, but only in terms of its earning potential. Real estate. Minerals. These were things nature furnished that he could find value in. The esoteric meaning was lost on him, not that he didn't possess a mind capable of grasping the philosophical aspects of creation, but due to his egocentric character. It didn't do anything for him. He failed to appreciate what existed when there was worth to be gained.

There was a chill in the air, as there would be for a few more weeks until summer made its full presence felt, but his steady pace and Mercer's alcohol warmed Mitch. Anyway, he didn't plan on a lengthy venture, just a fifteen-minute trek to expel the remnants of the day's arduous activities.

The compound stood in stark silence as Mitch made his way farther down the tree line and away from his bungalow. As he topped a short rise, the familiar sounds emitting from the dense forest came to an abrupt halt, as did Mitch. The calm delivered him a heavy blow, and his breathing slowed in response to his stagnant legs. He looked to both sides, his ears pricked to record the slightest sound.

There was nothing.

Mitch continued to walk, much slower though, alert to his surroundings.

The stillness remained.

A cricket picked up its symphony, temporarily, and then halted its legs.

Again, Mitch stopped. His heart thumped in defiance of a world in neutral.

He leaned toward the woods to amplify the slightest reminder that he wasn't alone. *Mitch Stanton. The symbol of solitude. The new age hermit. Concerned that he was truly divorced from life. Alone. Everything about the weekend failed to make sense.*

Confident he had reached a turning around point and thinking his electronics-free room was not all bad, Mitch made a one eighty and retraced his steps. The silence continued from the vast woods, and he now grew angry that he was letting the unnatural feel of the moment bother him. He had set out to channel some tension into the open air; instead, he was rebuilding a supply that would make the next eleven odd hours unbearable.

He damned his skittish behavior.

Glancing to his left now, his pace twice the former, Mitch let the darkness of the twisted branches and undergrowth take hold of his imagination. He saw movement, random shapes, and flashes of deep color. Without a sound, the woods were coming alive through his perception, and whether it was the silence or an acute awareness heightened through panic, he felt for the first time that he was no longer alone. His chest tightened; his heart thudded in protest of its confinement.

He looked down at his dampening shoes, the toes kicking up droplets of dew. His arms swung in cadence to the strides, which lengthened and channeled a growing burn in both to his thighs. The bungalow was still a good one hundred yards at the end of his path; in a minute he would be back in his room. There he could kick himself for allowing the night and the unfamiliar expanse of trees to play tricks at his expense. *It's all gotten to me. The retreat, the accommodations, the company. I knew this would be a terrible weekend, and now here I am on a late night walk with whatever backwoods creatures lurk among the trees. Damn Kellogg and his ideas. This is crap.*

And with that he was now sure something was pacing him, matching him step for step in mute mimicry. His eyes scanned the impenetrable gloom, its thick canopy denying entrance to the moon's soft glow. He started to jog, lifting his knees in hysterical response to the unseen image that shadowed him. Arms pumping, breathe pulsing from his open mouth, an abject look on his face, Mitch raced to the sliding door, any measure of pride lost in an all out effort to reach security.

He could now see definition in the bungalow, could make out the shapes of brick and gutter and shingle. There was the meager porch, illuminated by the bedroom light he had left on. It was within his reach, but the sense of dread grew as he neared the building. The stillness persisted in nature's thicket; nothing had changed. It was the prospect that he would be locked out, or worse, be assaulted at the brink of salvation.

He slipped and nearly fell face first but was able to right himself with scrambling legs and the flailing of arms.

And then he was on the pale concrete, pulling open the door in private triumph, and bursting into his assigned room, the one so graciously arranged by one Samuel Kellogg. He shut the door behind him, flipped the lock, and drew the curtains flush to the door frame. His mouth pulled in air in tremendous gulps as he began the slow process of calming his shattered nerves. He fell exhausted in the chair that once strained under the girth of Tony Mercer, closed his eyes, and let the room's four walls envelop him in safety.

"Oh, man, oh, man, oh, man."

His breathing slowed, calm ebbed into his frame.

What was that all about? he thought. *What's wrong with me? Scared of my own shadow.*

He put his hand to his forehead where it found beads of sweat had gathered in pronouncement of his exertion just moments ago. Another beer sounded good--a straight bourbon perfect. He would have to settle for a locked door instead. His distraught mind had just taken what started as an innocent stroll and turned it into a nightmare, the physical results of which left him drained. Mitch saw it as the culmination of an ill-fated weekend. It would be his last if it meant a new job and relocation. It was his instincts that had made him successful, and they had warned him about the retreat, where he now sat shaken. Never again would he deny those gut reactions.

A low growl came from the other side of the room, near the door. In his hurry to get inside and collapse in relief, Mitch had not taken notice of the large shape that stood transfixed in the opposite corner. His hands gripped the armrests. His confusion returned.

"Mercer?"

In an instant the shape was upon him.

Chapter 7

The Shawnee County Medical Examiner's Office, located in Topeka, was a state of the art facility that served four counties and held one of the largest forensic libraries in the area. Utilized by the University of Kansas in nearby Douglas County for its medical investigations' students, the facility was used for autopsies, housed the Shawnee CSI team, and was a site for other civil and criminal purposes.

Though external examination or immediate medical history served as a cause of death in many situations, instances of accidental or sudden death and homicide required an autopsy. Kansas ranked well below the national average in unexplainable deaths, yet the Topeka office was constantly backlogged. With four county medical examiners calling it home, the site was a beehive of motion, whether it was the constant parade of vehicles from hospitals, funeral homes, and the morgue or the feverish buzz of medical examiners, deputy medical examiners, forensic unit team members, and the occasional police officer. On this day, the reflective, smoked glass doors were opened to the head of the Auburn Sheriff's Department.

Since being served a down home slice of humble pie from his deputy, Ran had beaten himself up over his lack of effort on the Melton case. He had completed the typical cycle of denial through acceptance and had decided to make a personal appearance in Topeka to see if he could speed things along. Driving up in the early morning hours, his resolve to keep the case from going cold and reclaim his law enforcement manhood, Ran felt renewed for the first time since his arrival three years ago. The rash of homicides in LA had kept his skills finally tuned, his determination honed to a sharp edge; Auburn's lack of crime had dulled his senses, made him lackadaisical and ineffective. Monk's words had been a splash of cold water on his coma-like disposition, and with it provided a sense of purpose once again. The discovery of Melton's body had touched old wounds, triggered suppressed memories, and pushed him further into a depressed condition. The old Ran, the Ran who was the subject of department legend and newspaper headlines, the former detective who earned both the admiration and apprehension of his colleagues, had lain dormant for too long. There was a death that needed his professional attention, and a community that was counting on his expertise. It had been time for Ran to answer the call…for them…and for himself.

The full lab report from the Kansas State Bureau of Investigation was still not available for quite a while, longer than the revitalized sheriff felt he could wait. In the case of Sonny Melton, the crime had occurred within multiple jurisdictions, giving the KBI authority to process the data as it saw fit. The Topeka medical examiner was a natural choice, but the aggravated crime scene, unique qualities of the event, and notoriety of the deceased kept the bureau's hands in firm grasp of the investigation. Lucky for Ran he had a friend in Hunter Wilkins to keep him updated on lab findings. Though Ran was free to pursue leads and hunches in cooperation with state authorities, his awareness of their progress was not a priority. If he wanted to know more, if he wanted to push this investigation, it would require some effort.

Experience had taught him that friends could be made in the medical examiner's office, and the sheriff needed to find himself one. His encounter with Deputy Medical Examiner Clifford Weyland the night of the body's discovery had not gone well, in part because of Weyland's demeanor and Ran's temperament. Weyland had said nothing to instigate such a negative reaction from Ran; it was his smug expression at the scene, his better-than-this presentation that had angered the sheriff. The report the ME had given after completing his on-scene evaluation had been stiff and monotone, leaving the sheriff assured that his source of quick information and timely deliverer of results was still to be found at the facility.

Since it was the medical examiner's responsibility to determine the "cause, manner, and mechanism of death," the process was a painstaking one, relying on the forensic skills of a variety of individuals. There could be a half dozen individuals with a direct connection to the corpse, and within each could exist a propensity for helping an appreciative and sympathetic police officer. Ran had befriended a few on the West Coast, examiners and technicians who shared his passion for discovery, not as a sterile, biological event, but as a solution with far-reaching implications. Few in the forensic circle truly saw beyond the results their microscopes, test tubes, and DNA processors. What lay beyond these chemical formulas and genetic codes were salvation for future victims and retribution for those already victimized. Ran saw his talents and the investigative abilities of these people as tools of moral obligation, and why he had forgotten that recently, he couldn't say.

The first thing Ran would need to determine was forensic responsibility of the Melton case, and he feared that Weyland, having done the field work, was a likely candidate. The main desk of the workplace confirmed his first suspicion, though when Ran asked for an audience with His Highness, he was told the runty ME was away on a personal matter. *Yeah, probably getting fitted for shoe lift and a new personality.* He was instead directed to the office of the chief medical examiner, Dr. Ron Maxwell.

Maxwell, a scholarly, graying gentleman in his sixties, was cordial while professional, standing and extending his hand as Ran was led into his office.

"Thank you for seeing me unannounced, Doctor."

Ran was directed to one of two chairs in front of an ornate oak desk that he coveted while thinking about his own beaten workspace. The desk was housed within an equally magnificent office, with rich wood paneling and a deep earth-toned carpet. It was a fortress of comfort.

"Not at all, Sheriff. Lovely community, Auburn, from what I have been told. I've surprisingly never found the occasion to make my way over, professionally or personally."

"Well, Doctor, next chance you get, let me know, and I will give you the grand tour. Though I have to admit, it may only take five minutes, " said Ran.

"Offer noted," Maxwell smiled. "Now, how can we assist you, Sheriff? Can I assume you are not here to take a tour of our place?"

"Not in so many words. I am here about the Melton case. The young man that was found about two weeks ago in a field in Auburn?"

"Yes, Sonny Melton. Tragic."

Maxwell shook his head slowly in a quiet reverence. His humanity, in a job surrounded by death of every magnitude afflicting young and old, was admirable.

"I was wanting to see how close the inquiry was to completion. Is there anything available at this point that I could take back with me to help in my investigation? We are at a standstill, and I would appreciate some direction if your office can provide it." Ran maintained a respectful air, though it was not difficult with Maxwell, who, unlike Weyland, exuded a large measure of esteem.

Maxwell lifted a well-worn folder from his ordered desk, thumbing through the pages with a knowing precision. "Melton…Melton…Yes. Here we are…standard postmortem. Face sheet. Historical summary complete. Presentation complete. Postmortem changes. Features of identification. Pathological examination external and internal complete. Toxicology. Ancillary procedures, off-site laboratory tests, and results pending. What I have here, and excuse me for my technical rambling, is an up-to-date rubric of the autopsy report. I require of my deputy examiners a daily checklist on a case-by-case basis. It allows me to answer inquiries such as yours while assessing the workload and performance of my staff," Maxwell explained. "I have found it to be quite efficient in my capacity."

"From what you're telling me, the body has been submitted to first, second, and third-level processes and is pending KSBI lab, summary, and cause of death."

"Very impressive, Sheriff," the doctor said honestly. "I take it you have had some exposure to the our little world here."

"Los Angeles County Medical Examiner. Spent a few hours gleaning their records and picking their brains," said Ran.

"Then you know I have no official findings for release."

Ran leaned in. "Official, no. But I was hoping for something prefatory, anything to give me a sense of direction."

"I'm sorry, Sheriff, but it is not the practice of my office to expose forensics made within the confines of these walls, especially when our work is in conjunction with a state entity." Maxwell said. "I know you understand."

Ran nodded, "I am aware of the legal procedures and would not ask you to circumvent policy. I respect your position in the matter and realize you have a function to complete. But I can assure you that any information that left with me today would not be front-page news tomorrow, nor would it be used to jeopardize any further work that you need to conclude. All I was hoping you could provide me was a taste, really, of what I am dealing with here. I've been in this business a long time. What I saw was shocking."

"From what Deputy Weyland has reported to me, yes, a rather singular death, but my position remains," said Maxwell.

Ran could see that though the doctor had been gracious in his welcome, he was stubborn in his duty. "Very good, Doctor, I can see you are a man of principle, and I can appreciate that. I hope I wasn't too pointed in my appeal."

"No, no. Don't give it another thought. I admire your tenacity and commitment to this case and the people you represent. We all have a job to do. Sadly, we all have rules and regulations to follow as well, regardless of the fact we share the same goal," said the doctor, standing with his hand extended.

"Thank you for your time and consideration," said Ran, taking the medical examiner's hand gratefully though disappointed. "I hope I didn't put you off."

"Actually, I enjoyed the diversion. If you will allow me to show you some of the functions we are capable of here," he said ushering Ran to the door, "I would feel I haven't totally created an enemy in the Auburn Sheriff's Department."

"Far from it, and thanks, I would like a look around," said Ran, who saw a future ally in Maxwell, though he would take the facility excursion because he enjoyed the man's company and now wanted to see what the Midwest had to offer in the field of forensic science.

"I think you will be pleasantly surprised. It's not California, but it's very progressive, even for the stepchild of evolutionary education," the doctor laughed.

He was, of course, referring to Kansas' one moment of historical embarrassment and a step backward in forward thinking, the Scopes Monkey trial. Ran acknowledged the joke with a heartfelt, knowing laugh. "Let's start with your carbon testing on the piece of Noah's Ark."

The doctor beamed at the reference. "A sheriff with integrity and a sense of humor. My day of discovery is complete."

The two men walked along the reflective white tile of the hallways, stopping intermittently to view labs, cadaver rooms, and processing theaters. The Shawnee County Medical Examiner's Office employed sixteen full or part-time employees, ranging from deputy medical examiners to investigators and morgue technicians. Maxwell explained to Ran that, not surprisingly, limited resources were available in Kansas for the work being performed in the facility, and since there were no State offices that counties could turn to for outsourcing of their workload, the Topeka location was terminally behind.

"Efficient, though," the doctor beamed. "Considering the number of autopsies and lab analyses that goes on here, we have a remarkably fast turnover in relation to offices twice our size handling half the responsibilities."

Ran was impressed with what he saw and gained a new confidence in the event his department should need qualified, dependable forensic investigation. The facility was clearly managed with constant scrutiny, which explained its productivity and energetic staff. In harmony with a proficient use of available space, members of Maxwell's team seemed highly motivated and driven to produce reliable results. The sheriff had marveled at the Melton crime scene at the manner in which a lab team from the essentially rural central states could process a homicide arena in big city style. Even Weyland, though Ran was hard pressed to acknowledge anything positive in the man, had done his job admirably, as if deaths on a mythic scale happened frequently in his own backyard.

Maxwell introduced every available staff member to Ran, described the purpose of his visit, and in the process conveyed a fatherly image that kept his team alert and yet proud of their place in his family. Ran told Maxwell as much, commending him on his well-organized, systematic approach to his business. It was very similar to the approach Ran took, *had taken,* to law enforcement, so he soon found himself endeared to the elderly doctor.

One of the last legs of the tour took them to one of three autopsy rooms, where Assistant Deputy Medical Examiner Tara Phillips was completing work on a thirty-something vagrant found dead under a bridge in west Topeka. A small microphone hung from the ceiling near her head, which was turned down to her subject as she drew flaps of scalp, skin, and muscle tissue back to their original positions.

"Cause of death is decidedly sharp force injury to the head made with an instrument with a circular end, exactly one-quarter centimeter in diameter and at least six centimeters in length based on penetration. Time of death, in consideration of body temperature, rigor and liver mortis, and stomach contents, was approximately between 9:00 P.M. and 1:00 A.M., roughly twenty-four hours prior to discovery."

Dr. Phillips snapped her latex gloves as she spoke, drawing a sheet over the body as she concluded her summary of the internal findings. Scalpels, a rib cutter, toothed forceps, and various other dissecting tools lay at a rolling table to her left, the vibrating saw used to open the skull holding a particular fascination for Ran. The examiner was gowned and covered from head to toe. Her face was obscured with a surgical mask and clear goggles to prevent exposure to potentially infectious aerosols, her head sported a surgical cap as well, and considering where the corpse had spent its living and breathing days and nights, Ran figured they might all want to wear some protection.

Eventually she acknowledged their presence, but only after completing her summation, further testament to Maxwell's accomplished leadership.

The chief medical examiner explained that Phillips was a recent acquisition in his office, the result of months of begging the Shawnee County Commissioners to part with a few of their tax dollars so he could bring in a third doctor. She had come highly recommended from KU, a local girl, who had even done an internship in the Topeka office, and was a logical choice.

Dr. Phillips approached them, her hands busily unveiling the face beneath. When her warm smile and smooth lines preceded her introduction, Ran was pleasantly surprised. Though he knew she must be in her mid-twenties based on the history Maxwell had provided him, he had expected a hard, bookish figure to immerge from the medical garb. Though he couldn't be sure under the scrubs, she appeared athletic and extremely fit; her grip was firm and her eyes penetrating. Long blonde hair gathered in a ponytail behind at her back, and Ran marveled at her natural beauty. Free of noticeable make-up, Tara Phillips was a vision, and the sheriff had to gather his train of thought as the conversational hellos turned to him.

"Dr. Phillips. I understand you are new to Topeka?" he offered.

"New to this office, yes, but I was born and raised in the city. This assignment is a coming home for me actually."

"Dr. Phillips studied at KU and did her post-graduate work at the University of St Louis. She is a valued addition," Maxwell bragged, his fatherly hand ever so slightly on her arm as if presenting the catch of the day, his personal pride and joy.

"I was lucky enough to be able to return to Topeka. My parents, siblings, even some aunts and uncles, are here. It's good to be back," she smiled.

"Well, from what Dr. Maxwell tells me, they are the lucky ones. The good doctor was just showing me around the facility. Truly remarkable," Ran said.

Her eyes were alluring. "Yes, it rivals some of the larger forensic units in the Midwest. So, what's the Auburn sheriff's interest in our humble abode?"

Maxwell excused himself to take a call, notification of which having been hailed from a loud speaker attached in the upper corner of the hallway where they stood. "I won't be a minute. Doctor Phillips, if you could entertain our guest, but don't fall for his pleas for information." He smiled easily and disappeared around the corner.

"Pleas for information? So, you're here to speed the process, so to speak. And here I thought you had come to appreciate and learn about the fine services we are providing the four county region."

"Guilty as charged. I did come to see if I could get an update on a particular autopsy, which I was steadfastly denied, but Dr. Maxwell is so intriguing and convincing, I stayed around for the excursion."

They turned in unison and started slowly up the hall in the direction where Maxwell had just departed.

"Which case brought you from sleepy Auburn?" she asked. "I would think the only unexplainable deaths there would involve chickens."

She blushed after the words left her mouth.

"That came out wrong. What I meant was that Auburn is so…it's just not a town that has instances of…"

Ran rescued her, for which she appeared grateful. "No, I understand what you mean. Auburn's definition of horrendous crime has been the price of a stamp at Meyer's Deli and Post Office. Until recently. Not sure if your colleague Clifford Weyland mentioned the Melton homicide? Body was badly ravaged and disposed of in a field in Auburn?"

They made their way to a reception area near the front doors, where Ran was extended a seat. The latest recruit to the Shawnee County Medical Examiner's Office sat down with him.

Her beautiful, piercing eyes had lit up. "Was that your jurisdiction? I consulted with him on that case. It never came up in our discussion where the body was found. Baffling presentation. Really odd."

"You sat in on the autopsy?" Ran started up.

"No, I just provided a sounding board to some of Dr. Weyland's discoveries. It's common practice among medical examiners to seek advice. I'm sure it's not unlike police officers sharing opinions." Her voice matched her features--soothing and pleasant.

"True, we do collaborate on investigations, but I wouldn't have tagged Weyland as one to seek anybody else's advice. He strikes me as rather…independent."

"He has his moments of vanity, but really, he is an excellent pathologist," she countered.

Beautiful. Intelligent. Positive. Ran hadn't met anyone like her in, well, ever. He felt almost giddy in her presence, alive in ways that were foreign, unknown to past marked by privacy and singularity.

"And I can assume then, having heard Dr. Maxwell's preemptive warning, that neither you or Weyland can fill me in on your findings?" Ran asked.

"You assume correctly, Sheriff. I can only venture to guess that lab analysis is incomplete?"

Ran nodded, "Yeah, the KBI boys found it necessary to process the crime scene, and with it the lab work."

"Did Maxwell mention our toxicological report being complete?"

"He didn't mention any toxicology, but Weyland would have samples from the body evaluated as well, right?" Ran said.

She agreed, "By our technicians."

"Man, I'd really like to get some of that data. I have a town full of frightened residents, wondering if they are going to be next, county and state investigative departments ranking me last on their need-to-know ladder, and now a medical examiner's office with, of all things, professional integrity." Ran smiled. "Pretty poor, pitiful me, huh?"

"Not entirely. You have a job. You can't do your job without all the facts, and everyone else is holding the cards you need to play," she said. "I can appreciate your predicament."

"But you're still not going to help me, are you, Doctor?"

"I'm still not going to help you," she smiled. "But what I can do for you, and I say this because I sympathize with your predicament, is give you a history of similar cases that I have come across that may help your investigation."

Ran was stunned. "A history?"

"Comparable homicides. After talking at length with Weyland, I recognized the method and presentation of death. You forget, I've been outside the Sunflower State for quite a while--studying, interning--I've been exposed to a lot of recent criminology, which is one reason Weyland approached me. The evidence was new to him after ten years in good 'ole Kansas."

Ran found renewed opportunity, but was hesitant to put faith in her promises.

She went on. "I spent a great deal of time at the bottom looking up while I pursued my doctorate. Male Ivy League graduates getting preferential treatment and consideration while a Midwestern girl from Kansas struggled to gain the respect she believed she deserved. I took such offense to the system that I graduated head of the class. Thought I'd show them what a country gal could accomplish."

"Congratulations," he said.

She bowed her head playfully, "Thank you, Sheriff."

"But, Doctor, what about Maxwell's lock on all information prior to completion of all pathology and toxicology? Aren't you going to breaking the rules?"

Tara Phillips remained even and unfazed. "I will be sharing with you cases of similar pathology, not that from the Melton case. The findings I am speaking of are of public record. In some cases I encountered them in lectures and case studies."

"But if other homicides share this one's make-up, then in a way you would be imparting to me to some degree findings that have been put under lock and key." Ran shook his head. "I wouldn't want to put you out, Doctor. I am sure you have plenty to do here, from what Maxwell explained to me. Besides, I don't want to be responsible for any trouble you may get into, being new to the job and all."

"For an investigator, you certainly make a lot of unfounded observations," she said.

Ran liked her direct approach. Liked everything about her as he was shown each subtle nuance.

"Public record, Sheriff," she emphasized. "Nothing you could use to make an arrest in the Melton case, but possibly some…let's call it *informative direction*. While you are awaiting the final report on your case, you could at least do some research that will prepare you for what you will be receiving, in general terms."

Ran was amazed at her investigative prowess. "Are you sure you didn't take some law enforcement courses along the way?"

"It just sounds logical, and again, I am sympathetic to your situation."

"Okay, then, how do you propose we go about doing this? Meeting with me further will only cause Dr. Maxwell to throw up a red flag, and I wouldn't want to upset him or jeopardize your position here," Ran said.

She said, "How familiar are you with the culinary offerings of Auburn, Kansas?"

Ran was slightly taken back. "You mean dinner in Auburn, the two of us?"

"Don't read anything into, big fella. I've been stuck in this place for weeks on end. I deserve a night away and you deserve some information to assist your investigation. Sounds mutually beneficial, wouldn't you agree? Mrs. Sheriff won't mind, will she?"

The doctor stood, her conversation with Ran apparently at an end, whether he agreed it was or not. She was a remarkable creature in a hundred different ways. He had to add impulsive to her list of attractive characteristics.

"Well, no, I mean, yeah, I guess we could eat and discuss the homicides you are speaking of. No, on the Mrs. Sheriff. Have never found time for one." He hesitated. "Yes, definitely. When is a good time for you?"

"Saturday night. Seven o'clock. Do you know a good place?"

"Dalton's Restaurant is good."

"Dalton's it is. I will see you there, Sheriff."

She held out her hand for the second time that day, and he took it gratefully.

"Are you always this decisive, Doctor?" he asked. "Certainly not befitting a Midwestern gal."

She withdrew her hand and riveted his eyes in her own. "Better come with notepad and pen, Sheriff. You may want to take something down. Or aren't small town sheriffs schooled in the art of writing?"

She flashed her deadly smile a final time and turned back toward the hallway and her autopsy room, her ponytail swaying rhythmically to her gait.

Ran Price was dumbfounded, but in an affable way. He really didn't know what to make of what had just transpired, but he was too smitten to judge either her behavior or his uncharacteristic compliance to her suggestion.

He returned to the reception desk to have Dr. Maxwell informed of both his gratitude and departure, and then exited into the sharply contrasting midday sun where his car and a short drive back to Auburn awaited.

Ran climbed into the squad car and sat with the engine idling for a minute.

Dr. Tara Phillips.

Things were only getting more interesting.

Chapter 8

Caine sat naked before his trio of iMac 24-inch screens, supported by 1 GB of memory and 250GB of hard drive, his fingers flying across the keyboard like those of a piano virtuoso. A half-eaten sandwich, thick with layer upon layer of shaved meat, sat on a paper plate on the desk next to him. An empty plastic bottle stood with it, the sports world's latest hero emblazoned across its label promising renewed energy and proper flow of water molecules across cell membranes with artificially-flavored electrolytes. Ten straight hours of configuration, upgrades, installation, and troubleshooting had caught him up following a couple days of down time. Luckily, customers usually failed to realize that same-day resolutions of their problems was possible with most qualified computer technicians, but since most of his clientele were small business operators without IT support, they depended on his normally timely service and suffered the occasional issue requiring a two to three day fix. Long ago, when a much younger though highly intelligent Sebastian Caine recognized his *unique affliction*, he realized a normal job involving interpersonal contact would require a consistent presence he couldn't live up to. No right-minded organization, regardless of its leniency regarding employee time off, would allow for his unpredictable absence and lack of explanation for forty-eight hours. He knew he had to work independently, in his own business, and in a field where his hours of operation were flexible without jeopardizing revenue. Caine had toyed with the idea of being a writer, possibly a freelance journalist (he had a proclivity for the written word, considering he spent all of his time in hermit-like seclusion) but again, being confined to his home base was essential, and reporters required on-site research and personal contact in the compilation of their information, a chance he couldn't risk.

No, Caine had soon recognized that his life was destined for concealment and solitude, a self-enforced quarantine at a grand scale, so he had turned to computer science, with its parallels to mathematics (another discipline in which he excelled), programming languages, and most importantly, human-computer interaction. The collection of circuits, wires, and other hardware would never question his whereabouts, be accessible any time of the day, and provide him with financial opportunity. And so, he had absorbed countless documents and information on the subject, learned at a rate comparable to that of the very mechanisms he was familiarizing himself with, and started his business via a website and other remote means. In time he found that computer knowledge provided him with access to a plethora of useful information once he had learned how to hack into major computer programs undetected. Here he became versed in the methods, functions, and unspoken rules of the government and corporate world, learned their secrets and waded through their dirty dealings. He became a master of technological deception, an invisible Bigger Brother to Orwell's Inner Circle, and discovered the true nature of man's place in a democratic, capitalistic social order. The revelations were no longer shocking. It was in this electronic world he could see all, know all, and take whatever he required.

Not that Caine was in need of much--a place to live. To house his computers, food, and the clothes on his back were his only requirements. His transportation demands were minimal. Morning trips twice a week to one of the vast numbers of super stores that supplied consumers food, clothing, and general supplies were his only vehicular excursions, and while he was out, he would empty a post office box that provided him with the local paper and further added to his privacy. Consequently, the weathered though dependable Ford F150 in his driveway was perfect not only for its suitability for hauling bag upon bag of retail purchases but also its harmony with a rural setting.

He existed simply, free of the typical human anxieties that accompanied relationships, family, and job performance. Like a rogue animal, he lived on the periphery of society, visible only when fulfilling his basic primal needs, attached but unattached, in harmony with his natural environment until…well, until the rage.

Caine guided his complex system through its shut down, pushed the keyboard forward, and spun around in his leather swivel chair. The computer monitors cast a fading light into the dark living room, their soft radiance nosing its way into the deep shadows. He was finished for the day and needed to shave, dress, and head into Topeka to pick up a week's worth of food, his stock sharply depleted following a rather intense recharging. His intake was increasing with each episode, and the period between episodes had continued to shorten.

He wasn't worried, though experience had taught him to be vigilant, to respect the unknown nature of the rage and give it its just respect. It wasn't a matter of control; he had never been able to anticipate its arrival. What he held for the rage was a profound regard, a mutual tolerance. Caine maintained his anonymity and restored his decimated body while living what casual observers would consider a normal life, paying taxes and trying to survive the roller coaster of political agendas that kept the citizenry guessing; the rage met only one of his needs--it carried out its cycle of destruction unseen and then secretly conveyed him home (in a manner of which he was unaware though he had his suspicions). He had never been the subject of an investigation. Never been questioned about a crime or implicated in any involvement. Time and again the outcome was the same: an unexplained death filed as a cold case. Caine served as host to the parasite and years of service had made him an efficient supplicant.

The bathroom mirror held Caine's gaze as he stood in personal inventory. He was a large man, muscular and trim, with a dark complexion and Romanesque features. A full head of jet-black hair complimented his deep brown eyes and rugged skin tone. Those same eyes followed the taunt lines of his shoulders and arms, the muscles gorged and packed tightly in athletic repose. His bulging chest emptied into a washboard stomach and trim waist, then exploded again into legs worthy of a highly trained weightlifter, though Caine had never formally exercised in his life. Considering his food intake, it was a wonder he lacked such little body fat and retained a youthful healthy appearance. He couldn't remember ever being ill; even the slightest cold had failed to find a home in his frame. Caine knew the reason for his remarkable body was tied in some way to the rage, but he didn't question the product of a physiological and psychological metamorphosis that he little understood. The body, he thought, as he turned slightly side to side to determine if there were any outward signs of trauma from his most reason clandestine undertaking, was an additional reward for housing this thing that took hold of him like a walking dream.

He recalled little if any of the journeys his body took while it was outside his influence. It was as if he were comatose or in a deep, dreamless sleep, his conscious self locked away behind a heavy door of lucidity behind which he heard an occasional noise of indiscernible origin or witnessed flashes of activity that came back to him much later in jumbled pieces of confusion. It had been that way from the beginning;

the only thing that had changed was his ability to deal with the events in an efficient and safe manner.

After shaving, Caine went to his bedroom, the only other place in the house that was furnished, though like the living room with its computer desk, television stand, and simple recliner, it too was sparse and eerily empty, lacking anything that could be mistaken for a comfortable setting. Occupying the far corner, its disheveled sheets in disarray, was a lonely twin bed. The near wall held a multi-drawer chest that was of heavy oak and held dozens of recently-purchased underwear, socks, and t-shirts. Countless scratches and gouges covered the once rich surface, damage acquired from years of relocation. To the wall at his right, Caine slid a closet door that was constantly leaving its tracks and hanging up on the cheap, long shag carpet. This compartment, like its counterparts the refrigerator and pantry in the kitchen, was crammed full of Polo-style shirts, retro bowling and boulevard shirts, camp shirts, and other styles of sportswear; pre-washed jeans, khaki pants, and slacks with pleats or single pleats; and shoes of various function--tennis, dress, and casual. He could have clothed a small army with his wardrobe, but because of his late night burn parties in the backyard and an abhorrence for anything used, the racks of items seemed to rotate at an incredible rate.

Dressed and out the door (his first exposure to the outside world in almost four days), Caine piled into the truck and made his way toward Highway 75 which he would then take south, crossing Soldier Creek into the city limits where he would pick up 70 West after the Kansas River toward his ultimate destination. The store he had discovered on Topeka's northwest end was to his liking, meeting all his needs with variety and easy access. Within minutes he was walking across the parking lot of the store, his gait like that of a bear but with a grace and ease that made onlookers take a second glance. His was undoubtedly a handsome man; he had long registered the stares he received from women and the infrequent man with little interest, his desire for sexual fulfillment completely absent. With the libido of a ninety-year-old man, the intellectual Caine had concluded his biological design was geared toward one function. Energy was built up and stored for one purpose--it wasn't to be expended in a sweaty union of meaningless copulation. Besides, maintaining a distance from others was a prime objective.

He grabbed a grocery cart, classified the single wheel that shook violently in opposition to its companions as yet another symbol of the imperfect world he lived in, and stalked the aisles with a purpose. His familiarity with the store kept him off many of the specialized rows; his attention was centered on baked goods, meat, dairy, and produce. Children darted by him, urgently pursuing their mothers with a desired box of cereal or candy treat. Elderly women stood entranced with product labels challenging their fading vision, their carts forgotten in the middle of the aisle in road block fashion. Managers called for cleanups and register help. Stock boys faced shelves and replaced their empty holes with half-hearted effort, their minds elsewhere. Caine ignored it all as he wasted little time filling his cart to overflowing. By avoiding people's eyes and appearing in a hurry, he knew he could complete his task quickly and escape the buzz of scanning machines and talkative customers.

Nearing the end of his safari, Caine was loading the bottom rack of his cart with cases of water and sports drinks when a tiny voice halted his progress.

"Excuse me, young man, could you reach something for me?"

Caine turned his head to see a small, grey-haired woman at a ninety-degree tilt. Dropping the product he held, he righted himself to his full six and a half feet and stood towering over her.

She pointed to the upper shelf of the aisle. "The large cranberry juice there. Could you reach that for me?"

His attention turned to the shelf where a variety of plastic jugs resided, each colorfully proclaiming its nutritional value in percentages and taste.

"The sixty-four ounce bottle, please," she said, her voice a soft flutter somewhere far below him. "I have asked them to keep those lower."

Caine's pilgrimages invariably required him to engage in dialogue with the outside world without the use of his impersonal computer system. He had found eye contact to be an instigator of such communion and avoided with practiced success. But every now and then, whether it was in the checkout line, pumping gas at Hoyt's only convenience store, or signing for prearranged deliveries at his door, Caine was required to use his voice, instead of his fingers, to network.

"Certainly, ma'am. I would be more than happy to," he said, reaching for her request.

Natural. Warm. Inviting. Polite. His voice was deep and resonate, appealing to the ears of those around him. It carried with it a measure of charm and was reminiscent of the great big screen heroes of a bygone era: Bogart, Hudson, Cooper, Brando. It relaxed those who may be intimidated by his Herculean size, and Caine understood that odd behavior was the best way to be remembered. It was during these inconvenient exchanges that he softened the edges, drew the curtain on the discomfort he felt among them, and became amicable.

"Thank you, young man. I hate to have bothered you, but they just don't…." she continued as she took the bottle from his massive paw.

He interrupted, "No trouble at all. Anytime."

Caine, his cart in the lead, continued up the aisle. The old woman stood momentarily watching him go, marveling at his great size, but then she recalled the cranberry juice in her hands and deposited it in her basket. Looking back up, she saw her savior was gone. *Such a nice young man.*

With his shopping complete, Caine headed for the checkout where he paid for the mountain of items with his debit card. He carried little cash, never wrote a check, and paid for everything he could over the Internet. Like his computer business, electronic payment was detached and aloof, the way he preferred it.

The cashier, a high school aged girl, had commented on his purchase while stealing glances at his cut frame between the repetitious drawing of bar codes across the glass before her. "Been awhile since you shopped, I guess."

Caine produced his best smile, mechanical and contrived, but from all outward appearances, genuine. His steel dark eyes penetrated her juvenile stare. "Yes, I've been out of town for some time. I was running low."

"For sure," she said in her best Midwestern version of West Coast dialect. "Like, I've never seen anyone buy so much meat. Are you having a party?"

He tried to hold his attention to her infantile rambling. "What? Oh, yes, a party. Big barbecue. Friends coming over to welcome me home."

"Sounds fun," she cooed.

Following a few more empty exchanges, Caine loaded the back of his truck and gratefully headed home. The midday sun was dulled in his dirty windshield and would have impaired the visibility for most men, but Caine was far from most. In addition to his Olympian body, he possessed uncharacteristically acute senses. Smell, sound, sight--they were all at a level far superior to the average man. *Another gift from the rage,* he had concluded. Standing in his backyard at night, a recent outfit feeding flames that licked the rim of his blackened burn barrel, Caine would use his unparalleled vision to scan the horizon where he would spy small animals scurrying about in their foraging at a distance of two hundred yards. And when the flames died down and their sizzle with them, he could hear those same creatures among the dense undergrowth of the wooded area at the rear of his property, their padded feet sending the snap of a twig on the air for his ears to envelope. He could determine with certainty the meals being prepared a mile down the road, their inviting aromas issuing from homes and in the air to his downwind nostrils. Nothing escaped his sensory elements when he was in his normal state, and he could only imagine their keenness during the height of his affliction.

Among his purchases that day he unloaded into the house had been a copy of the Kansas City Star, not his normal means of gaining local news, but he had not seen anything on the television or Internet that would account for his recent episode. There were instances when he had concluded that nothing happened, that for some reason, possibly lack of opportunity, nothing had transpired in the course of the night that warranted media coverage, but this was not one of those times. Caine, regaining his conscious self after the first day's hard sleep, finding himself disoriented on his living room floor, always found signs, or none at all, that indicated to him whether it had been a successful hunt. Smears of deep red on his face, around his mouth and nose. His clothing covered in dirt and dark smears of what must be blood. Muscles completely expended, making sitting up a challenge. These were his indicators that the media would soon divulge stories involving a missing person case or evidence of a brutal attack. On occasion he awakened to find himself relatively clean, only scant signs of mud and grass, his hair and clothing unkempt but not drastically so. His musculature sustained heavy damage in either case, though, as if the metamorphic process alone was enough to tire him substantially.

There had been plenty of time for a person gone missing case to be revealed, though the media in its political agenda often prioritized the importance of each case depending on a number of elements. Age was often a factor; an innocent young child, taken from its front yard as it played, was common candidate for a lead story. Beautiful college co-eds tended to draw public curiosity as well, the unfortunate victims of crazed boyfriends or quiet sociopaths who pined for them from afar.

The NAACP frequently complained that the waspish ownership of leading media giants was resolute to give the disappearance of black Americans much in the way of airtime or print coverage, but Caine doubted the veracity of that assumption. The country's minorities could be found in all media sources, but usually for different reasons. Protestations from religious leaders, the participation in or victims of a variety of crimes, or their socio-economic conditions--these were their venues. Print and video journalists reported the news; they avoided creating it at the risk of unemployment. It wasn't their fault that African-Americans and Hispanics were being passed over for abduction in favor of Caucasians. Caine wasn't a bigot; he disliked the population equally.

Like the noon telecast of state and local news, The Star offered him nothing in the way of disappearances or bizarre deaths, so he tossed the paper aside and returned to his computers. The semi-circle of technology was a haven for him, and he settled into the chair intent on further discovery. He spent the rest of the afternoon running queries on the usual search engines, tapping into local media websites, and all the while repairing the intermittent problems his clients suffered. His interest was superficial really; he had never been tied to any crime or ever expected to be. What he wanted to know wasn't the *who* or the *how* but the *where*. The buffer zone the rage had consistently provided him had shrunk drastically with the finding of Melton's savaged corpse, and Caine wanted to be sure that perimeter wasn't constricting further. It would mean another move, one of many he had made over the years, but he had grown used to, even fond of, relocation, which meant a newness. Even eight months in Hoyt, Kansas had grown too familiar to him and wore like an old suit.

It shot up on the monitor to his left just before six o'clock from Kansas City's KCTV, a CBS affiliate. Caine had registered with all news sources to notify him of breaking news, and now here it was. The report was a press release from the public affairs office of the Kansas City Police Department:

The Kansas City Police Department is seeking information regarding a missing Kansas City man. On Saturday, Mitchell Stanton went missing from the Lake of the Forest Conference Center at Camp Theodore Nash near Lake of the Forest in Bonner Springs, Kansas, west of Kansas City. Stanton was expected to complete a business conference on site Sunday but failed to return after retiring to his room for the night. Stanton failed to show up for subsequent appointments on Monday, causing his employer and co-workers to be concerned for his safety. Stanton is known to always keep in touch daily either by phone or e-mail with business associates. His 2005 silver Saab remained in the parking lot of Kellogg Investment Group as Stanton and others were driven to the conference via company drivers.

The Kansas City Police Department is asking the public's help in locating Stanton. Anyone with information regarding his whereabouts should contact the KCPD.

Caine consulted his map. The lake was roughly fifty miles from his home and well outside the boundary recently established by the Melton kid's demise. He knew this was a promising sign of a return to normalcy, if normal could ever be applied to Caine's life, but there was still the matter of the body and its resting place. It could easily be on the lake property, discarded in a ditch or left mangled near the water's edge, eyes staring up emptily at the Kansas sky. Or, and Caine knew he would have to continue his vigilant search for new information, the remains of Mitchell Stanton might lie closer, narrowing authorities' sphere of investigation as the incidents began to compile.

He crossed his arms and leaned back in the computer chair. Caine, with all his intelligence and physical prowess, had one quality that circumvented them all--he was arrogant. The arrogance kept the concept of threat completely out of his mind, though he was wise enough to keep track of his paths of destruction, wishing to simply dismiss himself from the possibility of speculation as to his involvement. But *fear*? Never. He hid to maintain a life of solitude he preferred, free of men's condemnation and infernal back-fence talk. Years of survival while prowling among the species he belonged to but looked upon with disdain had made him complacent. *These weak creatures with their materialistic pursuits and inferior compositions!* He walked among them, despised them for their pettiness, took their lives when the rage saw fit, and feared nothing from them.

Besides, he couldn't be sure that Stanton was the rage's second victim in two weeks; people went missing at a rate of thousands per year. Something told him, though, that this was the result of his latest trek into the night and subsequent days of recovery. But the real concern, the one he was avoiding with these geographical matters, was *frequency*. Caine had been pushing aside the real reason he was feeling an unfamiliar stress, a sensation foreign to his narcissistic perception of the world. Since his arrival in Kansas, the infirmity he had grown to view as an attribute had surfaced only three times prior to this, taking him unaware an average of every two or three months in a pattern consistent with his prior places of residence. *But two weeks?*

Fourteen days and smart investigative work could lead to conclusions he would rather avoid, namely, the presence of a serial killer. Mention serial murders and the police's efforts would be compounded exponentially through the assistance of the public, ever watchful, ever suspicious. Caine had his anonymity and freedom because he was cautious, nomadic, and self-assured. He resolved to monitor the situation more diligently, and if necessary, retire to his next residence, already purchased and made ready.

He stood and walked confidently to the kitchen.

Chapter 9

Ran arrived at Dalton's Restaurant fifteen minutes early, angry with himself over the unexplainable nervousness that had kept him awake the night before and pacing the house most of the day. Saturday was usually a day away from the office for the sheriff, but he had come to the office twice under the guise of needing to look at some files, though he knew he was just passing the time until his meeting with Dr. Phillips.

Unsure whether to dress in civilian attire or in his uniform, he had finally chosen the khaki sheriff's outfit for two reasons: he wanted to project a professional appearance since Dr. Phillips had alluded to respecting his investigative determination, and he didn't need the collective gossip of the fair folks of Auburn including his personal life in its daily editions. Not that he expected the doctor to arrive in scrubs and latex gloves, but he didn't want to appear to be taking their meeting as anything other than business, an exchange of information.

He convinced himself an early arrival would be practical so he could locate a booth that ensured some privacy while secretly fearing to be late and therefore rude. She was doing him a favor; expecting her to wait for him was unconscionable.

The restaurant was uncommonly busy and Ran wondered whether he would be able to find a table at all as he scanned the crowded room, but then there she was, waving at him from a booth toward the back. She was half-standing, her smile more penetrating than he remembered, and Ran headed toward her, confused and a little embarrassed.

"A little early, aren't you?" he said.

"I was glad to get away for a while. A little overenthusiastic, I guess."

She sat back down in the vinyl bench seat, and Ran slid in across from her.

"I went ahead and got us a table if that's okay. Unless you have something Dalton's reserves for its sheriff?"

She was in a light blue sundress, her hair now free and falling on her supple shoulders. The fluorescent bulbs caught the locks in beautiful highlights. A little make-up had accented her eyes, cheekbones, and ample lips, but Ran believed her natural beauty could survive without the slightest assistance from it. Dr. Tara Phillips didn't need flash and color to attract attention. She was fresh and bright and alive, and Ran was mesmerized.

"No, no, this great. And I thought I was getting here ahead of time to find us something."

"Sorry if I overstepped my bounds. I didn't really think it mattered who got here first," she said, looking around her with a childlike fascination. "Auburn. I should have come when I was younger. It's a nice place."

"We like it here," Ran answered, looking about him at the full tables to indicate the residents. "It's been a nice change of pace for me as well."

She smiled, "I had the impression the other day you were out of your element. Not in the morgue. You seemed comfortable there. At home. What I could also tell was you weren't corn fed local. Let me guess-- Northwest? West Coast?"

"Los Angeles. Three years removed," he said. "Shows, huh?"

Ran looked down at his folded hands.

"My roommate in med school was a byproduct of the California wine country. I thought I caught some regional bits here and there," she said, her eyes now settling on his. "It was a pleasant change from the Kansas drawl."

"I really thought I was picking up some of the Jayhawk in me. I guess you can't totally abandon your past."

"Totally."

Ran laughed comfortably with her, feeling relaxed for the first time since meeting her days ago. Dalton's was coming to life now, its sounds and smells infusing Ran with vigor, and the presence of Tara Phillips only added to his stimulation.

"Hello, Sheriff Price."

It was Patty Stark, apparently their waitress for the evening. She placed silverware and menus in front of them.

"Hello, Patty. How are you?"

"Busy as ever, Sheriff." She was stealing glances toward the doctor, her interest obvious. Ran had frequented Dalton's since taking the job in Auburn, having eaten on the run for years and in no way ready to start cooking for himself regularly. He had breakfast at home, usually got lunch or a late night burger from the Dairy Queen, but if a sandwich or his only culinary feat, chili, were not desirable, then it was a home cooked meal at Dalton's. At no time had he ever sat down with anyone other than Monk, choosing to eat alone before heading home where he went out for an evening jog, then drank a beer and settled down to television and bed. The town had accepted him as a single man and cherished him now as a confirmed bachelor. A noticeable man, dark, rugged, and mysterious, Ran had drawn interest from a few of Auburn's unattached but had not reciprocated that attraction. He projected a professionalism in his duties but also an unwillingness to open up and expose the person behind the badge. As a result, Ran had established himself as a respected enigma and private individual. Even Monk and Polly were kept in the dark about Ran's life outside the office and the years prior to his arrival.

"Patty. This is Dr. Phillips from Topeka. She is here on a police matter," he said as he patted the notebook he had brought with him.

Ran wished he could capture those last words and replace them with ones not so explanatory. He didn't owe anyone a reason for his dinner guest and hoped Dr. Phillips had not picked up on his unease. This was not his first business dinner, but Ran felt like a foreigner in a strange land, unfamiliar with local custom. The doctor had him completely off balance.

The women exchanged their pleasantries and then Patty was off to get their drink orders.

"I get the distinct impression you usually come here alone," the doctor said.

"Yeah, I'm here after work sometimes on the way home," Ran said to the napkin that went on his lap.

"I'm afraid we have caused quite a stir, Sheriff," she sad looking around. "I don't know if you will be able to avoid the rumor mill after this dinner," she said sarcastically, a sly grin on her radiant face.

"They'll get over it. They're just used to seeing their sheriff at a table for one," he joked.

"So, what's good here?" she said, shifting the subject away from Ran's obvious discomfort, sparing him from further speculation as to what the townsfolk of Auburn had decided about his rendezvous with such an attractive partner.

After their drinks arrived (they both had tea, though the doctor had requested extra lemon), they ordered chef salads based on Ran's recommendation. He noted Patty's evident reaction to their identical meals and knew this had secured his name prominently in the Auburn grapevine.

"So, Doctor, is pathology everything you thought it would be?"

"First, call me Tara, and yes, it's as exciting as I had imagined it would be."

She made it easy on Ran, and he wondered whether he was that transparent, whether the immature little boy he once was, fumbling and nervous around the opposite sex, had made his triumphant return engagement. Again he chastised himself and vowed to refocus his attentions on why he was there. A killer out there, somewhere, and the doctor, *Tara*, had offered to help him on the road to discovery. For now he needed to forget she was beautiful, forget he could sit in her company all day and just listen to her silvery voice, and put the mangled corpse of Sonny Melton and apparently others in his mind's eye.

"When I was growing up all I could think about was being a private detective. Encyclopedia Brown. Nancy Drew. I read them all and secretly lived their lives of solving mysteries."

Ran drank in every word.

"After high school and a little reality check on my future, you know, sitting all night in a beat-up sedan eating cold pizza and watching the hotel room of some wayward husband, I considered the potential of science to appease my inner Sherlock, so forensic pathology was just a natural fit." She traced solid lines in the condensation on the side of her ice tea. "It means long hours, little time for friends, no social life for sure, but I wouldn't trade the work for the world. I really feel like I am doing something significant while satisfying my own curiosity."

Ran agreed, "I must say you have fully described the life of a sheriff."

She seemed encouraged with a confederate, leaning in as she continued, "I know that. We both spend our days studying evidence and trying to find answers. But for us it's more than that. The world really can't know what commitment we make. It's how I feel about my work. People outside the forensic community can't imagine how the human body can be a road map of revelation. It is the harbinger of histories and secrets that await interpretation and detection. I look at these men and women and children that have been brought to me, and it's like they need me. It's my job to bring closure to their lives, as if death were only a preamble. Sounds silly, doesn't it?"

"It doesn't sound silly at all," Ran said. "I stare into the same faces and those of their loved ones and feel the same pull to find answers, to bring closure like you said. I can't imagine myself doing anything else."

"No, you seem to me to be doing exactly what you were meant to do," she said.

"It's this dull brown uniform, isn't it?" he said, thrusting his chest in mock dignity. "I strike a regal pose, wouldn't you say?"

She laughed, "No, I'm serious."

And she was. Ran believed her conviction

"I could hear it in your voice the other day at the morgue. You were sincere but single-minded. You wanted answers and were determined to find them but much too proud to grovel. Very sure of yourself, too. Kind of a 007 minus the tuxedo. And even though I couldn't help you, I wanted to help, so here I am."

Ran barely noticed the meals placed in front of them as they went on. She was speaking about him, for him, and in the dark recesses of his past he was beginning to find the final hidden pieces of his long dormant purpose for living. She had painted his principles with words and shed light on the true Ran Price. After sharing a brief narrative past and absolutely nothing beyond two conversations, they had found a common ground that long-standing relationships were built on. This time they both appeared uncomfortable with the proceedings and now it was Ran's turn to play savior.

Flipping open his notebook that lay next to his scarcely eaten salad, Ran said, "All right, Dr. Watson, putting aside each of our life's calling, as important as we agree they are, what can you tell me about these similar deaths?"

His Holmes reference drew a playful grin from her, and once again they were bound to duty for duties sake. It was here that Ran, whether consciously or in some spiritual epiphany, vowed to reshape his persona, to recapture the zeal by which he lived, in concert with his profession, and somehow include, though it didn't all hinge on this final objective, Dr. Tara Phillips in his life, even if it were only in police matters. She made him feel--he would have to struggle for the word--*vital.*

Ran learned that after receiving her doctorate in forensic and environmental pathology from the University of St. Louis, Tara had completed four years of resident training in various locations before becoming board certified and returning to Topeka. Her residency had taken her as far east as North Carolina and the Wake Forest University Baptist Medical Center where she was exposed to advanced autopsy procedure, scene investigation, and trial procedure, and south to Emory College where she worked closely with the Fulton County Medical Examiner's Office in Atlanta. Her exposure to clinical pathology and importantly, autopsies, was advanced, many because she had an unwavering thirst for experience, secondly, the medical establishment was losing qualified forensic doctors faster than they could recruit new ones, so students of the science were thrust into service and provided with as much real world exposure as they could handle. As a result, Tara was privy to crime scene reports, police investigations, and other criminal proceedings.

"It was a welcome baptism by fire," she said. "It was real. The cases were nonstop, and we never looked up for a minute. I loved the pace then and still do."

Not to be outdone by her fellow residents, Tara kept a grueling pace, involving herself in countless cases and thriving on those that offered a challenge.

"If a ninety-year old man with external presentation and medical history both indicating heart disease as the cause of death was wheeled into the morgue, I would fane lab commitments in order to free myself for the next subject, hoping for something more demanding." She picked at her salad, more interested in the pathology of human beings than that of the concoction Dalton's called their *Summer's Cool Crisp Escape.* "I needed more than the typical autopsy."

She appealed to Ran's reason. "Imagine coming upon a dead body with a bullet hole in the temple and an assailant brandishing a gun and yelling at the victim, 'I told you I would kill you but you just wouldn't listen.' That's how some autopsies made me feel. No adventure. The truth was already revealed because it was posted on a billboard for the rawest of pathologists to find in big, bold letters. Don't get me wrong. I wasn't after the praise, the congratulatory pat on the back thanking me for the fine forensic work. It was the hunt, you know, the journey to the answers. My friends cringe when I tell them that. But that's what I relish."

Ran could empathize. He took pride in solving a murder, true, found satisfaction in bringing a criminal to justice. But it was the thrill of the chase, the hide-and-seek, that he fed on. They were bloodhounds, he and the good doctor, built for pursuit, and ultimately, exposing the truth behind Death's interruption of life.

She went on, "I encountered every manner of death in those four years: disease, homicide, accident, suicide. It really sharpened my skills, made me valuable. But it was the murders that intrigued me, not because I had some morbid fascination with it, but because it was the only cause of death where answers were not readily available. Sure, an aneurysm requires some analysis and deduction, but inevitably there it is, the ballooning artery that says, 'You got me. I did it.' If it is an accident or suicide, you guys can usually piece together the crime scene and replay the events to everyone's satisfaction. When someone is poisoned, or strangled, or beat in the head with a fireplace poker, only forensics can lead to answers and guilt."

"When I was completing my officer's training in Sacramento and looking ahead to life as a patrolman or beat cop, I cringed at the possibilities. I always wanted to be a detective and made a promise to myself that I would do whatever was necessary, put in the required years, study the required material, to make that my reality. Like you, I wanted to be presented a riddle and be dared to solve it. Distributing traffic tickets and working police lines at rock concerts was not in the cards for me," said Ran.

"Okay, so I was right about you and James Bond," she said.

"Shaken, not stirred," he quipped.

"I have no doubt."

Eating a foregone memory, their conversation had taken center stage.

"I held out for the special arrivals that came without apparent cause or explanation," she said. "Murder by unknown instrumentation, poisonings, dismemberments in an attempt to hide identity, or bodies with specialized trauma, or those with substantial deterioration due to time or the elements. These were the cases I cut my forensic tooth on, and I saw an entire encyclopedia of ways to do away with your fellow man, believe me."

Ran said, "And now I have no doubt."

She smiled, "Sheriff Price, you are quick. When do you find time to learn such an attractive dialogue?"

"That would be during my indoctrination into Scotland Yard. Must be versed in all aspects of the language. Never know when you might have to spar with such a brilliant, and to once again borrow a word, *attractive,* pathologist such as yourself."

It was now her turn to blush. "Have you ever witnessed an autopsy, Sheriff?"

"*Ran*, and yes, Tara, I have seen an autopsy," he said. "Well, not from beginning to end, but I have been brought in on occasion or asked to view various peculiarities in a murder case-gun powder burns...strangulation features."

"It's a very intimate thing."

The reaction on Ran's face signaled his confusion.

"What I *meant* by that is an autopsy is a time when communication is at its most personal. That body lying there on the table is speaking to me. No inhibitions, no attempts to deceive or hide the truth. I am seeing this person for who they are and what they were, in a way that a mother or spouse couldn't ever know them. And it's during that communion that I have the responsibility to understand what they are trying to tell me, or in this case, show me." She shook her head and poked at her food. "In med school they would put us in front of these cadavers and send us off on an exploration of the inner workings of the human body, getting us familiar with every system and organ. Very sterile. Cold, really."

"I've always wondered how you guys can spend all day inventorying a body," Ran said.

"That's just it. Until I started forensic pathology, that's all they were--like dolls on a conveyer belt. They were all the same. The same inside and out. A never-ending flow of John and Jane Does. But they had nothing new to show me. After the first few they were no longer speaking to me." She laughed uncomfortably. "You probably think this sounds crazy."

"Not at all. I've met plenty of medical examiners who doubled as spiritualists," Ran said playfully. "Seriously, I think I know what you are saying. It got to the point where I could fill in the blanks during murder investigations. I just knew how everything would play out--revenge, greed, lust. It was easy to pin down."

"Exactly. So when I began true autopsies, especially criminal, the exchanges resumed and I fell into my work and career with a renewed attitude. The bodies I started seeing were again trying to tell me something and it was up to me to find out what," she said.

"It was toward the latter half of my first residency, in North Carolina, that I saw something unique, and granted, I hadn't been exposed to years of cases, but I felt I had been witness to just about every means of death. This wasn't consistent with any remains I or those I worked with had seen before. Brutal. Savage. The body was defiled. " She dropped her fork and grabbed her napkin as she leaned back in the bench seat. "I saw others over the next few years--Winston-Salem, Atlanta, even Little Rock. All the same. It was as if a pack of animals had ravaged the corpse, though there was never evidence of wild carnivore on or near the body. The most recent case I saw was here, in Topeka."

Patty came by and refilled their ice tea and shuffled down to the next of her tables. She had arrived at an awkward moment; her two customers sitting back, obviously done with their meals, staring at each other speechless. They hadn't even looked up when she poured from her pitcher. *Sheriff Price is smitten.* Of that, she was sure.

Ran's hesitation wasn't because of the graphic nature of the murder; he had seen Sonny Melton's mutilated body in great detail and had the early lab results from Hunter Wilkins. What left him momentarily stunned was that a pattern of these deaths existed. *Were the county or state departments aware of this? Had federal authorities made the interstate connection? How was it that he had no information on the possibility of a serial killer?* He knew he was out of the loop from an administrative point of view, but he had a homicide in his jurisdiction, and if there were indications of future incidents, he had a right to know. Auburn had a right to know.

"What did Weyland want from you?" he said.

She said, "Dr. Weyland knew from my entrance interviews that I had diverse experience with criminal pathologies, especially devastated remains. Sometimes you get a body that has been burned or underwater for a significant period of time. Makes identification and cause of death difficult. After reading his preliminary notes, I asked to see the body, and it was then I confirmed what the notes had suggested.

"The problem all medical examiners face in such a mutilated post mortem is not only how they died but by what manner. If someone places their hands on your throat and squeezes or ties a rope around your neck and hangs you from a tree limb or puts you in a car and runs a hose into it from the exhaust pipe, death was caused by a lack of oxygen to the brain. The body acts as a blueprint for reconstructing what biological processes were affected and in what way."

"So Weyland wanted to get your opinion on what method was used to kill Sonny Melton?" Ran said.

"What Dr. Weyland specifically needed help with is not the subject of our meeting this evening," Tara reminded him. "I'm just trying to establish a composite framework for these cases."

"Right. No Sonny Melton questions," Ran responded in agreement, crossing his hands on the table in mock obedience.

She looked at him shrewdly, but seemed to see he meant no disrespect. "What I found in half a dozen autopsies was that death was due to blood loss, both internal and external, from a massive number of traumas. Now, none of these traumas was lethal in and of themselves, but when combined with the others and denied medical treatment, they were devastating."

Ran had begun his note taking. "No weapons?"

"Unless you consider teeth a weapon?"

Ran recalled his conversation with Hunter. "No cuts or blows to lethal areas?"

"Damage, yes. Significant trauma to the head and chest. But lethal? The injuries brought death in combination. What I encountered repeatedly with each case was a frenzy of attack upon the body: gashes, bites, tears, blunt trauma, dislocations, rough separations, but no clean cuts. No deep penetrations. Initial conclusions were that the victims were killed by conventional means and then set upon by nature's scavengers. We found no evidence of a weapon nor did we see any canine, feline, or insect activity as to blame for the excessive damage. There just wasn't anything that offered clues other than some human saliva and hair samples. It was, *is*, frustrating. We can tell you the body went through the human equivalent of a wood chipper, but nothing more," she said.

Ran could hear the passion in her voice as well as a hint of failure. Unable to hear what the victims' bodies had been trying to tell her, Tara Phillips must have felt she wasn't owning up to her end of the private deal she had made with her dead clients.

"Is it possible for a man, or a group of men, to inflict the measure of injury you witnessed with their bare hands? I've seen the result of a gang beating, and that included chains, bats, and knives. It pales in comparison to this."

"Keeping in mind the degree of trauma, the lack of any artificial weapons, and what would have to be a sociopathic disregard for life, it would take a number of men working in unison to cause this level of depravity. *One* man?" She pursed her lovely lips and looked out through the darkened window at a calm Kansas evening. "Given time, one man could cause this injury. But it would take way too long. In the investigative reports from the crime scenes, I found no indication of opportunity for a prolonged attack. Most of the crime scenes were discovered within hours of the assault, in some cases only minutes had passed. No man alone could inflict that measure of aggression without time. Hell, he would have to stop and catch his breath for God's sake. The energy he expended would be substantial. What kind of man could bring himself to do that?"

Yes, Ran thought, *what kind of man.*

Chapter 10

If asked to remark on his drive home from Dalton's, Ran would have been hard pressed to describe it. The comfortable breeze captured through the open window of the squad car was refreshing and a welcome change from the cool nights that had recently given way, but it went unnoticed. The streets were alive with townsfolk in their front yards, sitting in lawn chairs as they protectively watched over their children play tag or chase fireflies in the moonlight, yet Ran failed to return their hearty waves. Auburn was entering summer with its usual small town attraction, and passing through its quaint setting would have stirred a sense of belonging and pride in most residents, but the local sheriff was preoccupied in chaotic thought. His dinner with Tara Phillips had been both illuminating and troubling; Ran had wiped the cobwebs off an emotion he had not felt in years while learning that the murder case he was absorbed in was not confined to his little borough. It was a collective whirlwind of excitement and confusion that left Ran mentally exhausted but equally motivated by the time his head hit the pillow in the wee hours of the night. Lying awake in his bedroom, the ceiling fan casting soft shadows of motion across his peripheral vision, he settled on two courses of action before succumbing to a dream-filled rest: he would follow up on the cases described to him during dinner, and secondly, he would make every effort to stay in contact with the doctor. One path he would travel assuredly, having traversed its recognizable bends and dips many times in his career, while the other was covered in a dense growth from years of neglect.

When he arrived at the office Sunday morning, a day he usually reserved for chores around the house and recharging himself from the week's perpetually slow work schedule, he first put a call into the Shawnee County Sheriff's Department and Tony Sartin. His friend with the county was unavailable, but another deputy took the message and promised he would leave it for Sartin, who checked in frequently, but unlike Ran, was actually taking the day away from work. Ran figured it would be later in the day or Monday before Sartin got back with him, so he settled into busy work for the remainder of his morning, answering a few calls he had received the day before and later reviewing the notes he had taken during his discussion with Tara.

They had continued to address the similarity of the cases she had encountered as a resident pathologist with that of Clifford Weyland's, though Ran was careful not to mention his case at all. Tara was doing him a huge service and he wanted to respect her adherence to the rules that bound her. What was clear about all of the victims was the savage nature of their deaths and the little amount of forensic material available to the police to pinpoint a person of interest. Enough DNA was present to map the genetic code of a single individual, but without leads, the genetic strands could have belonged to anybody.

"Did the genetic material of each incident match?" Ran had asked.

"That is what was puzzling. The genetic markers matched in some aspects, but not in others. You see that when subjects are part of the same biological pattern, like family…cousins maybe. What was clear was that in each case a single genetic strand was involved. Makes the theory of multiple assailants hard to prove, doesn't it?"

"Not necessarily," Ran said. "Others could have participated but to such a degree that they failed to deposit DNA on or near the body."

"I suppose," she said.

"What I don't understand is how the similarities of the murders and their MO's didn't red flag the criminal investigators."

She replied, "Oh, but it did. We had requests for comparison of the samples in multiple murders in both North Carolina and Georgia. No match. Surprising really. Measurement of the bite and claw marks were the same, the level of trauma showed a like application, fingerprints had commonalities though complete samples were not found, but the saliva, hair, and other physical evidence were not from the same code. Close, as I said, but distinctly different people."

"How would you describe the difference?"

"My training is not in laboratory forensics, remember," she sighed, "so I can't venture the reasons behind the chemical differences. I did spend time with those involved in the analysis, though, so I am able to generalize on their findings."

Ran remembered every word. True, he had taken excellent notes; years of investigative interview had honed his own brand of police shorthand. What had brought the conversation back in full clarity were the images that accompanied them. The entire night played like a movie in his memory: her coy smile, the soft light capturing the radiance of her skin, the way she drew her hair through her fingers and way from her face. It was all there, replaying in a small frame of flashback, the sounds of the restaurant faded to a disregard hum. Only her voice, her face.

"I don't know how much exposure you have had to DNA constructs, genomes, that sort of thing."

Ran said, "If they match, I have my man basically. I have been involved in mitochondrial DNA cases, some degenerative situations, but structure? Sequence? It looks like Tinker Toys to me."

"Tinker Toys. Nice visual," she laughed. "Well, I'm not too far ahead of you even with my experience. Sounds like you have a pretty good idea of the basics."

"Very basic."

"I'll put this in the most simple of terms, but ultimately even some of the best forensic chemists were uncertain of what they found." Free of condescension, she had given him a brief summary of the genetics of their assailant.

"What most people don't realize is that the DNA molecule that contains the genetic code for life is similar in all forms of life. The make-up of the strands, your Tinker Toys, is where the difference lies, and along the strands are individual markers that define each of us uniquely. It's basically a blueprint of life from which cells receive instructions as they divide and construct a single living organism. Special. One-of-a-kind.

"Our parents provide each of us with half the construct, the mitochondrial you mentioned, so bloodlines are easily seen through genetic coding. We can confirm paternal, maternal, or sibling relationships with accuracy because the imprints are undeniable."

"Can identical twins be singled out genetically then?" Ran asked.

"No. Even though there are slight differences in appearance and traits; for example, they have different fingerprints--their DNA is the same," she said.

Ran was confused. "So one twin could be implicated for murder if all that was left behind was DNA? No fingerprints or eyewitnesses?"

"Essentially, yes, unless there are mutations within the molecule."

"Mutations? Like disease?" Ran said.

"Right. Mitochondrial DNA mutations can be passed to a mother's offspring, though in twins there is the possibility during division that one child receives a large number where as the other only receives a fraction.

Now you have a genetic variance. Very common."

"So are you saying our boy is a twin?"

"Not at all. You brought up the twin angle, but it is a good basis for DNA explanation. Genetics is an on-going science; the engineering of gene patterns is effectively in its infancy, but we are learning more every day," she said. "What I am saying is that DNA is consistent. If you were to leave your genetic code in fifteen locations, lab analysis could place you and you alone at every spot. In the multiple autopsies I described to you, the code was similar, but unquestionably from different people. There were variations that pointed to numerous individuals of familial but distinct genetic coding."

Ran said, "Are you saying I have a family of degenerates taking turns killing on a cross-country spree?"

"I said familial, but not in the sense of a family tree with parents and offspring."

"Once again, color me confused."

Tara explained, "What was found, and for all I know the results were tabled, filed away, whatever, because they refute all known human biology, was that each sample showed a unique pattern of genetically transmitted features."

Ran shook his head in bewilderment.

"I'm sorry. I know this sounds like scientific mumbo-jumbo," she said. "Start with this: Mutations occur in the evolutionary process, and this causes changes in the gene pool. Some of the mutations are not desirable, and those are usually removed through natural selection. Other mutations can be favorable, and over time they accumulate, and the result is evolutionary change. If a lizard's offspring have a mutation that causes them to blend into their environment due to ultraviolet light exposure, that trait is maintained through the pool because it is desirable. Over time all of the lizard's ascendancy in the animal kingdom is a result of this mutation."

"Darwin's theory of evolution and natural order. The strongest survive."

She agreed, "The strongest, swiftest, most capable to adapt to environmental change. Mutation is not always a negative word. Humans have mutated for centuries into the dominant species that they are. The opposable thumb is a perfect example. Along the way we have eliminated those traits that are undesirable; scientists think a mutated gene led to our graceful jaw lines versus the ape-like, jutting jaw of our ancestors. The road to brain over brawn.

"These positive mutations are hundreds and thousands of years in taking hold as the gene pool is slowly cleansed. Keep in mind though that only a very small percentage of mutations have a positive effect on a species. Most mutations are detrimental and the evolutionary process eliminates some while others remain in the form of disease, mental and physical retardation, and debilitating or deviant psychological behaviors."

"Basic biology. Why do I feel like I never took the class?" said Ran.

"Because maybe it's been a few years and a crash refresher course is trouble for anyone."

"Thanks for the sympathy, but I was always a lunch and Phys Ed student by nature."

She said, "Oh, I don't think I can believe that."

"Believe it. A plus in both. I was in honors gym as a senior. First in the food line three straight years," Ran joked.

Tara laughed fully, an intoxicating sound. "I hope you don't believe that because I don't."

"Tried to add study hall to my schedule but had to drop it. Too demanding what with ping pong and meat loaf to stay on top of."

"Stop."

"Fine. Don't believe me, but you will not get to witness my hot roll jump shot. Truly breathtaking."

She repositioned herself in the booth, her laughter slowly subsiding. "Where was I anyway?"

Ran checked his notes. "Good mutations need centuries to take hold, but only a few are worth having."

"Yes, the quality of mutations."

"It's such a negative term. What is a genetic mutation anyway? I have images of Barnum and Bailey. You know, bearded ladies and two-headed calves," said Ran.

"Well, that's only a part of the genetic process. A mutation is simply a change in the sequence of the genetic material. There could be a copying error when the cells divide. It could be caused by radiation, faulty chemical processes, even viruses."

"Before you started talking about mutations, you said that your lab boys discovered, what…" Ran looked at his notes, "…genetically transmitted features. What is the relationship?"

Tara continued, "Bare with me. I'm almost there. As I said, these mutations occur over a long period of time, either helping or hindering the species, but evolving as the species moves from generation to generation. A mutation occurs within an individual, which is then transmitted to each subsequent generation to be further adapted, refined, or eliminated in progression."

For the first time Ran was seeing some light. "So a single mutation must be shared among thousands of DNA strands to have a lasting impact on the species?"

"Excellent. That is right where I was going," she complimented him.

"P.E., I'm telling you."

Tara ignored his reference to what she surmised was a mythical education. "If we traced the evolutionary pattern of a mutated gene, it would be through the DNA of literally hundreds and hundreds of individuals. Keep in mind that an individual's DNA strands, yours, mine, are not only unique but also stagnant. We are what we are, and the only way we can create change in the species is by transferring a copy of ourselves genetically to our offspring who, with the DNA from the other contributing parent, create a new, unique genetic code.

"Here's the kicker. The DNA that was extracted in each of the cases that relate to yours showed identical sequencing *except in relation to mutations.* The same code with variations in each case."

She went on, "The mutations were not hereditary. They had occurred within the life of the organism. And were continuing to occur, at a cellular level."

Ran was lost again. "Sorry. Back in *Land of the Lost* again. Are you saying that each killer had the same DNA but a special evolving mutation? Like twins gone radioactive?"

"No, because I saw at least a half dozen lab results with this sequence. It would mean identical sextuplets were going around taking turns killing the same way, down to the biting and blunt force, each with his or her own special mutation. It's beyond impossible. The shear magnitude of the scenario would make any dedicated scientist scoff in search of other answers."

Ran said, "So what are other answers?"

"There aren't any," Tara said. "That's why the DNA findings were put aside as the result of corrupted or degenerated samples. A logical conclusion in the face of incidents breaking the laws of nature."

"So where does that leave us? Prove the Brady Bunch is out there killing in cycles?" Ran joked, though he regretted the flippant nature of his words and hoped Tara had not taken his tone as hostile.

"There is one other explanation, though it is a farther reach than the other theories. It would be career suicide if I even suggested it."

"Fire away," Ran said. "After the last few weeks and tonight, nothing could surprise me."

"You won't believe it."

"Try me."

"Hyper mutation at the cellular level within a single organism, or in this case, human being."

"Hyper mutation?"

She explained, "A person whose DNA strands are mutating at a rate consistent with, say, a caterpillar turning into a butterfly. Only these mutations are unstable and volatile, manifesting themselves in episodic violence only to dissolve and reconstruct in progressively negative patterns. No beautiful wings and the wonder of flight."

Ran put it in terms he understood to clarify what he had just heard. "A man whose molecular structure is evolving in a matter of days through unspecified mutations, mutations which normally need eons of evolutionary development? You're saying that my killer could be walking around with a new DNA profile everyday, possibly driven to murder by a mutating gene?"

"I told you you wouldn't believe it."

The phone rang around 3:30 that afternoon. Ran was trying unsuccessfully to get his head around the profile Tara had suggested for the murderer of Sonny Melton, struggling to even consider what amounted to an X-Files episode, and had figured he would have to wait until tomorrow to talk with Sartin, but his friend, like him, was eternally bound to his work.

"Tony, thanks for calling on your day off."

"What day off? You mean the same one you seem to be enjoying?"

Ran had recognized dedication when he first met Sartin during a county law enforcement briefing for all new officers within Shawnee's sheriff's and police departments. Ran had immediately taken to the sheriff's professionalism and ability to treat a small town officer as a peer instead of an inferior. Sartin was genuine and trustworthy, and for a long-time law officer who had seen the corrupted nature of the force, Ran valued their friendship.

"I came by the office after taking the boys fishing this morning and saw you called. What's up?" asked Sartin.

"Well, I was hoping I could come up this week and discuss the Melton case with you, see where your boys may be on the crime scene, access

NCIC, you know, information my two-man operation seems unworthy of having," said Ran.

"Ran, you know you are welcome here anytime. It'd be great to see you and I can bring you up to speed on the investigation from our end, though there really aren't any new developments. Just waiting for the autopsy and lab work like you, I figure. As far as NCIC, when are those tightwads on your council going to introduce Auburn to the twenty-first century?"

"Most likely in the twenty-second," said Ran. It took high-end crime to warrant the technology his office needed according to the town council, and money, which they didn't have. For now, they had believed putting what funding they did have into manpower while making the department reliant on telephone inquiries should they need information about crimes or criminals from criminal justice agencies. Ran had appealed to their common sense, explaining that a routine traffic stop could escalate into a dangerous situation if he or his deputies were not aware that a vehicle may be stolen or the driver had an outstanding warrant, but until he could demonstrate situations where that had been the case in sleepy Auburn, they would remain in the Stone Age.

"What are you looking for through NCIC?" asked Sartin.

Ran hesitated, not because he was considering withholding information from his friend, but struck by the image Tara had created of a mutant killer.

The National Crime Information Center was a computerized system made available to federal, state, and local law enforcement, compiled and updated through the FBI. The data provided is obtained from all crime agencies, including foreign sources, and certain courts. Through NCIC law enforcement could find information on everything from missing and wanted persons to criminal records and vehicular details. Searches on the data bank even provided the names of suspected gang members and those implicated in terrorist activity. It was an invaluable source of crucial, timely information that Ran had used like a Christian the Bible, but he had only delved into its records twice since arriving in Kansas--the first time to register Irene Dunn following her disappearance, and the second to check on a pick-up left unattended for three days at the Piggly Wiggly. (It had turned out to be stolen from nearby Emporia, though the thief had never been identified.) In neither instance had Ran actually tapped into the system himself, relying on Tony Sartin and his acquaintances at the SCSD to access the databank. It would be like revisiting an old friend. In Los Angeles he had worn out two keyboards as a result of his late night surfing sessions.

"Just taking some shots in the dark," Ran said dismissively. "I can't stand the wait."

"Well, maybe I can save you some time after I show you what dead ends we have encountered."

"Nothing worth pursuit?"

Sartin sounded frustrated. "We completed an extensive search at the scene, extended to perimeters outside the normal crime area, did hundreds of interviews, assisted the KBI in dozens of background checks on the victim's business associates, traced his entire day from the last time he was seen in the city to the bloodbath on 75. Zero. Nada. I'm not sure what other pavement you could pound."

"What about similar instances?"

"Well, sure, dozens of cases of mutilation. Most involved verifiable instrumentation of some kind or use of vehicle," said Sartin. "Only a few cold, though. Convictions and sentencing in most. You can find a case like this in every state; there is no limit on the number of certifiable nut jobs in this country."

"And neither you nor the feds could draw parallels?"

"Nothing that indicated serial occurrence…unless you count some psycho in Minnesota who butchered six people in a two-day stretch with a set of cutlery he bought on QVC. Claimed Satan told him to make the purchase and start Thanksgiving early."

"Nice, Tony. Real nice."

"Everyone is stumped. Until we hear something from the ME, everything is in a holding pattern."

Ran knew that what Tony Sartin was telling him was on the up and up. If there was information being guarded, then the Shawnee sheriff's deputy was as in the dark as he was. Ran still wanted to check the cases Tara had referenced, and he felt somewhat disloyal by not revealing the real purpose of his trip to Topeka, but at the same time Ran wanted to maintain the doctor's anonymity. As soon as he told Tony about the cases in North Carolina and Georgia, the source of the details would be required should they pan out. For now, Tara's assistance would remain undisclosed pending the findings of the Melton autopsy and the private investigation Ran planned to conduct through NCIC.

"I think I'd like to come up anyway. I'm just sitting on my hands on this one and I've got to do something," said Ran.

Sartin laughed, "Sounds just like you. Sure, get on up here and spend the day. It'll be good to see you. We'll have lunch and see if we can't put our heads together on this one."

"Thanks, Tony. I'll see you tomorrow."

Ran hung up the phone and sat in thought, his elbows on his desk, his chin resting on the steeple his fingers created. Tomorrow he would leave word with Polly to let Monk know he would be out for the day. Chances were good, according to Tara, that they would receive the full post mortem and lab analysis of all samples from both the crime scene and the field from the medical examiner's office Monday, so any documentation should remain sealed until he could look at it. He was counting on his visit to Topeka to shed some light on things while at the same time giving credence to the possibilities that Tara had unveiled.

Twenty years of police work, fifteen years of homicide investigation, some of which was grisly and worthy of purging the stomach, had hardened Ran and exposed him to what he thought was every measure and type of brutality and human condition, and yet he felt he was spinning out of control, without direction, while looking for any familiar landmarks to orient himself. His sense of unsteadiness was multi-fold. He was without the technical means he had taken for granted to carry out a proper investigation; the available information was sketchy at best, calling for conjecture and supposition; his pursuit of answers had put him in contact with a woman who had ignited feelings in him long since abandoned in the dawn of his career. Ran was driven by organization and detail, believing that each step should be forward as he traveled a road of enlightenment toward the ultimate prize--resolution. No case had ever gone cold under his scrutiny, and he wouldn't start this late, and in all places, the rural Midwest.

There was no perfect crime in Ran's world. Inevitably, a lead or a clue or a record emerged, pointing the way and unraveling the web of question marks and revealing the inevitable--a declaration of guilt. Ran was traveling for the first time without a road map and no sense of direction. His fellow officers were equally perplexed and offered him little during one of those rare instances when he needed their insight and humbled himself before them. Now, more than ever before since his arrival in Auburn, he wished he were back in his native arena, attacking a case with reliable tools he had grown accustomed to. Dependable tools, like informants, who never disappointed. *What did he have here? Nothing. No signs to discover that pointed the way, and even if they were available, he couldn't read them because this was not his hunting ground, it never really had been. It just took a major crime to illustrate for him that he was a foreigner in a foreign land. Forget Monk and his guilt trip. Polly and her expectant glare. Let them solve their own problem; it wasn't his. There was nothing here for him.*

Tara…

The doctor had offered him an unbelievable story line to consider. It was farfetched, borderline supernatural, and in many ways not worthy of his efforts.

But she had made the impossible seem hypothetical, and she had shared the information not as a way to poke fun at his predicament but to shed medical insight on a potential link to other instances. What if the mutant gene theory was ridiculous speculation without scientific merit? The potential that his killer was tied to other cases made the effort worthwhile. Who knew? Maybe a fresh approach was necessary to bring a common bond in all the cases, including his. And now that he had met the doctor, had spent time with her and fallen under a pleasing spell, his place in Kansas appeared more meaningful, with greater purpose.

He closed his notes and headed home, intent on riding the wave of his new resolve.

For the second time he had to remind himself that he had a job to do and an obligation to what was now his home.

He would not forget that again.

Chapter 11

The rage was beginning.

Sitting in the middle of his living room floor, Caine had taken all the necessary steps in preparation for what was to come. The period of transformation afforded his conscious mind ample time to ready himself, and he had learned over the course of many years what measures to take to assure a safe transition.

He normally recognized the onset of his affliction around midday, marked by a dull headache and steady rise in body temperature. If he was away from the house (and he always made sure he was within minutes of returning), Caine would calmly complete whatever he was doing, filling the truck with gas or checking out at a retailer's, and make his way back to the safety of his secluded ranch-style home. There was no need to rush; the process took the remainder of the day to complete itself, and by nightfall he would be unaware of his activities until he tried to piece them together days later.

There, on the wood floor in an open area away from furniture or walls, he would allow the predator of his will to advance, slowly, while he contemplated its approach and purpose. In years past he had often found things in disarray upon conscious return. Thinking he was experiencing the onset of the flu or something health-related, he would retire to bed, only to find the mattress and box springs in shambles. Reclined in a chair or leaning back against the sofa had earned him the same results. He concluded that his body went through some kind of fit or physical assault, causing him to disrupt objects within a confined area. In time, treating himself as if the victim of an epileptic seizure, he opened a space roughly eight feet in diameter (and far from his precious computer system) where he would greet the rage in sardonic acceptance.

The reality of seeking medical aid had not missed his list of options, though something told him it would prove a waste of effort while exposing him to potential inquiring of a damning nature. He had self-prescribed various remedies initially--aspirin, pain relievers, cold suppressants--but to no avail. The heat of his body only increased, drawing a heavy, thick sweat from his pores as it radiated from somewhere deep inside, growing, spreading, seeking to ignite his entire frame in a spontaneous combustion. The building rhythm of his heart found a pounding accompaniment within his skull as if something in both places demanded release. Bearable at first, the distress he felt would move from a dull discomfort to an agony that would have welcomed death until he mercifully slipped into nothingness. Certainly doctors could observe him, wire every form of machine and device to his body to track the course of his malady, but history had shown him that nothing could prepare them for what came after. And if he demanded restraint, warned them of the danger that would come, would they honor his plea and protect themselves? Of course not. They would stand by their superior training, know what was best for a patient who was obviously suffering from paranoid delusions, and eventually betray his secrets, putting him on the run. No, the scientific community was not his answer.

He had in fact enclosed himself in an empty room, locked the door and barred it with an extravagant number of key and combination locks in the hope of thwarting the rage from escape to the outside world, only to awaken and upon inspection find the bar lifted, the locks opened and laid uniformly along the baseboard. There would be no signs of aggression, no splintered wood or ruptured handle. The force within him apparently reversed the conscious process, manipulating the resting Caine, acquiring his knowledge to disarm the barrier and free itself with purposeful ease. The introduction of a second party to assist him in confining himself was not an option. He or she would feel compelled to respond to his cries (which he believed his new self would be most capable of doing) or seek help and advice from others out of compassion, and he would be back to square one. Caine and the power that ruled him must remain anonymous. Something beyond his rational self told him this in no uncertain terms.

The life he had created was his best, his only, choice. Discovery meant loss of freedom, and what little free choice he enjoyed while living with the rage would be lost to him. Under the control of judicial authorities, legal representatives, or even medical heroes bound to save him from himself, there would be no more Sebastian Caine, only a number of record in some institution, enclosed in a padded cell or, more likely, the topic of debate in the ongoing argument over capital punishment. In either case he would be forever held captive in a world not of his choosing. If he was going to be enslaved, it would be on his terms, or at least on terms that allowed him moments of respite. His disorder at least afforded him a measure of liberty. He had grown to accept it as a disability. It was his blindness, his paraplegia, a handicap that required adaptation in order to coexist with society. He had accomplished this with an incredible degree of success. The outside world was manageable; as long as the rage maintained a consistency, though he had recently seen signs of instability that would require his careful monitoring.

In the years prior to the start of his epic journey, Caine had already established himself as a loner, working as a computer programmer for a mid-level oil and gas company in the South, his family long since dead and gone, the victims of disease and obsessive chemical dependence. An only child of a stern, overbearing father and submissive mother, and object of children's ridicule because of his immense proportions, he had abandoned the familiar hills and snow-peaked trees of a cloistered New England lifestyle and headed to east Texas where he could put his technical skills and unknown name and face to work in an industry recovering from a national crisis and finding a new foothold. He had just wanted out, away from the painful memories, free of the eyes that looked down on him with mock sympathy while secretly avoiding anything resembling human contact. The first two decades of his life had been forgettable monuments of despair and solitude, growing up an outcast among peers and even his own home, and Sebastian had sought a fresh start, not to capture a childhood of friends and precious moments unrealized, but to shed himself of the old skin of his miserable past and bathe himself in the unspoiled that he knew must exist beyond the borders of his collective experiences. Little had he known that his previous life and escape were preparing him for the future he would share with his other self.

His first episode had occurred without grave consequences, and it was some time later before he recognized that he wasn't alone in a conscious effort to remain concealed. While leasing a small two-bedroom on the west side of Beaumont, his newfound life well underway, he had come home feeling near death, assured that he would be calling in sick the next day. A round of store-bought remedies and four agonizing hours later, he had staggered from his soaked sheets and collapsed on the floor in unbridled fear, unable to make it to the kitchen phone and an appeal for assistance. His mind was a feverish whirlpool of agony, and in the closing moments of his grip on reality, he had screamed a helpless cry.

He ascended from the blackness much later, his conscious self bringing with it dreamlike images of dark, wooden vistas and open hills of meadow and valley. Here he raced with blissful and determined ease, feeling the soft, wet grass beneath his feet, and drew in cool air that bit in his chest and offered a moment of euphoria. Every muscle was alive, with each contraction propelling him along. The night provided a solidarity he found familiar, comforting. In this moment in time he had never felt such freedom. A oneness pervaded to every fiber of his being. Among the trees and gentle slopes of nature's design, he found harmony, a sense of belonging that surged through him. For the first time in his pitiful life he was at home. There was no discomfort or exclusion; nothing in this place offered exile or rejection, only acceptance. It was all very alien to him at the same time, but he welcomed it with joy, an equally foreign emotion.

The scene soon became a blur as his pace quickened. The movement felt natural and he settled into it with measured strides, the threat of weariness an impossibility. His strength was immeasurable; bursts of power and force drove his legs like pistons. His arms pumped in cadence to the effortless motion as he sailed across a colorless landscape. Just beyond his mind's eye, over the next swollen river and through a stretch of forest was his destination, the target of his flight, and he could feel his imminent arrival. There laid the fuel that drove him. It was in this final leg of the journey that he understood his role in the disjointed picture show that played upon the screen of his waking brain. He was in pursuit, part of a hunt in which he was the aggressor. And for once, he was superior. Sebastian Caine was worthy of dread in the eyes and hearts of those around him. His prey would look upon him with trembling alarm as he approached. Closing the gap, he could feel his balled hands flex back and forth like talons. His lips drew back revealing blood stained teeth that would soon clamp and tear and rip. Vessels pulsed and stood wormlike on his taunt skin. Suddenly, topping the next rise, he beheld the sufferer--meek, trembling, a symbol of imperfection. The terror that froze its lesser frame was painted on a face of disbelief. This was the moment of ecstatic relief. It was here that Sebastian would change the humiliation, the expulsion that had forced his withdrawal and placed him on a harsh island of forsakenness.

And then chaos. An unmerciful attack liberating a sea of wrongdoing. The vista of beauty became washed in red, both with the fire that blazed from his eyes and the life force he loosed upon the earthen terrain below him. Coursing up and out of him came primitive moans and bestial wails of pleasure. The assault was endless, the satisfaction, infinite.

Before he was fully conscious, Caine clung to the dream, willing himself back into that wondrous panorama where he ruled the night. But it was quickly lost, slipping through his mental fingers and falling into a deep chasm of fantasy. He tried to project himself down, down to the kingdom of his dominance, but the vision was gone. Out of it came the sharp ringing of a phone, and the world's bleak reality slapped him hard in the face.

He struggled that first time to make sense of what had seemed so real, not knowing it would take many more encounters with the rage to begin to get a grasp on what was happening and accept the fate of his tomorrows. The call that had drawn him back after his maiden trip was his boss at T & B Oil and Gas, demanding to know why he had missed two days of work without the slightest contact.

"Two days?" he had muttered.

"We were about to send the police to your house if you went another day without answering," the Senior VP, Jerry Schneider, had said. "Have you been gone? Why didn't you let us know your story? We can always work something out if you need time off, but you've got to let us know ahead of time."

"I've been sick."

"Too sick to pick up a phone or send an email? This is not good, Caine, I have to tell you. I can't keep Adams off my back another day. I better see you in here first thing in the morning or we're going to have to go another direction with our IT department."

"No, no, I'll be there. Just...I've been sick and..."

"Tomorrow, Caine, or not at all. You've really put my butt in a sling here," said Schneider. "I mean, two days? You're lucky you still have a job."

He had given himself a cursory inspection following the conversation, having struggled to the bathroom to survey the damage. He felt totally spent, as if two days of sleep had done little to relieve his weariness, and the twenty odd steps to the mirror seemed like a great distance. When he flipped on the light, someone he did not immediately recognize greeted him. Hair wild and unkempt, the phantom that hunched across the sink from him was pale skinned. Black streaks of something had dried along his face and arms. His clothes were torn and ragged, the stitching along some seams having burst outward. The same dark smears tattooed the shirt and pants in long thin lines and wide swipes. His first thought was transmission fluid because it looked just like the stuff that covered Roger Boynton who used to work on his father's old Plymouth in Maine. His shoes were covered in dirt and carried grass stains up to and over his pants. Caine was ravenous, but the pull to sleep was just as great. He drug himself back to the living room where the frayed carpet held some of the same staining that covered his body. He knew he should get to an emergency room and found out what was wrong, but something told him to stay home, willed him to deal with it here, in the confines of his house. Other than the carpet, he found nothing wrong that first time. The front door was locked; his then Buick Century sat stoically in the driveway.

He made repairs to himself and the carpet that evening. Following a long, hot shower in which he dozed off repeatedly, only to be startled awake when he dropped the soap or his shoulder impacted the wet tile above the bathtub, Caine nearly emptied his refrigerator and freezer, his stomach too impatient to wait for frozen foods to fully cook before he was tearing into them with a hunger he didn't recall ever feeling. He was a big man, had always had a good appetite, but the amount of food he put away that night was frightening. His thirst was extreme as well, and after a gallon of milk, a twelve-pack of diet soda, and a liter of orange juice, he still felt dehydrated. Had he had more to devour, he would have done so without difficulty, but his compulsion to stay inside far outweighed his desire to seek further sustenance. It was then he learned to keep ample supplies at all times, never knowing when his debilitated body would need replenishing.

Drained, in need of more sleep, he had gone into work that next day and salvaged his job, though the quality of his performance left much to be desired. His concentration on motherboards and wiring was supplanted by flashbacks of his nightmarish reverie and its real, palpable aftermath.

He was fired three months later following his second episode, the results of which were quite similar, including the reaming he had taken from Jerry Schneider, who spoke of a lack of dependability, consideration, and being *just plan weird*. He had heard through the industry grapevine some time later that a former colleague of his at T&B, a quiet fellow who took some of the same verbal abuse Caine had tolerated, had been murdered in some freak accident at a cabin where he had gone hunting or fishing. A bear or something.

That began a string of new jobs and firings for Caine, who soon understood the nature of the episodes and the need for him to not only move on to another part of the country but to find a job more suited to his talents and ailment. He had traveled the Gulf Coast, eventually making his way up the Atlantic seaboard, but progressed west from there before reaching the site of his painful upbringing. Through the Carolinas, up and down the middle of the U.S. as far as the Ozark Mountains and the Ohio Valley, he had eventually landed in Kansas, strategically placing himself outside a small town on a remote property where he could work and transform unabated. He had come upon a perfect job situation while listening to two former colleagues argue over the potential of off-site computer programming and repair during lunch in one of the many companies he worked for before finally striking out on his own. Along the way he had dozens of episodes, some memorably violent while others were free of the carnage and left him with mental impressions of an invigorating journey (the lack of blood on his clothes and skin confirmed this), but with the growing number came understanding and a vague acceptance. He would soon recognize how dependent the rage was upon him, and conversely, how it served him, delivering a form of retribution that he could not find on his own.

Now, once again, as it had so many times before, the mystical swell of his other self was making its way up from its sinister abode, to lay claim to Sebastian Caine, escape its bonds, and exact revenge on an unsuspecting world. It had become a ritual of sorts. With hours of the preliminary changes still ahead, Caine made the simple but necessary preparations for its arrival. An email to all his clientele that he would be shutting down his systems for a maximum of forty-eighty hours for internal repairs would explain his failure to reply to their service requests while hopefully avoiding any backlash to his business for going off line for so long. His response time otherwise was prompt and courteous while providing fast resolution; these features were the reason he had only lost two full-time customers since becoming self-employed. It seemed his untimely lapses in service were bearable in an uncompetitive market of high-priced computer geeks who chose to specialize versus diversify. Caine had concluded early in his business venture that appealing to a mass market was the only way to stay afloat.

With his hard drive and monitors went every light in the house. A passing motorist would be witness to a desolate house without yard light or street lamp, the old truck a hulking shape in the driveway. Caine was certain he left the house in the cover of darkness and found signs that suggested he returned in the same measure of concealment. It only made sense that the rage would operate in this manner, using shadow and sunless sky to exact its purpose. His last wakeful memories were consistently captured in a pitch black, the faint dusk of the evening light long since gone from the edges of the blinds and curtains that sheltered the interior of the house. Revived from the journey many hours later, he would note the now dry footsteps shaped of dew, mud, leaves, and grass that lead from either the front or back door. These were found locked when he gained consciousness, just as he had left them, when he began the cleansing process of house and self. It was apparent the rage worked in conjunction with his acts of avoiding identification. Caine knew he was never one hundred percent sure of being cloaked in secrecy. Any unforeseen event could trigger a fallout. What of the statistically low chance a burglar targeted his home and made entry? He would find few items, other than the computers, to make off with, and they were easily replaced. Should Caine be in the midst of restoration, well, his invader would find no resistance and potentially relish his ability to come and go unmolested. If, on the other hand, the uninvited guest came upon him now, as the rage took possession, the problem would surely be eliminated.

The now-locked doors were not an effort to cage his wrath; it could not be contained, but were a symbolic act of enclosure from the prying eyes that lay just beyond. This was a private moment for Caine, an intimate transference of self to a higher power, his shocking imitation of prayer. There, on the wood floor, he found his Garden of Gethsemane, his mission about to be fulfilled, and where, human in his design, he suffered a supernatural anguish. Far from the inferior gaze of an unjust majority, he suffered. Every muscle soon spasmed in involuntary jerks and starts. His jaw popped and snapped with whip lashing effect. His limbs pulled and gathered as every joint became an anchor to violent motion. The dull ache that had invaded his temples and found residence behind his eyes was now building to a crushing crescendo. He fell back prostrate then flopped like a fish drawn from the sea and cast helpless onto a waterless world. The sweat was profuse, dampening his clothes and giving a slapping quality to the sound of his body impacting the floor. The pain in his head soon reached an unbearable degree, and in a climactic announcement of his departure from the conscious world, Caine let out a bloodcurdling scream that found its birth deep in his throat.

The cry was sustained for many minutes, until the high pitch of the vocalization began to alter. It deepened, becoming more guttural and thick, losing the human quality it once possessed to claim a more primitive, bestial manner, then abruptly stopped, an eerie silence on its heels. What had started as a wail had transformed into a growl, a fitting overture for the thing that Caine had become.

It lay perfectly still.

Acquaintances, if he had any, would still recognize it as Caine--the same broad shoulders and Nordic features. The timid giant who recoiled from ridicule and found solace in his retreat.

In time it sat up and then rose to its feet. In the dark recesses of the room it stood, its chest heaving with each deep breath, eyes cutting through the blackness to reveal every hidden corner. The exterior was a worn Sebastian Caine; behind those eyes lurked something new, a sinister, purposeful other.

Having oriented itself, the new Caine strode to the front door, unlocked it with a familiarity, and stepped into a cloud-filled night. The Kansas air was dry this night, free of the humid conditions that had ushered in the summer. Frogs spoke in concert across a nearby farm pond. The open field across the road was alive with the sound of insects calling one another from the vast expanse. The rage that was now Caine sniffed the air with an upturned nose, detecting the slightest of odors from hundreds of yards away. Its tongue slid across glistening teeth in anticipation as it made a slow, full turn, gaining its direction and objective through senses that were supersensitive, a composite normally seen singularly in such great magnitude.

Pausing then, only briefly, it set out in a southerly direction down the road, its stride determined, its heightened senses attune to the slightest rustle or movement.

The Caine thing's pace soon quickened, weaving the tapestry of memory that its alter ego would later recall.

Within minutes it was miles from its starting point, its destination waiting across the next riverbed, over the next hill.

Chapter 12

Ran arrived at the Shawnee County Sheriff's Department around eight o'clock Monday morning. With him was the information he had compiled during dinner with Tara Phillips, notably the locations and approximate dates of murders similar to his own dead end investigation. It was through NCIC, and a review of the Melton murder with Tony Sartin, that Ran hoped to shed some light on a case that, to this point, had failed to provide a single suspect. All he had were the preliminary forensic reports and accounts of deaths that bore striking similarities, but in each case the facts were obscure and hard to swallow. Ran had made a career relying on credible fact gathering and solid investigative work to piece together a crime. It was in Topeka that he planned to put that into action.

Having explained to the front desk officer his intent, Ran crossed the bright parquet floor to what he traditionally referred to as the bullpen, a large open area crowded with desks for any of a number of sheriff's deputies and other department personnel. Reminiscent of the holding area he shared with dozens of detectives in Los Angeles, Ran found the hectic room comforting and inviting. He scanned the law enforcement arena, coveting the computers that occupied every desk. Groups of officers huddled at various points, some obviously sharing stories of weekend exploits, their laughter rich and heartfelt. Others were already pouring over reports and data. The smell of strong coffee assailed his nose, and he was instantaneously carried back to a different time, not long ago or easily forgotten. Along three outer walls of the pen were offices, each with a door and full window for the high-ranking members of the department. Behind Ran and to the left of where he had entered was a wall of file cabinets and a small table with a coffee machine. Next to this was the greatest single source of ridicule of police work in the free world--a box of donuts. With his hand exploring its contents stood

Sartin. Ran couldn't resist the opportunity.

"I should have stayed in Auburn if picking between chocolate and maple was the duty of the day."

"Stick around. You could learn something about navigating toward the elusive raspberry jelly," smiled Sartin, who put his cup down to shake hands with his friend. "I expected you a little later in the day. Auburn closed for renovation?"

Sartin's slam on Ran's charge was allowed only within their relationship. Tony had told him on more than one occasion to ignore the petty jokes levied on the small town and its negligible crime rate.

"Complete overhaul. We're having the gravel on Main Street cleaned and polished one piece at a time. Could take hours, so I thought I'd come see how real police operate," said Ran.

Sartin turned to his office, "Grab some coffee. I'll meet you in my office."

Tony Sartin was a lieutenant in the Criminal Investigation Division, and as such, held an upper level position and the right to a desk behind a door. Ran joined him in an office that stood as a testament to the All-American family. Youth sports photos and staged poses with the wife and children littered the walls and every available space. A magnet held a colored rendering of childlike design on a file cabinet; its rough outlines featuring three stick figures, one of which held a disproportionately sized fish.

"So did you know the final autopsy report is due today?" said Sartin.

Ran knew through Tara, but was not willing to expose their new alliance. It only made sense that the Shawnee Sheriff's office would be privy to information first, based on their location and close ties to the medical examiner. Ran knew Sartin well enough to know he wasn't rubbing it in his face.

"Well now, Tony, how would those of us in the back of the line know what you boys up front are hearing?" said Ran.

Sartin grinned, "If I know you, you will eventually find a way to the front of that line."

"I'm not really counting on the autopsy to reveal anything compelling. You've told me yourself and I've seen it in the scene reports. There is nothing linking the murder to any likely suspect," argued ran. "No witness testimony. No substantial evidence. Tips have been nonexistent. This case strikes me as one needing a fresh approach, not the usual phone calls and foot work."

"Word came down last week that Melton is throwing a rich man's tantrum--threatening legal action for police incompetence. Claims we're letting it go cold. The sheriff to the captain. The captain to me. I hope you're wrong about the autopsy," said Sartin.

Ran agreed, "I'd love to be wrong, but this case just feels different. Are you not puzzled that not one person of interest played out? That there are no suspects? This kid and his father were hated by hundreds of business associates and despised by half the state if I'm not mistaken. Alibis, computer and phone searches, interviews. Every investigative angle has been utilized within your department. It reeks of going cold. And then to add to the problems, the body is dumped under the same unrevealing circumstances miles from the encounter. Again, not a clue to go on. I think we need to work outside the box on this one, Tony. I really do."

"With all this manpower here," Sartin gestured to the open room outside his window, "we still can't devote the time and energy you are talking about, Ran. Captain Tolles has added a third detective to the case after the stink Melton raised, but in time they're going to have to file it away and pursue investigations with promise. That's why the autopsy is so important to us. Like you, a little direction would be welcome."

Ran said, "I don't want to sound like a defeatist or superior legal mind, but I just don't have a positive feeling about the autopsy by itself. But, if we were able to link it to other autopsies and crimes of a similar nature, well, then maybe would have some direction."

"You're talking hours of needle-in-a-haystack investigation. We will probably give that a cursory try, but until something turns up, I can't see the case getting a great deal of play after a few weeks if the autopsy proves a flop."

What Ran had to his advantage was a laundry list of potential *needles*, and with it he could enter the search well ahead of Tony's detectives. Three things kept him from revealing his information to Sartin and eliciting his department's assistance: one, he couldn't jeopardize Tara's involvement; two, he wasn't prepared to deal with the same doubt he offered the doctor when she presented her theories (the lowly Auburn Sheriff's Department didn't need another reason to be viewed as subpar and unworthy of respect); and third, and Ran had convinced himself it had nothing to do with pride, he wanted to solve this case himself, as he had done for years in his previous employment. He worked better alone, didn't feel constrained to pursue leads he thought viable because a partner determined them a waste of effort, and could keep a pace bent on discovery that few officers he had worked with were able to manage.

"So your captain won't have a problem with me using the county's

NCIC access?"

"Not at all."

"I will limit my donut consumption, I promise," said Ran.

"If you know what's good for you," Sartin said standing. "Come on. Let's get you on-line and out of my hair. Remember, I need you out of here by five o'clock. Housekeeping is picky about their time."

The two men shared a laugh as they headed into the bullpen. Ran nodded to a few detectives and deputies he had met before, some in the confines of the office, others during the recovery of the Melton remains.

Sartin led him to an empty desk toward the back of the room. Ran was pleased to see the monitor faced the near wall, its contents not on display to the curious. He wanted to follow this lead on his own, free of the conjectures and ruminations of others. It wasn't so much an anti-social behavior; it was his make-up as an investigator, and it had never failed him. Even when the trail led him to the front door of a leading Los Angeles politician, where a concerned voice sharing in his discoveries could have shown him their potential ramifications, he had pushed forward, eventually ending his employment and nearly his career. He trusted his skills--alone and without impediment.

Given the required entry information and password, Ran was left to access the NCIC files. His notebook lay open next to the keyboard displaying the specifics of Tara's memory. Ran wasn't sure what he was looking for as he accessed records from the first state on his list. Few investigators were aware of the evidence that would jump from their pages and demonstrate a commonality. In most cases they looked for a reoccurring theme or name or location to bring things together. It was never the same thing twice. One set of circumstances might show that a killer used the same ligature in multiple crimes, and those bindings were purchased from the same store and matched remnants presently occupying a place in the back closet of the perpetrator's home. Another instance may reveal that all three victims employed the same pool cleaning service over a span of two years, and in that time a former employee with a lengthy criminal record had serviced the homes on more than one occasion. It was a matching game on a grand scale and Ran savored the challenge.

On the drive to Topeka that morning Ran had concluded that he would start searching for the more credible scenario Tara had proposed, though every conclusion she had drawn was remote. He hoped to confirm within as many cases as possible the similarity of DNA coding of the assailant and the manner of death of each victim, then plot a geographic and time line. If he could find substantial proof that indicated serial murders, he could then advance the search to include demographics, occupation, and family history of the victims, time and location of each respective murder, including the body's final resting place, and any significant connections in testimony and forensic findings. It was a great deal of work, even with an accurate list of cases, but Ran was determined to find something useful. And should he uncover validity in Tara's second theory? He would cross that supernatural bridge when he got to it.

One of the most important aspects of crime scene investigation, far more vital than a layman's media-driven guess like the walk-through, contamination control, or evidence collection, is the documentation of all information and proceedings. From the initial response and recording of actions and observations to the crime logs and final scene survey, documenting the scene is crucial for on-site investigators and the later independent evaluations that are often made in time-consuming cases or those that go to a cold file. Ran had not been on the national information system in quite a while, but within a matter of minutes he was cross-referencing files and accessing the records of many criminal justice entities. It was hard work of a sedentary nature, and nothing that he could find himself doing on a daily basis, but when a case called for it, he relished this chase of keystrokes. Every new window represented new opportunities, and by lunch time Ran was feverishly absorbed, so much that he failed to notice Sartin standing behind the computer screen.

"Are you going to work straight through lunch?"

Ran was not surprised four hours had passed. "I think I might. Is it all right with you?"

"You aren't in our way. Just thought you might want to stop and stretch," said Sartin.

"I think I will just work through, thanks," Ran said, to this point not taking his eyes from the monitor.

Sartin knew better than to press it. "Any luck?"

"Depends how you define luck. I've found some of the things I was looking for, but I've only grazed the surface, Ran responded, finally stopping and resting his eyes on Sartin. "Would you mind if I printed a few things off? I promise I'll bring you a ream of Auburn's best to make up for it."

"No problem, and forget the paper. Listen, I'm running home for lunch. The kids are home over the summer, and I like to spend as much time with them as I can find," said Sartin. "I'll be back later. Can I bring you back anything?"

"Just hurry back, Daddy. I need you here too," joked Ran.

"You bet. If you're good, I'll bring you a Popsicle."

The truth was, Ran *had* found many of the files Tara had alluded to, and in the same vein, it *was* only the beginning. He was impressed though not surprised at the accuracy of Tara's dates and locations. With a minimal amount of searching, he was able to find the murders she had pinpointed as comparable to his case, and she was dead on in regard to their similarity. In many instances, as he fervidly worked the mouse over its pad, Ran could have been observed shaking his head in disbelief. Not at the lovely doctor's investigative instincts and intuitive nature though. Ran was at a loss as to how his peers had not looked deeper into what he recognized as a string of highly coincidental events. He realized that in many jurisdictions manpower was a common problem. There just weren't enough qualified investigators to keep up with the growing violent crime rate in the country. It was a progressing disease that the country, sadly enough, had grown to accept and, like physical illness, lived under the blind assumption that it would never happen to them. As a result the financial commitment necessary to support a well-staffed and highly trained department of police was not always present. Ran's own Auburn was a prime example, though a smaller version of the same failure to see a need happening in large cities from coast to coast. Murder, kidnapping, armed robbery, and every other type of violent crime was on the rise. The average citizens believed a stronger lock on their front door, an alarm on their car, a whistle on their key chain, and a more vigilant neighborhood watch were the answers. Little did they realize that though these were effective measures, crime was staying ahead of prevention as lawbreakers were becoming more knowledgeable and daring.

Ran was going to need to discuss with Tara some of the medical information he was finding, and so the request to make copies. There were some signature forensic markers that were reoccurring with each case he examined, and their significance was not for his untrained mind to deduce, but he felt there might be something worth further explanation. It was true he wanted to see Tara again, and further discussion of the topic that had brought them together was to him a legitimate reason to call and arrange another meeting. And should that get-together involve another dinner, something more formal, well, that was purely a happenstance. Even if the autopsy report were issued today, a meeting with Weyland would be both painful and unproductive. He needed her knowledge about the cases he was now absorbed in. To this there was no argument. *He also wanted to see her.* Also, no argument.

From a seasoned investigator's point of view, Ran had found a number of compelling pieces of information that gave credibility to a serial killer theory, regardless of the DNA evidence to the contrary. The manner of death, as bizarre and heinous as it appeared in Shawnee County, was a constant, from the chunks of flesh bitten and torn in animalistic style to the massive blood loss. Additionally, all the victims had been found in a location miles from the murder scene, their broken and crushed bodies seemingly discarded when their value to the assailant had run out. The lack of witnesses was consistent, but in many of the cases there where persons of interest, and Ran recorded their names in the hope of duplication or something that would tie the cases together, but found none initially.

As an investigator, Ran had been trained to look for the less than obvious, the subtly hidden clues that could break a case wide open. He evaluated the victim's jobs, sought parallels in the periods leading up to their deaths, and checked their backgrounds for histories that matched. Nothing. From what he could tell, those before him had done an adequate job of compiling information and pursuing the normal courses of action. These deaths, to his dismay, shared another stark reality--they were destined for the unsolved drawer in their local jurisdictions. It was too much to ask a department to expend energies beyond a reasonable amount of time, and in every case it appeared federal, county, and local investigators had stayed with their cases as far as they could carry them. A few had been further examined by newly-formed or long-standing cold case teams who looked at the same information Ran now absorbed across miles of cable and wire and had also come up empty.

Around two o'clock, Sartin reappeared. "Coffee?" he offered, setting a Styrofoam cup down on Ran's desk. In his other hand was a file folder.

"Thanks."

"Autopsy's in," he said casually, as if he knew the revelation would have little bearing on Ran's present endeavors. "Just arrived by courier. "I expect you should be getting the same. Do you want to take a look?"

"Have you looked at it yet?" Ran asked, stretching his back and taking the cup of coffee with sudden relish.

Sartin opened the file. "No. Thought you might want first crack, and to honest, I would love to see you doing something other than staring at that screen. Your rods and cones are going to be permanently damaged."

"You go ahead. I'll take a look back at the station when I am at a point to switch gears, but you will tell me if something jumps off the pages, right?"

"You'll be the first to know," Sartin said. "In fact, I have decided that from here on out, anything noteworthy in my life, whether it's a promotion, my son's first home run, or my wife inheriting a fortune, Ran Price will be the first to hear about it from me."

Sartin turned away with a devilish grin on his face.

"Hey," Ran said to Sartin, who stopped and turned back, "forget the promotion news. They're going to bust you back to deputy when they find out you've been sneaking home to see your family. Disgusting display of father/husband values."

Sartin rolled his eyes and continued back to his office. "I'll let you know if I see anything Price-worthy."

Alone again, Ran picked up the desk phone and dialed the main number at the county morgue. "Dr. Tara Phillips, please."

"Just one moment, sir. May I ask who's calling?"

"Sheriff Price, Auburn Sheriff's Department."

"One moment, please."

The detective who stood firmly by independent investigation was slipping without much struggle into a state of reliance. The insight Tara possessed was vital to his understanding of the muddled facts he had gleaned from NCIC, and though he had worked with pathologists in the past, their input had come on a factual level in an interrogative format. *What evidence do you have of suffocation? Was the victim's body placed at the murder scene to make it appear she died there? Is it possible that the assailant struck the deadly blow from behind?* In this case he was actively engaging her help in theory and supposition, asking her to evaluate the evidence and draw conclusions outside the forensic world. True, he needed her medical awareness, but she possessed an intuitive quality that he had seen in only one other person--himself. She looked passed the given, around the corner and up the street. Putting aside her looks, wit, and easy-going nature, all which were extremely attractive, Ran was able to see the need to break tradition and extend the olive branch of teamwork. If, and it was a big if, she was willing to continue providing him with her expertise. Based on their first encounter and subsequent meeting at Dalton's, it appeared she was a doctor with a detective trying to escape. Pathologists were naturally inquisitive, so it was not surprising that she seemed to have a predilection for mystery. Dismissing his attraction was difficult, but Ran felt certain that her involvement was crucial to his solving the case.

"Sheriff, Dr. Phillips is in a meeting. Can I take a message?"

"Yes, if you could have her call me at the county sheriff's office. Tell her I will be here until five. Thank you."

He hung up and then dialed Polly. "Have we received anything from the medical examiner's office? That autopsy report is circulating as we speak," said Ran.

"Nothing yet, Sheriff. It's been quiet most of the day."

"Well, call me here or in the squad car when it arrives. I want to have access to it the moment I return. You'll be gone when I get back. Just let Justine know."

"Will do. Sheriff. Sheriff?"

"Yes, Polly."

"You had a call from Dr. Phillips at the morgue. She said she would get back with you. Maybe it's about your report."

A rush of anticipation flooded Ran's body. Tara had already tried to contact him. It sent waves of varying emotion through him. Did she have further information to give him, possibly about the now released Melton autopsy, or was she simply wanting to talk with him, maintain a line of contact on a more personal level?

Man, was he infatuated. She was first and foremost a professional, as was he. Of course she was calling him about business. He had to stop carrying the flame she had stirred within him to the battlefield of law enforcement. There would be time for that later, if there was even a possibility of her interest. Auburn, with its down home charm and inferior position to the crime that filled the streets of LA, was proving to be a bigger challenge than Ran had ever anticipated.

Ran spent the rest of the afternoon looking for cases outside of the group Tara had given him, hoping to chart further evidence of a serial killer. He found six more murders that met the requirements to be included in his list, though their locations were random when placed on a small U.S. map he had brought with him that morning. Starting with his four points in Kansas, North Carolina, Georgia, and Arkansas, his new locations did not always lie on a line intersecting these, removing the remote possibility that Ran could divine a connect-the-dots route, indicating the killer was moving along an either preconceived or determined path that was predictable. The only conclusion he could draw having add the new points was that Kansas was the farthest site west. Some of the murders were in large cities, others in small towns. Some were coastal; others were in mountainous inland states. Yet another indecipherable set of facts. Ran reminded himself that sometimes investigators tried to find something that wasn't there, tried to create purpose where none existed. There may be no common denominator in regard to murder locations. They could be as random as the victims.

A dozen murders in all. Others were most likely out there, undiscovered either by him in his computer search or police in their investigations. The former was the more likely due to another commonality: the bodies were never buried or hidden in remote areas. Their discovery wasn't necessarily wanted; it just didn't seem to be a concern. And again, cross-referencing of DNA showed initial promise but was wasted effort in the end. One quality stood out when Ran arranged his cases chronologically; the time period between occurrences had been lessening. The first date, a murder in the Texas wilderness, was over four years ago. It was followed by a gruesome death three months later in southern Louisiana and ten weeks after that in the Florida panhandle. The death of Sonny Melton had occurred four weeks after the killing of an Ohio handyman. His body had been discovered a day later, in of all places, a store parking lot on the outskirts of Youngstown. The length of time between cases was definitively shrinking, and with this knowledge cam a new concern for Ran. *What danger was there that another victim was days away from meeting the same fate, and would that victim be drawn from the Auburn pool?* He couldn't wait to find out. He had to begin drawing some conclusions from the evidence he had, combined with the autopsy and Tara's input, and he had to do it now.

Ran gathered his paperwork, plucked the rest of his copies from the Xerox, and headed to Sartin's office to thank him for the use of his computer. His friend was gone, so he scribbled a note and walked out of the bullpen. He was now beginning to feel a sense of urgency. Details of each case swirled in his mind, joined by his imagination's creation of future crime scenes, in the heart of Auburn. His frenzied thoughts carried him toward the front door of the building where it took the front desk officer three tries to get his attention.

"Sheriff Price. Phone call. Medical examiner's office."

Tara.

He reached for the receiver with relief.

Chapter 13

Summers in Kansas tended to be long and hot, sometimes very hot, but Topeka and its surrounding communities were enjoying the start of an average July with highs in the eighties and lows in the mid-sixties. The precipitation that dominated the spring months, including some of the strongest thunderstorms and tornadoes in the nation, had failed to return to the aired plains of the state in quite a while, and residents, though pleased with the comfortable temperatures, were hoping their cracked lawns and dry fields would soon enjoy some saturation. Wildfires were plaguing the western two-thirds of the state due to the long drought, and late night dew did little to refresh the thirsting vegetation that was beginning to brown with neglect. Wheat, sunflower, soybean, and cotton production was suffering tremendously, and the state's cattle and sheep ranchers were also feeling the crunch. Things would have to turn around soon or the economy would suffer a major economic blow.

Sheriff Ran Price, if asked whether the lack of rain was for him a major concern, would have laughed at the implication. Having returned to Auburn after a short conversation with Tara before leaving the Shawnee County Sheriff's Department and rather lengthy ones with Monk and Tony Sartin on his police radio, the very idea that enforcing campfire and burning restrictions was a priority for fear of grassland fires was ridiculous. Ran had a much more pressing matter, with the potential for disaster far greater and the long-term effects more frightening. The rain would come, maybe sooner than later, if forecasters were on target with their oft-adjusted predictions based on weather patterns and satellite imagery. Or it could be late August, when crops would by then lost and farmers left wondering how they would survive the coming winter months, but they would at least have their poorer, less optimistic lives ahead of them. There was no need to focus on *potential* threats.

The storm that had already descended was the one to fear.

Tara had of course seen Clifford Weyland's full report, from its first level historical summary to its lab results, comments, and cause-of-death statement. The entire report had rung a familiar knell for her and added further detail to a design she had seen started years ago. Her voice had sounded controlled but anxious, and Ran suggested they meet that night to discuss the findings, to which she had readily agreed. This time their business would be conducted in a private venue, Tara's office, away from prying eyes. There the doctor and sheriff could voice their thoughts and concerns without interruption and, if necessary, view the remains still housed in the morgue until tomorrow. Ran, having dropped by the office and then home to shower and change, had told her he would be back to Topeka around eight o'clock.

Monk had spent an inordinate amount of time explaining the arrival of the autopsy report to Ran, along with its implications. When the sheriff returned to the office from his day of surfing the NCIC system, he found the deputy anxious to look at the Melton autopsy report that sat unopened on his desk, making terminal reference to it from the moment Ran had returned to Auburn. As he sat checking his messages, Ran could feel his deputy's expectancy as he hovered in the office, his fingers pounding a nervous rhythm on the leather belt that housed his firearm and other personal equipment.

"So did you learn anything new in Topeka, Sheriff? Anything outside of the medical examiner's report? They did get the same report, didn't they? What did they think about it?"

Monk was operating on hyper-drive, eager to rifle through a report of which he lacked little understanding, but all the more determined to dive headlong into a new pool of thought regarding the first violent crime in his hometown in over fifty years.

Ran perused his messages, giving little suggestion he was interested in the brown envelope that rested before him. It was a mean-spirited attempt to see how long he could ignore the report before his deputy exploded in anticipation, but secretly he willed himself to continue the charade while he too longed to spend time with its contents. What Monk didn't know was that Ran was waiting until he sat down with Dr. Phillips to begin interpreting the data. She could answer his questions as they arose and keep the report within a layman's sphere of understanding. Even Ran, who had seen his share of autopsy reports and had listened to hours of forensic testimony in the courtroom, needed a medical wall off which to bounce his questions and confusion. Tara would be that provider.

"Yeah, I think Lieutenant Sartin said they had it around noon. He hadn't had a chance to look at it by the time I left," said Ran.

Monk pressed, "What do you think we're going to find? I think a bunch of guys went after him with all kinds of things: picks, bats, maybe even rakes. I was thinking to myself the other day on patrol--could have been a biker gang passing through. Grabbed Melton and beat him for the thrill. Dumped him later over here on their way through."

"That's an interesting observation, Monk," said Ran. "That would explain the condition of the body, somewhat, but do you think a pack of Harley's could pass through Auburn without any in our community hearing it? Old Man Dunham knows everything that happens around his place."

Monk's assured expression faltered.

"Do you think a gang of bikers could enter and exit the field and not leave a trace, especially on a blood-soaked highway?" Ran tried to avoid talking down to his deputy, whose previous experience in a murder case had been trying to find the killer of Morgan Alter's prize bull, a time before Ran's arrival to Auburn. Turned out some drunk hunters had shot it for a deer. "No, I think it is something far less obvious. Maybe the autopsy will give us some hints as to who that may be, but I don't think all of our answers are going to come from the report. We still need to rely on investigation and a measure of luck to find our suspects."

"I'm getting ready to run my evening round," Monk said. "I can be back here by seven and we can take a look."

Ran stood and reached for the envelope. He appreciated Monk. The man was dependable and willing to do whatever was asked from him. He was eager to become a better deputy, and Ran saw great potential in him. This was just not one of those learning situations. "I think I'll just head home with this and see if anything substantial jumps off the pages."

He could see the disappointment in Monk's expression. "Maybe tomorrow I can sit down with you and show you some of the basic information contained in autopsies," Ran said, giving in to Monk's evident reaction.

"All right, Sheriff," Monk capitulated. But then a second later, "I need to spend some extra time along Southwest Eighty-fifth anyway. High school kids have been drinking up on Jenkins Lake, and I just know one of them's going to drown."

Ran smiled, "Put the fear of God in them, Monk."

"Will do, Sheriff."

The deputy, now with a renewed purpose, had seemingly forgotten about the autopsy report. Both men had then left the office, each to fulfill their goal.

The call from Tony Sartin, one that kept Ran sitting in his squad car long after pulling up to the sheriff's department in Auburn, had involved news that further complicated their investigation. A Kansas City businessman's body had turned up in Leavenworth County State Park about thirty miles east of Topeka. Apparently the victim had been last seen at a conference near Bonner Springs before he went missing. Fishermen returning to their car from a day of catfish and bass found the corpse, evidently dumped, in open terrain. It had displayed some of the same trauma witnessed in the Melton case and a preliminary investigation was underway. As of then, no murder scene had turned up.

"They thought someone had disposed of a deer carcass after hunting illegally in the park," Sartin had said. "When they noticed a hand with a gold ring on one of its three fingers, they dropped everything and raced to the ranger's office."

"Same MO I could gather. Extensive blunt force trauma, claw and bite marks, and little blood remaining. Looks like our perp to me."

"Anything at the scene suggest entrance or exit?" said Ran, already knowing the answer.

"Nothing, and when I talked to Sheriff Porter over at Leavenworth County, he acted like the only signs that someone had been there was the leveled grass the fishermen indicated was their path. Spooky how familiar it all sounded."

Ran agreed, "No doubt it's tied to ours. I assume they will be transporting to Shawnee County for the autopsy?"

"You bet. Should be in some time early tomorrow I would think. May give us a lead since it mirrors our case," said Sartin.

"Two zeros still amount to nothing, Tony. What do they have at the conference site?"

"Victim's room was undisturbed except for a bent frame on the sliding glass door. Management couldn't recall whether the damage was preexisting. No sign of struggle. Looked like he walked away. I checked the investigator's summary. Mitch Stanton, successful broker. Didn't have a reason to up and leave, especially his personal effects. Bit of a loner. Peers said he was unhappy with his required attendance at the conference, but not enough to risk losing his job and envied status in the company."

"So he was in his room and then, boom, he's gone," said Ran.

"A sweep of the immediate area showed no sign of foul play either. Yeah, just gone," said Sartin.

Ran was confident something was there. "I'll bet a wider sweep gets them something. Any chance they will return to the conference location for further analysis?"

"I'd bet on it, now that they have a body. I know Porter. He's a good man. Very thorough. I'll keep you posted."

Ran exuded doubt, but the news brought with it some optimism he didn't immediately embrace.

Sartin said, "I read the autopsy report."

"And?"

"And I'm not sure what to make of it. When you get a chance, let's talk about what you think," said Sartin.

Ran wasn't ready to tell anybody what he thought, but he was confident that by the end of the night he would have more answers to the growing list of questions that faced people. "Sounds like a plan. I will get back with you, and thanks for the update," Ran said.

"Why do I feel like you know more than I've already told you?" asked Sartin.

"Go play with your kids," Ran said. "I'll call you tomorrow."

Ran was back on the road to Topeka by seven-thirty, his notes and the unopened Melton report in tow. Along the way he considered the new information Tony Sartin had hit him with while also determining his next move. His NCIC search had confirmed Tara's account of a history of deaths remarkably similar to that of Sonny Melton, though investigators had run into a snag when comparing DNA profiles. That, plus the complete lack of eyewitnesses or other clues, had landed the cases in cold case file cabinets across the eastern half of the United States. Ran was now in the process of creating a new file, comprised of all the murders, to which he could add new information while continuing to cross-reference and hopefully discover something yet unseen within the archives. He was confident it was there; it was just a matter of asking questions of the data. Experience taught him the answers were usually on the surface, highly visible, like a floating speck of dismissed debris, waiting to be drawn from a turbulent pool of facts and figures. It was what kept police work interesting to Ran, and what he had been missing for the last three years.

Word of the second death in the area said a number of things to Ran. For one, their perpetrator or perpetrators were close, though not for much longer. The clusters of deaths came in twos and threes, so Ran believed northeast Kansas was nearing the end of its attraction. He didn't have to consult a criminal profiler to know that those involved in the deaths were nomadic, settling like gypsies for a brief period to commit atrocities only to pack up and move to the next killing field before drawing too much attention. Ran knew his time was limited; they would have to develop their case quickly or risk missing the chance to identify suspects and ultimately link them to the growing list that Ran believed only he was aware of. Second, it was obvious the level of injury inflicted on the victims had remained a constant; what Ran knew was that such extreme attacks, when the number of wounds extended into the dozens, suggested the assailant or assailants knew the quarry intimately. When a woman was found dead as a result of multiple stab wounds, authorities automatically sought out a spouse or companion as their person of interest. If an elderly man, missing for weeks, is discovered in pieces in three separate suitcases in a shallow grave, profilers looked to his family for answers. Violent offenders, their actions usually the result of strong emotional reactions, were predominantly acquainted with their victims and the fury often manifested itself in lengthy, traumatic episodes. These killers, or Tara's DNA doppelganger (though Ran was still hesitant to give her theory any real consideration and leaned toward the idea that more than one individual was involved), likely knew the victims, and some mental state, be it a psychological misfire or an emotional outburst due to a genetic flaw, was driving the destruction.

One thing Ran kept going back to was the unique geographical pattern he had charted while in Topeka for his all-day sit down with the NCIC system. The locations of the crimes covered the East Coast, South, Ohio Valley, and, most recently, the Great Plains. When plotted based on chronological occurrence, the events showed a roughly circular orientation, starting in the Gulf region, zigzagging through the South and up the Carolina coast, and crossing west. It didn't appear random (the killings progressed forward in their relationship, never showing a backtracking or crossing of path), though there was nothing Ran could pinpoint to explain the pattern. If he were asked to guess the next region of activity, he would assume a westerly course was logical, whether southwest into the desert or abruptly toward the Colorado Plateau. There was evidence that the killer could close the circle, completing his circuitous route where it seemingly all began, either in Texas or Louisiana. He found evidence of similar deaths in both states, but the investigative reports were shoddily handled. Ran could not be one hundred percent sure that this was the point of Genesis, but all things led back to there. Among his many plans were phone calls to both areas in the hopes of speaking with officials who had led the investigations. As was every lead now, it was a reach, but Ran knew not to leave stones unturned.

Geographic profiling was a relatively new field of criminal inquest, working on the assumption that the locations of crime scenes could give investigators clues to the perpetrator's residence, job, and travel routes. There did exist a computerized system known as the CGT or Criminal Geographic Targeting that took spatial details such as time, place, and distance and produced a paradigm called a jeopardy surface. This construct provided probabilities superimposed upon a map and allowed for police to pinpoint areas for increased surveillance and patrol measures. Ran had become familiar with the technique during a number of serial killings in the Los Angeles area. In each instance the CGT provided areas of interest that police concentrated on. In one case the system identified the suspect to within a square block of his residence. This through a careful study of transit maps, demographic data, and witness statements. Use of the CGT was available nationally, though few departments had criminalists adept at manipulating the information into something usable. Ran had already put in a call to an old friend before heading to Tara's office. It was with her that he hoped to confirm or cancel the individual cases he had compiled then submit his findings for profiling. Concurrently he would hope to gain knew insight from Melton's autopsy and seek word on any developments in the most recent murder outside Topeka.

Ran could feel the wheels of progress beginning to turn beneath him.

He arrived at the Shawnee Medical Examiner's Office around eight o'clock, their agreed time, but he had a strong feeling Tara would already be waiting for him. The night desk attendant, a squirrelly little man with thick glasses and a poorly contrived comb over, was already aware of the sheriff's arrival and directed him down the nearest hall to Dr. Phillips office. The building was terminally quiet, but it took on a special calm this late in the evening. Apparently death waited until morning to reveal its causes.

Ran found Tara behind her desk, her hair pulled back and lab coat still on, busily typing at her computer while staring at a document to the side of the keyboard. He was immediately riddled with guilt at having agreed to the night's meeting since Tara had not shared Ran's luxury of a shower and change of clothes. Nonetheless, she looked up with a broad smile.

"Grab a chair. I need to just finish a few more entries and then I'm all yours," she said.

Ran stood at the door. "Tara, we can definitely do this another time. I had no idea you were having to work into the evening."

"Don't be silly," she said. "I've got a pizza on the way and Cokes in the frig. It was my idea anyway, remember?"

"Pizza? Look, Tara, I wasn't planning on you going to such lengths for me. We can certainly..."

She looked up quizzically but continued to type. "Such lengths? Delivery pizza and Diet Cokes? Boy, you're a cheap date. I can promise you I will expect much more extravagance when it is your turn. Sit."

Ran mulled her response as he crossed to what was a comfortable chair to the side of her desk.

Date? Your turn?

He savored the words.

From where he sat Ran was able to gaze upon Tara in profile, and at that vantage point, the bachelor sheriff, married to his job for most of two decades and rarely slowing down to even consider the opposite sex, concluded, though he was fairly convinced already, that she was absolutely stunning. It was in that brief moment that Ran decided he would put aside his insecurities, risk the possibility of rejection, and take a leap of faith. He was a man of instinct, and what that inner sense told him was clear: regardless of the outcome of the Melton case, whether he was able to tie the murders of over a dozen people together and liberate them from the cold files or not, he would forever consider himself a failure if he didn't at least try to take his present relationship with Dr. Tara Phillips in a new, more personal direction. His life to this point had revolved around a history of dead ends and mistaken assumptions. If he was wrong, it meant one step back. Tara would probably let him down easily, and their professional relationship would remain intact, with only a slight tear in the fabric that held them together. But if he was right, and she wanted to move things along to another level, well.... He tensed at the idea and felt a surge of anticipation with his commitment.

Tara completed her task, neatly stacked a set of papers in a file tray with her supple hands, and rotated her chair a quarter turn to her guest. "Well, you look much more comfortable out of uniform, though I can see a hint of exhaustion in your face," she said.

Ran looked down, then quickly back into her eyes. "Again, I would not have agreed to this if I had known you had to work straight into this evening. You obviously have had little time for yourself."

Tara shook her head. "If our time together is going to consist of endless apologies, then it's going to be painful for both of us. I am free the rest of the evening, I want to help you with the case, and I love pepperoni pizza with extra cheese. This, my friend, is not a working dinner by any means."

"Well, as you suggested, I promise a work-free, appropriate dining experience for you next time."

Leap.

She smiled wearily though genuinely, "I believe I will hold you to that promise."

"It will be my absolute pleasure," Ran said. "I'm talking four-star, now. *Supreme* pizza and an ice cold beer."

Tara laughed, "Oh, my. I don't know if I can allow that expense for the little I have done for you."

Ran joined her in the relaxing moment, then added, "Seriously, I would love to be able to take you somewhere nice, without the talk of business, if that sounds okay."

Leap.

Her whole face brightening, Tara said, "That would be perfect."

For a few seconds the inherent awkwardness of the situation caught up with them, and they each sat silently, until Tara broke the quiet. "So, the Melton autopsy. I guess you have looked it over, and what else did you bring there?"

She referenced the stack of files he held over one leg.

"Honestly, I have not looked at the autopsy because I thought your evaluation would save me the frustration. I spent the day gathering information on the cases you outlined plus a few others with similar details," he said. "I would like to take a look at those with you too and see if we can't come up with some common ground for all of them – from a forensic point of view."

"Sounds like a plan," Tara said, standing. "Why don't we move into the room across the hall; it has a large conference table we can spread out on. The food should be here any minute, and there are sodas down in the kitchen I can run and get."

Ran stood as well, waiting for her to lead the way. He quickly took in the character of her office and was not surprised to see that it mirrored its occupant. Formal certificates and licenses occupied one wall, where a short, antique half-moon table stood with a few glass and pewter photo frames. Ran was quick to note that the subjects of the stills were all old, probably parents and grandparents. The opposite wall was in stark contrast to its scholarly counterpart. Abstract, almost playful art hung in random presentation, their frames simple and modern. A child's crayon drawing was tapped crooked toward the bottom, its salutation expressing love for "Aunt Tara." Ran imagined her family to be very important to her, so much so that she had returned to her hometown to begin her career. A woman with her strong commitment would never jeopardize that bond for the sake of another, would never put herself ahead of them, and he was further drawn to her because of this obvious dedication. He vowed in that instant that no matter where the future led them he would never ask her to choose, never try to draw her away from her allegiance. It would be like asking it of himself.

Within minutes they had covered two thirds of the conference table with files and records. The pizza arrived soon after, and they enjoyed a quick meal and comfortable discourse before turning their attention to the dozens of printouts and hand-written notes lay out on the shiny mahogany table. Unspoken, they each reveled in the pursuit.

Chapter 14

For the first time after one of his countless transmutations, Caine regained control bathed in panic. The complete exhaustion and hunger he was normally greeted with as he lethargically climbed out of the cavernous world of rage was accompanied by a strong anxiety, a feeling he wasn't immediately sure was residual or part of his conscious world. If it was the latter, he wondered whether he should get to his feet and assess his safety in the now – check all the doors and peer through slits in window blinds and drapes to assure he was alone within the outer perimeter of his property. On the other hand, should this unfamiliar concern that lacked purpose be an extension of his time outside of himself, he felt there was little he could do to remedy the situation. To this point in his many journeys, the events that transpired while he was unconscious came back to him only in fleeting frames of image and occasionally high-speed flashes of movement and landscape. Had he been subjected to intense questioning he would be unable to recall details that could provide a substantial clue as to his whereabouts during the blackouts. The distinct impression he was vulnerable was undeniable, though, so he opened his eyes to what he hoped was the security of his out-of-the-way house.

As was usually the case, Caine peered out at a deep darkness that sat heavily on his surroundings. He squinted involuntarily, his eyes trying to hurry the adjustment to the only available light that snaked its way through the top of the living room windows and sat in a dispersed fan of gray on the low ceiling. The silence was deafening, also a familiar reception and one to be expected on the desolate stretch of road in Hoyt, Kansas. His initial response was one of relief, though the perception of dread that had clung to him in parasitic fashion lingered, so regardless of his monumental fatigue, he knew he had to satisfy the concern.

Caine struggled to his feet and with limited strength gave the home as close as an inspection as possible. Hunched over and willing his spent musculature to activity, he shuffled from room to room, checking doors and carefully peeking out windows. Everything appeared normal, but the feeling persisted as he stumbled back to the living room and collapsed on the floor. He was dizzy and had not given himself the time to acclimate like he usually did. The house fell quiet along with its apparent lone occupant yet again, and the early morning darkness continued to blanket the world beyond Caine's walls in muffled silence.

His reclamation of Sebastian Caine unerringly had left him secure in the knowledge that his other self had taken steps to keep its activities unknown to all but the unfortunate few who met it with terminal consequences, while he stayed true to finding a place of private sanctuary where work and sustenance were constants. This was the unspoken agreement, a contract neither party had either discussed or signed but adhered to with an almost vicious loyalty. The fear that met his awakening could simply be a misunderstood emotion that had clung to his ascent, a strong surge of adrenal response that had failed to subside with its creator, crossing over into Caine's lucid existence.

Whatever the source of the strange reaction, it wasn't something he could just ignore because a cursory glance of his abode had found nothing of consequence. Caine remained wholly confident as he considered his options while lying lifeless on the cool wood floor. He could abandon his present location (though he had still not completed the final steps in securing his new place), removing himself from any potential suspicion; he also had the choice of biding his time to determine if what he felt was truly a threat or a new quality of his transformations. It was during this time that he would still have to monitor the investigative progress of the local authorities, though, as he had witnessed time and again, their efforts would surely prove wasted.

The shortening time between episodes showed that the rage was becoming unpredictable. It was clear that he could no longer expect an even playing field before, during, or after each experience, but to panic was ridiculous.

With sleep pulling at him in unrestrained waves, Caine allowed his trust in his other's unblemished record of concealment to make the decision for him. Just to be safe, he would complete the necessary transactions for the next point on his journey within the next few days. That way, if the concern persisted or the frequency of occurrence continued to shorten, he could gather his minimal possessions and relocate himself and his dark alter ego.

As the foreign emotions began to subside, washed away by the confidence of almighty superiority and faultless planning, Caine began to relax and drifted off into a recharging rest, having assured himself that he was unreachable, draped in the impervious shield of the rage.

Even though they shared a love for investigative pursuit and the thrill of discovery, it was difficult for Ran and Tara to put aside their easy conversation, which was itself a period of exploration, and turn their attention to the darkly contrasting information that awaited them.

Tara had removed her lab coat and now sat back with a look of fulfillment mingled with regret. Ran marveled at her natural beauty, a constant after a full day of post mortems and autopsy reports. Their meal had been less than spectacular, but the ease they felt in the other's company was evident, enough to make fast food dining a five-star experience.

"Well, sir, where do you want to begin?"

Ran considered their starting point. "I've got all the information from your cases plus the cumulative evidence I found in other instances. We also have Weyland's final report on Sonny Melton. No matter how many autopsy reports I have seen, even with a lexicon to help me decipher the process, I still come away confused, so your expertise will be crucial there."

He weighed the choices. "I think we should do this with a chronological emphasis. Though a pattern seems to be evident, following the chain of deaths, bouncing each new instance off an established history may reveal further detail, both medical and sociological. I put a call into an old friend in California – a special profiler. I'd like to be able to give him some solid information tomorrow."

"Sounds like a plan," Tara said, leaning into the table with an air of anticipation.

Ran looked at her seriously. "Understand, if you have had it for the evening, just say the word and I will take my self back to the office and let you rest. I still can't believe I am letting you do this after the day you must have had."

"Just try to leave me out," she said with sincerity that Ran found invigorating. "Besides, this was my idea, Sheriff."

"Yes, ma'am," he smiled.

Ran shuffled through the papers until he found the case with the earliest date, the brutal slaying of a Louisiana businessman just outside Baton Rouge.

"All right, this is the farthest back I was able to find an instance similar to the others. I've made multiple copies of crime scene evidence, lab analysis, and autopsy reports. I think we should go with our strengths on these," Ran said, handing her a short stack of paper clipped statements. He had slipped into the detective's role as quickly and easily as Bruce Wayne in a phone booth. "If you would concentrate on the forensics and pathology, I will go back over the crime scene evidence and witness questioning. If something jumps out at you, don't hesitate to point it out. I'll keep a master list of parallels and noteworthy data that we can eventually apply to the Melton case and ultimately turn over to my profiler friend."

"Yes, sir," she smiled, saluting him with a military wave from the forehead to counter his obvious professional manner.

He stared at her in embarrassment. "Sorry, I guess I get a little over the top."

"I was just kidding," she said. "I couldn't get over how quickly you transitioned to police officer. Don't feel like you have to apologize to me. I admire your commitment, Sheriff Price. I admire a lot of things about you."

The redness that burned at his cheeks kept its grip. "I've done this for so long, and most of it alone. I forget to leave the blinders off," he said. "You're doing this as a favor to me, and you don't deserve the snap to."

"I'm doing this because I want to help, and I care about your results. Remember, I'm intimately involved with the things outlined on these papers. I share your desire to see this figured out," she said.

He relaxed, impressing with her honesty and understanding.

"Explain this profiler to me. How can it help?"

Ran said, "Criminal profiling has gone on for years, but geographical profiling is only a recent field of investigative method. These guys can look at raw data in serial episodes and predict an offender's likely location, using mathematical models and maps. My past exposure to the system has required a minimum of four or five offenses in the same vicinity for a complete analysis, so I'm not going to get the best I could hope for, but who knows? Something may come of it."

"You've kept some ties back west, haven't you?" said Tara.

Ran nodded, "Hard not to after so many years. There are some good people back there; some I regret leaving behind."

Tara leaned back again with her copy of the first incident. "Ran, what happened in Los Angeles? Why are you out here in what was until a few weeks ago a desert of criminal activity?"

"Just another example of my determination getting in the way of common sense," he said offhandedly while separating a page into columns with his pen. He added, "Looking back, it was inevitable, I guess."

"Can you tell me about it, Ran?"

"There's really nothing to tell. I made a poor decision and it landed me here," he said.

Tara had only known him briefly, but she could register the bitterness that invaded his usually positive dialogue. He was soft-spoken to the point of humble with her, often humorous, and his authoritative presence was tempered by a genuine kindness. He gave her the impression that he saw her as a peer, an equal in service to the public, and she favored him for this simple respect. What had happened to him years ago in LA was still a fresh wound that hurt when uncovered. She was beginning to care about this man at a very personal level, and a sign of that was feeling his pain. Her empathy pushed her to help him overcome it.

"Ran," she said softly, hoping he would respond, "what happened?"

And in that instant, as Ran stared at the doctor, her open concern for him evident, he knew he could tell her anything, share with her the deepest of his fears, regrets, and mistakes, and with that she would not judge him or criticize. She would simply listen.

He put down his pen, pushed back from the table, and letting out a short sigh, he told her his story behind steepled fingers. She would be the first to hear of his private past since arriving in Kansas three years previous, and they each privately prayed it would be the start of many more personal admissions.

"I was working the death of a local prostitute who had apparently overdosed on heroine in her hotel room. We saw it all the time," Ran said, and Tara could tell by his facial expression that he was drifting back to that unfortunate yesterday. "Drugs were everywhere, and most of the girls would go straight from their john to their dealer. Not a pleasant life, to say the least. Sometimes the drugs were laced or tainted, and users would end up at the county morgue with tracks on their arms indicative of years of addiction. When uniforms arrived at the hotel, they were immediately red-flagged by the condition of both the body and the room, so a crime scene was established and Homicide called in.

"I agreed with detectives that a struggle had taken place – the nightstand was turned with its drawers toward the bed, indicating it had been hurriedly repositioned; a lamp shade was dented; and there were fresh concave impressions in the cheap drywall, as if shoulders or hips had contacted it sharply. Our girl was known in the precinct, and though her fellow professionals confirmed her drug habit and a growing depression over her lifestyle, we worked it as a murder investigation. Are you bored yet?"

Tara had maintained eye contact to this point while Ran's attention had been fixed on his hands. She confirmed her interest and he continued.

"I would be remiss to say that my fellow investigators were as determined to solve the case as much as I was, and I really couldn't blame them. She was one of the dozens of Los Angeles' seedier elements that ended up in a body bag on any given day, and it was normal to dismiss cases like hers. Gang members, hookers, those involved in drugs – death was a part of life for them, a choice really. A chance they were willing to take to survive. It hit me differently, though," Ran recalled, "and I think it was because of the expression on the young girl's face as they were drawing the sheet over her for removal. She looked so...cheated. I don't know, as if this was not what she had planned. It's kind of hard to describe."

"It seemed like she was trying to tell you something?" asked Tara.

"Yeah, like she wanted an answer to the *why* of it all."

Tara agreed, "I often feel the same way with my cases. There is a look of appeal in their expression."

"I had seen hundreds of dead faces before, but I had never felt such a pull from the victim to explain what had happened to her--why the sun would no longer be shining on her face."

Ran's recall to that point supported Tara's belief that the sheriff was a truly caring man. "Well, I went after the case full bore. Interviewed anybody and everybody that knew her or had been with her prior to her death. Lab results confirmed a deadly level of heroine in her system, and the medical examiner noted the fresh injection site was inconsistent with her normal areas of delivery. He found old scarring between her toes, which was not uncommon for girls trying to hide their addiction and maintain an attractive look. Forensics found numerous partial prints that we ran against DMV records, and I interrogated various suspects and checked alibis. For weeks I came up empty, and I was staring at my first cold case in years of investigative work when I got a call from an informant, a junkie I had befriended during my days in a squad car in West LA. He was pretty strung out, and I feared his twenty dollars worth of information was just a made-up story to satisfy his habit, but it turned out what he gave me was legitimate."

Ran paused briefly. "He was a good kid – just got with the wrong crowd. I got a call a few days later he had been rolled in an alley. His throat was slashed. They do it to themselves, you know. Kill their own for a few bucks." He shook his head. "Addiction makes them primitive – savage."

Tara could see his pain, could see Ran fighting back the raw emotion.

"He gave me the name of a two-bit piece of work, Manny Ringo-- pimp, hustler, a real gem. Ringo danced the No Man Shuffle. 'No, man, don't know what you're talkin' about,' 'No, man, I ain't never had a girl work that side of town,' 'No, man, not my problem.'"

Tara watched a subtle transformation as Ran's hands flexed and his eyes cut into lines of intensity. She could only imagine how he must have responded to Ringo's denials.

"It took some coaxing, but Ringo finally gave me what I was after."

Ran got up from the table and walked over to the darkness that covered the room's only window. He lingered there, staring into the nothingness of a Topeka night, his hands resting firmly on his hips. "One thing you learn as a detective in LA is that very few leads find you; it takes a lot of legwork and connections. No one is interested in helping the police because history and the media had given us such a bad name. All the police beatings and corruption took their toll. You just have to stay after it – do what is necessary, legal or not, to stay in the game. Legal or not."

A pause of infinite measure brought an appropriate quiet to the morgue's conference room. "A few phone calls and interviews later I had the name of a young man from Beverly Hills who had inquired at a bar about girls interested in partying. College boy. Bartender remembered him. Said he was there off and on with his fraternity brothers to coin a new definition of Greek social. Just a bunch of rich brats looking to break some rules and let their actions get lost in the lawlessness that was, is, the fringe of LA society.

"After no more than ten minutes of closed room interrogation, this kid caves, says they were just looking for a good time and things went bad. They hadn't planned on anyone getting hurt. He spills a name, luckily before Daddy and his high-priced attorney arrive to shut down the proceedings. Kyle Bentencourt."

Tara thought she had heard the name, and when Ran turned to look at her, he saw the recognition.

"Yeah," he nodded, "Bentencourt, as in State Attorney General Sam Bentencourt. The same guy that prosecuted police in the anti-gang division back in the mid-nineties for stealing drugs, planting evidence, and shooting unarmed suspects. Rampart Division gave all of us a black eye after that, and some of them went to jail. Well, when I show up at his door looking for his son, you can imagine the reception I received."

Ran crossed back over to his chair and sat down heavily. "Of course, the father makes his son unapproachable, starts pulling strings in the division, and threatens a repeat performance of the Rampart incident. I have what I believe is solid evidence linking the son to the dead prostitute--college buddies trying to salvage their futures, a street dealer who sold the heroine to the kid, and various pieces of forensics far from circumstantial. Unfortunately, I didn't have the support of my superiors who were feeling the crunch from higher up the ladder. I was able to get a grand jury hearing, though, and after a plea deal; the boy got six months of easy time and five years probation. Bentencourt had promised I would regret pursuing the case, and he succeeded in getting my detective's badge lifted for what was described as "gross misconduct during witness interrogation." Seems he got to Manny Ringo who was more than happy to see me burn.

"Well, I wasn't going to push papers and sit at a desk permanently, so I just resigned my service and walked. I was through with police work, completely disappointed in the men I had served with and their lack of commitment to me and law enforcement. Three months later I was here; the pain had subsided and I was ready to get back to the only thing I knew. A week in Auburn and I wondered what I had gotten myself into, but then this case came up, and I was reminded what it meant to be a police officer."

Ran finished, and then, "Meeting you has helped me completely shut that door."

They sat in another moment of silence, one that Tara eventually ended. "Ran, I'm so sorry. A man does everything the job asks of him, and the people that should offer support only abandon him for the sake of their own undeserved positions," Tara said. "But you're here now, and the people of Auburn respect you and the job you're doing for them. You have friends on the force and in this office willing to see it through. I'm here for one, and I think you know that I'm glad things led you to Kansas."

He looked at her for a long time, unwilling or unable to turn his eyes during a moment that would have normally left him uncomfortable. "Thank you, Tara. I'm glad I'm here, too."

As the moment drew to an end, Ran gathered strength from the purging and felt years of painful memories washed away with the revelation. Having shared on a deeply personal level and now bound by more than a criminal investigation, the two redirected their efforts and dove headlong into the cases. They knew the evening would be a long one, but Tara's insistence that Ran bare his burden infused them with new vigor. While the doctor poured over the pathology, Auburn's sheriff reread countless crime scene notes and witness responses.

During the next four hours, the pair scrutinized, retraced, and quietly questioned the information Ran had gathered, leaving nothing to chance. On numerous occasions Tara exited the room, only to return with a stack of file folders or thick, collegiate, leatherbound texts. Ran observed her off and on with somber pride, encouraged by the determination she brought to the project in a style very reminiscent of his own. They exchanged very little dialogue in those hours, and it wasn't until Ran pushed away from the table for the first time since they began that there was any indication either had reached an end point.

He stretched and flipped his pencil on the stack of worn papers in completion. "Including my time at Shawnee County, I think I've stared at this stuff for twelve hours. How are you doing?" he said.

Tara was intent on a particular page within the file before her, moving her attention from the document to an open book and back again as if following a tennis match. "Good. Almost done. Let me just check one more thing."

Ran said, "Okay, I'm going to run to the restroom. Do you need anything? Can I get you a drink, something from the vending machine?"

"Huh? Oh, no, nothing. Thanks."

She was absorbed, and it was one of the many qualities she possessed that had lassoed Ran over the brief period they had been acquainted. He left her to her bloodhounding and walked down the bright, well-lit tile toward the facilities at the end of the hall. Behind him and at the end of the opposite hall, faint but enough to bring his head around, came a shuffling of feet and muffled conversation. Ran was able to discern a familiar face among the busily involved men gathered around a gurney, and he walked briskly toward them. If what he had been told earlier was true, the stretcher's cargo was of vital interest to him.

"Ran? Why am I not surprised?" Tony Sartin said with a look of amusement when he noticed the sheriff's steady advance.

"Is that who I think it is?" said Ran, nodding to the medical examiner's assistant and two deputies stationed about the conveyance on which rested a black body bag.

Sartin smirked, "You know it is, Sheriff. Are you telling me you've been waiting at the morgue for our arrival? I am definitely buying you a puppy tomorrow so that you have some distractions in life."

Their banter was incessant, but it was what defined their solid friendship.

Ran countered, "Could you make it a goldfish? The walks would be shorter."

"Seriously," Sartin asked, "you know I would have called you first thing."

"I was up here on a related matter. Is this the Leavenworth County homicide?"

"Yeah. By the way, this is Deputies Rice and Bulware," Sartin said, introducing his officers.

After a few minutes of small talk, and while the morgue assistant was steering the body of Mitch Stanton into a vault room where it would be kept until a detailed post mortem could be done, Sartin instructed his deputies to wait outside while he talked with Ran.

"Well, does it look like a repeat of Melton?"

Sartin looked down at his blurred reflection cast at an angle from his feet. "It was inhuman. We loaded that body bag with pieces, and I don't even think we located them all." For the first time Ran noticed that Sartin looked physically drained. "Examiner's going to be working with a jigsaw puzzle when he spreads the contents on the table. I've never seen anything like it, Ran."

"Anything preliminary?"

"Well, like Melton, we have some bite marks, what I consider some good fingerprints in blood on the extremities, deep contusions and fractures, but other than that, it is going to take a more thorough pathological examination for forensic evidence. The location of the find was similar. Not much there in the way of evidence. How can someone come in and out of numerous outdoor crime scenes without leaving even a partial footprint? I'm telling you, Ran, I don't think we are getting anything additional from this one."

Ran thought for a moment. "Well, good prints may be a start. Any idea who is working this one?"

"I think I'll give this a fresh perspective."

It was Tara. Having completed her evaluation of the lengthy autopsy reports and wondering where Ran had gone, she had come upon them unaware.

"Lieutenant Sartin." She smiled at the Shawnee County investigator.

"Dr. Phillips," he replied. "Good to see you."

"As I was saying, I think I will make a formal request to Dr. Maxwell.

Seeing how Dr. Weyland worked a similar case, maybe I can sell him on another opinion."

She looked at Ran with satisfaction, something he realized Tony Sartin was taking interest in.

"We...we were just looking over some of the pathological data I gathered from your office today. Dr. Phillips was answering some of my questions regarding medical evidence," Ran explained.

Sartin's "I can see how that would be helpful" look left Ran feeling very vulnerable.

"Okay, Lieutenant, we are going to complete our evaluation. Doctor." He nodded to her and Tara turned to begin her retreat down the hallway.

"Good to see you again, Tony," she said.

"Always a pleasure."

Sartin grinned knowingly at Ran, "*Always* a pleasure."

"Don't you have a jaywalker to apprehend?" Ran joked in a whisper.

"Ran Price. Taking full advantage of the ME's wonder girl. I would have never fingered you for a playboy," Sartin said with mock sincerity.

"Shut up," Ran returned in the moment of brevity. "Seriously, I think this will be productive."

"For you or the stiffs," Sartin offered for his final sally before heading to the door.

Ran threw some final words through the closing door. "I'm contacting Internal Affairs. They're in need of a division clown."

Chapter 15

Tara was waiting in the conference room when Ran returned, her demeanor completely professional. Ran was concerned that the scene in the hallway had not played out in his favor, afraid Tony Sartin's ribbing may have discouraged her interest and exposed him falsely as a typical man of ego, childishly strutting a conquest among friends. He was not that person and hated the very thought that she could be perceiving him that way. Had the very innocent moment been translated as a disrespectful exhibition, Ran would be crushed. He had to say, had to do, something, anything, to expose her present mindset. It would be impossible to continue the rest of the evening, and beyond, without assuring himself.

"That Tony Sartin is something else. I didn't know you knew him," he tried.

"You blushed," she said without looking up from the paperwork before her.

"I what?"

"Blushed," she repeated, glancing up. "When Tony was giving you a hard time. It was sweet."

"Well, I..."

"And besides, I deal with Shawnee County detectives more often than not. I met Lieutenant Sartin days after joining the medical examiner's office. He's a good man," she said.

"Yes, he is," Ran stumbled. "I just wanted to be sure you didn't take that the wrong way...you know...what he said."

"Boys will be boys," she said. "Don't worry, Sheriff. You're still in the batter's box."

"You really do like to see me blush, don't you?" Ran said.

Tara agreed, "It's very assuring."

And what could have been troubling and awkward was swept away under a broom of candor. Ran, his mind once again at ease, redirected his attention to the file folders and loose piles of printouts.

"Before we dive headlong into discovery, are you sure you don't want to do this tomorrow?" Ran said. "We can certainly pick up from here later. I know you had a long day, and..."

She said, "Don't be silly. I'm good. Besides, I've found some things that may interest you, and I would hate for you to have to delay the investigation any longer than necessary, especially if what I have to report helps. No, I think we need to do this now."

Ran loved her tenacity. "Okay, let's do it then. Why don't you start, and remember, medically inept over here."

"You have a better grasp on forensics than you give yourself credit, but I'll try to make it painless."

"Doctor, you may proceed," Ran said, sitting back while simultaneously gesturing with a sweeping motion of his hand that the floor was hers.

"You'd make a great replacement for Vanna White," she kidded.

Ran smirked, "I'd have to opt out on the dress though."

Tara shifted some papers, ran her finger down the legal notepad she had been filling all evening, and began. "Suffice it to say I was already familiar with some of these autopsies and lab results. I simply had to refresh my memory on some key elements. What I didn't have before was such a large sampling of evidently similar cases, and because of that, I have been able to create a composite post mortem while drawing conclusions that only repeat occurrence can support. In other words I have taken elements of reappearance from each sampling and combined them to complete a representative model of autopsy and forensic lab findings." She looked at him with concern. "Am I making sense?"

"Perfect," Ran assured her. "You basically took the similarities from the cases and created a cross section of the case history."

"Shared wavelengths confirmed," she smiled. "As if I could have doubted it."

Ran said, "Stay right where you are, teacher. Any more advanced I'll be banging my head on the table."

"Right," she leveled with sarcasm. "Are you just begging for intellectual assurance or what?"

"Ran try learn. Ran learn good."

"Okay, smart guy. Enough. You need to get ready for the details because it is hard for my medically-trained brain to wrap around."

"I am a sponge. Give it to me slowly though," Ran said in all seriousness.

Over the next hour, Tara highlighted the specifics of her assessment, at times going into deep levels of analysis with jargon that sent Ran backpedaling and in need of more basic terminology. There were moments when his detective side, the rational, factual police officer persona that had dominated his existence for many years, couldn't help but challenge her theory, but she persevered in spite of his doubts. When she had finished, Tara sat expectantly but with a self-assurance that only supported the information she had laid out for Ran's appraisal.

"Wow," was all Ran could utter when she had finished.

"I'll say," affirmed Tara.

"And there is no way you could have misinterpreted the information?" Ran said, and then immediately wished he could swallow the insensitivity that accompanied the statement. If words had substance, he would have pounced on them before they met her ears. Instead, he sat forward waving his arms in denial, a reaction not only to his response but the look of disappointment that dropped like a shadow across Tara's face.

"Wait, wait, that came out completely wrong," he scrambled for clarification. "What I meant is there any way the data could produce different results? Is there more than one possibility? Oh hell, I know what I'm trying to say, I just can't get it out right. Forgive me."

The dark storm that had begun to envelope her countenance began to recede, replaced with a look of utter exhaustion.

Tara began, her efforts over the long night evident, "I'm not mad at you, Ran. We're both tired, and the facts and figures are starting to run together. When I drew my conclusions, I feared you would have problems with my line of logic, the same trouble I was having. Your reaction just confirmed it."

"It's not that I question your reasoning, Tara, and you know I can't thank you enough for your time on this. Meeting you has been...the first real positive thing I've experienced since leaving LA. I think you know that, and when this is all over, I hope we can continue to spend time together, you know, in a way other than this." He presented the paper flood that covered the table with a sweeping motion of his arm. "But right now, I'm a detective, and I can't change my perceptions when it comes to police work. What you are saying is...well, *unbelievable*, especially coming from a member of the scientific community. I was hoping we would be dealing with something concrete, something I could get my head around."

"Imagine where I am right now," she agreed, the softness having completely returned to her angelic though weary face. "Everything I told you flies in the face of years of medical schooling and training, not to mention common biological knowledge. The pragmatist in me is at odds with the idealist. The science says there is another answer; experience has shown me that in this case natural law does not apply. We are dealing with the unknown here. I believe that with all my heart."

Ran recalled his conversation with KBI forensic tech Hunter Wilkins. The Melton crime scene had produced confusing results: levels of hormonal discharge representative of a dozen men; blood loss equivalent to that seen in multiple victims; and tissue samples indicating a perpetrator with animalistic instincts. That had been the start of what had become a case with arcane implications, and now here was the hypothetical conclusion of a qualified, dependable pathologist whose opinion he valued greatly in support of a theory ultimately reserved for the certifiable. Ran was treading on unfamiliar ground and the lines of rational thought were blurring even further.

"Tara, I hear the conviction in your voice, and I am in no way discrediting your findings. Like you, I deal with substance. Facts. Tangible evidence. This mess is asking for some cryptozoological deduction, and I am having a hard time going there."

She sat quietly for a long moment, and Ran could see her wearied mind gathering itself for a final summation in defense of her claim. He wanted to accept her word, wanted it more than anything right now. His steadfast logic denied him.

"Ran, this is ultimately your investigation, and with that said, you have the unenviable job of dismissing information, including my scenario. I can promise you that I am going to push to be the examiner on the Stanton case. I think there is more to this than meets the eye, and I would like to try some evidence gathering techniques that are new to pathology and I find no indication of having yet been attempted. Remember what I told you about the dead speaking to me. Well, I think there are volumes of information that are just waiting for the right ear.

"If you decide that I belong on a website devoted to knee-jerk speculation and mystical interpretation, I will understand perfectly. Far-fetched doesn't begin to describe my conclusions. We haven't known each other very long, and like you, I would love to change that after this is finished, but I feel...I *know*...I am right. Helping you with this case is important to me. I wouldn't go out on a limb otherwise."

He valued her at that moment, not only for her commitment to him and her place in his life both now and in the future, but also for the measurable lift she had delivered to his outlook on the case. Tara was right. He could play judge and jury with her proposal: cast it off as useless guesswork of the preternatural or value the source and give the message its true justice. Undeniably, the logical detective approach had proven ineffective. Maybe it was time to trust something, someone, outside himself.

"Okay, let's say I work from your angle. I wouldn't know the first way to use the information. I've never pursued anything other than human suspects," said Ran.

"And you will still be looking for a human being, but one unlike any you have ever tracked down and handcuffed," she replied. "This one makes Jack the Ripper look like a petty thief."

"Tara, I hear what you are saying, but man or not, I have nothing concrete to go on. No names, no last known whereabouts, no witnesses, nothing. All I have are a bunch of victims and some lab samples unknown to medical science. I didn't compile anything substantial on my end," Ran said.

She perked up, "What *did* you find?"

"A lot of inconsistency really." Ran reached for his legal pad and dragged a pen down the bulleted summary.

"I mentioned to you earlier a definite pattern of movement when the crimes are plotted chronologically. The first possible event occurred in Texas; the remaining murders took a counterclockwise path along the eastern half of the country, for the most part, to eventually land here, in northeastern Kansas. I am hoping my profiler friend can shed some light on that one. I'm thinking a guy that moves that easily, that frequently, is either a transient, a laborer, or in a line of work that keeps him on the move, like a trucker or salesman. He could simply be finding work from town to town, probably contract work that leaves no paper trail, enough to keep him going while he feeds his need to kill before relocating. Worst kind of perpetrator to track down--the one in constant motion. Doesn't look like he stays in an area long enough to be noticed. No roots, no ties. Shows he's intelligent, too.

"There are no clear similarities of either the locations of the murders or the resulting areas where the bodies are found. I've got victims killed in both public and private locations: neighborhood streets, highways, wooded areas, you name it, though never in homes or structures, while their corpses are turning up miles away in fields, shopping center lots, quarries. *This* guy," he tapped his pen in drumstick fashion on the pad, "was discovered the day after his death behind a Laundromat. Looked like he had been tossed away like an empty soda can. That victim they brought in tonight: he was in a ditch along a walking trail. Again, I will leave it up to my profiler, but there doesn't appear to be a thread tying these locations to each other."

As he had done for her, Tara let Ran speak without interruption, though she catalogued questions in her head while he proceeded. "Witnesses are effectively non-existent. A few people questioned claimed they might have heard something, might have seen something, but when pressed they couldn't be sure or give any specifics. Though the carnage at the crime scenes is extensive, the mere fact that no one has come upon the act in progress tells me the killings are swift and measured. The perpetrator is looking for a window of opportunity, holding out for the moment of greatest privacy, and then attacking quickly, bringing an end to the event in a matter of seconds really. I think it explains the body's removal from the scene, as if the perp has some unfinished intimate business with his victim that is best accomplished elsewhere. Logic would deduce the killer, then, is cunning and strong. It would be safe to say as well that he probably has been denied opportunities. The conditions have to be just right to claim a victim.

"And of the victims, I find only generalities: they are all men, twenty-five to forty-five. In every case they are away from home, sometimes traveling, and are always in areas of seclusion when attacked. They do not share any acquaintances or anything work-related. Going over their personal histories, I found nothing that more than two of them had in common, for instance military service or something as obscure as the grocery stores they frequented. They were strangers, which means they were most likely unknown to the perp, except for whatever twisted quality he perceived in all of them. Maybe the fact that they were alone in a semi-secluded area was enough. Reminds me of a hunter in a deer stand: the prey is purely coincidental."

"Or a predator in the wild," Tara interjected, her first comment since Ran had started, and one she had not planned to utter until he was done.

"Or a predator in the wild," he repeated in agreement, though he said it with little enthusiasm. "I think it is safe to conclude that the victims were random, sharing only a proximity to the murderer when the time was right. Additionally, it would require man hours that we don't possess, nor do I think this is even possible, to figure out of the dozens of general populations, an X factor, an individual who lived in all the kill zones concurrently at the times of the deaths, and most likely resided within them anonymously or under an assumed name."

For the next fifteen minutes, Ran highlighted other nuances of the cases, shedding little light on what they already knew and failing to expose the slightest investigative direction to follow. He concluded in an evidently depressed manner that he could only hope the geographic profiler, who would receive all the relevant information by midday tomorrow, would provide them some concrete information. He was obviously nonplussed, and after years of success, was treading on unfamiliar ground. The dependable leads of the past were vague and failed to indicate a course of action, while the only scenario he was being asked to consider was, in his respectful estimation, fodder for The Twilight Zone.

Tara let him brood momentarily, if only to strengthen her own position, before she remarked on his report. He looked beaten, and the cloak of surrender that seemed to encompass his expression hung on him in unaccustomed fashion. She knew him well enough to know he would press on, regardless of the odds, but in his obvious perception, the case was escaping his controlling grasp. Tara hoped she could give him the support he needed to see it through, but it would take a complete reversal of his logical thinking. Getting him to seriously consider the macabre, the scientifically absurd, would mean pushing against decades of experience rooted in the absolute, the substantive. Her medical training, though firmly planted in the perceptible realities of the world, had not failed to impress upon her the potential of life. In her admittedly short career, she had been witness to things inconceivable in the context of not only her schooling but also her general understanding of biological episodes. Life, as she had grown to acknowledge, adapted, broke the labels of conformity placed upon it by man's science, and rewrote the rules. It could not be defined within a finite structure of principles. Life, as research demonstrated, evolved, reacting to its environment in a manner that guaranteed its continuation. Radical change in DNA structures were usually attributed to some contaminate that drastically altered chemical strands within a species, as in radioactive exposure or mercury poisoning. But science also taught that organisms are constantly scanning their genomes for inconsistencies or abnormalities so that repair can be initiated for correction. Was it beyond rational thought to then conclude that those same organisms, whether they are viruses or humans, can adjust their DNA structures to resist damage or elevate their perpetuation? Some species were known to change their sex while others evolved remarkable features to combat predators. The human race had experienced change over thousands of years. Tara felt it was not outside the realm of biology that a single human organism, within its lifetime, could have affected drastic DNA changes in response to some outside stimulus, whether it was for survival or some other reactionary purpose. Her job was to make Ran simply consider the chance. What she couldn't provide him was an open mind. He would have to bring that favor to the party himself.

"I don't know much about the police investigative process, but it sounds to me like you have looked at this from every conceivable angle," she started.

Ran nodded, but his face spoke volumes of doubt. "What I have to accept is that other, more specialized investigators, are going to be heavily depended on to open up some solid leads."

"I agree, not that your dependence is a reflection on your work, because you have done a great deal here, but because this case is unique. There is no precedence other than cases with marked similarity occurring within a tangible time line and geographic path. What does your twenty plus years of instinct tell you? Let me start with that," she asked.

"Well, I think instinct is what has brought me to this point: utilizing your pathological expertise, gathering information from proven resources, reaching out to trusted professionals. If you mean what do I think I'm dealing with, I have to rely on experience. Our boy is a serial killer, with a full-blown psychological bag of troubles that would keep Freud busy for a lifetime, but intelligent, and I would guess physically impressive. There was some event in his life that pushed him over the edge, and his victims are mental representations of that scar on his psyche. By tearing them to shreds, he temporarily destroys his demons, puts the pain to rest until it flares up again. His public side, the calm, normal half that must interact with the rest of the world without drawing suspicion, realizes he must stay a step ahead of authorities, so he moves in short, predictable spurts, assuming new identities and locations until his darker half emerges to reek havoc again."

Tara said, "And why were you needing the opinion of a profiler? Sounds pretty solid to me."

Ran disagreed, "Supposition really. It doesn't begin to tell me how I can narrow my search."

Tara, her legs gathered under her in childlike fashion in the padded chair, her energy the spark that kept them going well past midnight, began her maneuver. "You mentioned intelligence more than once. Do you base that on his ability to avoid detection--no fingerprints, no eyewitnesses, staying one step ahead?"

"Sure, and that he appears to calculate his victims' accessibility and qualifications for choice. Nothing seems random except for the victims, as long as they match his demented profile for execution. Everything else is preconceived – the place, the time, the outcome. He's still out there because he is smart."

"Like book smart or predator smart?"

Ran considered her question. "Both, I guess. I'm not sure what you mean."

"Well, would you consider the suspect educated or simply familiar with his environment?" It was important to Tara that she not sound professorial or pretentious.

"He's done this many times; he knows the playing field. If you mean does experience outweigh IQ, maybe, but I think it would be a combination of the two."

"In what way?" Tara led him.

"I think his natural intelligence conceived of the idea, the plan to feed his sick need to rend flesh, how to best single out and ambush his victim with little to no opportunity for discovery," Ran said with obvious disdain. "After some trial and apparently zero error, he finds himself comfortable in his time-tested surroundings, recognizing elements of threat and confident in his methods."

"So he adapted to his situation over time?"

"Sure, in so much as he put his plan into action and worked out the kinks until it was, as we can see by our lack of solid evidence, foolproof."

"But we have evidence."

"We have bodily fluids that suggest more than one killer. We have partial prints with incomplete and in some cases mismatched markers that make the federal print system useless. What we have is a whole lot of nothing from a forensic standpoint."

"And this isn't the first time you've dealt with a serial killer, is it?" Tara asked.

"No, I have some experience with them. I think the difference here is a complete lack of hard facts to narrow the search. That is what my profiler will hopefully provide."

"What have you relied on in the past, specifically, to help you isolate a suspect?"

Ran seemed uncomfortable in this line of questioning from Tara. "The usual things. Solid lab results, eyewitnesses, paper trails. The things we don't have. Today's technology makes it difficult to maintain anonymity, but he's managed to do it."

He stood up and stretched, an apparent signal that he was weary of Tara's interrogation and ready to call the evening complete. Tara refused to acquiesce, though, and ignored his attempt at dismissal. She hopped from her chair and walked around to him.

"If you were the suspect, based on your knowledge of police work, how would you avoid the incriminating clues?"

"Tara, I've kept you way too long, and if this is about our theory of..."

She persisted, hands on hips, "How would you avoid detection?"

Ran was shocked at her determination, but at the same time appreciative of her commitment to the case. Knowing Dr. Tara Phillips awaited him in Kansas, both professionally and personally, would have made his exit from LA much easier.

"I...I would do exactly what our man is doing. Choose remote locations to minimize witnesses, stay on the move so as not to become a familiar face, clean the area of clues. But even then, years of repeated offense would eventually catch up with me."

She was afire. "Why?"

"Why? Carelessness, a feeling of superiority. Success in crime breeds arrogance."

"Then why, in all these years, has this typical serial killer avoided arrest, escaped the egotism inherent in criminal triumph?" Tara prodded.

Ran began to pace the room, watching his feet while he considered her challenge. She watched him dutifully.

"First, he's not typical. Rather unique in many ways, which has slowed my progress. Second, the forensics does not make sense. We've entertained the prospects of multiple killers, a single Goliath, even your DNA changeling. Science has not provided an answer. Whatever we are dealing with, whatever has led others and us by the nose across half the country for multiple years, is, admittedly, an anomaly," Ran said, then raised his head to her granite physiognomy.

She smiled, for the first time since he had re-entered the room after Sartin and his men had deposited the latest victim. "He's what?"

"An anomaly." Ran couldn't help but grin at her methods. "Okay, so he could be what you described. It's just so...unscientific."

"Wrong, sir. It is perfectly scientific. Nothing more so than the laws of probability and genetic mutation," she smiled, relaxing in the subtle posture they had assumed.

"You are a crafty one, Dr. Phillips. You realize you missed your calling. You are a far better investigator and interrogator than pathologist, and you do the latter extremely well. Would you consider a deputy's position in the crime-ridden community of Auburn? Pay is probably less than your current salary, but, hey, the hours are just as terrible."

Tara crossed the floor and stood within feet of him, staring up into his puffy eyes, red from hours of staring at monitors and reading file upon file. She had maintained her singular beauty after an equal amount of work, and Ran did not fail to notice.

"He's inconsistent with everyone I've ever pursued. An aberration," Ran concluded.

Tara said, "It's not that surprising, from a medical view. Just requires a little thinking outside the box."

"Way outside," Ran added.

"So you'll give my tall tale some credibility?"

"Now it's just a matter of proof to back up our claims."

He took her shoulders in his large hands. She felt right in his grasp, a perfect fit. "You win. We'll run with your idea and at the very least, get this investigation rolling again. But not tonight. You look, well, incredible, despite the long day, but very tired. How about running all that biological stuff by me again tomorrow? In the mean time, I will get this paperwork out to the coast for analysis."

She smirked but knew he was right. They needed help from every angle.

"The more opinions, the better," he said. "Now, let's get you headed home."

"Since you're so open to opinion all of a sudden," she stopped him, "I have one more for you to consider."

"And what would that one be?" he asked, rubbing her arms now methodically, cupping her elbows with a gentle squeeze.

"I think it's time you kissed me."

Ran smiled, "You won't have to bully me into agreeing with that."

He held her tightly for many minutes before reluctantly steering her to the door. They parted with difficulty but affirmed that their time would come--only more reason to bring closure to the task at hand.

Chapter 16

Spears of brilliant light from the midday sun penetrated the squinted eyes of Sebastian Caine and existed in sharp contrast to the dull heaviness that had dominated him mentally and physically since consciousness had reclaimed him hours previous. He had dragged himself out the door not for a change of scenery (the dark, cool recesses of the house were much more conducive to his recovery) but out of necessity. The growing frequency of his transformations was biting heavily into his work schedule, putting him far behind the demand of even some of his most established customers and forcing him to the computer supply store in Topeka for electronic components. He had already lost two fairly new clients in the last few days and couldn't risk further hits on either his income or reputation. Word traveled quickly among the movers and shakers of many small business IT departments, and if talk spread of his inability to provide timely remedies to problems that were becoming less of a challenge to operators in the growing field of remote computer systems repair, he would be hard-pressed to maintain the standard of living that allowed him to coexist with his affliction.

And, now, for the first time since he had become a harbinger to it, Caine was wholly concerned about the rage and its purpose. It wasn't a fear necessarily; he had grown to value its presence and the feeling of superiority it had instilled to his self-image. The rage was something he had never controlled, so what assailed his confidence had nothing to do with dominance. What troubled him now, as he negotiated the truck west to 75 South, was the unpredictability, since it had always been faithful in discretion and timeliness.

The two had bonded in a surprisingly short amount of time considering the demands put forth on Caine as host, having come together at a moment of mutual need, an epic merging of mortal and immortal souls to the benefit of both. What had evolved, and possibly made the union so quickly effective, was the way in which each member of the grotesque alliance had taken the role of parasite. Caine had only briefly considered the enormous life-altering changes he would have to undergo to accommodate such a visitor, the constant relocations and the pressing demands of his business, before realizing what positive things were happening to him. New to his psychological make-up, the air of egotism fit him like a new suit and provided distinct nobility that wept from his pores in noticeable measure. He had never felt so good about who he was and the position he occupied among the sub-species with whom he shared space but little else.

His whole life, as far back as he could remember, reeked of submissive behaviors and an endless cycle of intimidation. A mirror image of his withdrawn, battered mother, Caine had learned from an early age the meaning of inferiority and what it meant to be dominated emotionally and physically. Martin Caine, a hard-working dock supervisor on the busy shores of the Atlantic coast, had instilled in his son, long before the child entered public school, an unhealthy respect for him. Like his own father, Martin recognized that the back of a hand best served notice to the weak members of his household that he was in charge, that the roof over their heads and food in their stomachs was a result of his efforts, and they should count themselves lucky he allowed them to remain in his care.

Young Sebastian regarded him with quiet hatred but self-preserving, outward deference, finding little compassion from a mother already cocooned in the numbing shell of alcohol, her long-standing defense against years of abuse. A strict Catholic upbringing denied her willful access to the freedom of divorce, and her maternal instincts had effectively disappeared in a cloud of denial. Mother and child shared lives of unhappiness and singular despair, but Sebastian, climbing into bed night after night with tear-stained cheeks, craved the protective shroud of an understanding parent, vital to his future development, yet within the framework of his family, he found none.

Armed with an inferiority complex bordering on social prostration, Sebastian had found the same world existed outside his torturous house. Hoping to find peers in a world marked by insult, abandonment, and pain, he ventured into his education with hope. But as is the proclivity of school-age children, when a member of their herd demonstrates weakness or possesses physical attributes deemed worthy of ridicule, the attacks are merciless. Sebastian was big for his age, remarkably large in many respects, a foot taller than his closest rival and well over fifty pounds heavier. An outsider would have marveled at the massive boy's inability to defend himself, which was why adults normally treated the suggestion that the man-child was under attack, but years of degradation had shrunk everything but his growth. An intellectually superior version of Steinbeck's Lennie Small, the hulking figure was jelly in the face of boys who, ironically, sought to nullify their own deficiencies by making fun of those of others. Ostracized at home and school, living on the perimeter of social inclusion, Sebastian found no source of friendship or human compassion, nor did he have a venue to release the great despair that welled inside him.

The anguish grew as did the boy, and in time he became desensitized, boxing away the dread and pain he had accrued in a remote corner of his psyche where it festered but remained cloaked in isolation for years. By the time he was a teen, Sebastian was known as a harmless Goliath with certain social handicaps that kept him occasionally teased but largely ignored. Apparently, the disabilities that kept him categorized as a misfit had not affected his ability to learn, for his grades were exemplary. He demonstrated mastery in the sciences, a deductive ability that relied on reason and interpretive fact, a place void of subjective response and emotional creativity. In the world of ancient rock and reproductive protozoa, he found escape; through textbooks of rational theory and proven experimentation, Sebastian discovered a place where only observation mattered. Here, interaction occurred through a microscope and not in awkward social circles. The environment was stark, clear, and definable. Chemical reactions were dependable; laws of physics were grounded and faithful. He could rely on science like a friend, and it became his constant companion, free of judgment and open to error.

Caine welcomed college with the death of his father, whose overworked heart and alcohol-sodden liver succumbed to a level of abuse he had provided his wife and child for many years. The overbearing Martin, in response to what he would have called his duty as breadwinner, had left behind a sizable life insurance policy and years of social security, of which the boy and his mother would benefit.

In a quirk of life's great enigmas, the death of her stern taskmaster should have delivered the joyous bells of freedom and rebirth to Caine's mother, but she inexplicably drowned herself in the dulling oasis of a bottle and was herself the honored guest of the second family funeral in six months. The expressionless orphan was extended half-hearted regret from relatives rarely seen, and since he was of age to determine his own fate, Caine was left to ponder his next path alone, as he fittingly always had been. The social opportunities that were afforded to young students in the university setting were lost on him, but the allure of computer sciences opened a new world of discovery and would forever bear his attention.

Without family or friends to share in his educational endeavors, he was able to complete a degree in just two and half years, a masters coming in another twelve months. Absorbing the technology with fervor, Caine, though still a social misfit, was a prime candidate for leading computer companies throughout the country at a time when programmers and creators were in heavy demand. Feeling the need to displace himself from a world that had forever made him feel unwanted, he spurned the advise of placement counselors and professors and headed south, selling off the family house and affectively severing all ties with his past. He traveled fifteen hundred miles from the familiar yet harsh world he had always known with guarded optimism, not necessarily hoping for a fresh start, but simply a clean slate.

The truck rolled to a stop in the parking lot of the computer store he had discovered during surveillance months before his residency in Hoyt. Among other necessities, an accessible parts location was paramount to his business's survival. Overnight delivery, though a viable alternative, meant unnecessarily inviting outsiders to his home, and their arrival was unpredictable. Woods Computer Outlet employees had grown to recognize the hulking behemoth that now filled the sun-drenched entrance to the store. Reserved but highly knowledgeable regarding his computer needs, Mr. Caine could be counted on for a prompt verbal list of needs free of interaction that could ever be misconstrued as warm, open human contact. He spoke in a manner reminiscent of the very components he sought--cold and mechanical. He had quickly gained the privately used nickname 'Terminator' among the Woods' staff, an appropriate label for a man of Caine's mechanized behavior and substantial girth. Had he walked into the store on this singular day clad in biker leather and sunglasses, no one would have been completely surprised.

As was his habit, Caine bypassed the obligatory customer perusal of featured and sale items that accosted visitors within a few yards of the store's threshold and went straight to the counter at the back. Here the stocked items he required could be quickly gathered and delivered to him in a timely fashion, and though he didn't demand kingly attention, those serving him were pushed to action. From their Olympian heights, Caine's cold, dark eyes hustled and drove with unseen tendrils of intimidation. It could have simply been that his creepy nature hurried them to shorten his stay, but anyone that had ever packaged an order for the Terminator privately feared a reaction without precedence.

Today the unwanted privilege fell upon Wes Duncan, no small man himself, broad-shouldered and well over six feet, but nonetheless dwarfed in the shadow of Woods' best and worst customer. It was not the first time the honor had fallen to him.

"Mr. Caine. How are you today, sir?"

The question carried little weight, as its deliverer neither felt the suggested interest in his customer's disposition nor did he expect an answer, and the receiver would ignore the pleasantry as if it had never been uttered.

The black eyes burned an imaginary hole through Duncan's lower forehead, which he immediately rubbed in a subconscious attempt at relief with his forefinger. The order, as always, was presented in a monotone, deep resonance. Experience had taught Wes to retrieve a pen because the unwritten order would be long and only begrudging repeated.

"Two memory modules, a dozen ribbon cable connections, Penryn CPU, an Intel entry server board, four 2GB memory, Thermaltake Silent 775 Cooler, an ATI Radeon graphics adaptor, the 1900, not 1650 Pro, and a 350 watt power supply. Bill it."

He stood unwavering as Wes looked back over his quickly scrawled grocery list to verify its contents were discernable before turning around and passing through the entrance to the supply room behind him.

"I'll have that for you momentarily, Mr. Caine," he threw over his shoulder in feigned appreciation for the valued service, all the while hoping the new cooling fans had arrived in the morning order. Familiarity guided him from shelf to shelf as he collected his technological prey in a handled and shallow wooden box. As he feared, the fans on back order, specifically the 775, had not arrived. Wes was not sure how the Terminator would react, but all he could do was apologize for the inconvenience and speculate on its arrival, which should have been that day. *Besides*, Wes asked himself as he headed to the front of the vast supply room and back to the counter, *what was the worst he would do? Demand the manager or storm out proclaiming it to be his last visit?*

Wes boldly repositioned himself in front of the hulking Caine, whose posture had not changed in the six and one half minute interval since their transaction began. He began charging the items in the computerized register.

"Everything available except the 775. We had a case expected today, but it is not here yet."

Wes continued to compound the total charges, uncomfortably but expectantly waiting for a harsh reply. When it didn't come within a few seconds, and no perceptible movement was discerned within his periphery, Wes glanced up at the granite bluff that was Caine's face, wishing to end his quickly growing anxiety. A second quick take drew him in permanently and confirmed his initial look, and with it Wes stopped processing the order, stopped drawing involuntary breathes, and stood transfixed.

The store's activities ceased to affect his senses; a dark cloud of awe dropped over him and sealed him in the moment. Wes Duncan lingered in a black tunnel that drew him unwaveringly into the cavernous maw of Caine's altering expression. The store clerk could have been at arm's reach from a thunderous lightning strike or metal-wrenching car wreck and not been pulled away from the sight before him. What he stood witness to was not only a perceived change of emotion unfolding on the face of his customer but a physical alteration as well. Darkness fell as a backdrop for Caine entirely, and Wes became an unwilling but grossly enraptured spectator to a vision reserved for nightmares and Hollywood's special effects gurus.

Caine's black eyes drew back as if sinking in cavernous holes, slowly, methodically. Wes found himself drawn with them as they ultimately revealed a spark of light and morphed into growing bonfires of swelling life in the concaved sockets. The brow simultaneously moved in opposition, becoming pronounced and expansive, the skin drawing back to reveal taunt tissue mass enveloping hard bone. The jaw line too opened to an inhuman diameter, flexing outward and side-to-side and carrying with it bloodless lips that peeled back to expose shockingly white teeth of an almost canine quality. Cheeks and nose and ears took new shape and blended with their new landscape.

He'd seen these magical transitions in the cinematic horror of movies like *American Werewolf in London* and *Altered States*, been directed to the frame-by-frame metamorphoses skillfully created on YouTube, but he was not lost in technology. This was stark and undeniable, but reason would not allow him to totally accept what his senses confirmed. Caine remained, bits of his features still recognizable, but on the whole, he was something else, something primitive and monstrous. Before him, cast sharply against a dark blend of nothingness, hung the evil of Biblical myth, the atrocities of Pandora's box, and the culmination of man's greatest sinful nature. Wes Duncan was the random attester to mankind's future, the one foretold in countless cultural histories.

And then it was over as soon as it had begun.

The event lasted either two seconds or two minutes; Wes was totally unsure. His eyes now stung with the pain of overuse, and he pulled away to the bright screen before him, its display fuzzy and unstable. He blinked repeatedly, trying to free his visual organs of the stains they carried away with them. Nature would not allow him to settle with only a memory of the perversion he may or may not have beheld, so he sought fearful confirmation of that sight he had just consumed, and was greeted with the Caine of past experience.

The Terminator stood motionless, his face belying his transformation only seconds earlier, though to his terrified observer, the hardened features that normally made up his cold expression were broken, giving way to what appeared to be confusion. Caine, for the first time since Wes had dealt with the man, looked...scared. But then that mask, too, was suddenly gone.

Wes waited for a repeat of the freakish phantom that had revealed itself earlier, but was met with only the monotonous expression that had carried Caine to the back of the store seemingly eons ago.

Wes finished the order, held out the collective contents of most of Caine's needs along with an itemized receipt, which his customer took with a cold reception.

"I'll come for the fan later," Caine mumbled while taking his items, and then turned and strode across the store in long, aggressive steps. Wes watched the door close behind the gargantuan figure as it became surprisingly lost in the bright reflections of the day's sun.

Wes Duncan took a deep breath in sharp similarity to that of a newborn child. He also had just glimpsed a brave new world.

Chapter 17

The Auburn Sheriff's Department was alive with more activity than even Polly Sheridan could recall. The very fact both phone lines were occupied with police-related business *at the same time* was a testament to the code blue conditions being experienced that day. Normally, calls were of a personal nature--a request for grocery items, news that couldn't wait for the end of a shift, or various other matters not requiring law enforcement assistance. The infrequent call for police intervention was most always of a non-emergency nature, rarely signaling the need for blaring sirens and weapons at the ready. If two worker bees constituted a hive, then the offices of the ASD were abuzz with frenzied life. The sheriff had been on the phone most of the morning, between calls referring to large county maps pinned hurriedly on his regularly bare walls or shuffling for the hundredth time through files worn from hours of handling. The veteran dispatcher, her crossword puzzle magazines pushed aside while their role of constant companion was temporarily on hold, was also busily dealing with incoming and outgoing calls that required both her experience and maternal charm.

Ran had arrived at the office uncharacteristically ahead of Polly, started a fresh pot of coffee, and transformed his office into a work space that resembled the preconceived sets on some of the more popular detective shows enjoying mass appeal on television recently. Even the fax machine was fired up, one luxury the department was begrudgingly provided, and Polly was surprised to find that its ink cartridge hadn't dried up with years of disuse. She had no more put her purse down than Ran had outlined for her in writing some of the contacts he needed her to establish in the course of her shift, contacts that required a professional approach that veiled what could best be described as subtle half-truths and craftily designed appeals for information normally reserved for big city law enforcement. The sheriff had briefed her on the proper approach. Their investigative involvement was minimal--a body had been discovered in their community but rendered deceased in an area outside their jurisdiction. Polly would have to balance their position of importance with necessity by exuding authority and offering little detail in Auburn's role in the cases. Before the morning was half over, the dispatcher had placed and received more calls than she had in her previous twenty-two years of service combined and done a remarkable job of convincing high level officials that she, a grandmotherly dispatcher in what amounted to Mayberry R.F.D., Barney Fife included, was attempting to gather vital names and information for a high-profile criminal investigation.

Excited about the challenge, receptive to something outside her normal workday, and honored with the sheriff's confidence in her, she became "Deputy Sheriff Polly Sheridan, Auburn Sheriff's Department." And with that transformation, the office and its inhabitants came alive with change. Detective divisions blanketing the eastern third of the country, medical examiner's offices, sheriff's departments, police departments, serious crime units, homicide bureaus, and crime lab professionals were targeted, and Polly relished the role of bloodhound. She required documents from some, contacts from others, while spreading her phone number across the region like a modern day Johnny Appleseed. Ultimately, she functioned as the go-between for Ran, who consumed the fruits of her labors, taking dozens of callbacks and greedily receiving the faxes that covered his office in a non-traditional form of wallpaper.

"We're interested in a cold case in your county from three years ago. Looks very similar to a homicide investigation we are pursuing here. Sheridan. Yes, Auburn. Excuse me? We are in a coordinated effort with the Kansas bureau and Topeka's Shawnee County crime units. If Detective Summers could contact Sheriff Price, we may be able to shed some light on both cases. Yes. Well, I appreciate it. We are up to our necks here too. Thanks."

For Ran's part, the pace that had introduced itself to the department fit comfortably like a well-worn suit and kindled fond memories of times too long absent. He was in his element, surrounded by a flurry of activity as the hunt began in earnest. The addition of Polly and charging her with important tasks was part of the new Ran Price, an administrative skill and dependence so effectively taught to him during his time with Tara, who showed the former lone wolf that reliance was not a sign of weakness but an effective tool in criminal investigation.

"Sheriff. Tom Avery on line two. I think it's the guy I left a message for in Canada."

Ran snapped up the receiver. "Tom. Thanks for getting back with me."

"*Sheriff* Price? Now I understand why I haven't heard from you in a few years. I caught your name here and there but never got the whole story. Tucked yourself into an easy retirement with benefits, huh?"

Avery had pulled many of Ran's cases from the precipice of unsolved during their ten-year professional relationship, bringing his uncanny ability and proven technique of profile analysis to narrow the search for unknown serial murderers. His success was undeniable and in high demand. Ran was understandably concerned that the profiler would be swamped with inquiries and investigations on top of overseeing his Geographic Profiling Analyst Training courses at Canada's Oxford College, so he was encouraged when his call was returned the same day.

"Long story, sir. Long story. Maybe if you get me through this one, I'll fill you in on all the sordid details," Ran said.

Avery laughed, "Sordid you have to guarantee or my time is not available."

"You got it."

"What can I help you with, Ran, and please don't let it be another pizza delivery guy."

Avery had been instrumental in the identification of Chester Turner who killed eleven people during a twelve-year rape and strangulation spree in crime-plagued Los Angeles. He had delivered pizzas for a living during the span. Eight of the killings occurred within a few miles of Turner's residence in South LA, a geographic fact that Avery had used in his analysis.

"No delivery guy this time, at least I don't think so. No, this guy is operating on a regional level, and has for years. And if I'm right in the information I've already complied, I have every reason to believe he is slowly going national."

"Whoa."

"I don't know if he is a suit taking care of his sick fantasies on business trips or a vagrant wandering the countryside. Nothing ads up. In fact I would be surprised if some of these details haven't already been given to you. It's a classic case for your expertise."

Avery was amused. "Listen to you. Laying it on thicker than normal, don't you think? It's always a tough one when you're reaching out."

Ran had to admit to his desperation. "I could really use you on this one, Tom."

"And you have me. Besides, the profiling business is a little slow right now. Serial killing must not be in vogue," Avery responded. "But seriously, sounds like a challenge. Let's have it."

And Ran complied, for the next twenty minutes, outlining the history and detailing the nature of the crimes. As he had suspected, Ran referenced to some cases that Avery was familiar with, vaguely, having done some preliminary work on them, only to be informed that the investigations were taking a different course. That course, as Ran was learning during his examination of the previously abandoned cases, had taken an exclusively medical direction, most likely because autopsies and lab results were pointing to multiple aggressors.

In theory, geographic profiling was a waste of time if the cases, though similar, involved more than one killer. The label of "copycat" had eventually appeared during the stringing together of the events, a logical conclusion, though in Ran's mind, a resignation to what was perceived as the impossible. Before Tara's hypothesis, he would have followed the same path of investigation.

"I know it sounds preposterous, and after you get the paperwork, it's probably a sure bet. But I want you to track this one as a single perpetrator. Whatever you can give me, because right now, I have nothing but supposition. And you know me by now, that's far from something I can put handcuffs on," Ran said.

"I haven't heard this side of you before. Is this something personal?" Avery asked.

"Let's just say I want this one, Tom, and if this all works out, we'll sit down sometime and I will really fill you in."

"It's a deal. I'll see what I can do," Avery promised. "Can you give me a few days? Maybe more? Sounds complicated."

Ran smiled for the first time that morning, "Days? I figured on weeks. Yes, take what is necessary, but I'm glad you caught on to my urgency."

"If your boy is moving at the rate and distance you believe, impatience is perfectly understandable. He could be someone else's problem pretty soon, and with any knowledge of jurisdictional privilege, he may be manipulating the system to further his own agenda," Tom conjectured. "Look, I'm not making any promises, but understand one thing: the bigger the haystack, the harder it is to find the needle. Staying a step ahead of the authorities is a matter of logic mixed with a little sixth sense, and I have to think he is confident while not feeling untouchable. He obviously knows something about the criminal and medical investigation process."

Ran sobered quickly, "I agree. Based on the agencies that have had a look at this, he seems to know at a highly intellectual level what mistakes not to make while feeding his primitive lust. I've been asking myself what more a small town sheriff can do that hasn't already been done."

"A small town sheriff with big city expertise. Don't sell the wolverine short," he chuckled lightheartedly.

"I don't know, Tom. I've just got this feeling. It's like I'm going to miss my opportunity if I don't act quickly. Maybe I'm reading into it, but it's like the investigations to this point have always been a step behind – missing a final piece. Dumb, huh?"

Avery countered, "I know you well enough, Ran. You've never ignored your own sixth sense. Don't start now. Let's figure out how you're going to get this stuff to me, and I'll get the ball rolling from my end."

"I'm counting on you to complete the puzzle, Tom, or at least point the way to making it fit."

"As if the profile business didn't need any more pressure."

"Thanks, Tom. Really. Thanks a lot."

Ran felt measurably better as he replaced the receiver, confident in Tom Avery's commitment and skills. Few things rivaled Ran's belief in hard-nosed detective work, but he had witnessed the successes of geographical profiling and recognized its place, along with forensics, in police work. The Auburn Sheriff's Department and others like it were benefiting from the advances being made in criminal inquiry, but Ran couldn't shake the doubt that it was still not enough to put to rest his present investigation.

Avery needed locations, times and dates, and a brief summary of the crime scenes and victims' biographies. Geographic profiling relied on mathematical probability and characteristics of locales in order to create a map that would help narrow the area in which to find a suspect. Once a profiler had focused the search, detectives could refine their own, looking for individuals who lived and worked in the specified area. Avery's challenge was two-tiered. He would not only have to map multiple areas since the crimes had occurred over half the country but also combine those findings into a model geography that represented all the crime sites. This artificial map would have to be interpreted and matched to Shawnee County, that was *if* Avery concluded that the suspect could be found within a manageable perimeter. Ran's reference to a business traveler mixing work with pleasure was a possibility and could significantly reduce the profiler's chances.

With Polly's day filled with the phone lines, Ran had played secretary and gathered the necessary information from his growing files and combined it with current documents that were keeping the office fax machine in overdrive. The sheriff had promised a complete record for the profiler by the afternoon, which he would himself fax to Canada. If all went well, he could potentially know something in a few days, coinciding with Tara's autopsy of Mitch Stanton, but even that was still up in the air. She had promised to speed things along if given the opportunity to perform the task, and Ran had every reason to believe in her, theory and all. He had failed to share her speculations with Tom Avery, telling himself he didn't want to influence the outcome of his profiling, but privately admitting the off-the-wall nature of her hypothesis would likely invoke doubt and possible ridicule. It was a protective instinct, of her and himself. Her for the deep affection he carried, and himself for even entertaining the fictional nature of her supposition. His years of experience repeatedly told him to seek a more logical answer; his heart wanted nothing more than to support Dr. Tara Phillips.

Their previous night had sealed the fate of his detective's mind.

Tara had been thorough in outlining the details of her hypothesis while staying as elementary in her presentation as the information would allow. She was fully aware of the scientific and medical knowledge required to grasp her deductions, and Ran had promised to give her his undivided attention with an open mindedness to concepts that were sure to strike him as irrational and quite ludicrous. Those had been his intentions, at least. Keeping himself receptive had been challenging, and in the end, after a few moments of uncomfortable disagreement, he had begun to see the possibilities of her idea.

She had sat with an almost commanding posture as she began, the light from the conference room enveloping her in a reverent shroud, and Ran imagined her elevated as if on a pulpit, while her words showered down on him in the illusionary setting. It wasn't until later he realized the great risk she was taking with her career and any possible future they may have together.

"All right, I am going to have to give you some background information for all this to make sense, and even then there is no assurance that you will accept what I am about to say. So, are you up to a little evolutionary biology?"

"Teach away, ma'am. I am your humble pupil," Ran responded. He made himself as comfortable as possible in the stiff meeting chair. They had had most of the building to themselves that night, though there was always the chance of interruption from a phone call requiring their immediate attention. As it turned out, they had remained undisturbed.

Ran had readied himself for terminology and scientific hypothesis that would most likely leave him either hopelessly confused or so unable to grasp the scenario she suggested that his input would be meaningless. Quite the contrary had resulted, and looking on it now in the confines of his office while Polly fired away at another out-of-state department, he knew that their relationship had undergone a tremendous test, one that he believed they had passed.

"Evolutionary science tells us that change occurs in a species with each successive generation over a vast period of time. Traits are passed on from an organism to its offspring in a cycle of life that is ultimately driven by change, for it is necessary to the survival of the species that it adapt and thrive within its ever-changing environment."

"I am with you so far."

"Okay, let's start with the basics. Have you ever heard of *natural selection*?"

"Darwin. Junior high science class."

"Exactly."

"Do I get an A?"

"Not so fast, Einstein. We have only touched the surface," she smiled.

Ran feigned disappointment. "I would like to cash my chips in while I'm ahead, and based on my scientific knowledge, this is as good a time as any."

"Raise your hand if you have any other comments; otherwise, let me get this lesson rolling," Tara joked, but Ran could catch a hint of seriousness that he quickly obeyed.

Tara continued, "Natural selection involves the passing down of favorable traits to successive generations while making the undesirable traits less common. It is one of two mechanisms that really drive the evolution process. In an effort to guarantee reproduction and a stronger population, heritable traits show up more commonly in future generations while undesirable traits become rare."

"Survival of the fittest." Ran bathed in subtle confidence, only to have Tara steal his thunder.

"Well, that is a rather crude assessment of the process. To put it better, *survival of those best equipped to survive*. Even unfit organisms can reproduce and populate the environment, so I try to avoid the term when talking about genetics. It is crucial that *heritable* traits move to subsequent generations, those traits that better prepare an organism for life. It then stands to reason that if these organisms are being spawned, then the population is growing with *meaningful* evolution."

The human species doesn't need the genetic trait for greater and greater physical strength to pass on if we are becoming a mechanized and technology-driven society. That trait, though a standard for *fitness*, brings little to the table when other traits, like intelligence, are more desirable. In human history the species has evolved to match the demands of its environment and its established place at the top of the food chain. Heritable traits have moved with us to push that evolution. The key to natural selection as it pertains to evolution is that genetic qualities that support a species in its survival will move to future members of the population. All of this is tied to DNA and genetics, which I will get back to in a moment."

Tara paused in an evident gathering of her thoughts. Ran appreciated the approach she was careful to take so that he fully comprehended. "Now, tell me this: what is your understanding of *genetic drift*?"

"Never heard of it. See, I should have gone with my instincts and cashed out earlier," Ran complained half-heartedly.

"Stay with me. Genetic shift is the other factor I mentioned in the evolutionary puzzle. This concerns the frequency of genes in a population, and ultimately their transference to future organisms, through probability. Chance. The idea is that variations in the genetic pool will occur due to purely random events in the life cycles of the species."

Ran asked, "Are you saying that some traits are passed on by pure luck of the draw? I guess my gambling analogy was not that far off."

"For our discussion here, yes, luck plays a huge part in the transfer of genetic traits in a species, whether those are good or bad," Tara concurred. "We see this coming into play more frequently in small populations, as chance will tell you that the odds increase with the numbers. If I asked you to pull the ace of spades from a typical 52-card deck, your chances are slim but definable. Decrease the deck by 40 cards, and you are more likely to succeed. What is key here is that there is always the possibility, however small, that negative genes can make their way down the generational chain. Probability teaches this."

"So, a chance event, say a falling piano, can affect a species' future development?"

Tara said, "Well, in a small population it is more likely. The chance that genetic variations are affected by a single event in the human species is almost impossible. The law of large numbers makes the chances astronomical. But I don't want to discredit the importance of genetic drift. Probability would allow for a gene to survive, regardless of its heritability."

"Which again was...?"

"Heritability is the measure of variation in the phenotypes of a species based on variations in the genotypes of the individuals."

"Oh, right...what? Did we cover this earlier? Phenotype? Genotype?" Ran was hopelessly lost.

"Ran, I told you this was complicated. Just bear with me. It's not easy giving a genetics lesson in a matter of hours when it takes years to understand, and even the best geneticists have only breached the surface."

She wasn't frustrated with him or his response, just the magnitude of the endeavor. Each question required her to backpedal and branch off in a new discussion of biology, and she understood Ran's confusion.

"I'm sorry. I never was a very good student." Ran worried that he was angering her.

"It's all right. I have a little more experience in this, and I need reminded when I am getting over your head. If it were the basics of interrogation or the criminal code up for discussion, our roles would be truly reversed," Tara said.

"You have me wondering if you have me beat even in that regard," Ran said. "All right, I was good up to pheno...phenos..."

"Phenotype. The physical characteristics that make up an organism. These are observable and vary in the population due to variations in the species' genotypes and environment. The genotype is the genetic signature of the individual and constitutes all the dominant and recessive genes available in the DNA structure. We can look at an individual and know which variation of a gene it is utilizing. Let me give you a simple example. Your phenotype exhibits use of the gene for brown hair. Your genotype for hair color, though, may have three *alleles*, or separate variations of a single gene – blond, brown, and red. Brown was the genetic marker used in your make up, probably because it is a dominant gene."

Ran nodded to signal clarity.

"But the allele for red hair is still part of your genetic code, and probability allows for that genetic variance to survive to future generations, whether it is important to survival or not."

"I think we can make it in this world without redheads, don't you?" Ran quipped.

"Unless society determines that red hair is desirable, and all individuals with other hair colors will be systematically eliminated. From an evolutionary standpoint, the gene for red hair will become a quite inheritable feature over time."

"Point taken," Ran said.

"To further clarify phenotype, the way this allele reacts to the environment further determines the physical characteristics of the organism. My blonde hair may lose its luster with prolonged sun exposure while another person's may lighten and take on a more attractive glow. This further qualifies the individual and ultimately affects future traits."

Ran couldn't imagine Tara's hair ever losing its beauty. "Okay, I think I have righted the ship of knowledge in my favor. I got that part."

"Congratulations. You just passed Evolution 101. Ready for the next class?"

Ran bragged, "Are you kidding me? Bring it on. I obviously have the genotype for advanced scientific understanding."

"I think your wise-guy gene is dominant," Tara responded. "What are the odds of that being suppressed?"

"The probability is minimal I am afraid. Just part of the genetic package."

Tara seemed to relax with the banter. "Things are going to get progressively more difficult, so here goes. A factor important in all this evolutionary change is mutation, a necessary contributor to variation in the gene pool. Mutations are thought to be the thing that natural selection acts upon."

"Wait. I thought a mutation was like a disease. How can that be desirable?" Ran asked.

"The connotation of the word is a simple misunderstanding. A better term for what happens genetically would be *modification*. We have an entire fossil record that shows us how mutation has allowed a species to survive. With mutations we get a change in the genetic material of an organism, but these changes can be advantageous or unfavorable. If the mutation assists the species in reproducing and therefore surviving, it is a genetic change that will likely become a permanent quality in the population. Evolution requires adaptation within a changing environment, and mutations can be a response to the need for change. In the process, many *alleles*, specific genetic traits, and often ancestral, are suppressed or completely eliminated, though we can never forget the influence of genetic drift in all these events.

"Millions of years ago there may have been a huge population of white, black, and grey field mice. Their predators--birds, snakes, and foxes, for instance--found locating them quite easy given the available genetic codes for hair color within the mouse species. One day, a pair of mice give birth to an individual with a mutated gene for hair color – brown. This mutation proves to be an advantage for prey living in fields of open ground and sparse vegetation, so it survives and passes the now favorable trait to its offspring and they to theirs, and so on. Soon, brown hair is a dominant trait in the population as vulnerable members, the white mice for example, are progressively removed. In an evolutionary reaction to the adaptation of the mice, predators mutate in an effort to survive – a bird's vision improves, a snake develops heat sensors and motion detectors, and the foxes are benefited by auditory mutations within their species. These mutations were helpful to the organisms' survival so they were used. Deleterious mutations, those that are not favorable, will usually die out, or at the very least, reduce in frequency. Albinism is a disadvantageous mutation that is hardly seen in the animal kingdom. Natural selection ensures its rarity, while genetic drift explains why we still see examples of it."

"So far, so good," Ran verified.

"You forgot to raise your hand."

Ran's hand quickly shot up in perfect imitation of an impatient schoolboy. "Ms. Phillips, I am a better person for being in your class."

"Shut up, Mr. Price," she countered with a smile.

"Yes, ma'am." His hand rocketed back into his lap.

"There are a number of reasons for mutated genes – viruses, exposure to radiation, errors in the copying sequence during cell formation. What is key to our understanding of mutations is that they don't happen overnight, and in most cases take thousands, if not millions, of years to be a dominant trait in a population. Human mutations can even lie dormant for a long time before surfacing."

"Let me interject. Are you trying to draw the conclusion that our killer is the victim of a mutation, a suppressed, undesirable one that chose now to make its grand appearance?"

"That is exactly what I am saying. "

"But you said yourself that mutations take millions of years to catch on. No way our boy is an overnight wonder," Ran said.

"Scientifically speaking, he could be. But that is only the basis for my postulate. Let me continue."

Ran had decided to let Tara present her theory without argument or debate, but the rational detective in him was finding it difficult.

"Please, Ran, give this a chance."

"You're right. I'm sorry. Continue."

"Very few mutations are actually beneficial, which is why organisms have developed inhibitors and cell repair kits to fix defects. It's just another example of evolutionary adaptations. Since mistakes in DNA can lead to disease or permanent damage, cells have developed a number of pathways for recognition of errors and fixing problems. A mutant, then, is really just an organism that has suffered a structural change in its DNA and been unable to correct the error. If it proves beneficial, evolution may encourage the change, but in most cases the instance is a flaw that is quickly remedied through natural selection. What is important to my theory is that some mutations could be long-dormant alleles that have been unseen in a phenotype for many generations--an ancestral gene that stood the test of natural selection and genetic drift."

Ran wanted to comment but held his tongue.

"Remembering that mutations can be helpful modifications, we have many examples in nature of mutations that perpetuate the species, like my brown mice example. Among these are transmogrifications, the ability of an organism to change its appearance or state. Mimic octopuses can appear to be over a dozen different sea creatures as a defense mechanism. There are many examples of insects that completely change as they move from the larvae to adult stage. Look at frogs. Prior to lungs and legs they are tadpoles with a tail and gills. These are all genetic qualities that have developed over time as the organism adapts to its surroundings.

"Looking back at the files you gave me and my own experience with cases similar to those, both here and in other places, all the contradictory evidence leads me to the premise that we are dealing with one man, an individual who can change his blood type, finger prints, and seemingly every chemical quality that allows forensics to identify him. Given that, it is highly probable that he is capable of a complete physical transformation. Imagine if you can a human organism carrying the genetic disposition for metamorphosis."

"To what? Change his entire appearance and genetic design? Transform into something completely different? I can't buy that. Tara, I'm sorry, but no. I can't."

Ran had heard nothing to that moment that asked him to completely abandon his concept of the natural world, but this pushed him out of the parameters of believability. It was bad enough that it was his nature to question everything, but here was an idea that flew in the face of reality. He stood for the first time and crossed the room in dramatic denial of what she was suggesting.

"But why? Because there is no history of human metamorphosis? That alone can't cancel out the biological prospects of a never-seen, suppressed gene emerging within a human organism."

"Tara..."

"I explained to you the genetic process of evolution. Look, dwarfism is a genetic trait, and some have theorized it is an ancestral one suppressed since the rise of early man, but one that frequents our population nonetheless. Science has proven that primitive genes are still part of human DNA, either through evolutionary duplication or purely descended."

"But..."

"Humans are and seemingly have been at the top of the animal kingdom since their dawning. Is it ridiculous to theorize that an ancient gene survived after millions of years of natural selection and probability to emerge now under the right conditions? One that has never been observed because the adaptation has never been *needed*?"

He had folded his arms in an unconscious, defensive exhibition. "Myth. Fairy tales and bedtime stories. There is no way you can convince me that I need to be looking for a man who can transform at a genetic level. Utterly impossible." Ran was shaking his head in stark denial.

Tara pressed, "There are adaptations, which require hundreds of generations to develop, and then there are acclimations, which can happen in the life cycle of a single organism. Listen. If you moved to the deserts of Africa, constantly exposed to a harsh climate and little water, you would suffer but survive. Your body would learn to adjust to constant sun exposure and dietary change. The organism thrives. What if our guy had the ability, at the DNA level, to acclimate through gene transfer? To change at the chromosomal level to survive?"

"But he would have to be able to repeatedly transfer the genes, change his...phenotype, to interact successfully in society. Humans aren't octopuses. You haven't given me an explanation for how he is accomplishing that feat *in his lifetime*," Ran argued while his arms now flew about in demonstration. Simultaneously, though, he was regretting his tone.

Tara seemed unaffected. "Our understanding of genetics and human biology supports my argument, except that one point."

"The guy would have to be a *werewolf*. Come on, Tara."

Ran knew he was being cruel in his judgments, but it was too fanciful to stay quiet. For her sake, he tried to calm his reproaches.

"In some respects he is, or as close to it as you can get. He is cannibalizing, mutilating, and demonstrating animalistic urges and aggressions. But unlike the folklore of the werewolf, our man is shape shifting not as the result of a wolf bite or full moon but more likely in response to a legitimate environmental stimulus. My theory," Tara chuckled to ease the moment's tension, "does not allow for supernatural or mythical elements, but if I had to draw an analogy, he's more like the Incredible Hulk."

Ran appreciated her attempt at easing the tension. "I dragged you into this,' he said, "so it is unfair of me to completely dismiss what you are saying. Let me get this straight, as I am hearing it: You are telling me that in the course of human history, a gene that allowed for human metamorphosis was passed through countless generations, a mutation that was never required in the entirety of human existence, only to be called to immediate service by a serial killer with the unique ability to voluntarily alter his DNA."

"Well, I don't believe its voluntary, but yes, that's the highlights."

"So he has no conscious awareness that he is brutally murdering and has been for many years?"

"I didn't say that," Tara explained. "I said it wasn't a voluntary genetic transfer. There came a moment in this individual's life that environmental concerns and threats to his survival were so great that he was driven, at the genetic level, to alter his phenotype drastically and instantaneously. Getting back to the fossil history, we have no evidence of immediate genetic change. None. So I can't explain the interplay of what are now equally dominant genes, but somehow his DNA is changing, which is a dangerous thing."

"I think Mitch Stanton would attest to that."

"No, I mean for the organism. There is either distinct allele swapping taking place or specific gene duplication on the chromosomes--possibly entire chromosomal mutations may be involved. Regardless, the repeated cellular restructuring will ultimately weaken the integrity of all the effected systems. I think it's also safe to say that the reduced amount of time between documented events, and I am going on what you were able to provide me, indicates that the process is accelerating, and in so doing, significantly damaging the organism's life cycle."

"Would you say he is conscious of the change even though he does not initiate it?" Ran asked, having curtailed his defensive posturing.

"I would guess he tolerates it. You see, it's like a disease. Involuntary, a negative mutation in his DNA. Only this one turns itself off and on like a faucet."

"Bipolar genes. Very unpredictable," Ran joked, and he sank back down in his seat in a heavy sign of submission. "I would have to believe he would know that this change is happening; how else could he explain the periods when he wasn't himself."

"Based on his movement, he is most likely encouraging the physical and psychological changes, protecting it and himself from discovery. He may not totally understand what is happening to him, and most likely he retains little if any memory of the occurrences, but a part of him knows that he has to be discreet. Bipolar was a fair assessment, but it's more like dissociative identity disorder, a split personality; sociopathy, which would explain the violent tendencies; and a rare genetic disorder marked by instability and rapid cellular restructuring all rolled into a homicidal ball."

"So what do you suggest we do to find this guy?" Ran asked.

"You may have to do nothing. There are two distinct possibilities with this Jekyll and Hyde scenario: one, and I think this is the more likely; the cellular damage will become so profound that his internal systems will cease. Complete organ and tissue failure. Or two, and to answer your question, I have no idea, the transmogrification stops as the body suppresses the genetic flip flop in order to spare its existence, leaving him in one of the two DNA constructs. Assuming that his first self, the one that apparently interacts in society as the acceptable version, is the more familiar DNA thread, one could conclude that he will revert to that form permanently. On the other hand, if the second self is stronger and able to force its presence, it is highly possible that this could become the dominant persona."

"You're certainly not making my job any easier," Ran said.

"Ran," she got very quiet here, almost at a whisper, forcing him to listen closely to her words. "What you are dealing with is a superhuman, a man who has escaped the boundaries of human evolution and become more, something...monstrous. You can't rely on what you have trusted or what has proven effective in the past. This is beyond anyone's experience, and from a biological standpoint, an *abomination*."

The shrill ring of the office phone pierced the envelope of reverie that Ran had created of the previous night.

"Sheriff Price."

"Ran. It's Tony. How are things going?"

"Hey, Tony. Well, you know, trying to make some headway."

"Wanted to get you up to speed on the Stanton case. The search came up empty on a kill site. Strangest thing. The guy is last seen in the lake area and his partial remains are found in the same, yet the combined efforts of our CID and Leavenworth County officers found no trace of attack in a 20-mile circumference. Really frustrating."

"Yeah, that's odd, but then again, everything about this has been puzzling."

Ran tried to appear disappointed while hiding his lack of surprise at the failed efforts.

"What have you been able to find?" Sartin asked.

"Well, we are really in a holding pattern here. Just trying to compile some additional information from jurisdictions involved in the cases I pulled from your systems earlier. Nothing new so far."

Ran felt guilty keeping Sartin out of the loop because he may find himself needing his help later if everything fell into place, but his desire to keep Tara out of the picture far outweighed any commitment to his profession.

"You wouldn't be hiding anything from an old friend, would you, Ran?"

"You'll be the first to know, Tony. Honest. Until then keep me posted and I will do the same."

Sartin concluded, "As far as I know the autopsy is still pending, but maybe that will shed some light. There was at least more to work with than the Melton remains."

"Barely."

"Well, maybe there will be something. Right now it's all we have."

Tara had promised to inform Ran as soon as she was able as to the status of the post mortem and whether Maxwell had agreed to appoint her to the case. He knew that if there were answers to be had, she was the most likely pathologist to find them.

"I'll be in touch, Tony."

Ran went back to prepping the materials for transmission that Avery would need for his profile.

Chapter 18

The truck and its interior failed to offer the cool darkness that Caine needed as it broiled in the asphalt parking lot of the strip center. Here, in the oven that was the cab, he sat clenching his sweat-stained face, too disoriented to start the pick-up and too frightened to lower the window. The confident figure that had strode into the store earlier was a far cry from what had emerged. Stumbling and blinded by tears of excruciating pain, he had somehow found the pick-up among the ever-growing number of vehicles that had arrived after him, fumbled for his keys, and enclosed himself in the metal cocoon.

It was nothing like the familiar welcome of his temperate living room, with its murky isolation and frigid wood floors that bathed the fire of change in a cocoon of tranquility. But what was he to do? Never before had the conversion shown itself in the full light of day, and more importantly, never in public. *In public!* Caine's mind suffered the possibilities. *What was going on? Why was this happening?* What had occurred not five minutes ago in the electronics store caught Caine off balance; though the relationship he had shared with the rage had never been comfortable, it had at least been manageable. Mildly predictable in ways he had been able to work around. But lately it was showing itself more frequently, abandoning its pattern that protected both of them, and now this.

He shook uncontrollably in response to these thoughts as he fought off the confusion that had enveloped him at the store counter. What he had felt in that brief moment, though intimate, was totally out of place. He had always enjoyed a normalcy, a namelessness in the sea of human population. It was what made living with his other side harmonic in many ways. Caine could partake in everyday life: work, shop, tend to his needs, all without the fear that his darker side, the side that lived in sporadic periods in the cover of night, was going to make an appearance in the light of day. He had grown to trust this unspoken agreement, learned that a few changes in his habits and an acceptance of life on the move was the price he must pay for his freedom and a new sense of self.

Though striking in appearance and demeanor, the Sebastian Caine of society had always been gratified that the rage had left him to manage in the world of civility, to work and live in relative obscurity. What it did with its occasional nights was disruptive and left him a vagabond, but he had adapted, adjusted with remarkable ease. Their relationship, for all its horrific qualities, was strangely bearable, and in some ways, gratifying. He had agonized over its onset years ago, and now wished for its affable return.

With the perspiration pouring from him in cleansing torrents, he sat rigidly and recalled that day in eastern Texas when his life was forever changed. For him the years of banishment, the personal hell fostered by selfish parents who practiced little in the way of nurturing and strengthened through wave after wave of social response to his size and eccentric behaviors, had dissolved when the man Caine went in flux, forever changed. Out of the dark recesses of his battered self had emerged another, one marked by arrogance and a fierce sense of purpose. This Caine was confident and vital, its make-up in sharp contrast to the pathetic recluse with whom it shared a body. Initially repulsed by the reflection staring back at him at the end of each episode, he soon accepted the changeling for what it was, and for what it gave him. Over time the transformations brought on by the other had a direct effect on the original, as frequent exposure left residual qualities for the better. The young boy who cowered at the hand of an alcohol-soaked father and the hurtful jeers of pubescent bullies, who found no maternal solace in the cold, shriveled heart of his emotionally-dead mother and sought safety in the confines of his room at the end of each bitter day, was for the first time in his misery alive with a strength as yet unrealized.

That first experience had left him terrified and exhilarated, on a roller coaster ride of physical and emotional satisfaction. It was during that initial blackout when Caine discovered his true place in a world that, up to the moment, had offered him nothing but rejection. It was a rebirth, and Caine would treat it as his moment of salvation. The necessary changes that his new self required were little to ask for a life rediscovered. Yes, it had been a struggle at first—the constant travel, the fear of being uncovered--but the rewards gave it all meaning. He was alive, no longer a leper. No longer a stranger to the sensual world—a world of experiences and feelings denied him for too long. Now he was the master, the one in charge, and the bringer of pain. It was invigorating, and he brought the cast off traits from the other Caine into his conscious life, self-confidence and a pride that bordered on narcissism. To the Greeks it was *hubris*, an egotistical self-concept that encouraged invincibility and delusions of immortality while suppressing the instincts of fear and self-preservation. He would learn to cherish the surge of indestructibility that flowed through his veins as the fog of a night's hunt lifted and to hold onto the sensation for its unfamiliar yet pleasing quality.

But it was all crashing down around him, and as he sat in a pool of his genetically-alien fluid, he was reintroduced to emotions long forgotten—those of helplessness and dread. He fought to suppress them as he had done before, but denial was more difficult to summon this time. He had felt the rage and the distinctive path it followed in the slow captaining of his voluntary control of self while standing at the counter in the store. (He could only speculate as to what the employees and customers may have seen.)

Though brief, the transfer had begun, and only Caine's determined efforts and quick departure had kept it at bay. He had never exerted such force to inhibit the rage—the first time it materialized, he had been ignorant of its ways, and subsequent events had been received out of curiosity, and later, gratitude—and was unsure whether he could do it again.

He shifted on the truck's bench seat, his shirt and pants now drenched in sweat, though his hands remained fixed over his face, the fore and middle fingers methodically rotating his temples. If anybody had passed by with a hint of interest, they would have been mildly struck with the sight though unsure of just how long the man had been sitting so oddly in the parking lot. Their interest would have invariably been cancelled with their own reasons for being in the lot, that of whatever purchase they had come to make. Besides, he looked like a big man capable of solving his own problems surely.

In time the long-forgotten feelings of self-doubt and vulnerability passed, to be replaced with assurance and reaffirmation of his pronounced place among those inferior to him. Just as the rage had easily been thwarted from materializing, so too had the rather human emotion of fear been expunged.

How he could have ever let the isolated occurrence bother him was a puzzle he failed to see necessary to solve. *Hadn't he always stayed a step ahead? Hadn't the two benefited from their union all these years?* Nothing would change, and he was soon convinced that the events were simple aberrations whose return was highly doubtful, if not completely impossible.

They were one, he and it—forever tied and terminally co-dependent. Their futures relied on each other with faith as the basis for the communion that linked them. There was no need for conversation, petty exchanges between the two that was the practice of inferior creatures like man. No need for contracts or sworn statements of commitment that was the means of union in the world he had long forsaken but begrudgingly still lived in to provide for their needs.

They shared so much, and did so through a connection at a level only they understood. The rage had given him so much, had reversed the pain of living, and made him realize he was unique, above all others. He/They lived at a higher dimension of being, and nothing would change that now. Neither of them would allow that. *Ever.*

He was able to remove his hands from his face now, and was soon aware of the tremendous heat that surrounded him. Caine reached for the window handle and methodically lowered the glass to let a warm breeze carry the outside air into the stagnant shell he had occupied for quite a while. The change in temperature was immediate though not the comfort his house provided and for which he now longed for. Patrons of the various shops that lined the strip center came and went, unaware of the man who now sat in judgment of them. They with their weak minds and even weaker bodies, letting society dictate to them right and wrong, what to like, how to dress. And most found their presence on earth the result of a higher power, a presence greater than themselves, to whom they gave allegiance and thanks. *Didn't they know they should look to themselves for strength? Why were they so quick to hand over the reigns to someone else?*

He had taken responsibility for himself and look where he was— greater than all others. More powerful. No longer the sheep but the shepherd. The victim had become the predator. He lived among them but beyond their understanding, and as was his responsibility, beyond their reach. The years of existence as the new Sebastian Caine, conscious as two selves, had shown him the true nature of all things, and he was sure that soon some greater purpose would be revealed to them. This was just a journey toward a point of ultimate reality.

He pitied these underlings and their unfortunate lives, and looked upon them through the truck's windshield with contempt. *Poor creatures.* Like the Caine of the past, they were marked for a fate bound by assent and a lack of determination. They were void of a desire to rise above the day-to-day and…become. If they had the potential he possessed (and he seriously doubted their abilities), then where were his brethren? When would they evolve with him toward the next plateau?

He had discovered his potential; unwilling to settle for mediocrity, a force long untapped had surfaced, undoubtedly through some unconscious will of a Caine ready to change, and was now the driving mechanism of his future. *He was the hereafter.*

The man who had sat in the truck in the parking lot for almost half an hour now leaned his head out the open driver's window and opened his mouth as if to make a proclamation. He hesitated, grinned noticeably, and returned fully to the truck's interior.

Caine considered his options. Though the electronics store was both reliable and convenient, he would simply find another one to fulfill his technological needs until he was to move on to the next stop in his journey. He had already identified the place, made the required arrangements, and guaranteed its suitability. The drill had been followed many times before; it was just a matter of implementation. Soon he would be hundreds of miles from here—safe and secure in the knowledge that he had left behind any possible opportunities of discovery.

It was his half of the bargain. He had always been dependable. The other was simply voicing its need to move through its short appearance here today.

It was evident they had overstayed their welcome.

Caine gathered his keys, started the engine, and headed home, his resolve now firmly in place.

Chapter 19

For Ran the most difficult part of the investigative process was the waiting. Once Polly had either made or returned every phone call on his list, after he had faxed the numerous files Avery would need in his profiling, when every record had either been received or had been requested, he found himself in a very familiar spot. Criminal investigation relied on so many things, and among them were the efforts of a variety of people to systematically connect their individual pieces of the puzzle to help complete the larger picture. This distribution meant a great deal of the jigsaw was out of Ran's hands, and thus out of his immediate control. Dependence continued to be the thorn that hobbled him, and though the move to Kansas had seemed a way to eliminate the problem, he found himself facing the issue yet again.

What made the passing days bearable was the quality of people he had working with him. Polly and Monk were loyal and free of a haughtiness often seen in big-city departments where position and authority were matters of politics. Auburn was blessed with civil servants who cared as much about their town and its inhabitants as they did their service to them. These were a homespun folk with a familial tie to their charges and were willing to do what was needed to deliver the protection required.

Men like Tony Sartin and Tom Avery were career criminalists with an innate desire to see justice handed down to society's darkest elements. With every capture and conviction, these professionals felt a little more at ease, having done what they saw as their duty, in freeing the world of one less destroyer. They were also role models for a safer future, bringing their skills and experience to the next wave of guys in the white hats.

Ran had worked with dozens of persons just like these, and he was proud to call all of them friends.

Tara, though, was quite a different story. Aside from her obvious dedication to pathology and the unerring ability to provide the forensic information required of her by today's investigative process, she meant more to Ran than anybody he had ever come in contact with in his years of police work. Sure, he had encountered numerous women in various departments, had even dated some with whom he seemed to have a special connection, but it had never felt like this before. He was completely enamored with Tara, from her stubborn confidence to the singular striking beauty that occupied him the majority of the time he spent with her. She was dynamic, and exuded a natural charm that was magnetic in its attractiveness. There was no denying his feelings, and based on the previous night, he believed she shared his interest.

It was unchartered territory for Ran; he had lived as the quintessential loner, normally too preoccupied with his work to find time for emotion. Tara had lifted that veil of reclusion and found a way inside, a way to touch him deeply. Her initial concerns were that the distraction would jeopardize the investigation, but it had done quite the opposite. Bringing an end to the decades-long series of unsolved murders was vital to their future, and he was more determined than ever before to close the case and begin life anew with this special woman. Little had he known upon his painful departure from the familiar West Coast that he would discover his destiny in the form of Dr. Tara Phillips.

The night before had been a testament to what he hoped was a new beginning.

Right before heading out to grab a bite to eat and somewhat discouraged he had not yet heard from Tara, Ran stood looking out his office window at the nondescript activity that was taking place on a sun-drenched Jay Street when Polly called for him.

"Sheriff. Line one. Dr. Phillips."

His heart raced. "Thanks, Polly."

"Personally, I was going to give it a couple of days before calling. I didn't want to appear desperate," Ran said.

Tara's smirk found its way through the phone. "I expected as much, Smartguy, so I thought I better move things along before last night was forgotten."

"Trust me. Last night is a permanent fixture in my memories, at least until dementia sets in."

"You are such the romantic," Tara laughed. "I can't wait for Valentine's Day."

'I've already decided on the Winnie the Pooh cards. My favorite says, 'I want to be Eeyore Valentine.'"

"Oh, my, that's horrible."

"I'm actually a better cop than poet, but I'll keep trying," Ran quipped.

"And though I hate to leave this oddly-appealing conversation behind, it is in fact the cop stuff I wanted to talk about."

"Ah, just my luck. Here I thought I was making some headway."

Tara was reassuring, "You have made great strides, Sheriff. Believe me, but I need to let you know about the Stanton case. Good news."

"You got it?"

"I got it," Tara confirmed. "Despite Weyland's protests, Maxwell is giving me a shot, on the promise that I include Weyland in a comparative analysis of the Melton results. What a baby."

Ran was sure the chief medical examiner would not deny his up-and-coming pathologist a chance to thoroughly evaluate the Stanton remains. His years of experience, not to mention a strong desire to keep his plum position in the face of some recent grumblings regarding the efforts of his department, made the choice simple. Weyland's hollow conclusions had provided few answers and only helped in Maxwell's decision.

"That's great. When do you start?"

"This afternoon."

She sounded very upbeat.

"Meaning you'll be done..."

"With the physical examination? Sometime tonight, but you know the lab results will be weeks away," she said. "I am hoping I won't need those, though."

"What do you mean?" Ran asked.

"Now that I know what I'm looking for, I want to believe I'll have some answers before the day's end."

Ran was lost. Nothing new when talking medicine with Tara lately. "I don't understand," he said. "If Stanton was anything like Melton, you don't have much to work with. What is a shredded corpse going to show you without tissue and fluid sampling?"

"Oh, I'm not denying the need for samples, but what I'm looking for are things that I can quickly examine on my own, specifically hair and prints."

"What do you mean 'quickly examine'? Like under a microscope?"

Tara explained, "For one, and I think there are some simple observations and tests I can run to help accelerate our cause. Remember, Ran, I have some earlier experience with his victims, and now that I have seen the previous course of post mortem taken in these cases, plus my own beliefs, I know what I am looking for. If what I need is there, and I am confident it is, I can tell you something as early as tomorrow morning."

Ran's heart resumed its fast pace. "The morning? Wow. I hope you are right. I was thinking it would at least be toward the middle of next week."

"I don't think we have that kind of time," she said. "As we discussed, if the pattern continues, he is going to be moving on soon, and if he gets outside your jurisdiction, I don't know what our chances are of getting anybody to believe my claims."

Ran pursed his lips. "*Our* claims, Tara. Ours."

"No, I know you still have your doubts, and that's…"

Ran stopped her. "Tara. Listen. I gave last night a lot of thought, about everything, and I'm standing behind your theory."

"Well, I don't want you putting your neck out just because we shared something more."

"No, that's not it. Yes, that is part of it, but…," Ran faltered. He wanted to tell her so much. He wished she were there.

"Look, Ran…"

"We agreed to make time when this was all over, to see if what was happening could be…more, and I understand and support that. True, it's hard not to jump to your defense in the face of what has, is, happening between us, but believe me, I was up all night considering what you said, separating the *us* from the job I have. My duty to the people here.

"I looked back over all the files this morning, took into consideration everything you described last night and the days before, and honestly, it all fits. Crazy as it sounds to this veteran cop, it all makes sense. I never thought I would be saying that."

Only a long silence from the other end of the line, then finally, "Thank you, Ran. I feel I am right about this, but it sure helps knowing you are with me. Problem is, I don't think I will ever be able to convince the likes of Maxwell of my theory, and I know you would be laughed out of Auburn if you told the locals to lock their door to the threat of a creature of fantasy. That's why it is so important that I give you the means of catching him without the need for revealing our methods. Hopefully what I am able to discern, coupled with the help of your profiling friend, will let you end this, and all you will have to claim is a hunch. That's a big part of detective work, isn't it? Hunches?"

Ran smiled, "A huge part. Without intuition, I would be lost most of the time. It's what told me to side with your idea. I just have this feeling."

"As long as you are listening to your internal policeman. If all it takes is a kiss to get you to agree with me, I can see us locking lips over everything," Tara joked.

"See how intuition works? You are right on target, and I am your slave."

They shared some needed laughter.

"Believe me, Tara, I have drawn the line between professional and personal. Let's catch a killer. What do you need from me right now? I am chomping at the bit while everyone else is working away. I feel useless."

Tara said, "You've done all the leg work. Let us take care of our areas of expertise for now. Soon enough you are going to have to put it all together and finish the job."

"Speaking of that, what can you possibly deduce from hair samples, and all the files showed inconsistent fingerprints. What are you hoping for?"

"I'm hoping to find some pieces that will create a whole," Tara explained. "If there are any hair samples, and granted, none have been found, or even considered, I can at least determine race, maybe even gender and age. And yes, the fingerprints that have been isolated were either partials or were inconsistent from case to case. But I'm not looking to lift a print to run through a records search. I'm looking for one to X-ray."

Ran's eyebrows pinched in confusion. "X-ray? Is that possible? What would that do for you?"

Tara expounded, "You obviously cancelled your subscription to *Chemical Analysis* magazine."

"Sure I did. The swimsuit issue was a real letdown."

"I'm sure it was. Luckily, I have kept up on some of the latest techniques in forensic discovery during your absence, and X-ray is a technique that goes far beyond matching a fingerprint to a bank of records. With a spectroscopic microscope and an infrared array detector, the chemical make-up of the print can tell us all kinds of things."

"What is it that you are exactly looking for?"

Tara went into detail. "One of the big problems with the standard means of fingerprint detection, dusting, which you already know about, is the loss of important chemical traits inherent to the print. The powder can in many ways even alter the print, destroying valuable forensic information. By using a simple lifting gel, we can now take a print and retain all of its chemical composition. The print is hammered with infrared rays in the microscope allowing for individual elements to be exposed. These are then fed through the detector for identification and volume, which helps us determine everything from the suspect's diet to anything they may have come in contact with prior to depositing the print, like gunpowder or narcotics. It's basically a chemical picture of the print's owner. We can even determine the time of the crime based on the decomposition of the chemical agents involved. Really incredible stuff."

Ran said, "And you know how to interpret all the data?"

"Pathology is my job. Chemistry is my hobby," said Tara. "Can you stomach being seen with a geek?"

"Just beautiful ones. They have to be beautiful, otherwise…I think you could relate to my embarrassment," Ran said with as much seriousness as he could muster.

"I see what you're all about."

"It's a man thing. You wouldn't understand."

"Oh, I understand perfectly."

Ran redirected, "So you will be able to tell me what specifically about our man?"

"From the map is developed a chemical photograph. From that I can tell you whether it is a man, but so much more useful information. His age. Blood type. What he has digested, be it food or drugs. If he has handled anything that is unique to his occupation—special materials or products that would leave a residue marker behind. All kinds of things. I can drastically reduce your suspect field overnight," Tara concluded.

"And the Shawnee Medical Examiner's Office has these tools?" Ran asked.

"No," Tara answered as if she anticipated his question, "but I knew where I could get them. In fact, I requisitioned them from a supplier days ago."

Ran smiled, "Pretty confident you would be handling Stanton, weren't we? Is Maxwell going to okay the equipment? Sounds like stuff not normally available in a Midwestern medical examiner's office."

"He'll raise a fuss, most definitely have them sent back, but not before I have made use of them. They arrived today actually. Maxwell will not review the monthly charges until the end of the month, so I may even be able to return them before he explodes."

Ran was now concerned. "You better not have put your job in jeopardy with that move. I wouldn't be able to live with that," he said.

"I'll pass it off as an amateur mistake, motivated by a strong desire to find answers. The charges will be reversed. He'll get over it. He's always had a fatherly approach to our situation anyway," Tara said. "Not to worry."

"Okay, if you think it's all right," Ran calmed slowly, "but how are you going to explain the stuff until then? I mean, it's going to be out there for everyone to see."

Tara said, "Well, a spectroscopic microscope and its components are slightly bigger than a standard scope, so that won't be an issue. The problem is the detector. It's really nothing more than a black box that ties into a computer system, but that is where technology and I part ways. I'm not sure I can bypass the present computers as they are configured and introduce the detector properly. I may end up crippling the whole system."

Ran thought for a moment. "How quickly would you be ready to use the computers?"

"Late tonight, I would imagine. Why? Do you have some IT skills I wasn't aware of?"

"No, but I think I know somebody that can help us. Let me get back with you. Are you going to be near a phone in, say, thirty minutes?" Ran asked.

Tara confirmed, "I'm going to be here all night. I was going to get started after lunch. Do you really think you can get somebody here on such short notice?"

"I will use all my abilities in persuasion."

"They worked on me," Tara said.

"Ah, you were nothing," said Ran. "The promise of work-filled nights and little sleep? Easy pickin's."

"Such the romantic. I can't stop saying it."

"I'm plotting my next move as we speak."

"Just get moving on that computer help for now, Romeo."

"You got it."

Overcome with guilt with determined to do what was necessary to bring an end to the string of brutal murders that been crisscrossing the United States for over twelve years, Ran called the Shawnee CID unit and asked for Lieutenant Sartin. He had promised a resolution to Tara's problem and was bound to helping her in any way possible, even if it meant further manipulation of his good friend Sartin. Ran told himself that it was for all the right reasons, but it didn't make the call any easier.

While Ran waited for the lieutenant to pick up, Monk peeked in the office door. "Sorry, Sheriff. I'll come back later."

"What is it, Monk? I'm on hold."

He came fully into the room, his hands in their customary positions on the sides of his wide police belt. Ran had laughed to himself the first time he had met Monk, who then as now was decked out in the latest tactical gear available for law enforcement. It was ironic that his deputy would be so extremely outfitted for an area that had not seen a violent crime in many years, but Ran had soon determined that Monk needed the special gadgets and toys that were strapped to his exterior not for the security they provided him but for the self-esteem they fostered. Though he had not suffered ridicule from anybody in the community of Auburn where he was born and raised (quite the contrary—he was well-liked across the board), he had never felt a sense of achievement, that was until he earned an associate's degree in criminology from a program in Kansas City and returned to his hometown to begin his career. The uniform and its accessories were a symbol of that accomplishment, and he carried himself and the talismans with a dignity and pride not seen in most large police departments. Ran had seen this same type of excessive wearing of equipment, but among the men he had known to duplicate Monk's ensemble, it was used as a means of intimidation, a way to impress the general public. Fellow officers generally ignored the flamboyance, allowing their colleagues to approach their jobs as they saw fit. Ridicule found little acceptance in the brotherhood of law enforcement.

Monk's adornment was genuine; he was proud of his position as a public servant, a guardian of the people he cared for deeply, and for that alone, Ran could not have liked the man more. And so, with his Kevlar bulletproof vest, garish Safariland hooded holster, Accumold covered handcuff case, Frictionlock expandable baton, and combo edge folding law enforcement knife, among other things anchored to his slight frame, Monk stood before the sheriff's desk with his head predictably lowered at half mast in an unnecessary show of respect to his boss.

"Sheriff, if I could ask you something real quick, I'll get back on patrol," Monk said in hushed tones.

Ran said, "Sure, Monk. What is it? And I'm not talking to anybody, so there is no need to talk quietly."

"Sorry," Monk whispered. "Sorry." Significantly louder.

Ran looked at him with expectancy.

"Uh, I just wanted to tell you that with all the activity surrounding the cases we have been dealing with lately, I feel like I'm not helping.

Polly's out there busier than ever, and you're coming and going all the time. I don't see how patrol is…"

Ran shook his head. He could see where this was going, and though it was inconvenient right now, he took the time to assure Monk of his value, not because Monk needed positive strokes, but because he truly felt useless.

Most sheriffs would have reamed an underling for such petty whining, but Ran had never learned to come down on anybody other than criminals. He sometimes wondered whether he had the leadership skills to be in charge of a department. In California Ran had rejected promotion and avoided positions of command for just that reason. Since coming to Auburn he still viewed his title as honorary and his authority as an inconvenience.

"No, no, Monk. You're wrong." He shifted in his seat and let the mouthpiece lower toward his shoulder. "We can't let Auburn go without its needed surveillance while all this is going on. Believe me, I am relying on you to keep the day-to-day operation of this department in full gear until we either ID the killer or are certain that our community is safe from any further threat. You are the symbol of protection out there right now, and I know everyone in town sleeps a little better knowing the sheriff's department is out watching over them."

Ran could see the cloud of disappointment lifting from Monk's face. "I appreciate the extra shifts you're pulling with me preoccupied. I couldn't be doing this without you, Polly, or any of the department."

Monk nodded slightly. "Thanks, Sheriff. I just want to be doing my part."

"And you are," Ran said with a small grin. "Now get back out there."

He gestured to the door and brought the phone back to its proper place. Monk turned obediently to go with a "Yes, sir."

"Deputy," said Ran.

Monk halted and looked back.

"Thanks."

It was really all Monk had needed to hear. He was out of the office and through the front door before Lieutenant Sartin was saying his name in Ran's ear.

"Tom. It's Ran. What's up in the world of real police business?"

"Hey, Ran. What's the good word?"

"Little. Very little. How about on your end?"

"The same. I hate to admit it, but we're in a holding pattern until something breaks," said the lieutenant. Ran could read the frustration in his friend's voice and recognized it as his own.

"I had a captain in LA tell me that detective work was ten percent determination and ninety percent patience," said Ran. "I never felt good about that distribution."

"I hear you. So what is Auburn's finest doing to pass the time? And don't tell me you're being patient."

Ran wasn't sure how much longer he could exclude Sartin from the path he and Tara were taking, but realized that even though their conclusions were unorthodox, the route they were following to prove their theory was not so radical. He had decided before placing the call that he could divulge a portion of his investigative direction while sparing the Shawnee County officer a story of mythical proportions.

"Well, I called over to the ME to see if they could nail down a day that we could expect some results, and that new pathologist, Dr. Phillips, told me they would like to try something different."

"Dr. Phillips. She's that *awfully* attractive lady I saw you speaking with the other day at the medical examiner's office, isn't it? Going over some medical evidence, I believe was the story," said Sartin.

"Yes, as a matter of fact, it is. Was. Why?"

"Oh, no reason."

"Tony, don't even try to go there."

"Go where? As an investigator, I just couldn't help but notice the time that Auburn's sheriff is spending with Shawnee County's newest pathologist. I am confident that her good looks are in no way a factor."

Ran knew his friend was playing with him, and he wondered whether their relationship was so obvious to others. "Okay, okay, you've had your fun. Now do you want to know what she has in mind?"

Sartin laughed, "I'm a married man. I know exactly what she has in mind."

Ran tried to ignore him. "Since you seem to remember the time we were all together at the medical examiner's office so well, then you surely recall that I told her I would like some good prints off the Stanton body?"

"I think you said something like that, but you were uncomfortable and stuttering, I can't be sure what you said."

Ran pushed ahead. Sartin wasn't going to make this easy on him, and as much help as he had given Ran now and in the past, he could do nothing but let the ribbing continue. "In order to get us those prints and more, she wants to utilize some new technology, real state-of-the-art stuff."

"Sounds good to me. Are you sharing this to keep me informed or is there your regular ulterior motive?" said Sartin.

"Now you have hurt my feelings. The other I could tolerate, but this questioning of my purposes is going too far," Ran feigned injury.

Silence on the other end.

"Both, Tony. Both. She was given the autopsy, which she is about to start, and told me that to help in the results, she mentioned the new fingerprint analysis."

"So what do you two need from me?"

"This is a new imaging technique. May help us develop a more refined composite of the perp," said Ran. "I guess it could tell us more about his race, blood type, those things. I figure anything is better than nothing."

Sartin said, "I agree. We are sitting on our hands over here."

"Part of the extraction involves hooking up an electronic gadget to the existing computer system. She is afraid she will screw everything up if she does it," explained Ran. "She needs the equipment installed this evening."

"Why then? Why not contact the county and have them send out an IT guy to get it running?" asked the lieutenant.

Ran was ready for this. If Tara made a request through the proper channels, it would require Maxwell's approval. She wanted to connect and disconnect the detector before the next morning, long before Maxwell could catch the unauthorized activity.

"The equipment is not coming until tonight. Requisitioned and delivered via courier, and she really doesn't want to have to wait until tomorrow if she can tell us something sooner."

It was sketchy at best, and Ran could feel the thin veil that hid the complete truth being pulled away as Sartin considered his story.

If Sartin was suspicious, which Ran felt he had to be considering his job description, he didn't reveal it. "So you need me to what, have one of my people over to the medical examiner's later to put this thing together for her? Boy, are you not the white knight these days? This is all very uncharacteristic of you, Sheriff. Are you sure there isn't more to this? Something personal, I mean, because when I think about how pretty she is, well, I…"

Ran interrupted, "Carry on if you feel the need, but really, I simply told her we would appreciate anything she could get to us quickly, and this would make that possible. If you ask me, she is doing us a favor, and I figured we could help her help us."

"Ran, you know I am always ready to do what is necessary. Do you, does she, think she can get us some vital info from this thing?"

"Apparently it is the latest in chemical analysis when only fingerprints are available for forensic analysis. All things considered, it's worth a shot."

"I have to agree with you there. We have nothing right now to hang our hats on," Sartin sighed.

Ran said, "It made sense to me to do what I could. Of course, what I can do here inevitably involves you."

"Ok, just give me a time," said Sartin, "and I will have someone out there."

Ran explained the where and when for Sartin's tech.

"Thanks again, Tony. Can I go ahead and thank you now for my next request?"

Sartin said, "No, I would never hear from you otherwise."

Ran felt the sharp stab of Sartin's last comment, making it harder than ever to continue to keep him somewhat uninformed. A lot of what he could share would undoubtedly depend on what Tara discovered. Either way, he hoped he could find a way to repay Sartin and his department in the future. They had made his transition into small town law enforcement that much easier.

"I have been getting a little in debt lately. What would you say to a celebratory steak dinner after this is over?"

"Does that include when it goes to the cold files?"

Ran said emphatically, "We're going to end this, Tony. I can feel it."

"Well, I hope that is your West Coast experience talking, because we're not feeling real good about it over here."

"I don't know, Tony. I just think a break is coming soon."

"It better," said Sartin, "or we may be running into each other at the morgue more often. Pretty lady or not."

"You," Ran said, "are just jealous."

"If I didn't have a perfect woman at home, I'd be you're toughest competition. No need to be jealous here."

"I'll call you as soon as she has something."

"You *will* do that."

Ran thought the chances were fifty-fifty.

Chapter 20

The Shawnee County Medical Examiner's Office was, ironically, alive with activity as medical personnel, maintenance, delivery persons, and various legal representatives were scurrying about as if preparing for a snap inspection. The reception desk was the hub of the controlled chaos, a point where questions were dutifully answered, documentation provided, and the occasional loitering visits from fellow employees uncomfortable with the increase in the normally lethargic pace that usually dominated their occupations.

There was nothing special about the day to initiate such tumult; it just seemed that the entire northeastern half of Kansas had decided to coalesce in this one afternoon in the very place Tara Phillips needed it elsewhere. The number of bodies for autopsy was lower than normal, and Maxwell was gone to Kansas City for a conference, keeping his regular crowd of groupies from assorted departments and organizations at bay, so the influx of flurry in what was rarely a busy place was highly disconcerting.

A state categorized mainly by its agricultural history and in some educational circles for its connection with *Brown*, both the Civil War dispute between abolitionists and pro-slavery activists highlighted by the death of John Brown and the infamous segregation battle with the state's board of education, it had experienced little in the way of conflict or violence in the last fifty years. Its capital, Topeka, was better known for American Wild West museums and tributes to the Oregon Trail that had conveyed countless wagon trains to and from the new frontier than it was to modern day issues best found on television's investigative shows like *True Crime* and *Forensic Files*. It was a geopolitical body molded in the fashion of its centuries of occupants—hard, determined, and loyal to the cause of civil and religious propriety. The inhabitants of the twenty-first century version of Kansas were a simple lot, family-oriented, holding firmly to their roots with the neighboring states that collectively occupied the form-fitting Bible Belt. Far from trendsetters or national leaders, the people known as Jayhawkers who lived in the Garden State, so named for its rich soil and beautiful landscapes, were now reliving the period known as Bleeding Kansas, when violence and upheaval ruled the territory during the battle for individual freedom. The state had known peace for so many years since, and the tranquility it enjoyed was a symbol it carried proudly.

And so it was upsetting to the slow-paced nature of Shawnee County and its bordering parishes that a madman was walking among them, spreading fear and drawing the protective arms of parents around their children that much tighter. For Tara, it was more than clear that she was not in Kansas anymore; they had been thrust into the sociopathic world already affecting an ever-degenerating nation and were being asked to come to grips with the stark reality of evil's firm place in every corner of the globe, even modest Topeka, U.S.A.

Of all days for this place to come to life, thought Tara as she made her way across the building from her office to the autopsy rooms located on the other end. Here she would find the body of Mitchell Stanton, and hopefully some answers. It had been surprisingly easy for her to take charge of the case, and from what she could tell, Maxwell had been considering her before she arrived in his office that morning. She was aware of his conference and knew that if she got there early enough, she could discuss the autopsy with him. She counted on tight schedule to push him to agreement, but it had proven quite simple.

She had presented herself as the picture of pathological professionalism--hair back in a conventional bun, pressed white lab coat, a file folder clutched in her arm, the symbol of medical proficiency, though she didn't want to appear too desperate, so she first remarked on his pending seminar. Kansas City was welcoming chief medical examiners from across the country for a two-day forensics extravaganza. It was something he lived for, and she could see he was harried to complete his morning reports and issue various assignments prior to catching his plane.

"Dr. Maxwell," she said with a note of surprise, as though she didn't expect to find him in his office. If the chief ME was anything, it was predictably efficient. "I assumed you would be headed to the airport by now."

Maxwell searched his top desk drawer for something of importance. "Doctor. Yes, I am leaving shortly. Just tying up some loose ends." He continued his hunt.

Tara continued, "Did I understand the subject this year is the use of forensic palynology and its value in criminal or civil investigations? Fascinating. I hope you have time to share on your return."

He paused in his search, snared by a subject he couldn't avoid, and Tara knew it. Forensic science. Maxwell's hands stopped their busy work, and he looked up at her for the first time since her arrival.

"Yes, palynology. Do you know something of its application?"

Tara, not by coincidence, knew quite a bit about the subject. She had glanced at some materials on the Internet the night before to better her chances. "The use of pollen evidence that can link them to the seen of a crime. A technique made viable in New Zealand recently. Very interesting, and here in the Midwest, a useful tool."

Maxwell smiled, "You are well-versed, Doctor, and I agree whole-heartedly. With the vast amount of diverse vegetation and plant life that we encounter, pollen evidence found on defendants' clothing could represent another nail that we could use to hammer shut a suspect's coffin."

Tara attempted to dazzle. "I think you will find during your conference that the technique applies to the presence of pollen in dirt samples as well. I think I read of a case in Europe where a defendant's boots had traces of mud on them that contained various pollens, among them that of a 20-million year old fossil hickory grain. A forensic geologist was able to pinpoint a small area where the mixture of pollens could be found, implicating the suspect and gaining a confession. Again— fascinating."

"Well, well, well, Dr. Phillips. That is quite impressive. I knew you were fresh with the latest techniques, but I never pegged you for a forensic junkie. I thought we were a dying breed," said Maxwell, who had abandoned his desk drawer and was completely absorbed in the conversation.

"The field is changing rapidly, and I want to stay in touch. The things I was doing in residency are in many respects obsolete today, and as you mentioned, I am relatively new to the business."

"New but very capable, Dr. Phillips. You have proven your worth here so far."

Tara saw her opportunity. "Speaking of that, and while I have you here, Doctor, I was wondering if you had made a choice of pathologist for the Stanton case or if you were going to wait until you got back. I certainly would like a crack at it if you hadn't considered another direction."

Maxwell reflected, still lost in the reverie of microscopic pollens and ancient granules of forensic discovery, "No, I was undecided on that, though I had considered doing the work myself since there seems to be a great deal of interest in the case. This conference is going to keep me out of touch for a few days, so I don't think I should let it wait.

Tara felt her balloon of hope deflating, though she was ready to go to bat for herself if necessary.

"Tell me, Dr. Phillips,..."

"Tara."

"Tell me, Tara. How would you feel about Weyland handling this one? He already has a history with it."

Tara tried to maintain her professionalism. "I could see where Weyland would be the logical choice, but I was hoping I might have the chance to shed some new light on these cases…if we are talking about a serial suspect, that is."

"Weyland has the experience. He has the previous exposure," said Maxwell. "Seems like an easy choice, but I'm listening. Why should I go against my instincts and put you on the case? I'll have Weyland in here as a permanent fixture of complaint when I get back."

"I have a previous history as well," Tara confessed.

"I'm still here," Maxwell said without flinching, "but you better hurry. I have to catch a cab in ten minutes."

"During my residencies I assisted on cases very similar to the two we have here—massive tissue and blood loss, no crime scene, little to no forensic evidence and what was catalogued was ambiguous," Tara said, speaking with a conviction few could ignore. "I watched some of the best pathologists in the country come up empty, unable to contribute to what eventually became cold cases. I would hate to see that happen here. I am familiar with the procedures attempted, and with all due respect, Weyland didn't shed any new light. I just want the opportunity, Doctor. The chance to offer a different approach."

"It goes against my standard procedure," Maxwell said.

Tara pressed on, "I understand that, and I appreciate the efficient department you operate here; I can't imagine working anywhere else. Weyland has the years on me. But I'm asking you to reconsider. I won't let you down. There is evidence there, evidence that hopefully could lead to a conviction. I think I am the person that can find it for you."

She had been respectful while self-assured. His interim silence following her appeal was encouraging, as if he was considering the possibility. Finally, he spoke.

"Tara, I've been waiting for this moment for a while now--for you to come to me as an equal and stand behind your expert skills and strong forensic knowledge. It's what defines us as researchers and investigators—a deep belief in our abilities to expose the truth."

She masked her delight. "To be completely honest, I wanted you to take the Stanton case all along, but I wanted to hear it from you."

"Thank you, Doctor. I won't let you down."

Maxwell smiled, "Just promise me you will find time for yourself after this one. I can't have you burning yourself out. What would everybody think of me for overworking my star pupil."

Tara wanted to vault over the desk and hug the old man, but decorum got the better of her. True, she was happy to have been entrusted with the case for what it meant to Ran and herself, but her elation was more than doubled by Maxwell's words of confidence in her. She was valued, and nothing made a person feel more alive in their work. "If it is all right with you, I will get started this afternoon. There is nothing else pressing."

"Fine. Oh, and can you do me a favor," he said. "Save me some heartache on my return and include Weyland in your findings. He's a good man, just…inflated in the pride department. I'll leave formal word before I go that Stanton is your baby. Good enough?"

"Request gratefully accepted," said Tara, and she turned to go.

"Doctor Phillips?" the chief medical examiner stopped her.

"Yes, sir?"

Good luck."

"Thank you, sir. Thank you."

She had floated on air back to her office to deliver the news to Ran and prepare for the most important autopsy of her young career. Her special purchases arrived soon after, and she spent most of the morning outlining the post mortem and reviewing previous autopsies for inconsistencies and findings. She had not wanted to waste her time walking down the same road as Weyland and others.

The autopsy suites at the medical examiners (there were two) stood in pristine condition awaiting their use, bright examination venues marked by white tile floors and rolling, stainless-steel tables. An inventory of each would find one wall-supporting shelf upon shelf of medical accessories. Spotless Craftsman tool boxes stood here and there, the resting place of tools that had changes little in the hundred year history of autopsies: scalpels, bone saws, toothed forceps, rib cutters, a Stryker saw, and countless needles and collection trays. These were the devices of clinical and forensic autopsy, and pathologists wielded them like magical wands. Tara had encountered some doctors in her short career that actually went to hardware stores to find additional equipment. *Delicacy*, one had told her, *isn't always required.* Overhead hung two massive Halogen lamps elevated by jointed arms that allowed for easy movement. At the far end of the room was the autopsy bay where the main table stood, connected to a large collection sink mounted to the wall. Everything that Tara would need was within arm's reach in the bay, and it was here that Mitchell Stanton's remains now rested.

Tara was already in her scrub suit and now donned gloves and a protective face shield before beginning her work. The body had been stored in its original body bag in a refrigerated locker awaiting examination, and she had authorized the preliminary work to be done earlier in the day, culminating in the presentation of the former Mr. Stanton in his final state. Gary Livingston, the Shawnee County diener on duty, had taken care of the duties, following the special requests of Dr. Phillips in the process. Normally the diener was responsible for opening the body bag and taking detailed photos. If the exam was clinical and evidence was not required, the clothes were then removed and the body cleaned. Later Gary would clean the autopsy bay and its instruments to ready it for the next exam.

But this was to be neither clinical nor normal, and as a result, Gary's job had been simple. After weighing the corpse, X-rays were taken while it remained in the bag, which was then cut open to reveal its contents that went through a thorough series of photographs. Stanton had exited this world the way he came in, so the removal of clothing, which Tara would have done anyway, was not needed. She had wanted the body moved carefully in the whole process to preserve every detail, every subtle quality that could be lost with careless handling.

As she entered the furthest suite, she found Gary adjusting the intense lamps that hung ominously above the slanted table, and saw he had met her requirements. Where normally lay a complete body, clothed if part of a forensic exam, rested the splayed body bag revealing a twisted, bare mass of ripped flesh and splintered bone. Tara could make out only a single limb, and based on the muscle tissue that clung precariously from it, she determined it was a leg. The torso looked as if it had imploded, some great weight having compressed it from all sides, as the rib cage lay exposed in concaved decimation. Connected to this was a disfigured head no longer anchored by a spine but by ravaged sinews of neck tendons and cartilage. It was turned unnaturally to the side, the point of the jawbone resting on the table in support of the skull. The entire picture was surreal and made Tara think of victims of boating accidents she had witnessed during her time in North Carolina—distinctly organic but nothing more. The skin was relatively free of blood smear, though Tara could see bruises and tears through streaks of dirt.

"I'm just finishing up, Doctor. Quite a mess, huh?"

"Not one of his better days, I would guess," said Tara, moving over to the table. "Now that the body is exposed, I thought I would have more to work with."

"Looks like he got caught up in a tug-of-war with an angry family of bears," said Gary, who rolled a smaller, sheet-draped table over near Tara, its surface covered neatly with the tools of the trade.

"Well, I don't know about that."

Though his observations lacked in compassion, Tara allowed for his and anyone else's conversation during an autopsy. For her it was a clear reminder of the life that existed in a sanctuary of death.

"Doc, word is this poor guy is connected to the death of Sonny Melton. Is that true?"

Tara had already started an informal external exam. "That's what I am hoping to find out, Gary. Would you be sure to close the door when you leave? And I am expecting a late delivery--some medical equipment. Would you be sure it makes it to my office, please?"

Gary liked the new doctor and was quick to satisfy her requests. "You got it, Doc. Anything else?"

"Yeah, if you see Dr. Weyland out there, don't mention I have already started. I'd like to be able to concentrate on this."

"Pretty important, huh?"

Tara looked up at him for the first time. "They're all important, Gary, but this one is going to take some time."

"I'll try to keep you undisturbed, Doctor," Gary said as he headed out the door. "Count on it."

"Thanks, Gary," she said, her attention having returned to the task at hand. She planned on a long afternoon and evening, so getting started now instead of in the morning would widen the window of opportunity that she and Ran agreed was closing quickly.

Tara reached above her for the suite's microphone and switched it on to begin a recording of her efforts. In forensic autopsies, an external exam would now commence, a visual description of the remains followed by the gathering of evidence in the form of hair samples, materials like paint chips or gunshot residue, gatherings from fingernails and hands (not an option here), and fibers. The bag and clothes are then removed and bagged as evidence, and a detailed analysis of the body is carried out. In some cases a special UV radiation is used to enhance secretions on the skin, a distant relative of the process Tara planned to conduct.

She knew Maxwell, and Weyland especially, whom she had surprisingly not seen since earning the opportunity to do the post mortem, would evaluate her work closely, so she conducted a textbook and thorough exam. What she would leave out of the report was the infrared scan of fingerprints and the subsequent use of the detector to break down their components. This would all be done later in the evening when Tara could improve her odds of privacy. The UV radiation would pinpoint her targets, which she could catalogue and return to later after completing her required work. She felt no guilt; conversely, Tara was enthusiastic about the adventure that lay before her. This was what her years of training and subsequent nights of study of new research and strides in the field were for—to determine the identity of this bringer of pain and carnage. She was bathed in anticipation and excitement. It was her nature to be curious, to go the extra mile in search of answers, so the undertaking was like going home. Tara found herself in a comfortable environment, a place where she was needed and her fine tuned skills put to their best use. This venue, a source of disgust for some and heartache for others, was her showplace. The light's that cast their brilliance on the table before her were the spotlights of her performance. It was show time and she was more than up to the challenge.

"The body presented to the medical examiner's office is in a black body bag and is free of clothing and any additional materials from the scene of its retrieval.

"The body appears to be that of an adult white male consisting of a torso, head, and single leg. Each part and its attached tissues are the subjects of massive trauma, and bruises, tears, and what appear to be bites are visible. The body parts collectively measure 35 inches as a result of a collapsing of their normal framing.

"Soft tissue remains around the face. The nose, ears, and eyes are absent, and large areas of hair and scalp have been removed."

Tara delicately turned the head to a position more natural in relation to the torso.

"Blunt force trauma is evident to the orbits, maxillae, nasal bones, and mandible. Exposed skull and facial bones exhibit fracturing and separation, while all the teeth remain intact."

She continued her external analysis, noting the condition of the decimated torso.

"Extensive blood loss is evident. Chest walls are completely involved and partially destroyed. The anterior ribs are visible and pushed inward. Only ribs one to four are complete. The remainder is fractured or missing. The lungs, heart, and liver are missing. A large abdominal tear shows all digestive organs are gone. The resulting cavity houses none of the tissue normally present."

The report was following along the same lines of Weyland's recent efforts and those of the autopsy reports Ran had gathered for her. For Tara it was a flashback to her days as a fledgling pathologist hoping to set the world on fire with her coming out party. Devastating cases like this had shocked her system and brought her down a few notches from her pulpit as pathology's future savior. These were more troubling than the cases of victims of high-speed car wrecks, their bodies twisted and often decapitated, burned bodies exposed to intense heat and fire, or the casualties of senseless and passion-filled attacks marked with bludgeoning, leaving the body unrecognizable. Different because of the lack of forensic evidence in every case. Pathologists across the country welcomed autopsies in which physical contact had obviously occurred between the attacker and the victim. Here were ample supplies of tissue, hair, blood, and fiber samples that pinpointed the guilty with undeniable accuracy. The reason the cases she and Ran were focused on were either cold or headed in that unfortunate direction was because available evidence provided little information. There had been fingerprints, partially smeared in a scant amount of blood and left as a dried legacy on the victim's remaining skin. They proved worthless when matched to national records, and additionally, the prints changed slightly from kill to kill, causing the prevailing belief that the cases were not linked but only copycat versions of previous attacks. It wasn't unheard of. Fluid samples not of the victim attained in every case were only trace amounts and highly problematic, offering a variety of pieces that refused to come together in any coherent way. Tara did not discount the work done by her colleagues—quite the opposite. They had forged a path that gave her a clear place of departure, and with that assistance, she offered Stanton's remains less than her best effort while privately emphasizing the search for tale tell fingerprints visible only under UV light and whose contents would be extracted with the infrared and finally separated in the detector.

Remarkably left to her duty the entire afternoon, Tara completed both the external and internal exams, having gathered a plethora of samples for lab analysis in the hopes that their assailant had deposited something new in the latest of his attacks and far surpassing the measure of information Weyland had gathered.

Removing her mask and gloves in an effort to take a much-needed break, Tara stepped into the hallway and leaned against the wall with a heavy sigh. She was tired from a lack of sleep but her adrenaline had kept her going. She considered a diet soda from the break room before returning to the suite, only to be stopped by Shawnee County's deputy medical examiner.

"Dr. Phillips. How are things progressing?"

Weyland's question was short and accusatory, but Tara stood unaffected. "Clifford. You're here later than normal."

"Well, I thought I would hang around and get your preliminary assessment. Dr. Maxwell did tell you I was privy to all findings, did he not?" he said with his air of superiority.

"Yes, yes, he did, and I am more than happy to do just that," she answered, knowing full well that the best way to get him out of her face was to give him what he wanted know so she could have her freedom later, a time crucial to her investigation. "I was just going to get something to drink. Shall we walk and talk?"

Weyland seemed disappointed that Tara had not gone on the defense, while he was ready to throw his authority into the ring of discussion, seeking her white towel of compliance. Sexist and more than overbearing, he failed to bother Tara who possessed a strong sense of self-measure.

For the next fifteen minutes, Tara spoke of her findings, an estimated time of death, and probable cause pending lab results. She provided Weyland with enough information to satisfy his ego, and soon she was back in the exam theater, having ensured she would be left alone for the rest of her time with Mitchell W. Stanton. The next few hours would be crucial, and in the end, she hoped she would have the data they so desperately needed.

So much was counting on her, and Tara embraced the throwing down of the gauntlet.

Chapter 21

By the time he had made it back to Hoyt and his unimpressive three-bedroom ranch house, Caine had replaced his feeling of control with a monumental anger that left him consumed in a frenzied state only familiar to the rage. Slamming the paneled front door and gnashing his teeth with a bitter snarl, he had put three near-perfect circles in the bare walls with his fists before gaining marginal restraint, and he now stood anchored in the middle of his dark, damp living room in an animal-like crouch. The control that had allowed him enough time to make it home was now replaced with something else, something that shook him to the very core of his essence. What he felt was boiling inside him and growing in intensity, causing every muscle in his solid frame to tense while his head felt explosive with the pressure. It was not completely foreign, though, this feverish state; during his transformations, when he was lying helpless, struggling to maintain awareness if only for a moment longer, and a vast darkness was rushing to envelope him, the early stages of the change gave him an idea of the power that waited to consume him. It was these fleeting seconds that he clung to as the allure of the great will that was assuming ownership of him was more than anything he had ever felt before. But in every instance prior to this one, Caine was incoherent and fast approaching unconsciousness as the other took charge of his body to possess both him and the night.

But this was not the familiar beginning of the change. The coursing flow of raw fury that held him was not debilitating, not driving him to the floor in writhing pain to take full command and, after a night of carnage, return to the safety of the cavernous house. It was as if he owned this frenzy. This was his emotion, not an extension of him, and he soon began to savor its taste. With it came a sense of superiority that he had only shared in the moments following his return to self or in the dreams that entertained him during his days of recovery.

He soon paced the floor like a caged tiger and began to marvel at the incredible feeling that washed over him. He pumped and flexed his arms in triumph and hammered his feet in a show of defiance.

To be this, he thought. *To possess this.*

Caine was born of incredible size and strength and cast a shadow rarely seen outside the athletic arena. He possessed the force of three men, his arms, chest, and thighs swelling with a natural musculature that was the envy of those who secretly glanced as he passed among them. Now charged with an animation that made him feel invincible to the point of superhuman, his body was alive with what felt like the power of the universe.

I know what this is. What I am becoming. This is the rage, together with me. Here, surging inside. Caine believed he was more than the vessel now; he was the operator of a power greater than anything he or anyone else had ever witnessed. His blood burned in response to the task, and he bathed in its brilliance. *It is here with me now—as one.*

At the electronics store, he had zoned out as if in a daydream; whatever had happened there was lost to him, though he had gauged it as being only a short blackout. Not here. He was completely cognizant of what possessed him and realized he would have to learn to manage its severity should it choose to return or stay with him permanently. It fit him well, like a new suit, and he believed that if this was a trial run, the rage testing his capacity to stand with it, than he was responding correctly. Caine sensed a mastery of the rising animal and began to rein it in slowly with a will he summoned from a lifetime of regret. If what he was experiencing was a blending of his selves, he was confident in the prospects of dealing with this latest altering of his life. Hadn't he been able to adjust to the rage when it was first thrust upon him without warning so long ago? No one was better suited for this modification than Sebastian Caine, the willing companion of a previous change that would have left most people scurrying to a psychiatric ward, panicked and seeking medical care. He had practiced patient acceptance, and based on his success with that approach, there was every reason to do so again.

He chastised himself for his earlier concerns, when the thing that he worked so hard to hide touched the surface of the day. That event, coupled with the frequency that had concerned him, had been nothing more than the rage stirring its dark coffin, signaling him that it was prepared for the next step in his metamorphic rebirth—the ceremonial transfer of power across the ethereal border that separated his two selves, thereby dissolving the conjoined state and making them one. He was ignited by the prospects and flexed his arms in celebration.

This must truly be the energy it feels, he thought, his lips peeling back from his long white teeth as he raised his fists to the ceiling in a personal show of might and covetous exuberance.

Oh, the strength. The singular power.

He regretted not possessing this lofty might in the days of his youth, a time of skittish compliance and timid reaction to those of authority. His parents, his schoolmates, had all treated him with disdain and fostered the self-loathing that he donned like a well-worn coat every day of his life. He was threatened and bullied incessantly and secretly harbored a hope that he would be delivered from it in an almost apocalyptic fashion.

To have had this power then. To have crushed them all, grinding their pathetic bodies into the dirt.

He held his massive claw-shaped hands to his face; the long, jointed fingers bent in a show of potency and gathered at palms set deeply and riveted with intensity. He could see every detail of them though the house was nearly pitch black as heavy sheers and drapes covered every window. In this frozen moment of penitence, Caine pictured his hated father's terrified face caught firmly between his massive paws like a vise, blood beginning to run from his ears and eyes as the red liquid coated the digits compressing his skull. Dear old father screamed in agony and begged for mercy, assuring anyone that would listen that he could change, but his cries fell upon the deaf ears of a son far too long berated and beaten in the name of tough love.

Here is where true discipline in revealed, old man. Too late for promises.

Lifting the now lifeless frame of the man toward the sky as if it were a celestial offering, Caine imagined his mother's pitiful wails of sorrow, seeking forgiveness far from deserved. He would do away with her as well in a fitting moment of justified revenge.

Where were you, Mother, when he whipped me night after night in a drunken rage? You kept silent and escaped into the same bottle of despair, didn't you, while your only child paid for your husband's failures? You chose to share in his addiction and his ruthless attacks on your child, so join him in his death.

Soon, he imagined, this newfound strength would be unleashed on the others, the badgering peers who laughed at his awkwardness and pelted him with words of insult and humiliation. They too would suffer in a bloodbath of contrition and share in the pain that had soaked his pillowcase every night as he cried himself to a fitful sleep. Retribution could be found in the heat that filled him, but he realized it was too late now to exact these punitive actions, and in that he found permanent disappointment.

Someone must pay. Someone will *pay.*

He wanted to release it, vent the explosive urge within him, let the volcano of fire that surged just beneath his control to erupt and lay waste upon an unsuspecting world. Yes, they could all suffer for his misery. They had all turned away--teachers, neighbors, and relatives--shielding their denying eyes from the holocaust that was his existence. Avoiding the trouble of involving themselves as they found comfort in renunciating any responsibility for him. He had been a child, a lonely young boy unable to defend himself from the horrors of the outside world, and no one had ever come to his defense.

Except the rage.

Caine dropped to his knees, every muscle visibly taunt while overcome with the combination of anger and rooted shame in the parents from whom he had sprung and the cowardly response he had offered in response to the abuse. His fists balled and he drew them to his eyes in this moment of conflict, the need to strike out and render flesh clashing against the anguished child that would forever seek human comfort and peace. He was a cyclone of emotion and genetic frenzy, and for a man who valued his intellect and superior reason, the traits that had kept him going during those most troubling times in life, he found himself lost in the turmoil.

To this point the rage had seemed to serve as an adequate catharsis for the past atrocities leveled upon him, the dark side that he reverently protected while it lashed out in the role of the destructor. Their union had been effective. The results, gratifying, but apparently no longer. He had quickly concluded that the power was meant for him, that a blessed transfer was taking place, the baton of supremacy royally passed into his eager hands. But now he was struck with a new thought and was immediately jolted by its implications. What if the changes were for a different resolution? What if the rage was surfacing for absolute control, not giving him its power but adjusting to his consciousness before expelling him for eternity while it mastered both roles? His brain was a jumble of mixed thoughts in the depths of the physical jumpstart occupying its residence.

One of two things was happening to him, and he now weighed each as his rational self kneeled in submission to the physical and emotional doppelganger that he was sure was choosing to breach the wall that separated his selves. Those parts--the self-employed recluse meeting the technological needs of companies that knew him only as an electrical signal that tapped their systems and solved their problems while enjoying a mobile anonymity, and the other half, a primal beast that ruled the night, foraging the countryside in its ravenous pursuit of victims that would culminate in a satisfying orgy of death--were both Sebastian Caine. They would either come together to create a superior version that possessed the dominant qualities of both, sloughing off the traits that made each susceptible to defeat, or, and Caine momentarily lost his unnatural high, the rage was choosing to take full ownership of the shell they shared, eradicating the inferior self and assuming complete control.

His breathing became labored and his heart thundered in his chest as if in response to the possibilities he was now considering. To be in soul possession of this great power was enticing, *if* he could learn to harness its force, and he believed he could, regardless of his track record to this crucial point. Command was thrust upon him earlier in the day apparently, and he had performed pitifully, running from the store like a frightened child, a replay of the boy he once was. The shattered drywall that graced one side of his scantly-clad living room was a testament to his continued failure to reign it in, though he had to admit to his lucidity now, propped on the floor as the energy surged through him in wave after wave of omnipotence.

I wasn't ready. I didn't understand. Caine couldn't be sure that the rage was interested in providing him with a second chance, if making him the master was even its plan.

I can be this, he screamed in his head, trying to direct a telepathic appeal toward the other side, the dark place where the rage resided. *Give this to me.*

The prospects of banishment from his own body, his essence wiped out in a wave of the rage's mighty hand, frightened him, and he fought back against the show of weakness. Caine brought his fists down heavily on the floorboards, which snapped in response to the violent collision with his hardened flesh. The destructive force was, fittingly, like ambrosia.

"Give this to me," he bellowed with a commanding voice that until that moment had never passed his lips. "Let me have the strength with which you rule the night. Release it to me so that together we can walk by day and hunt the darkness."

It was desperate request, but real and honest nonetheless. Caine knew he could not mask his feelings from his companion; it knew him as well as he knew himself. And because of his bare emotions, he believed he was heard, that his words were carrying across the expanse that divided them, and that their passion was clear.

Caine was seeking a supernatural communion, though a response from the other side would have been shocking. The rage had always been more of a state of being to him, a mystical phantasm that was energy without shape, a current lacking form. It had been spirit to him, existing on a parallel plane and capable of transfer when the urge came upon it. He had never tried to interact with it except in the biological pool of his body where the interchange took place. Everything to this point had been understood, as if the role he must play was mapped out and impressed on his subconscious. He didn't know how, but he somehow understood that the dialogue would remain one-sided; speaking to the empty darkness helped dispel the feeling that he was alone and gave substance to what he was trying to contact.

This place stood as a confessional, and he sent his petitions in the hope that they would be answered. For what seemed hours, Caine sought a supernatural confirmation of his request.

Chapter 22

Ran remained at the sheriff's office through the evening. He had sent Polly home despite her insistence that she stay, assuring her that her efforts during the hectic day had been more than productive and that there was nothing more that they could do until the morning. He would need her bright and early at the phone to gather the fruits of her day's labor, and so she had left, though not without her signature show of displeasure with his decision. The veteran dispatcher was all bark, and Ran valued both her fire and maternal charm, especially now. He promised he would step out for dinner, a healthy one, before she had finally disappeared into the tranquility of a Kansas dusk.

Monk had enthusiastically agreed to work a double shift at Ran's request. The sheriff was overcome with a need to beef up security in Auburn, either a reaction to the potential truth in Tara's prophecies of a one-man armegedon or simply the sixth sense that he had grown to trust throughout his career. He instructed the deputy to tighten his regular surveillance and restrict himself to the perimeter of Auburn proper.

Laid out over three square miles in a rectangular pattern, Auburn rested in the flat agricultural plains reminiscent of its state's legacy. The majority of its inhabitants resided in a surprisingly tight pattern around the town's epicenter, which consisted of government and public service offices, the K-12 public school with its two ball fields and multi-functional auditorium that housed everything from athletic events to the annual Auburn Quilt Festival, and the few businesses that were able to thrive in a community of 2100, namely Landmark Bank, Bailey's Hardware, and Dalton's, the place where his enchantment with Tara had begun. The nearest airport and hospital were in Topeka, and most of Auburn's workforce made the short drive to the capital city to occupy positions mainly in the construction industry. The town had a brief law enforcement history, relying on Shawnee County to take care of what was the rarest of police needs, until it added two part-time officers ten years previous. The dispatcher's office had originated as nothing more than a town hall reception desk, taking care of everything from utilities questions to alerting the volunteer fire crew of a barn fire or severed finger.

It was only after Ran Price had agreed to head a sheriff's department of three full-time employees that Auburn had actually stepped into the twenty-first century of policing its own. The funding had come from the resourcefulness of the mayor who tapped the right federal grants and philanthropic institutions, and he was quick to remind Ran repeatedly that what was available was limited, so the equipment he had taken for granted in the big city stood as an elusive pipe dream.

With Monk making his rounds and the phones temporarily silenced, Ran had stepped over to Dalton's for a fast burger (a subconscious challenge to Polly's demand) before getting back in fear that he would miss Tara's call. She had told him not to expect any results before midnight, and that was only if she had enjoyed an uninterrupted afternoon and Tony's man had not encountered any difficulties, but he made his break short nonetheless.

The restaurant/diner was busy for a week night, and Ran hoped the hungry patrons and engaged wait staff would keep his arrival uneventful. But in a town that thrived on knowing the business of its neighbors and where the birth of a litter of kittens was common knowledge, the sheriff was wrong to assume he could get a takeout order unaccosted. Having made his simple dinner request, Ran sat in the small, benched alcove at the front of the business that functioned occasionally as a wait station when Dalton's had reached maximum occupancy, alone with his thoughts and free of questioning from his charges. It wasn't more than two minutes before Louis Tibbs, a life-long Auburn resident and Baptist preacher, had found him. The sheriff liked Tibbs for all his overbearing suggestions and frequent attempts at saving Ran's soul. He was genuine and straightforward, the son of a farmer who valued family and home, and Ran knew his obtrusions were more sincere than nosy. Recognizable by his jet black, flowing hair that most recently had been graced with a touch of gray and a subtle gold cross pinned to his left lapel, the preacher marched unabashedly into the small enclosure and presented his hand.

"Sheriff Price. Always a pleasure."

Ran stood in respect of the town's closest thing to a patriarch. "Reverend Tibbs. How are you this evening?"

"Very well, thank you. Brought the family to dinner after service," he said, glancing over his shoulder toward the back of the restaurant where his wife and three teenage sons sat in quiet conversation in smartly pressed clothes. Ran imagined their words reflected their attire--dutiful and humble.

Ran smiled in their direction. "I was just grabbing a quick bite before heading back to the office."

"Working late, Randall? And on a Wednesday night?"

Ran braced himself.

"Is there so much going on in our little town that you can't take the night off, possibly attend a service?"

"I have been very busy lately," Ran offered.

"There is always time for the Lord, Sheriff."

The Reverend Tibbs had tried for years to infuse Ran with a stronger commitment to the church, a place he frequented only at Christmas and Easter and the sporadic funeral that brought most small towns to a grinding halt. Ran was never uncomfortable or bothered during these moments, which Tibbs thankfully spaced out over their intermittent meetings, and saw it only as the function of his position as the religious leader of his community, a shepherd tending to his flock and attempting to retrieve those that had strayed. Everybody had their responsibilities in Auburn, as tedious as they may seem.

"Well, Reverend, you know as well I do that there have been two killings in less than a month in the area. It has kept us going more than normal."

Tibbs let his smile crumble into a serious frown. "I was, of course, aware of the recent events, and we as a congregation have prayed for those who have died and those suffering from the loss of their loved ones. I have had several members of the church express their concerns to me, and though we shouldn't ignore the evils that afflict our world, at the same time we must not allow those same evils to alter our lives. Is there cause for such great alarm in our little community?"

Ran responded with all due respect, "It is the very fact that these crimes are happening around us that I have stepped up the activity in my department, Reverend. We must both be vigilant in these dark times, wouldn't you say?"

"Quite," said Tibbs, "though we should never lose our focus that we are servants of the Lord first."

The preacher presented the diners to Ran with a wave of his hand. "We have a duty to them and to ourselves, you and I. Just keep in mind that their salvation is paramount and that God's intervention is the only true way to bring closure to the problems that face you and them.."

"I respect your position, Louis, as I am sure you do mine," Ran said, and though he normally took the reverend's sermons with the proverbial grain of salt, he found this conversation somewhat taxing. "Until this man is apprehended and the immediate threat to Auburn has ended, I am afraid I will be pulling extra time on nights like this one. It is why I was hired."

The Reverend Tibbs, for all his good intentions, still missed the point Ran was trying to make. "So, I can count on your attendance at service when these problems have resolved themselves, maybe even say a few words to the congregation? As a man of position in the community, your presence would mean a great deal."

Ran noticed Patty Stark heading toward him with a brown bag containing his own measure of salvation. "Looks like my meal is here," he said as he gestured to the waitress and effectively brought the exchange to an end. "I promise to give some thought to your proposal when this is all over, Reverend. I hate to cut this short, but I have to get back to the office."

Tibbs took his hand and parted with a final summons. "May God guide you in what you seek, Randall."

"I could use all the help I can get," he said as he handed Patty a five and launched himself into the shadows of the liberating night.

Auburn was solemn outside the doors of the well-lit Dalton's, and Ran enjoyed a lonely walk back to the office with a star-filled sky over his head and a soft, cool breeze grazing his face. There was an air of calm that, though expected in this quiet community, was most disconcerting. He perceived it as a precursor to something torrential, an omen of events that could level the town if it were caught unprepared and make his former job seem like a cakewalk in comparison. He had harbored these feelings for many days, but no more so than when he and Tara had parted that morning, her words and their warnings of doom still fresh on his mind. He imagined a giant boulder of destruction rolling toward Auburn, gaining speed with each revolution, as it steered unerringly to the decimation of all those in its way. In its wake were the people he had grown to cherish—Polly, Monk, the people of Auburn (even the overbearing Reverend Tibbs), and most importantly, Dr. Tara Phillips, whose safety was of upmost importance. These people were closer to him than anybody had ever been in Los Angeles, and not because he had denied himself friendships there. There was something about the open spaces and sense of reliance that people shared here. They looked to each other for acceptance and were as quick to extend help as receive it. It was a place of togetherness where people like Ran, who had adhered to years of self-reliance and independence, were gently forced to become parts of a whole, confiding in and banking on their neighbors. He had stubbornly grown to accept his fate, and one day, without resistance, saw himself for what he had become—a member of a small brotherhood of people who shared in their hopes and sorrows. They belonged to each other, and their melding had been an act of human nature, nothing more or less.

By the time he had reached the front sidewalk of the sheriff's department, Ran was both concerned for the continued safety of his town and determined to meet head on anyone or anything that jeopardized that security.

Part-time dispatcher June Frazier, her children all grown and spread across the Midwest, reported no calls to the sheriff, though this news was not surprising. He hadn't planned on feeling anxious about not hearing from her until after midnight; the compulsion to dial the ME's office was overwhelming, but he gave Tara her space and trusted she would you inform him the minute she knew something. She had gone so far as to suggest that he get some rest, that there was little he could do with any forensic information in the wee hours of the morning, but Ran was insistent that she contact him with her findings regardless of the time, and she had consented.

He was back to the waiting game after only a few, unsatisfying bites of a meal that failed to appease what nagged at him. With Tara and Tony Avery hard at work, he resumed his position as the self-proclaimed non-contributing member of the cast. Ran bathed in incompetence for the next four hours, shuffling between the files that had become frayed with constant handling, review of the countless county, state, and national maps that littered his office walls, and interrogating June about her family with time-consuming prattle. In Los Angeles he had spent these down times walking the streets, letting the sights and sounds of the inner city turmoil transport him from his restlessness. Auburn offered little in distraction, and Ran usually found himself at home in front of the television, a habit he hated but dependable all the same. It had taken him many months just to get used to the pace of the small town, and after a few weeks he was convinced he had made the wrong decision, only to settle into what was comparatively a living coma without further resistance.

A little before midnight, after Ran had radioed Monk to the house and given June the rest of the night off, the shrill ring of the phone moved

Ran with a start. He leapt to the receiver, his heart caught somewhere in his throat.

"Sheriff's office."

"Have you gotten any rest?"

"I could say the same of you."

"Well, I've been busy. Helps pass the time," Tara said. "You, on the other hand, could have at least closed your eyes for an hour or two."

"And miss out on all the excitement? Not on your life," said Ran.

"I'm not calling because I have anything yet." Her tone completely reversed. "I just wanted to let you know that I am done with the autopsy, and I located some usable prints on the torso that I scanned with the infrared and are now processing through the detector. Turns out my expectation of its analysis time was shorter than required."

"How much longer?" asked Ran.

"At least six hours. Maybe ten. The software is still timing out. Thing seems to be working great, though. The guy from the county office was here and gone in thirty minutes," Tara said. "Uploaded the program and connected the wiring with a cursory glance of the manual. Very impressive."

"Good. Sartin is a good man."

"For a small town sheriff, you certainly know people in important places."

Ran smiled, "I'm not sure about that, but I am glad they were able to help. Has Weyland given you any problems?"

Tara said, "Once I gave him a brief summary of my findings, he seemed satisfied. I think all he really wants is to have a hand in things. Probably didn't listen to half of the things I said."

"So how was it? Pretty bad?"

"The autopsy? Just what I expected," she said. "The manner of death mirrored the records you pulled and the cases I had already witnessed. There was no instrumentation, and the lab samples I prepared will only support past results. One thing I will be able to see from the labs is the extent of anomaly since Melton, but that will only tell us the progress of the genetic mutation. Until I can evaluate the data from the chemical detector, I can't really tell you anything yet."

"So we continue to sit and wait," said an evidently dejected Ran.

"I'm sorry, Ran. There is nothing more I can do right now."

"Oh, no, no. I'm not referring to you," said Ran. "You have gone above and beyond. I just hate being in this position of…idleness. There has to be something I can do other than sit here."

She could hear the disappointment coupled with agitation in his voice. "Face it, sheriff. You can do what I would like to do and go get six hours of sleep. It would do you a world of good."

Ran shook his head. "No, I can't sleep now. There is too much to think about."

Tara said, "And nothing to act on. Ran, you may wish you had some down time once things start coming in. Believe me, you're not going to miss anything."

"I don't know," Ran said.

"Doctor's orders. I promise I will call you first thing when I get back here. Say…seven?"

Ran relented, "OK, but seven o'clock. If I don't hear from you, I'm coming up there."

"Well, in that case, I think I will forget to call."

"You know, I am going to have to be there anyway to go over the results with you. What if I pick you up at seven instead of call and we can grab a bite beforehand? Sound like a plan?"

Tara agreed, "A plan I can't refuse. Seven o'clock in front of my office, then, but on the condition you go home and get some rest."

"I will," said Ran. "You do the same."

"See you in the morning, sheriff."

"Doctor."

Ran set the phone down and took a quick self-inventory. He was exhausted, but the plans he had just made with Tara acted like an adrenaline boost to his fatigue, and he felt like he could go through the night.

But what am I going to do until then? This place is dead, and until the new facts start rolling in, I am here twiddling my thumbs.

He figured Tara was right, and bet that this would be far from the last time, so he shut the lights off in his office, let the dispatcher know he could be reached at home, and exited the building to head home. As he climbed behind the wheel of his car, he hoped that sleep would come easy.

Something told him tomorrow was going to be a long day.

Chapter 23

For all his mental acuity, Caine was possessed by a singular emotional desire to take control of the power struggling within him. As the sunset over his solitary roof in the middle of an open stretch of Kansas field, he was now either unwilling or unable to recognize the burning truth of his situation. Thoughts of making his way to his next destination, far from the inquiries of authorities, were forgotten; concern over the radical variation in the cycles that ruled his life no longer present. Something was happening in the very core of his being, consuming him, but his elemental understanding of the changes taking place did not allow him to see that he was diseased, that the fire he knew as the rage, a fanciful step toward immortality, was really a chemical imbalance occurring at the cellular level of his tissues and organs.

The physical effects were a reality; Caine was experiencing a supercharging of every muscle in his body at a geometric rate. As he sat in the darkness, his skeletal structure was rapidly reconfiguring its design while his facial features were melting, reshaping, and drawing taunt across his mutating skull. The pain was exquisite, like the burn felt during a demanding bodybuilding session. Unlike the growth potential of anabolic steroids, though, the transfers taking place were instantaneous. He would soon be unrecognizable to anyone who had marked his appearance earlier in the day.

But the mental consequences of the genetic conversion brought the real damage. The thought processes that had guided him through his early years, and until now had captained the duality of his life and protected his two selves, were sloughed off like a snake's skin, to be replaced with the most primitive of intellects. From here on Caine would be forever driven by forces whose roots were found in the primordial ooze of man's beginnings. The genetic code that had piggybacked its way along humanity's climb to the top of the evolutionary ladder was making its full emergence after centuries of dormancy.

While Sheriff Ran Price and Dr. Tara Phillips were settling into their respective beds in an effort to catch a few hours of sleep, Sebastian Caine was *becoming*. The Caine of yesterday, of a mere hour ago, was no more, and never would be again. His concern over concealing the malevolence that stalked the nights was gone, as was the timid soul that maintained a remote computer repair business by day. They were now one, and the small measures of invincibility he had felt on occasion over the last few weeks dominated his thinking.

He stood fully erect among the trappings of an inferior species, and in the near pitch-blackness of the house, he saw everything in sharp detail. The computers hummed in an otherwise complete silence, their monitors void of life. Even the frequent jake braking of semis along Highway 75 had stopped momentarily in deference to the great event occurring in Hoyt. Caine heaved his chest to its full expanse as he drew deeply of the stagnant air through wide nostrils, a now primary tool in his evaluation of his surroundings. He soon turned in a slow half circle and set his eyes on the front door.

Beyond the barrier existed a familiar world of space and shadow that he knew well. There, he could revel in the richness and variety of pleasing sensations, race across vast fields of tall, swaying grasses, and drink from small pools where others gathered to recover from the heat of the day. It was in this panorama of open freedom that he found his greatest pleasure—the rapture of the hunt. Roaming across large sections of forest and open land, he stopped here and there and tested the current of the air that flowed just above him, searching among the millions of odors it carried for one, distinct smell, that of a vulnerable human male. Its aroma was clear and far-reaching, and Caine would travel many miles to reach his prey where he would follow it and wait for his opportunity. His patience was often rewarded, and the taste of the kill always proved worth the effort. Once he had decimated his target and tasted of it many times over in sensual delight, he carried it far from the prying eyes of others and deposited its remains with catlike care.

He was a thing of the night, and from this moment on, he would live that life completely.

He was drawn to what awaited him in the dark recesses of the night and burst through the door for the last time in a splintering hail of wood. He was greeted with the firm caress of the natural world, a reward for his conquest over the weakest part of himself--the sniveling, cowardly child that had once occupied the body he now claimed. It had hung on determinedly for many years, and he acknowledged in some way that it had served him well during his slow climb to the absolute control he now held. But its function had ended, its role of protector done. The night sky, in an ironic reversal, represented the dawn of a new day in the life of Caine, and he yelled triumphantly in answer to its calling. His tattered clothes hung in shreds across his mammoth frame, and the moonlight reflected off his exposed skin, damp with the metabolic and hormonal fires that burned beneath it. He chose a direction with an upturned whiff of the air, then set on what was to be the maiden voyage of the new Caine—bigger, stronger, better.

Chapter 24

Ran jerked awake in his recliner groggy and disoriented, his hands gripping the arms of the vinyl chair where he had collapsed earlier. The television, which he had turned on in the hopes of dulling his mind to induce sleep, continued its hypnotic glow and offered the only measurable light in the room. Outside the dark prevailed, and Ran could see the pinpoints of his neighbors' yard lights through the large windows he had failed to drape after arriving home. The only difference in now and the odd number of hours previous were the vestiges of a dream that had clapped to his consciousness like determined claws and brought with them vaporous trails of horrid images that he struggled to shake loose.

He stood shakily and turned his wristwatch to the light of the picture tube to orient himself. Five-fifty. Roughly half the rest he really needed, but enough, he concluded, to get him through the day ahead. Crossing with him to the hallway and the full bathroom to his right were nightmarish visions of suffering and death, translucent scenes of events he willed away. In them, a monstrous pair of hands and gnashing set of teeth laid waste to helpless people that he first couldn't recognize. But with each fierce specter came faces he knew, people he cared for, and when the semblance of Tara, bloodied and beaten, her face imploring him to action, assaulted him, he threw the vanity lights on and burned the image from his brain.

Now fully coherent, Ran started the shower, undressed, and stood transfixed for several minutes letting the hot water cleanse him of the night's memories. The day promised to be pivotal, and it would start with meeting Tara for breakfast and an accounting of the work she had done the previous evening. He was encouraged at the prospects of her discoveries but couldn't deny that simply being with her gave him greater satisfaction. Though it were not even feasible, Ran entertained daydreams of escaping the jobs they were bound to, jetting away to a place free of responsibility where they could concentrate on only one commitment, that to each other. They had failed to find time for themselves while caught up in the search for the demon that possessed their lives, and though he sometimes wished he was liberated of his sworn duties to protect and serve and could just walk away, he knew that it was pure fantasy. He was as tied to his role as sheriff as she was to pathologist, and it would require exorcizing the fiend that initially brought them together.

It was ridiculous to believe that he would hear from Tom Avery today. The profiler had seemed confident in a minimal time frame, but that was before he had seen the volumes of paperwork Ran had for his viewing. No doubt his findings were crucial; regardless, Ran would have to begin with Tara's work and go from there.

Out of the shower and back in his standard sheriff's uniform, Ran occupied his time with a house long in need of attention until he was to head for Topeka. Dishes, laundry, and the general picking up of clutter kept him busy over the next hour. Daylight had found its way to Auburn again, and Ran glanced at his watch repeatedly in anticipation of his departure while the town started showing signs of life with its occasional barking dog and passing motorist. He knew his charges were readying themselves as he was for the start of another day, but he was willing to bet that theirs followed a habitual course much different from his. They would prepare for a typical day, the only drastic alteration in it most likely what they ate; Ran would soon exit his door into a world of discovery. The morning could lead him down a hundred potential paths, and from there hundreds more. It was what fueled him in Los Angeles, and he was excited to taste the thrill once again. He anticipated the possibilities but was completely thrown off when the shrill ring of the phone broke the reticence.

It was Polly, and though he was surprised to hear from her, he relaxed in knowing she was back at her helm. "Sheriff. Hoped I would catch you before you left. You need to call Lieutenant Sartin at Shawnee County. It sounded urgent."

"Polly? What are you doing back at the office this early?"

"Are you kidding me? Most activity we've seen around here since the power went out for two days in the middle of the winter. Long before you got here, of course. You'd understand if you had been here as long as I have," she said.

"Well, I appreciate your efforts. Why didn't Tony just call me at home? He has my number."

"Said he tried, but got no answer. Would have left a message but your machine is full."

Ran looked down at the white box that flashed an F at him in demanding pulses, and he realized he had failed to empty it during the past few days when coming home was more about a change of clothes than catching up on his calls. He must have called while Ran was in the shower.

"Damn. Where was he? What did he say?"

"He just said he could be reached through the Sheriff's operator. Do you need the number?"

Ran said quickly, "No, I have it. Thanks, Pol. You can reach me in the cruiser for a while, then I will check in later. I will be in Topeka most of the morning for an autopsy review." Then, in an afterthought, "If a Tom Avery calls, find me at all costs through the medical examiner's office or possibly the county. Send Monk out looking if you have to."

Polly said, "You got it. Man, this is dispatching."

Ran depressed the button to end the call, a wry smile on his face in response to Polly's enthusiasm, and dialed Shawnee County. He checked the time and waited. "Sheriff's Department."

"Lieutenant Sartin, please. This is Sheriff Price from Auburn."

"I'll transfer you, Sheriff. Just a minute."

A call from Tony Sartin, until recently, had never carried so much weight. The minute he was promised seemed a lifetime.

As if he was thousands of miles away. "Ran. Where are you?"

"I'm at home. What going on? It sounds like you are at the bottom of a well."

"I'm out near Sherwood Lake—Cerrito and 33rd. Do you know the place?" said Sartin.

Ran knew the area vaguely. "About five, six miles north of us. Yeah, I know the area."

"We have another killing."

Ran's heart rate, already elevated, shot through the roof. "What? No. Where exactly?"

"A field just north and west of the lake. It's our boy again, for sure. Partial remains. No sign of kill site yet."

Anxiety swept over Ran in piercing waves. They had to find some answers.

"We have something else you might find interesting, though."

"What's that?" Ran asked.

"We have a witness."

"A witness?"

Ran's mind now raced. Finally, a break, and from the most unexpected of places. "Are you sure?"

Sartin explained, "Morning jogger came across the scene. Someone crouched over something in the pasture off the road. He stopped, not sure what he was looking at. Said he first thought somebody was checking out a deer carcass, but then our perp stood fully and turned to him. Had blood all over his face and hands. Clothes were in shreds. They just stared at each other. Our witness high-tailed it out of there and called us. He was pretty shaken up."

"I'll bet. How long will you be there? I need to cancel a few things. I can be there in twenty minutes."

"We'll be here," Sartin confirmed. "Until noon I imagine."

"See you in twenty."

Ran had two calls to make. The first would be simple: let Polly know his change of plans. The second he regretted because once again Tara would be adjusting her schedule to his needs. He hoped she would make this easy on him.

After failing to reach her at home, he found her in her office, not surprisingly.

"Hello there. You're not here are you? I didn't expect you for another thirty minutes."

"No, no. Still home. Did you get some rest?" Ran said.

"Yes, I did. Funny, but I dropped off here in the office. Forgot how comfortable the couch is. I hope you forgive my appearance. Luckily I keep a change of clothes for nights I crash."

Ran's guilt mounted. "How could I judge when you are taking more time out of your day for me? Which brings me to my problem."

Tara said, "Oh, no. What's happened?"

Her instincts for reading the living were as strong as those she had for the dead.

"There's been another murder, just this morning, a few miles from here."

"I was afraid of that. Everything pointed to a new occurrence. The clock is ticking, Ran."

"You found something, didn't you?"

"I think so. How long will you be?"

Ran considered the time he would need. "How's lunch sound? I still owe you a meal."

"That will work. Call me on your way in. I'm going to use the morning to repackage a few items that have been most helpful and do some comparisons with earlier data. You'll call me?" said Tara.

"As soon as I am done," said Ran, "and if it looks like I am going to be late, I'll let you know."

"If you are late, don't bother calling."

Ran stuttered, "I…but…if the…"

"I'm kidding, Sheriff. Go to your crime scene. It may prove important to what I have for you, so I will be interested in what you can tell me."

He swallowed the ball that had begun to gather in his throat. "You definitely got me there. I feel bad enough postponing on you, but I may have deserved that one," said Ran.

"What you deserve is the truth, and I truly don't mind. Wait until I cancel a romantic dinner to answer an urgent call. It's a reality we will learn to live with."

"I am more than ready to learn," said Ran.

"Ditto. Now get going."

Ran was in his cruiser and sailing up Auburn Road within minutes to the latest murder scene, the weight of the morning lightened after his conversation with Tara. She was quite unique, and he counted himself lucky. If what she had said bore itself out, the information he could gather at the newest crime scene may be significant in identifying their killer. With a witness to lend unprecedented details for the first time, the prospects were that much greater.

Turning east on 33rd, it wasn't long until Ran could see the flashing lights of numerous police and rescue vehicles. A roadblock had been set up on the west entrance to the scene, and he was quickly given access, where he parked his car to the shoulder of the ditch-lined, narrow two-lane and walked to the clusters of officers assembled in small groups some fifty yards ahead. As he neared them, Ran saw Sartin in animated conversation with a few lesser officers. From what he could tell, the lieutenant was dividing the area for door-to-door questioning in the hopes that others may have seen something. In a part of the country where early risers were the norm, the chance that someone else had information that could prove important to the investigation was viable. After he had distributed a few more instructions and put the necessary wheels in motion, Sartin waved Ran over to join him.

"And be sure there is a unit in front of Mr. Daniels' residence. Tell them I will be over later," Sartin yelled a final order to a deserting officer. "Ran, I thought you might get out here quickly. Can I fill you in? We just sealed the area and are waiting for a forensic team to show."

Units from the Shawnee Sheriff's Office, KHP, and Topeka Fire and

Rescue were present, but apparently they were now in idle until the lab boys arrived. Sartin commented with an air of frustration that the KSBI would be making an appearance, and he cussed the protocol he would be expected to follow.

The field just off the road was heavily strewn with yellow police tape, and from his years of experience, Ran's attention was able to fix on the epicenter of the crime area, where a small dark mass sat unremarkably. Like the two cases prior to it, the disposal area was stark and empty and provided little in the way of shelter. The depositor was bold, but the areas he chose seemed vital to his routine. Ran had considered it after looking over the historical records, and it hit him hard across the face at that moment. Discovery of the remains was important, almost necessary, in his macabre game. He took the mild risk of being seen to dump the body in a spot visible to the occasional passer-by--a field, a vacant lot, behind an abandoned building. Whatever the agenda, one point was clear: every kill was a breadcrumb on a trail. But to where? And why the trail? Did he hope to be caught, or was he simply taunting the authorities? Ran was counting on Tom Avery to answer that dilemma.

"How long ago did the witness make the call?" Ran inquired, his attention on the field.

"We got word from the 911 dispatcher at five fifty-seven. We had a car here eight minutes later and conducted a five-mile radial search twenty-five minutes after that. Nothing to report."

Ran considered the time frame. "What was the visibility at, what, five forty-five? Is your witness sure of what he saw?"

"Mr. Daniels, our witness, stated there was enough dawn light to make out some generalities, said Sartin. "He was still shaken when we got to him. I have to at least believe there was something there. I mean, we do have a body."

Ran nodded, "You said partial remains."

"We've purposely stayed clear of the immediate area, but from fifty feet away, it's quite obvious we are looking at another. It's a twisted mess, Ran. What kind of person could do this over and over?"

It was a rhetorical question really. They had both been in the profession long enough to have met some of the degenerates that handcrafted some of the more grisly crimes long-standing officers came in contact with. Sociopaths. Beyond understanding.

"We have to bring a stop to this, Tony," Ran muttered, his tired voice echoing the feelings of countless investigators across the eastern half of the country who had been touched by the string of murders and fallen victims to their own crimes--a lack of usable evidence to make an arrest.

Sartin remained stoic.

"Mind if I sit in on your questioning?"

"I was getting ready to head over there now that we have the area cordoned off. It's just up around the corner. Want to follow me?" Sartin asked.

"I'll be right behind you."

Ran jogged to his car and pulled up behind Sartin's unit and together they traveled the necessary half-mile to the house of a rather unique individual—the first person to have laid claim to seeing their murderer. Ran arrived with mixed feelings. He would reserve judgment until hearing the man's story, but based on the time of day, the possibility that what he had seen was nothing more than a curious animal, the deck was definitely stacked against him.

The suburban neighborhood just outside Topeka was home to a growing number of young white families seeking a quiet way of life but within short reach of their industries, mainly public administration and health care. Housing developments such as the one located near Sherwood Lake were springing up everywhere, and lying roughly thirteen miles from the city limits of the capital, it was projected that Auburn would be overrun within a decade, stealing from it its rural standing and directly affecting the future of its schools and public departments. For a man who had lived the majority of his life surrounded by concrete and high rises, it seemed Ran would welcome the injection of city influence, but he actually loathed the possibilities.

Throughout the area were houses on large plots of land; their residents afforded a semblance of privacy while still enjoying the amenities of urban living. Though new home construction traditionally favored ranch style and the occasional Victorian, Tony Sartin's cruiser pulled into the driveway of a Colonial style, two-story dwelling, a beautiful yet simple place on what Ran estimated as two acres. Birds chirped their welcome in the trees that were already beginning to draw their choppy shadows across the thick green carpet of grass that lay at the front of the house. The beds were full of geraniums, hibiscus, and marigolds, offering a rich variety of color attractive to the eye and the many insects that were drawn to their flowers. A wind chime rang lazily in the morning breeze. It was all very quaint, very peaceful. It would be easy to forget that a body lay butchered in a field just a short walk, or jog, away. There was no escaping crime. The days of carefree country living were long over.

A Shawnee County police unit was parked on the shoulder of the front yard; the officer inside waved to Sartin in recognition as the two men made their way to the front door. They were ushered in by an attractive young lady in her early 30s, who identified herself as Daniels' wife; her bright pink nurse's uniform and pulled-back hair informed them she was most likely headed to either St. Francis Hospital or one of the many single-day surgical centers in the city prior to her husband's close encounter. Based on her shortness with them, Ran could see she was annoyed with the inconvenience of her routine being disrupted. She pointed to the living room and followed behind them closely, as if urging them to conclude their business so that she, at least, could reconvene her life.

Daniels was sitting on a leather couch in what Ran saw as a cluttered living area. Whether it was his years of apartment dwelling or failure to put more than the necessary furnishings in his older house, he was overcome by the crowded conditions. Every wall, every few feet of floor space, was home to something, though the room itself provided no functional space for relaxing other than the sofa and a Queen Anne chair to its side. The officers stood in the menagerie after introductions, and remained in place through the course of the interview. Their witness was still shaken by the ordeal, and they repeatedly reminded him to calm down in his retelling of the events of the morning.

"Mr. Daniels, we need you to be absolutely sure of what you saw," said Sartin.

The distraught man ran his hand through his hair. He was still dressed in jogging shorts and a light muscle shirt. "I've told you twice. What more can I tell you?"

Ran interjected, "Take us back to the moment right just prior to your coming upon the scene. You are jogging down 33rd..."

"Just like every morning," Daniels said insistently.

"...and you can see the road in front of you clearly. It's light enough that you would know whether you were headed into the ditch. Then what?"

Daniels shot out, "And then I saw something to my right up in the vacant field. Probably fifty yards from me. I run that direction every day. *Every* day. I would notice something out of place."

Sartin took notes in his pad.

"I don't use an iPod or anything to occupy me. I like to concentrate on the road, the landscape. It's beautiful as the sun comes up."

"You were running west, correct?"

"Yes, the sun was breaking behind me. There was plenty of light. I know what I saw."

Sartin said, "Describe what you saw one last time, please, Mr. Daniels, and then we will leave you for the day."

"All right. So, I see this form in the field, and I slow my pace a little because, you know, it caught my eye. Totally out of place."

He stared down at his white Nikes, looking through them to the place of the terrifying encounter hours ago, his hands clasped just above his eye line in mock prayer. "I stopped because…you know…it just looked…wrong. I didn't know what I was looking at, just a dark shape out there, but it had a shine to it, too, like it was wet."

He paused here, the image dancing in his memory, and the two officers let him complete the telling a final time. "I was kind of walking, I think, but I couldn't take my eyes off it. I thought the closer I got, I would be able to tell what it was, but something made me hesitate," he shook his head. "I started getting scared."

He looked up at the men who had come uninvited to his home with pleading eyes. He didn't want them there, and yet he needed a human presence. He needed them to understand but feared even the telling. "At some point he moved…turned toward me. And then he started up from this slow crouch, went up for the longest time. I've never seen anyone that tall…just huge. I couldn't believe what I was seeing. His arms…enormous arms…and the blood was all over."

Ran had seen the look in Daniels' eyes one time before. It was during his last few months in Los Angeles. He was called to a scene on the east side of the city—a domestic dispute gone horribly wrong. An out-of-work father of three, stressed by the demands of his family and the harsh realities of the world, had butchered his wife and babies before blowing the back of his head off. It was something that even a veteran like Ran never got used to.

Among the first officers to respond to the location was a rookie; it was his first murder call and later Ran would learn it would be his last. As a detective, it was Ran's responsibility to assess the scene and begin interviews while uniformed officers secured the perimeter. The young officer was just exiting the house as Ran approached, his face completely pale. He shook uncontrollably and his head moved back and forth in denial of what he had witnessed moments ago. Ran led him to his squad car and sat him down, concerned that he may pass out or at the very least become violently ill. Kneeling beside the silent man, Ran looked into his eyes, the windows to a soul forever stricken with the horror that mankind is capable of.

He never forgot that blank stare, and he was seeing it again for the first time.

"I froze," Daniels continued. "I couldn't move then, until…he was looking at me. Straight at me. I felt so small, and then…white teeth." Remembering. "So many teeth, I thought. Snarling, threatening me. But then I realized it wasn't a threat…it was grinning at me. *Grinning*."

There was genuine terror on his face, and Ran quietly berated the wife for not comforting him. "I just started backward. Turned and sprinted home. Fell two or three times before I made it and called you. Never looked back. Never looked back."

"Mr. Daniels," Sartin said with a note of compassion, "thank you for your time. We 're going to go now, but we will have to contact you later if that is all right."

"Fine," he said. He was alone in his thoughts now, and Ran pitied him. His glass globe of reality, with its rustic landscape and country charm, had been violently shattered.

Sartin turned to go. "We'll be in touch."

Ran followed, but stopped short in the foyer. "Just a minute, Tony. Let me ask him one more thing."

"Well, hurry it up. I have a case to process."

Sartin waited at the door while Ran went back in the living room.

"Mr. Daniels, can I bother you with one more question? I'd appreciate it."

"What is it?"

"At the end of your statement, you said *it* grinned at you. What made you say that?"

"I don't know. I mean, it was a man, but for just a split second…he didn't look human. More like an animal. I'll never get that picture out of my head."

"Thank you, Mr. Daniels," Ran said, and he preceded Sartin out the front door.

The lieutenant looked at him. "So, what do you think?'

"Sounded credible. We've agreed it would take a large man to do what we have seen."

Sartin cocked his head. "Yeah, but he described a circus freak. No man could be that big. Had to be a black bear."

Ran said incredulously, "In Kansas? Are bear even indigenous to the state? I thought deer and elk were as far as big game went here."

Sartin nodded, "There are black bear west in Colorado and east in Missouri and Arkansas. What's so unbelievable that a group made its way up here? We have some dense areas."

"You're the native son, Tony," said Ran, not wanting to insult his friend, "but I thought the state was hills and plains. There isn't forest capable of supporting a bear population, especially around Topeka. Besides, we would have animal tracks at the crime scenes, not the empty ground and the fingerprints we have analyzed. I agree that he had to be wrong about his size; I'm sure the light messed with the detail, but I have no doubt what he saw was a man."

"Well, maybe. I don't know if he can be sure what he saw. And what about that wife? What a piece of work."

They walked to their vehicles.

"Have time to hang around for the lab boys?"

"I have a lunch appointment, but I would be glad to hear what they find."

Sartin patted his back. "Then let's go see if they are here yet."

Ran spent the next three hours surveying the crime scene with members of the lab team from the SCSD, and as Sartin had warned, detectives from the KSBI made sure they were fully briefed on all aspects of the case. Officers questioned residents in the square mile surrounding the field and came back without further information. No one else had seen or heard anything. The body was determined to be that of a middle-aged man, mutilated and unrecognizable. Until they could match him to a missing persons report and dental records or prints, nothing more could be known as to who he was or where he had originated. The area around the victim was customarily void of forensic items, and Ran and others damned their luck.

The short grass that blanketed the field did provide some information, and the investigators were excited for something. There was a clear trampling from the north and southwest, and after much debate, the forensic team concluded that the latter direction was an exit path, putting the assailant along a line of open terrain, though the Prairie View Country Club was within range, and all of this just five miles north of Auburn, which bothered Ran somewhat. Of course there was no way of confirming that the two paths had not been created prior to the event, and since they showed no discernable foot or shoe prints, the value of the paths was ultimately minimal.

With nothing more to learn until the body was processed, Ran chose not to wait for the medical examiners wagon and let Sartin know he would be heading to the city to follow up on the Melton lab results, which he had asked Tara to further evaluate, though he did not mention that it would be done in comparison to the Stanton autopsy completed just yesterday. Tara had not yet released her preliminary report but would have to do so soon.

"Is that your lunch appointment?" the lieutenant asked.

"Dr. Phillips is going to brief me on her findings. The lab work and DNA sampling proved inconclusive, but I thought after Weyland, a fresh approach might reveal something worthwhile."

"You, my friend, are a dog, but I am happy for you."

Ran tried to appear puzzled at his friend's words but couldn't mask the amusement on his face. "First, I am no dog, and second," he said with gratitude, "thanks. She is a great lady."

"She's no Mrs. Sartin, but I think I could get used to her deficiencies. Seriously, she has been a tremendous help on these cases, and you should be more respectful. She may just provide us with what we need to break this headache," said Ran.

"I'm sorry. I had no idea she was working to our advantage. Get out of here. Take that woman to lunch and buy her a nice meal."

"I will," Ran said as he saluted Sartin briskly and moved toward his car. "I'll be in touch. You do the same."

"Dog."

Auburn's sheriff went from a smile to a concerned frown. He had a good friend in Tony Sartin and a great woman in Tara, and he really wondered where he would be in his investigation without their help and input. Guilt reared its ugly head yet again as Ran struggled with their importance to him both personally and professionally. To a stranger it would appear he was using them, and there was nothing further from the truth, but he couldn't shake the fear that they too might perceive things that way. He made it a point to express his deep commitment to both of them as a friend, companion, and colleague so that there were no doubts regarding his intentions. Only together could they find an answer, and based on Ran's career history, that statement alone signified his care for them.

Ran called Polly to inform her of his whereabouts and learned she was knee-deep in responses from her many contacts made the day before. He instructed Monk to call him as soon as possible, and assured her he would be back in time to meet with her before she left at five. A final call to Tara confirmed his arrival at noon, and he met her outside the medical examiner's office from where they headed to a restaurant of her choosing. Before he could even begin to explain to her his morning and ask what she had learned, Monk's voice interrupted.

"Monk, I need you to take care of a few things until I get back in town."

"No problem, Sheriff. What do you need me to do?"

"Call Bobby and Chuck and ask them to start patrols on the perimeter of town. You stay closer and let me know if anything out of the ordinary happens. Got it?"

"Well, sure, Sheriff, but what is this all about?" Monk asked.

"Nothing I hope. Just keep an eye out on things until I get back."

Tara watched him through the entire exchange, and Ran knew she was wondering what had occurred to cause the alarm.

Ran returned the hand-held and then proceeded to explain the events at Sherwood Lake. He recounted the testimony of Daniels and the findings in the field, acknowledging that he was probably overreacting but wanted to play it safe.

"I know it sounds silly, especially in the middle of the day, but I just feel better with some eyes out there."

"I understand," she said. "After what I found last night and this morning, nothing would surprise me."

Ran sat up straight. "Well? Do you think you might have some answers?"

"I think so. It may be nothing, but it may be everything."

She had gotten in his car clutching a small brown file folder, which she held in front of her now in the passenger seat. "You'll have to decide for yourself."

"So the equipment finished its work?"

"Done and done. I have some lab analysis that I put a rush on, but it may not make any difference by the time the results are back. Left right up here," she pointed, and he slowed to initiate the turn.

"And?"

Ran began to feel the anxiety swelling in him.

"Let's sit down and eat something. I can explain everything then."

"I don't know if I can eat," Ran said.

Tara turned to him and said enigmatically, "I'd try. You may not get another chance."

Chapter 25

The tree line opened up to a wide expanse of valley marked with soft hills and grass-covered depressions. Here and there in the moon-filled light were small patches of wild brush, fed through the spring months with intermittent rains that saw nature through the difficult summers with their high temperatures and arid conditions. Small ponds were plentiful; their tepid waters were home to a variety of life and offered evening repose to small animals that had remained dormant until the sun had ended its torture of the day. The night was saddled with the familiar sounds of crickets and frogs that voiced their favor with the coming of darkness, and a breeze laced with the rich odor of farmed soil and recently harvested fields of grain sang softly through the oak and maple branches that dotted the display.

Disrupting the serenity of the tranquil night came the frantic movements of a near-winded man who appeared on the horizon at a runner's pace. Feet reverberating in the natural theater and his clothing and hair flapping about him wet and disheveled from the long distance he had seemingly covered, he gasped for air in what appeared to be a terrified escape. The uneven ground made his gait choppy and unsure, though his concerted efforts seemed to guarantee his success. He looked back sporadically at an unseen pursuer, and his face reflected the fear his pace suggested.

From the depths of the darkness that surrounded the heath came a new sound, a deep, guttural bellow that spoke of a predator, and like its apparent prey, out of place in the picture that had unfolded. It rang with anger and demanded attention, and the denizens of the night submitted in silent response. If the formerly peaceful meadow was an Eden, a sanctuary of life and living, then this was the black evil that lurked in its boundary of shadows, watching and waiting for a moment of vulnerability so to strike and leave chaos in its wake. A thunder of smashing timbers betrayed its location, and within seconds the disturbance was followed with a specter of make-believe and ancient lore. The shadows gave way to a malevolence that seemed to burn with its own light, a combustible fireball of speed and foreboding that shortened the distance separating it from its target within seconds. It was both man and animal in its stride—running upright but with a forward lean that defied gravity, its arms occasionally propelling it over fallen tree stumps or small crops of rock. And with it came an intelligence, a discernable sense that it was a force driven by a purpose. There was thought to its approach and reason behind each effortless movement.

Frozen for eternity was this fabric of time, a still image of life's perpetual race toward death —the weak, helpless victim and his unceasing attacker. The inevitable outcome was both terrifying and exhilarating.

The retreating man was hit with the force of a wrecking ball, struck with a blow that sent him tumbling for twenty yards in a violent rotation of flailing arms and legs. Dead before he came to a heaped rest in the thick pasture grass, the sacrifice lay still under the star-filled sky. As quickly as he had come to rest, his aggressor stood over him in triumphant surveillance—the pinnacle of the successful hunt, when the predator chose to fill all of its senses with death's essence. It was a moment of supreme satisfaction and fulfilled a primal need that only the hunter could understand.

It was the embodiment of evil described in a thousand different cultures—the gatekeeper of the underworld and the guardian of the dead. It was the Egyptian's Am-heh, the devourer of millions; the Babylonian bringer of death, Pazuzu; and The Beast in Christian mythology.

But above all else, far beyond its role on the life and death stage of man's existence, it was an agent of vengeance, and to that purpose it would be forever committed.

It roared in Pyrrhic victory.

He came awake fully alert. The years of unpredictability were over.

Unlike the past, sleep did not claim him for days on end, allowing him a moment's refueling before pulling him back into its dark retreat. Caine had gone dormant for just six hours, having recovered from the night's physical exertions and now ready to nourish his supercharged body.

This was a new beginning, and at its core was a life cycle that now functioned in the simplest of terms. He no longer needed to support the mutations that repeatedly ravaged his tissues and organs. Those years had been trying but necessary as the new Caine had systematically emerged, a delicate process that, if rushed, would have completely destroyed the structures on which it relied. His birth had been centuries in the waiting, and because of the evolutionary development of the human species, it had required a laborious surfacing and submergence, each time the cellular structures hardening and adapting to the primitive changes they were forced to suffer.

The rage, as the weaker self had so ignorantly called it, was the body's ongoing preparation for what was to be. Like the first creatures of the sea that tested their gills against the acrid world that existed above them, the progress required a methodical pace. Pain. Frustration. These were the elements of their journey, until a deep breath, and another, and another, until they were able to leave behind the confines of their watery prisons and venture out onto dry land. Here they would grow, thrive, and evolve, each generation better than the last. Children and children's children better suited to the environment that would ultimately be theirs to reign supremely.

The new Caine was now the keeper of the body, having completely replaced his lesser self. Functioning singularly, he required little rest, though a vast amount of food would continue to be necessary to stoke the fire that drove him. His body's ability to process just about anything he consumed made this easy, as he utilized the plant life and animals that covered the plains. He could also take what he wanted from the easily accessible homes and businesses of the species he now preyed upon daily. Of them he had no fear and only lurked on the borders of their habitation to better hunt their kind in anonymity. He could no longer walk among them since his appearance had made a dramatic change, and he was perfectly aware of his need to use the open country and the shadows of the night in the pursuit of his purpose.

The sun began to beat down on the lone figure as he stepped out of the cover of the tree line at various points in survey of his new grounds. He would spend the heat of the day in waiting after gorging himself, a time of anticipation for the night ahead. And this was what characterized his design, his reason for having emerged from an eon's-old cocoon. He would lay waste to them one upon one, so that each could feel the torment intimately. There, alone and with no one to turn to for help, every last man, woman, and child would succumb to a death that would be slow and excruciating.

This was vital to him. In truth he knew he could slaughter them in mass, but he would be deprived of the euphoria of the kill and the fear that he found in each of their eyes when they came face to face with their own mortality. Each would suffer, each would pay. He would take from them what he had been denied—life—and replace it with the emptiness he had endured since his own birth so many years of agony ago.

A perfect creation, the new Caine was a machine in organic form, like the computers he had left behind in his other existence. He would now, simply, kill. There was nothing inside him to burden the function—empathy, jealousy, even anger. Neither pride nor satisfaction could find refuge in this emotionally dead mutation any longer. Primal. Basic. Endless.

Death had an equal. The Reaper had taken a new form.

Chapter 26

After Tara had ordered an unusually large amount of food in contrast to Ran's chicken sandwich and iced tea, the two sat in an unfamiliar silence in the half-full restaurant, one of Topeka's newest diners catering to the influx of young professionals beginning to populate the city. The menu had an eclectic flair that reminded Ran of the New Age shops in Los Angeles with their organic wheat breads and tofu, but Tara had bragged on their soups and salads, and since he was more interested in what she had to reveal than what to eat, he had chosen his lunch with little interest and now waited on the special faire in a booth opposite her. He wanted to grab the file folder she had set next to her on her bench seat and begin finding his answers, but she had explained that she was up the entire night compiling and analyzing and just needed a recharge, so he decided to give her room to catch her second wind with a meal minus his badgering. He marveled over the inability of a sleepless, work-filled night to damage her beauty.

After the waitress had brought their drinks, Tara began, "I brought the results for you to attach to your case folders in case they are needed. The data is highly scientific, and I wouldn't expect anyone outside the medical community to be able to decipher their meaning, but I thought you would want them anyway."

She didn't make a move to transfer the folder to him as he anticipated, and Ran continued to let her dictate their time together. "What are the chances that you will get the geographic profile today?" she said abruptly.

Ran said, "Tom's a good friend. He knows I was working on a short time frame. Late this afternoon possibly."

"That will have to do, I guess," she said. "It should be enough time."

"Should be enough time? May not get another chance to eat?" Ran said. "What's going on, Tara?"

He said it as compassionately as he could.

"I worked through the night and just finished up late this morning, comparing my findings with Weyland's results and those of previous murderers in your records. I think I was right about what I told you. It's option two."

Her words were disjointed and out of place, and Ran could see the exhaustion beginning to make its appearance across her brow and under her soft eyes.

"What option two? Tara, I'm a little lost here," Ran said, and realized his questions were just complicating the situation. She had worked feverishly for what he figured was twenty hours straight, not having slept since the previous night, and regardless of her foreboding remarks, she needed some down time. "I'll tell you what. Let's get some food in you, relax a bit, and you can start at the beginning when you are ready. Surely whatever you found can wait until you have had lunch."

She conceded without argument, and they spoke of Ran's morning until the food arrived. Ran was surprised at his hunger, and they ate greedily until their plates were empty. After a few minutes, Tara, who had collapsed back into the vinyl seat with marked satisfaction, apologized for her vagueness.

"You know, I think I pushed my blood sugar levels. I feel much better now."

Ran answered, "Just adding to the pile of guilt I already feel, are you?"

By now they recognized the sarcastic playfulness of their counterpart.

"I think I have you right where I want you," she smiled tiredly.

Ran nodded, "That you do. And I am not going to fight it. But let's promise that in the future our meals will be free of talk of work. I don't think I ever want to do this again."

Her face broke into the familiar smile he had grown to cherish. "Promised. Let me get another Coke, and I'll start filling you in on my night…day…I'll let you know what I discovered."

"You got it."

Once both of their glasses were full, Tara reached for the folder that had lain forgotten next to her since their arrival. She had put so much effort into the case for him, and he hoped this would have to be her final science lesson. It was time he got back to work.

"What I have here," she glanced at the dull brown file in her hands, "is really something better understood and explained by a forensic DNA expert, so you will have to bear with me. Some of the data are outside my realm of knowledge, but for the most part, I can assure you that what I have learned is accurate and the results are repeatable. There is no doubt in the scientific method."

"Lady, you don't have to convince me," Ran said. "I was sold on your skills a long time ago."

"Well, thank you for that," she smiled, "but what you have to realize is that if this information is required in a legal matter, say a trial or court hearing, the work will most likely have to be repeated since it originated in the lab of a pathologist. I am hardly a certified specialist. We are talking exhaustive lab science here. Hell, Ran, I was using equipment I had never seen before, using techniques and technology I have only read about."

"Ok, ok, so you are not Dr. Baird. But you are the closest thing I have and I am happy for it."

Tara looked surprised. "How do you know Michael Baird?"

"Every homicide detective coast to coast knows Baird. When he was the first doctor to testify in a criminal case using DNA testing, we all felt a little weight lifted off our shoulders," Ran said reverently. "The guy is the reason we cleared over twenty cold cases in the first two years following that conviction. Late eighties, I think."

"1987," Tara said.

Ran looked at her quizzically.

"I'm a fan," she admitted.

Ran assured her, "Tara, whatever you have found, no matter how much you think it requires substantiation, is more than we would have ever had without your help. I have no doubts in its accuracy, and I can promise you without having heard it that it's better than anything discovered in dozens of similar cases to this point."

He had reached over and covered her diminutive hand with his before he knew it, wanting to ease her doubts with more than words. She looked at their bonded hands for a long time, and then up at him with a warm gratefulness.

"This work is important to me, and I'm sure of it. I just want you to be sure too."

"Let's hear it so I can take the next step. I have a feeling you have broken this wide open."

"All right, you asked for it," she said.

She opened the file to what looked like computer printouts with a variety of numerical graphs and tables and neat, handwritten notes in the margins.

"First off, the autopsy was unremarkable as I told you, for the most part. The body exhibited the same trauma we have seen in previous cases

– ripping and tearing of the flesh, bite marks, blunt forced trauma, massive organ loss. Lab work will undoubtedly be repetitive as well."

"For the most part?" Ran repeated her. "What was different?"

"Well, I looked at Melton further, compared some secondary findings with Stanton, and noted some subtle changes."

He sat in silence to let her continue.

She went on, "As you know, a majority of the post mortem process is visual examination. Even though we have made great strides in the last thirty years with DNA analysis and forensic investigation, an autopsy is still 90 percent observable discovery."

Ran nodded, "You can blame television for that. *Quincy, ME* just isn't sexy these days."

Tara looked at him bewildered, "Who's Quincy?"

"It was the show about the medical examiner. Jack Klugman played him," Ran struggled to gain her recall, only to realize that she had probably been no more than six when the program aired, not an age for the late night viewing of medical shows. Still, he felt compelled to trudge on, only to make his point. "Every show was the same. Quincy would do his autopsy, draw conclusions before any lab work had been completed, and then play detective for the remaining forty-five minutes to prove himself. Kind of like *Columbo*."

Tara shook her head as if he were speaking Cantonese.

Ran saw that his analogies were dropping like wet bags of sand. "Forget it. I have single-handedly shown my age in all its miserable glory."

"Yes, Grandpa, you are such the old codger. Tell me, what was it like before electricity? Did you search for criminals with a lantern, or did you just wait until the light of day?"

"Watch it or I will report you to the state board for practicing medicine before you could vote."

Tara laughed, "To be honest, I have never been much of a television watcher. Takes away from the imagination."

"I'm sorry. I got you totally off track. You said you observed some differences?"

"A few. Without in depth comparison as part of the serial theory we have developed, they would simply be facts in the external exam," she said. He loved how she spoke *to* him, her eyes rarely wavering from his to peripheral locations as many people do when they are engaged in conversations. Hers was a manner of deep interest and respect, as if the importance of whom she was talking to was not lost on her.

"Let's start with the bite marks. Nothing unique in their manner, but when I compared their measurements, I found Stanton's skin showed an increase in bite *size*."

"You mean the killer took a bigger chunk out?"

"No, I mean the tooth pattern had increased. Measuring from canine to canine, the bite had increased in width. Basically, his mouth was bigger."

"Is that possible?" Ran asked. "Can an adult's teeth and gums grow after maturity?"

"It is obviously a result of the genetic change occurring in him. His transformation prior to Stanton's death resulted in a larger man than previous morphs," she explained. "This was substantiated by the grip marks I cataloged as well. His hands had greater circumference when I compared the measurements from the bruising."

Ran didn't like the way her presentation had started.

She said, "Our boy has grown."

"Any idea how much?"

"That just so happens to be one of my late night computations. As far back as the history goes? Considerably, on an evolutionary scale. By as much as ten percent," she said. "I compared my measurements to anatomical charts on adult males, and for now I would put him at six-eight to seven feet tall. His weight is less defined, but considering the muscles mass needed to perform the actions we are seeing on these bodies, he is in excessive of three hundred pounds."

"Andre the Giant."

"Who?"

"Never mind. You said *for now*. Did that mean what I think it meant?"

She tipped her head, "There has been discernable increase in his size between the last two cases analyzed. More so than those preceding. I would bet that this morning's victim will show further growth."

"Jesus," Ran whispered.

"That's not all," Tara added, referring to her notes. "The size is translating into strength."

"Bigger muscles. You said that."

"No, strength. Muscle size does not always dictate strength, though in his case, it is probably a good indicator. It must be the hormonal activity contributing to the changes I found. In some places, Stanton's bones were not just broken or twisted, they were crushed."

Ran was concerned. "Crushed? Like under a great weight."

"More like under a great force, like a vice."

Ran stopped, "You mean to tell me that he compressed Stanton's bones with just his grip? Quite a handshake."

"Quite, but I don't just mean his hands. His jaws show incredible pounds per square inch force," she explained. "I calibrated the damage down to one of Stanton's femurs. Three thousand pounds."

"I would assume that is a lot?"

"The average human bite exerts a force of 300 pounds. A German Shepard measures in at around 750."

"I guess a James Bond analogy would be fruitless right here?"

She lit up. "You mean Jaws, the guy who could bite through metal cable?"

"Ah, hah. So you have seen something on television."

"Theater, actually. You can't deny me a good Bond film."

"I'll remember that," he remarked, but the sheriff was visibly shaken by word that their killer was capable of such brute strength. Concern was shaping into fear, but Ran had never shied away from his responsibilities.

"Keep it coming, Doctor. Does it get worse?"

"Yes and no," she responded. "Let me get the unpleasantness out of the way, and then I will detail for you what the equipment found."

She was in charge now, just as she had been the first time they had shared a lunch. Her knowledge erased any stereotypical gender roles, and Ran hoped his position in their relationship would soon realize a place of importance. He bordered on emasculation, though he didn't blame her. It was his petty reaction to the situation. She was the authority when it came to the science of their problem. Soon enough the detective in him would have what he needed to step forward and take his place behind the wheel.

"In every case, including Stanton, there was indication of disruption of the internal organs. Access to the internal cavity was gained through the softer tissue at the stomach, below the rib cage, where a few heavy blows and tears could expose the gastrointestinal area. From there, it is a simple matter of peeling back the edges, revealing liver, kidneys, and the like. We have always had a heart and lungs to evaluate—until now. The area under the ribs was scooped clean. Stanton was an empty shell."

"That makes no sense," Ran pondered. "Up until now he has attacked in what appeared to be a frenzy, like a mad animal, biting and striking and ripping, then hauling the remains away to leave them miles from the kill zone. Now you're telling me he is butchering the bodies like Jack the Ripper, cleaning them out like a Halloween jack-o-lantern?"

"No, that's not what I am saying. The cruel slaughter is still primary.

That hasn't changed. What he is doing is taking the time to extract every organ in the body, which is not surprising given my theory."

She could see that Ran couldn't understand why the methodical removal of the entire inside of the body's trunk was expected.

"Come on, Mr. Television, you can't tell me you haven't watched some *Animal Planet* or *National Geographic* episodes? Have you ever seen a big cat kill a gazelle or a zebra?"

Ran thought, "Sure, I've seen shows like that, but what does that have to do with…"

She saw the light go on behind his deep-set brown eyes. "They always go for the internal organs. Usually the limbs and outer carcass are left for the scavengers."

He looked at her hard. "Is he eating the organs?"

"My guess is no. I think he is simply following the encoded genetic blueprint of the dormant DNA. It is a primitive, instinctual act, which is why I think he has reached absolute transfer. Option Two."

"That's the second time you have mentioned Option Two. What am I missing?" he said.

Tara said, "Remember I told you I thought one of two things could result from the mutations? Well, this is the second one—the ancestral gene has emerged, permanently most likely."

"So instead of tearing himself apart at the genetic level, he has…"

"Given in to a new DNA structure. He is no longer the original, fighting to maintain his presence in the face of the other."

"Whoa."

"You're no longer looking for man, Ran. You're looking for a superman, one of incredible size and strength. And if we don't figure out where he is, myself and every pathologist across the country are going to start becoming very, very busy."

She had reached the end of her information much more quickly that Ran had planned. What she was telling him was that his search for a human perpetrator was over. He would be on safari from here on out. Northeast Kansas had just become the nation's largest hunting grounds.

"But what about all the fingerprint analysis? What can you tell me from that?"

"Plenty. I was just getting to it. I just want you to understand that you are not dealing with the average, if there is an average, serial killer. He is operating as an animal now, a lone wolf, but unlike the canine, he isn't going to stop when his stomach is full. He is driven by a different hunger, a simple need—the desire to kill. Bloody, brutal, vicious destruction. It's a thirst he has to quench, and I don't know if that is possible."

She was ever so serious. "Killing is his singular purpose. There must be some latent reason that he is driven to it, but like any predator, he is going to be cunning."

"How can you know all this, Tara," Ran now challenged. "I'm not questioning your methods, but I just don't see how a few fingerprints and an autopsy can reveal such epic conclusions."

Tara was unmoved. "Deductive reasoning, my dear Watson. It's what we pathologists do for a living. Let me tell you what the infrared and detector told me, with the help of a new little gadget a friend sent me, and maybe you will agree."

"Right. Keep going."

"I found a number of complete prints on the neck, shoulders, and back of the victim using a chemical reagent and the UV imaging equipment. Once I lifted the prints with the surface gel, I had to lift skin residue from virgin areas of the victims skin as a control against my prints."

Ran understood. "You needed to separate the two skin residues. Remove Stanton from the equation."

Tara said, "Exactly. A patch of skin on his inner thigh proved to be free of exposure to a majority of the environmental contaminants he came in contact with, including the killer. These samples were then placed under the spectroscopic microscope that divided each into its chemical make-up. Sample B's totals were then deducted from Sample A, and I was left with the killer's print and its chemical agents. I transferred that to the infrared array detector and let it do its work. The resulting analysis could then be compared with known levels of human secretion to identify his qualities in dozens of ways."

"Such as blood type, gender, stuff like that?"

"That and more," Tara added. "You will be surprised what the detector can deduce."

"Hit me with it."

Tara held up her hand. "Just a minute. While my print was getting worked over, I went an extra step, thanks to the friend I mentioned."

Ran interrupted, "Now about this friend. Is this someone I need to be getting jealous about, because I'm feeling a hint of it, and I am not normally insecure, so help me out here."

"Isn't that sweet of you," Tara said, "and extremely unnecessary. My friend is a girl I trained with. She works in the offices in Kansas City, and she was kind enough to courier over an item I have been dying to try. So, to answer your question, no, but I think I like the reaction. Keeps you on your toes."

"Great. As if I needed more to worry about."

Tara smiled. "Have you ever heard of *touch DNA?*"

"No, but by the sound of it, is it along the same lines as finger printing?" Ran returned the question with one of his own, though he knew after it had left his mouth that it was a childlike statement. The answer was obvious.

"Yes. It refers to areas where an invisible touch may have occurred," said Tara, who never spoke to him as the ignorant detective he sounded like sometimes when it came to forensics. "From that area we can scrape discarded skin cells and process them for DNA analysis. Fascinating really."

Ran asked, "How can there be skin cells from just a touch, and even if there were, our surface is skin, so scraping is going to take cells from there too."

"Our bodies are shedding skin cells all the time; the slightest touch can be a depository of usable DNA," said Tara, "and with the spectroscopic microscope, we can separate the cells from each donor. And that is where my friend's new toy comes in--an electromagnetic genosensor."

"I won't ask."

Tara said, "I had the county tech guy hook it up while he was here. It was surprisingly compatible with the other equipment and tied into the computer easily. Technology has really come a long way, hasn't it?"

Ran nodded his assent.

"When I sent my Stanton samples to the lab for testing and DNA analysis, I knew it would take days even without waiting in line," she said, "but the genosensor can perform the same task in just hours."

Ran said, "Hours? Then why don't they use this geno thing everywhere?"

"Because the data is superficial. Detailed answers take time, though we are making great strides in shortening the process. The genosensor provides a summary of the DNA construct without the fluff. Straightforward genetic mapping. It's like a road map with only the major highways—if you want the two-lanes and neighborhoods, you have to wait. But I felt our time frame wouldn't allow for the detailed report, and if we could learn anything useful from the short version, well, it couldn't hurt. We always have the lab report following in a few days. I just had to see if the mutations were further damaging the structure or expanding toward a conclusion."

"And what did it tell you?"

"It told me the transmogrification was probably nearing completion. A more recent sampling will confirm it," she said.

"You mean he will soon stop changing into the other form?"

"Yes, because if the analysis is correct, and I have no reason to believe it isn't, he has permanently taken the other form."

"Is that possible?"

"Possible and probable," the doctor conceded. "The cellular structures were, for lack of a better description, taking on the fixed qualities of the mutant DNA. The bricks were nearly all in place. I was surprised at the evidence. I didn't think that the human genome could withstand such an explosive assault on its chemical balance, but it has apparently introduced itself gradually, preparing the chromosomes for the switch. Quite incredible, really."

Ran gave no signal that he wanted to respond. He was lost in understanding, not the words from Tara's mouth, but the implications.

"The genosensor confirmed that the dormant gene has moved to the final step of total conversion. I am willing to bet based on this evidence," she said while referring to her papers, "that the man who was once afflicted with this genetic mutation is no longer. He is now…something else entirely. And if not now, very, very soon."

"So everything that you or Tom Avery will be able to tell me about this guy is moot at this point. My suspect has left the building," Ran quipped, though there was no laughter in his voice.

The restaurant had suddenly become very small to Ran's perception. The walls were inching in on him. Every ear in the place was tuned to their conversation, and he would soon be asked hat he was going to do now. What would his next move be to stop the killing? His answer was lost in the weight of a dull headache that was working its way across his temples and settling behind his eyes.

Tara rejected his statement. "No, you can use what we give you to track the man to the point he checked it in, then pick up the trail from there. It could lead you to him. He may not totally abandon his previous existence."

Ran said, "You're right. It is a starting point, more than we have had, but I can't shake the feeling that the chase has changed dramatically. The rules are all different now. After what our eyewitness told us this morning, I have to believe the change is done. He is the other."

"He is different physically. His intellect and emotion are likely altered, but I would think, even with the change, there exists some of the original, even at a subconscious level. The eraser couldn't have totally eradicated what was dominant for the majority of the organism's life span. Evolutionary biology tells us that we retain some of our past, however miniscule. There may be something still there, something that will help you."

"We can hope."

"Right now that is one of our greatest allies. That, and your intuitiveness. I am sure the detective in you can follow the trail we give you."

"Thanks for the vote of confidence."

Just as Tara was going to explain the specifics of her findings, the identifying markers that would serve as his breadcrumbs, a young man approached their table. He was all of fifteen, and behind him two other boys of high school age stood in anticipation of their friend's words.

"Excuse me, Officer. Is that your police unit outside?"

He gestured through the farthest window of the restaurant toward the parking lot where Ran's cruiser sat.

"Yes, it is. Is there a problem?"

The boy looked overly nervous, and he glanced back at his comrades for reassurance. They stared with no show of assistance. He turned back and said, "Well, my friends and I were riding our bikes by and heard your radio. There is a voice on there. Pretty loud. Asking for Sheriff Price. We thought you might want to know."

Ran was already standing, and Tara could see the concern in his face. In all his hurry to get inside and hear what Tara had to tell him, he had failed to take his remote radio in with him. Years of inactivity had only contributed to his negligence.

"Thank you, young man, boys, I will take care of it," he said looking at each of them. Then to Tara, "I'll be right back. Finish your drink. I shouldn't be a minute."

Tara watched him exit the main doors and cross to his car. He sat there for a few minutes, and then stood hurriedly, jogging back toward her. She saw that something was wrong.

He walked quickly to the table, peeling a few bills from a money clip as he came, and said, "I have to get back to Auburn. I'll drop you on the way."

"What's happened, Ran?"

"A robbery. Nothing special, except for Auburn."

"What was robbed?"

"Dalton's. The place we ate. Freezer truck out back was emptied.

Strangest thing," Ran said.

Tara looked distressed, "What about the rest of my findings, Ran? When will you be able to hear them? I'm worried about the time."

Ran thought for a second. "What does the rest of your day look like?"

"I'm free. Maxwell is out, I have nothing else pressing, and I have already made arrangements for the borrowed equipment to be returned. I can call the office and let them know I will be out for the remainder of the day. What did you have in mind?"

Ran said, "Come with me. You can tell me the rest on the way, and then I can drop you at my office while I check out the progress on the robbery. I could have you back home early."

"Or we could hang out at your place and discuss where to go from here," Tara said. "Besides, I would love to see your bachelor's pad."

"The prospects of you in my house, though inviting, are frightening considering its condition. I would hate for you to see the way a bachelor really lives. My disco ball is a little dusty."

Tara would have none of it. "Are you kidding me? I grew up with three brothers. Nothing would shock me," she said standing. "Let's go. I will use the radio in your car."

Chapter 27

With summer temperatures continuing to hover in the low nineties and the threat of rain long absent from the forecast, Kansas vegetation stood parched and brown in dry earth that screamed for relief through broad fissures that broke its surface in jagged lines. The climate was historically unpredictable, with most downpours coming in the spring and early fall. The Topeka area had what was known as a humid continental climate—hot summers and cold winters, with an average rainfall capable of sustaining large fields of crops and livestock. Also the frequent hosts to violent tornadoes, many in the area would have welcomed a severe thunderstorm and its nourishing rains regardless of its potential for damage. The oppressive heat and lack of precipitation had gone on for weeks, keeping farmers on edge and school-age children locked indoors at a time when playing outside was an important part of their vacation from teachers and books. Most activity was confined to the evenings, after the sun had nearly completed its descent and touched the horizon, its day of giving life and ironically taking it away complete, only to reemerge in nine hours to do it all over again. Heat exhaustion, grass fires, and water rationing were the norm when the season acted up, and residents of the Midwestern community argued over its status as one of the most extreme summers in decades.

This explained the jovial surprise of Ran and Tara when the windshield of the sheriff's cruiser began to be dotted with large droplets of rain as it pulled onto Highway 335 and headed southeast toward Auburn. While they had been inside, a dark front of heavy clouds had rapidly approached from the northwest, and Ran realized five more minutes would have guaranteed him a mad dash to the car to fully close the driver's window, left cracked in the humid midday, a habit he had acquired in his days on the West Coast. Fortunately, the boys had heard the radio as a result.

"Wow, that came up quickly," Tara remarked as she stared out at the foreboding scene.

Ran agreed, "Looks like it could get heavy, but there's no denying that we need it."

The traffic on the freeway was already responding to the ever-increasing downpour, slowing in direct contrast to the growing amount of water on the asphalt that was beginning to show signs of pooling in the random depressions that afflicted the road. Within seconds, Ran had turned his wipers to maximum to deal with the downfall and the sprays repeatedly thrown backward in the treads of trucks and cars that were also navigating the route.

"This may take longer than expected," he said.

Tara said, "Trust me, I can fill the time. Are you ready for some forensics, or do you need to concentrate on the road?"

"I'm good, but I'll have to pass on the note taking."

"I can repeat it later if you need me too, but most of the information is in the paperwork," she assured him. Tara reopened the folder.

"During these last few weeks of examining old files and talking about the cases, one thing has always bothered me: Why have my colleagues, even one of them, failed to come to this same information? It has gnawed at me and gnawed at me. I'm thinking, 'Is every pathologist that has come into contact with this series of victims as limited in their investigative skills and techniques as Weyland? Surely there are some solid doctors out there who are curious and determined enough to at least draw some of the similar conclusions I have.'"

She was reflective and open, and Ran could hear her concern. "Don't get me wrong," she continued. "I know I have a lot to learn, and I certainly don't consider myself the end-all medical examiner in the profession, but it just seemed so obvious to me that some of my conclusions would be shared. It's staring us in the face. Why has it remained so elusive? And then it hit me."

Ran's eyes were fixed on the road in front of him, the conditions continuing to worsen, but from his peripheral vision he could see that she was speaking out the passenger's window, more to herself than to him, in a moment of deep rumination.

"The treasure was placed in my lap to discover. The records you found. The unmistakable genetic changes that have increased in frequency and measure. My good fortune of having presided over quite a few of the cases in the examination room. Even a blind man can locate something if it is thrown in his path and he is steered in its direction," she said with humility. "Any one of them could have reached these results if they had half the clues I was provided."

Ran could feel her disappointment in her own self-concept, and he refused to let her take herself down. One of the things that he loved about her was her confidence. Her fatigue was playing with her.

"You can't be serious. The only reason I will have the slightest lead is because of you. I seriously doubt any other pathologist could have brought the creativity and determination you gave this. I have known my share, and you bring something special to the table," Ran said, searching for the best word. "You are…tenacious. Very little deters you. It's what has pulled these cases from a future in the cold files and given me a chance."

He could feel her staring at him now. "We have you alone to thank for what you are going to tell me, and I can already trust in its helpfulness. There are good pathologists out there. You are unique."

"Sorry, Ran, and thanks. I'm not sure why I went there. I know I'm good at what I do, but sometimes you just feel like all the discoveries in the world won't be enough."

Ran looked at her in spite of the weather. "I'll make sure it will be enough."

Tara sighed, "We are an odd group, my pathology brethren, but we make a difference, don't we?"

"A huge difference. We couldn't do without you," Ran said. "Except Weyland."

Tara laughed, "He means well. He's actually highly efficient, just not very personable."

"He is all business, I'll give him that," Ran said, "but if it's all just the same, I'll deal with you."

Tara repositioned the file in her lap indicating she was through with her brief, uncharacteristic self-evaluation and ready to get back the business at hand. "All right, back to our boy. Are you sure you want to hear this now? This weather is looking bad."

The sky had blackened considerably since they had left Topeka and the driving was treacherous, but Ran had waited long enough.

"What you can't get to now," he said, "we can finish this afternoon. Trust me. I can listen."

"OK. I'll start with what was easy," said Tara. "As if we needed confirmation, we are dealing with a male. A hair sample I found, black, by the way, together with the infrared, confirmed gender. He is clearly Caucasian, though all I was able to do was rule out ethnicity as opposed to define it. African-American, Asian, American Indian, and other dominant racial determinants were missing. Problem is, he could be a dark-skinned individual of Italian heritage or a light-skinned German. There is no telling.

"Are you ready for this? His age is anywhere from zero to thirty-five."

"Well, that will keep our search out of the local nursing homes, anyway," Ran said, his head bobbing to improve his angle of vision through the rain-washed windshield.

"The transmutation of the DNA strands made it impossible to be sure. Normally, at the end of the strands is a string of repeating nucleotides called telomeres. As we age, sections of the telemeres are lost, so it is possible to predict the donor's age based on the length of the telomeres. Problem is, I identified a strand that suggest an adult of 30 to 40 years, *and a strand that had a complete group of nucleotides, like a newborn.*"

Ran asked, "Is that Personality B rearing its ugly head?"

"No doubt," she said. "The new DNA structures are just that—new. He has involuntarily discovered a temporary fountain of youth for his aging body."

"Well, good. I thought I was looking for an American werewolf in Kansas. Turns out, he's just Buddha."

"You are the consummate comedian," she noted. "Here's something more to your liking. The blood typing was interesting to say the least. He's AB positive, not the most common. Probably six percent of the population. I am pretty confident that his blood type will be a constant while all else seemingly changes."

"Why's that?" Ran asked. "I don't know how sure we can be that anything is going to stay the same."

"Blood type is a constant. We have very few instances of blood types changing, and when it has happened, the circumstances were extreme, like a liver transplant."

"If you ask me, this has all the signs of an extreme situation," he said.

Tara agreed, "That is for sure, but in this instance I don't believe the organism would benefit from abandoning its type for a new one. By introducing new antigens to its body, antibodies would automatically form and bind themselves to the antigens on the walls of the red blood cells. The result is destruction of the cell walls and a total breakdown of the immune system. He has so many dangerous transformations occurring in his body, I don't believe the new DNA structure would allow for or desire a blood type alteration. The cellular structures are fragile; remember, I thought that his body would self-destruct as it was. From all the saliva and hair samples we have seen examined in the case files, AB positive has been a constant."

"AB positive it is."

"We know his appearance for the most part, though I would assume that his features have changed since the Stanton killing. He is most likely bigger, but the hair color, blood type, and gender are a constant. Now for the revealing stuff," she said with a tone of satisfaction.

"It will have to wait, Tara."

They were already entering Auburn proper, and the sheriff's department was just a minute up the street.

"I hate to do this to you, but you can wait at my office while I run over to Dalton's. Shouldn't take more than thirty minutes," he said. Then, "Unless you want me to take you by the house. Maybe you will be more comfortable there?"

"No, your office is fine. I can check in to my office and transcribe some of my observations in written form for you," she said, holding the file in front of her like a sacred relic.

"Really, it's no problem."

Ran brought the cruiser to the curb in his designated parking spot, hoped out quickly, and went straight to his trunk. The rain was still beating down in torrents. Soon he was at her door, a wide umbrella open and waiting to cover her short walk into the home of Auburn's law enforcement. She was taken with his chivalrous behavior, but at the same time not surprised by the show of care.

Once inside the front door, they both wiped their feet as Ran stood the umbrella against the side of Polly's rectangular enclosure. He had already called ahead to let her know he was headed back, and Polly greeted them both with a professional air that she normally reserved for the mayor and the occasional police visitor.

"Polly," he gestured to Tara, "this is Dr. Phillips with the Shawnee County Medical Examiner's Office. She has been assisting us in the Melton and Stanton cases and has agreed to come here to review some of her forensic findings."

Tara offered her hand and trademark smile.

"Dr. Phillips, Polly Sheridan, my chief dispatcher. She keeps this place operational."

"Dr. Phillips. A pleasure."

"The sheriff has mentioned you a time or two, Polly," the doctor said. "He can't say enough good things."

Polly glanced at Ran and allowed a slight smile to break her rugged exterior. "Sheriff Price has been known to exaggerate. Can I get you a cup of coffee?"

Tara said, "That would be great. Thank you."

"No, problem at all," Polly said as she made her way to the small table that served as a coffee station. "Cream and sugar?"

"Sugar, thanks," Tara said as Ran pointed the way to his office.

"Polly, I am going to leave Tar…the doctor here for a few minutes while I run over to see Monk's progress on the robbery scene. I told her she could sit in my office until I returned."

Polly countered, "Well, I think she can just stay right out here with me and we can each other company until you get back. Is that all right with you, Dr. Phillips?"

"That would be just fine," Tara responded. Then to Ran, "I can take care of my notes later when you are finished."

Ran could see that the ladies were interested in a little female interaction, so he agreed without rebuke.

"OK, then, I leave you in capable hands."

Turning to Polly, Tara asked, "Is there a restroom?"

"Just down the hall and to your right."

"Thank you. I'll see you in half an hour," she said to Ran and started down the hall.

"Half an hour," Ran repeated, and he caught Polly's eye as he gathered the umbrella for his return to the rain-soaked sidewalk.

"Very attractive," she said slyly.

"Dr. Phillips? Yes, I guess she is. Why?"

Polly openly detested shows of ignorance when the truth was obvious, but she took it easy on her boss in light of his lonely three years in Auburn. "No reason," she said stone-faced, "but if you come out of this with nothing more than an autopsy report, I will be very disappointed."

Ran tried to remain serious. "Come on, Polly. Ease up, would you? I have to go. Please see that she is comfortable."

"Will do."

"Polly."

"Yes?"

"Thanks."

"Don't I always take care of you, Sheriff?"

He dove into the hail of pounding rain.

Chapter 28

By the time Ran had arrived behind Dalton's Restaurant, the storm has eased to a steady drizzle but showed no signs of stopping. The rear of the building featured a rough gravel lot that held a large dumpster surrounded by five-gallon jugs and a few wooden pallets. The area was for employee parking and deliveries mainly, though customers would often venture their cars to the back when the parking along the front was full or they didn't want to walk from a parking space on up the street. Three cars were tucked toward the back of the lot against a rough chainlink fence swollen with tall brown grass and weeds. A white eighteen-foot refrigerator truck sat conspicuously in the middle of the lot, its back doors open. A collection of men was gathered under a short tin overhang that protected the first six feet out the back door of the business, their clothes heavy and dark with water. The were pointing and nodding at the truck in animated discourse, and everyone turned as Ran's tires crunched and splashed into the arena. Monk was among them, wearing a clear, rainproof sleeve over his deputy's hat, a small notepad occupying his attention. Ran also recognized Chuck Forrester, a part-time patrol officer and full-time plumber in Auburn. He was always ready to help the department with patrol duties, and as an added benefit, would drive his own F150 along the streets and outer dirt roads of the town, a large spot light with driver's handle and red flashing light prominently displayed on its exterior. Like Monk, he enjoyed the sense of authority and the prospects of battling bad guys that came with a deputies badge, but it was his commitment and dependability that Ran valued. Dalton's owner Joel Tucker was there too and a cook whose name escaped him. *Benny? Bobby?* The last member of the quintet was a stranger to Ran, so he figured he must be the driver. Ran knew he needed to assess the scene, determine just what Monk had accomplished in his investigation and questioning, and get back to the office. Though a robbery was uncommon in their small town, Ran was not overly concerned about the crime in light of the events that had been preceding it. There was so much left to do and time was not something he had to waste. A call to Tony Sartin on the identification of the body found near the Sherwood Lake community was one of a dozen things he saw as a greater priority than a vandalized truck. He also felt bad leaving Tara behind and hoped Polly would keep her entertained until he was done. Ran just wasn't sure how Tara would come away from the encounter. Polly was matronly and gruff at times, and Ran certainly didn't want the doctor feeling uncomfortable.

He parked the cruiser and walked quickly over to the cluster of jabbering men and right away wished he were somewhere else. They greeted him with a thankful but frustrated hello.

"Sheriff. What are you going to do about this?"

It was Tucker, his trademark apron strapped tightly around his ample belly.

"Joel. How are you? Boys?"

"I'll be a lot better when you catch who raided my delivery," Tucker said with a frustrated tone that Ran wholly ignored. "They trashed just about everything, Sheriff. What am I going to do for the dinner rush tonight?"

"And my truck. Ruined the back of my truck. I won't be able to run a load until it gets fixed."

The man that Ran supposed was the driver barked his irritation.

They were obviously exasperated, and Ran knew that they weren't upset with him but at their loss.

Ran answered, "Well, gentlemen, we're going to do what we can to figure this out. Let me talk with the deputies for a minute, and we'll see what we can do, but you know as well as I do that your supply isn't going to reappear, at least not in a sanitary condition."

He turned to the driver. "And the quicker we get done here, the faster you can get that truck to the shop. I would suggest both of you make other plans and let us figure this thing out."

It was not an answer that either man was hoping for, but Tucker knew Sheriff Price to be a fair man and would allow him to do his job. The driver seemed to be willing to follow his lead.

"Sheriff," Monk interjected, "if you'd like to step over to the truck, I can tell you what we have so far."

Ran first stepped over to his trunk to fetch a uniform parka, and then the three officers crunched across the short distance to the back of the truck where both doors hung in awkward ruin. "Man. Looks like they used a chain and just yanked it open. The hinges are bent in all four places," he observed. He moved the left door and it barked its complaint in an annoying rubbing of metal.

The interior looked like a bomb had exploded. Open boxes were strewn everywhere, some of them completely empty, and there were pieces of chicken, beef, and pork littering the walls and floor. Whoever had entered the truck had acted in a violent frenzy.

Monk said, "Call came in from Joel around 11:00. Driver pulled around here and went inside to have lunch before unloading. When he came back out, he found this mess. No one heard or saw anything."

"Not back here. Place is surrounded by trees and thick brush," Ran said, surveying the property through the rain. "What I can't figure out is how they created a safe angle to pull these doors. And the gravel wouldn't allow for traction. Maybe they used a bolt cutter, but that doesn't explain the damage to the doors. Gravel won't provide us footprints, and from what I see there doesn't appear to be a sign of tires spinning under the weight of a violent pull. Hard to figure."

"What about explosives, Sheriff?" offered Chuck. "It would explain the torn up meat all over the place."

Ran shook his head, "No, Chuck, I don't see any remnants of explosives here. There would be burn marks at the very least, and I don't see anything but wrenched doors. No, had to be a tow chain or something."

"We haven't talked to anybody inside to see if they noticed a strange vehicle coming or going," said Monk. "Figured that would be our next step."

"Before you do that, Monk, let's walk the perimeter of the lot and see if there are any indications that somebody entered or exited from back here."

The three men separated and slowly examined the sections of fence line. The old barrier was rusted and failing, but with nature's helping hand twined throughout it, it proved to be a formidable enclosure. After a few minutes, Monk yelled the other two over to the side fence he was examining.

"Right there, past the fence and just to the left of the tree trunk."

Ran could see it, about a dozen feet from the fence through the water-soaked branches and thick-leafed weeds, glistening from the rainfall that refused to cease--a chicken wing.

"Could it have been thrown way out here?" Chuck asked.

Beyond the spot they stared at was another empty lot that led straight out to a side street. Ran was looking at the fence now and the surrounding foliage. To him the area looked slightly disturbed. A small gap in the windbreak revealed what Ran thought could be another piece of semi-frozen meat. He talked as he scrutinized the location to each side.

"Maybe. The inside of that truck looks like a cyclone hit it. Still, this is pretty far from the truck's back doors and not the right angle."

He stood up straight and put his now dirty wet hands to his holstered hips. "Monk, I need you to finish your investigation inside. Find out what people might have seen, then continue the increased patrol. We may have to stay fully staffed for a few days, so let Bobby know. I'll take care of Joel and the delivery guy."

Monk said, "Yes, sir, Sheriff."

They started back to the restaurant.

"Sheriff," Monk said, referring to the truck, "does this have anything to do with the stepped up surveillance?"

"I don't think so, Monk," Ran said. "We had another killing this morning, north of town near Sherwood. I just want to be on the side of caution."

"Another one? Who?" asked Chuck.

"That's what I need to go find out. Take care of this, file your reports, and I will get in touch with you later," said Ran. "Monk?"

"Yes, Sheriff?"

Ran pulled him aside. "Be extra diligent. Be sure the men are too. I don't want anything happening here that we could have prevented."

"Yes, sir," Monk nodded in agreement.

Ran said, "I'm headed to the office to see what Shawnee County knows about this morning, then I am going home to get a change of clothes. I'll have my radio with me."

He walked determinedly to the back door of Dalton's where he satisfied owner and driver that he would do everything in his power to apprehend the perpetrators and then got back in the cruiser. Before heading back, he decided to contact Tony Sartin and see what progress had been made on the Sherwood crime scene and the identity of the poor soul left slaughtered in the field.

"Polly, how's our guest?"

"Just fine, Sheriff. We were just enjoying a few hometown stories."

"I am heading back soon. Would you put me through to Shawnee County, please?"

"Dialing. See you a few minutes."

Ran sat in the back lot at Dalton's, his car idling smoothly, waiting for to hear from the Criminal Investigation Division and Sartin to see if there was anything new that he and Tara could consider. The men had separated that morning agreeing that the victim, like the unfortunate dead before him, would be hard to identify that day, and it was very likely that the field was simply another dumping ground for a murder that had occurred miles away. This casualty of a serial murderer's private war, if the course stayed true to form, would be from another part of the county, possibly even beyond county lines.

Soon, Sartin was on the line. "Let me guess. You want to fill me in on the Stanton autopsy," he said less than jovially.

Ran was caught off guard. "*Stanton* autopsy? There's no lab work back on that yet. What can I fill you in on?"

"I know for a fact the preliminary report was completed yesterday afternoon, and that Dr. Phillips is out of the office today meeting with law enforcement regarding the matter," Sartin accused. "So I ask myself: Where is she meeting if not here? She certainly hasn't graced our department, *the one in jurisdiction*, with any report. What's going on here, Ran? You told me you were seeking a new angle on the Melton case."

His attempts to keep Tara out of the mix had caught up with him, and after pledging an alliance of shared information with his friend, Sartin was calling him on it. The difficult situation he had tried to avoid was staring him in the face. If he didn't handle it correctly, and that meant straightforward, no more hedging the truth, it could spell a loss in county assistance, a friendship, and Tara's standing in the examiner's office, not to mention any hope he had in solving the crimes. He knew that at some point he would have to bring Sartin and his manpower into his and Tara's closed circle of speculation if it proved true, but he hadn't planned on their admission just yet.

"Look, Tony, let me explain," Ran said.

"I'm listening."

Ran started, "I never intended to leave you in the dark on anything, especially after the open doors you have extended me. Dr. Phillips expressed some ideas to me in the course of the Melton investigation, and I have been following up on those while we wait for our luck to change."

"What ideas?" Sartin asked.

"Theories about the motivation of the killer, Tony. She is an excellent pathologist."

Sartin said, "So while we are over here struggling to make ends meet on these killings, you cozy up with her and get your own personal pipeline to the ME's office. Nice, Ran. Real nice."

"It's not like that, Tony. Listen to me. You know me better than that."

"I thought I did. Ran, after everything I provide you—the information, computer access."

Ran felt like a boxer had just jabbed his chest. "Tony, I have never kept information from you. I did ask her to evaluate the Melton report, and I knew the Stanton autopsy was complete, but it didn't expose anything new or significant that we haven't seen in the previous cases. What Dr. Phillips is suggesting, and what I have been trying to verify, is such a unique hypothesis that I thought it was best if I look into its possibilities and once I felt it was viable, to include you."

He could almost feel Sartin's impatience coming through the radio.

"When you hear what she has to say, you'll understand and agree with me that Shawnee County wouldn't have given it a second thought. Probably passed it off as a waste of time and energy, especially with the volume of cases you are dealing with above and beyond this killer. Auburn, U.S.A. writes one traffic ticket a week. I figured I had the time to give it a look and determine its validity. Only then would I have elicited your input."

Sartin backed off slightly. "What makes you think I would have ignored her theory? We have absolutely nothing here."

"Trust me, Tony. I know you. You're a lot like me. By the book. This is, well, out there."

Sartin paused, then, "So what have you found? Does your work support her?"

"I think so, but I still can't believe I'm saying that," the sheriff admitted.

"And this has nothing to do with the fact that our newest medical examiner is beautiful young woman?"

Ran felt the truth was all that would keep things afloat. "Not in the beginning. She had a history with cases similar to ours, during her residencies, and she knows her stuff," Ran said. "I do care about her, but I've been at this over twenty years. I know how to keep emotions out of the equation. She has a solid argument that we can't cast aside."

"Ran, you know the two of you could have come to me. I thought we were friends."

"We are, Tony. We are. I just had to be sure of this one before I let it out, and even with that said, I don't think it can go further than this right now. There are still some things to consider."

Sartin was silent for an agonizing few seconds. Ran didn't know what to expect to hear from the other end, but he prayed his friend would give them the chance to convince him.

"All right, Ran. I'll give the two of you the opportunity to explain yourselves. Can you be here tomorrow morning?"

"I can't speak for Dr, Phillips, but I'll be there. I can let you know later about her status," said Ran.

"Fine."

Ran said, "What's the latest on the Sherwood killing?"

"Oh, sure. I nail you for hiding things from me, and you want information. How does that work?" Sartin said.

"Come on, Tony. I explained myself to you. What more do you want from me?"

"The truth."

"That's all I have ever given you."

By the time Ran was back at the office, Sartin had updated him and confirmed their meeting the following morning. His mind was ablaze with the lieutenant's words and their implications, and though he wasn't seeing any significance, the robbery of the delivery truck was not sitting right with him either.

He gave Tara enough time to gather her things and tell Polly she had enjoyed their time before he was urging her out the door. By the time they pulled into his driveway, Ran had repeated his conversation with Sartin and assured her that he was a man they could trust. Tara was naturally concerned about the ramifications of a county officer knowing that she had been working in a less than proper manner. She had bypassed the proper chain of authority and gone straight to Auburn's sheriff with information that was not his to receive until it had gone through the correct jurisdictional channels.

"Tara, he will work with us, I promise. I've known Tony for a long time. Besides, we were going to have to reach out to his office at some point," Ran assured her. "There is no way I will be able to nab this guy alone, especially if it means working outside Auburn. We had to have county support eventually."

Tara replied, "It's not so much that the lieutenant knows as it is I broke procedure. I pride myself on adhering to rules and regulations, and I failed to follow protocol."

"If it helps any," Ran said, "you did it for the right reasons. Don't beat yourself up on technicalities. The county would have shut you down before you could have had a chance to prove your point. Maxwell? Weyland? You think they would have given your theory the time of day?"

Ran was fired up, angry at himself for encouraging Tara, and at the same time furious at the red tape that bound state employees to a rigid conduct that often delayed if not halted their efforts to move cases forward. She had recognized the need to act swiftly in the face of events that had gone on far too long, and Ran had apparently been the right circumstance for her to make her opinions know. Little had the two of them planned on taking things to the extent they had gone, both professionally and personally. It could be argued that they had shared nothing more than an investigative interest outside of their responsibilities. It was only when she had divulged the particulars of the Stanton preliminary report that a line had been crossed. Ran was sure that Tony Sartin would maintain a closed-mouth approach to their activities until he met with them in the morning, and though there were no guarantees that he would either support them or remain silent about their transgressions after the meeting, he felt his friend would at least appreciate their conviction, and that may prove enough to keep Tara's conduct unknown to her superiors.

"I need to call my office and inform them that I will be at the county sheriff's department in the morning. If the lieutenant is as open to ideas as you say he is, I want to be there to make my case," Tara said with a note of anxiety.

Ran started to open his door. "If it is all right with you, while you're on the phone, I'm going to grab a quick shower and dry clothes and then you can finish telling me what the hardware revealed."

Tara moved to the front porch where Ran had stopped short to allow her past and said, "That's fine. Should I make some coffee for us?"

"Sounds great. I'll show you where everything is, and remember, forgive the condition of my house," Ran said, unlocking the door and ushering her in.

"I'm sure it's nothing like you are letting on," Tara said, and she stepped passed him into the house.

If Ran had anything going for him when it came to unplanned visitors was that he was a simple man with few material needs, and since work was his passion, he was rarely at home to create a mess. The house was far from new, though, and as a result it needed the domestic attention that was not in him to give. He was efficient at keeping everything in its place, the same way he kept his office, so a consistent vacuuming and dusting was all it really needed, but weeks usually went by before the house received such attention. Not surprisingly, few people had ever been inside, mainly Monk, and that was on the few occasions when he felt he had something to make Ran aware of that couldn't wait until the next day, though it seemingly always could have. Tony Sartin had picked him up one lazy Sunday morning to go fishing and had used the bathroom on their return, but those were the exceptions. Ran was unconcerned about her reaction to his dwelling; in fact, he hoped she would make herself at home. The place was nothing special, and he had long ago come to grips with the financial conditions inherent to working in law enforcement. He and his home were reflections of each other—practical, efficient, and modest. They were functional and required little maintenance to serve. Ran had always accepted people and things for what they were, and he only asked the same in return.

Tara's genuine statements regarding the comfortable nature of the house only reinforced his opinion of her. She didn't require a dog and pony show to find something she liked in people or things, and if she said it, a person could count on it being the honest truth. Like Ran, her impressions were rooted in human kindness and hard work; the accessories were just fluff. Twelve thousand square feet or twelve hundred, it made no difference to her. What she valued was the person that considered the place home.

While Ran was in the back of the house getting out of his wet clothes and showering, Tara readied some coffee and had started on a much-needed second cup when he re-emerged clean and dry. He joined her in the living room after pouring himself a cup and together they savored a moment of peace before getting down to business.

"So, are you ready to pass out or do you think you can hang in for the rest of the afternoon?" Ran asked concerned.

Tara sighed and took another sip from the mug she was grasping in both hands. "I'm good. I will admit though, this couch is feeling very comfortable right now."

Ran agreed, " I have slept on it more than a time or two. I can vouch for it."

He didn't like that she was well into her second day without having slept. "Tara, why don't I run you home so you can get some rest?" he said, but she shook her head in protest. "We are committed to divulging everything to Tony anyway, so I can just hear it then. No reason to repeat yourself any more than you have to."

"No, no, I'm fine. The coffee is starting to do the trick. I think I'm good for another few hours."

Ran knew that in battles of will, she was quite the combatant, so he ended his argument after the single thrust and parry. "Okay, agree with me on this then: You finish explaining your findings, and then I take you back to your office so you can get some sleep. I'm getting a little concerned, Doctor."

Tara smiled wearily, "No reason to trouble yourself, but I will take you up on the offer. I hope you don't mind if I retire for the rest of the day so I can be fully alert tomorrow. I think I better be at my best."

"You'll be fine," Ran acknowledged. "I would never worry about your ability to make your point. You sold me, and I'm twice the skeptic Tony is, trust me. Seriously, I have work to do at the office, and I need to follow up on the robbery, which brings me to something I wanted to throw out at you. The crime scene behind Dalton's—very weird."

"All right then, but me first," Tara said, pulling both of her now bare feet up under her in cross-legged comfort. "If you will be so kind as to get me a refill, I will tell you about the infrared scan and then maybe we can tie in the murder this morning. Who knows, we may even solve your robbery."

"That," Ran said, reaching for her cup, "would definitely earn you deputy status around here. I think you may have missed your calling."

She grinned, "No. I think I like the way things have worked out for me."

"Me, too," Ran said. "I wouldn't change a thing about you."

Chapter 29

Having returned to the dense tree line that served as natural cover from the rain that blanketed the formerly parched landscape, Caine lounged in contentment, the undergrowth serving as his personal Elysian Fields. Temporarily placated, he rested on the slightly damp earth strewn with twigs and small rock after his first day of the new beginning. He lay passive but alert, like a coiled snake ready to strike if bothered.

There was no threat beyond the canopy he had claimed, only the lapping water of the lake where he had taken a long drink upon his arrival and the various houses and structures where his prey retreated when the skies grew dark and the swollen clouds poured out like an uncorked bottle. And beyond that, and farther still, but for now Caine took no interest in the happenings outside the area he had marked his own. In good time he would hold dominion of those places as well, enjoying the same authority he held here, and with equal rule.

His was a territorial claim, and his movements within it were marked with stealth and advantage. There was no reason to bring unwelcome attention to his actions; he would operate in anonymity and thereby discourage fear and concern that could lead to a defense posturing that he would rather avoid. Men were generally cautious, to a point, but rarely altered their patterns without concrete reasons. If the occasional passerby caught a glimpse of his deeds and provided nothing more than an outrageous tale, Caine knew the herd would fail to stampede. On the other hand, should many eyes fall upon him, or should a leader believe that there was a cause for alarm, his desires would become complicated and his needs harder to fulfill. With a lifetime of experience at his beckoned call, Caine knew the smart play was to inhabit the shadows while picking off the weak, the solitary, at his leisure.

What he desired to howl from the highest peak so that all may hear and believe was that he did not live in fear of them, the detestable and small creatures that unwisely lived under the assumption that they were the kings of the jungle, that they were prey to no predator.

His seclusion was by choice, not the will of the inferior. Here he could avoid their stares and reproaches. Away from their prying eyes he could find peace. He had never belonged among them, and it was apart from them that he would forever reign supreme. They disgusted him, with their pettiness and bickering and material concerns.

Above all else, he loathed their weakness—physical, emotional, mental. They stood as a testament to everything that was wrong with the world and valued none of it. His life among them had been like the slough of a snake that he had eagerly cast off in his journey to this ultimate existence. With it he had shed all the inferiorities that had made him fragile, having removed the old, frail coat of timidity and spineless submission and replaced it with a pride and strength that gave him direction. His was an immortality born of everything man lacked. He was the phoenix, and his rebirth branded a new era for him and all who claimed their unrightful place on the earth. This was the age of reckoning, and he was its author.

How easy it had been to kill among them, and how exciting not to seek to finish the task in seclusion but to start and end it there, within yards of their dwellings. And at the end he had faced one with triumphant eyes, daring it to stay, though knowing it would flee in fear as it had done, as they would all do that witnessed his greatness.

Taking the food had been exhilarating as well. Hungered by his exertions and seeking to take what was his, he had entered the truck easily, his senses brought to life by the sweet rich smell of the blood-filled meats. He had moved stealthily and with surety, and then eaten his fill without concern before taking an armful of the half-frozen beef and chicken, making his way back to where he reclined now.

The storm that spoke above him was all the company he needed, or would ever need, in this, his new life. He would stay in this land until he felt compelled to move on, not by force or threat, but with the instinctual desire to experience new opportunities, greater challenges. And when he found that place and laid claim to it, he would drown in the same pleasures that he had taken this day. And nowhere, not where he now sat in quiet reflection or in the next killing field, would he let fear rule him. That, he vowed, would never be the case.

And so he was pacified, for now, his hunger appeased. But with night would come the familiar yearning, and the need to satisfy its maddening call for retribution. It was a summons he would answer with a fierce determination, a charge to which he was wholly sworn. Like the primal demands of his body that eased once he fed and drank from the water's edge, this craving would be satiated through the hunt—and the inevitable kill.

Caine grinned in simple exultation.

Chapter 30

"So the prints were different. I don't see how that can help us. It's the reason no one has gotten anywhere with these cases. The only thing they have in common is their violent nature. There has never been anything to link it all together otherwise."

"The differences were actually helpful to the chemical analysis," Tara said. "Though the dermal ridge pattern was unique and failed to show a tie to the other cases, the sweat pores had increased in size and allowed for a greater amount of material to exit the body. I was able to qualify his eating habits, hormonal levels, even isolate certain materials that he had come in contact with prior to and possibly during the kill. Once the computer compiled the data, it was just a matter of cross-referencing with biological and environmental information that is available to us through the KSBI and the National Center for Forensic Science. Simple really."

Ran marveled, "Yes, simple."

"Seriously, Ran. It became a matter of research at that point. Time-consuming, but really just a game of quantitative matching," she said, as if it had all been an intriguing treasure hunt, her map a numeric table of values and percentages that led to previously assigned results. "For example, the protein levels were through the roof in human terms. The numbers were consistent with various diseases, even cancer, but knowing the DNA change that took place, I concluded that the values were the result of increased animal proteins and that was supported with a larger than normal volume of nitrogen excretion. Nitrogen is the waste product in protein synthesis, and our bodies normally remove it through urine, but his body, in some remarkable way, has adapted to the need for further nitrogen removal."

"The sweat glands," said Ran.

"The sweat glands. In fact, it looks as if his epidermal organ is functioning at a level much higher than it was originally designed to, a sign of the metabolic and genetic mutations that have taken place. Consequently, his touch is a blueprint of everything that constitutes him chemically, whether it is what he ingests or expels."

Ran said rhetorically, "So he eats a lot of meat."

"Animal proteins. What we call high-level protein--meat, fish, eggs, milk, even cheeses. But he could be gaining benefit from low-level proteins as well--grain, vegetables, and fruits. They may all be assisting him in his body's need for amino acids."

Ran nodded.

Tara continued, "The basic building block. I would imagine his body is like the old wood-burning steam engines of the late 1800s. His metabolism must be a fire burning deep within him, using up his caloric intake at an incredible rate. Initially it was a matter of supporting the cellular transformations that were occurring, but now I would guess he is simply a racing engine, and where there is power and strength and speed, there has to be fuel."

"But you don't believe he is meeting any of his dietary requirements during his kills. How can you be so sure?" Ran asked.

Tara said, "Again, the by-products of the waste that is passing through the cavernous pores that riddle his body. There was no indication of human ingestion. Chemical analysis determined the waste products were consistent with bovine, porcine, some bird groups, and a few others I was unable to immediately identify, probably because they were not domestic in origin. The bottom line is that he is and has been consuming large quantities of meat products and will continue to do so."

"Locate a local butcher with a repeat customer and I have a lead."

"A customer that no longer frequents the shop, but yes, that is the idea," Tara said. "I don't think he will be acquiring his meals the same way now that he has made the complete change. I would venture to guess the very sight of him would raise flags of alarm. No, he's going to be dining through other means, possibly relying on wildlife or just taking what he wants."

"Or breaking into a meat delivery truck."

Tara agreed, but then caught his meaning. "The robbery behind Dalton's."

Ran stood to see if Tara needed more coffee before refreshing his own. "A delivery truck was robbed earlier today. Mostly frozen chicken and beef. The doors were nearly torn off," he reflected.

"That kind of strength would not be surprising."

Ran went on, " I know we said you first, but I need to tell you about the murder today. This just seems to be the right time."

"While you were in the shower, I checked in at the office to relay my meeting in the morning. They mentioned the arrival of a body from the Sherwood Lake area. Similar to Melton and Stanton."

"Almost similar. We had an eyewitness."

Tara sat up as Ran returned to his seat. "To the murder?"

"No. Apparently he saw the aftermath, but I'm pretty sure he saw what you have been describing today, Ran said. "A man of incredible size. A Goliath. Our witness was nearly in shock, and he hadn't even seen the body of the victim. Turns out the body is that of a resident of the area, just a street over from the field where he was found. When I spoke with Lieutenant Sartin he updated me on the details. One George Stanhope, thirty-five, father of three. Must have gone out on his back porch in the middle of the night to smoke a cigarette before returning to bed. His widow said he often did that when he couldn't sleep, and she refused to let him smoke in the house with the kids."

Tara could see how personal Ran was taking this, maybe because of the fatherless children. His compassion was one of his likable traits, and she both pitied and related to him for his empathy. A genuine care for others was what made their jobs worthwhile.

"Later in the morning, probably right after I left the scene, she went outside to look for him after walking through the house calling his name. He was a banker and usually read the paper and wrestled the kids before going into work at nine. After seeing that his car was still in the garage, she stepped out the back door and was greeted with splashes of red all over the concrete porch and lawn furniture. Farther out into the grass she saw pieces of something shining in the sun, and at first she thought it was an animal, something dead that had been dragged onto their property by a night predator. Foxes are pretty common in the area, but she couldn't be sure. It was the blood that scared her, and since her husband had not followed his normal morning routine, she got concerned and called 911. Since county units were still in the area, their response time was instantaneous. Come to find out the man with whom she had shared a life for ten years had been gutted just outside their bedroom window next to a trampoline that their children played on.

"The kill sight was a hundred yards from the encounter with the witness, and he was seen at dawn, *knew* he was seen, and just stood there in defiance. I don't know, Tara. It's as if he wanted somebody to know he did it."

"He's marking."

"What?"

"Marking. His territory. Most animals use scent glands or urine to let others know they are claiming an area, but he is being much more *human* about it."

"How do you figure that?"

Tara explained, "Consider your history. The Romans lined the roads of their empire with the crucified bodies of their enemies, a warning to others to fear them and their empirical machine. Many primitive cultures mark their perimeters with symbols of power and ownership. Remember, Ran, this thing was human, what we consider human, so it will continue to draw from that biological past regardless of the changes that it has undergone. We must always keep in mind that though it acts like an animal, it will demonstrate human response in some situations."

"Daniels said it smiled."

Ran recalled the expression on the witness's face, vacant and confused. "The witness, Mr. Daniels. He said the thing looked at him and smiled."

"A perfect example of the human equation. He would have beaten his chest if he were a gorilla, howled if he were a wolf. It all makes sense."

Ran looked out his living window as the sun started to make its descent to the rushing horizon. Out there, a man-beast had staked his claim to a large piece of property of which Auburn was included. He was one man with a handful of untested deputies. The odds were definitely stacked against him.

"The variations in hydrogen and oxygen isotopes in his hair were inconsistent with the drinking water in northeast Kansas, but the low levels of fluoride and chlorine suggested his fluid intake was coming from an untreated source, like a stream or river," Tara said.

"Or lake."

"Any natural water source. We have known for years that the hair holds keys to water consumption and that a person's normal location can be pinpointed anywhere in the United States. By the time he killed Stanton, he was learning to live off the land."

Tara now stood with an unexplainable excitement. "Everything that has happened, for all these years, all the deaths and baffling crime scenes, the lack of repeatable toxicologies and fingerprinting, it has all been the preparation of his other self to emerge, permanently, and survive among us. It knew all along what it was to be, and his original self only served as a mechanism to support it until it was ready for the complete transfer. It had years of readiness and an entire human history of foundation to build on."

She spoke dreamlike. "And now it is here, Ran. It is here and it has chosen its home."

"Is there anything else useful in your data, anything that might help me see where this trail started?" Ran appealed, and he walked over and took her shoulders in his hands. "Tara, I still don't know where to begin."

"There are more chemical components. I found high levels of melatonin, the hormone that regulates sleep and aging. I don't believe he hibernates, but he apparently requires or did require a great amount of sleep. Makes sense with a metabolism as high as his. His skin cells lacked normal amounts of melanin for an average Caucasian male, which can mean one of two things: he is either albino, something I seriously doubt, or he stays out of the sun. Nocturnal. I wasn't surprised to discover dangerously low levels of serotonin and monoamine oxidase. The first is a neurochemical that controls impulsive behavior and aggression. The second is an enzyme that regulates antisocial behavior. They were both at unproductive measures, but I was unable to determine whether these amounts were depleted through the metamorphosis or already existed. It may help lead to records of a history of sociopathic behavior in the original self, but I can't be sure of its origin. The rest is really just supposition which the geographic profiler will probably address."

She walked away and collapsed exhausted on the couch. "I wish there was more, Ran. I really do."

He joined her and spoke sincerely. "It's enough to get us started, Tara. For tonight I will alert my men to vigilance until we can mobilize Shawnee County tomorrow."

"I hope we have avoided another death, but I just don't know," Tara said.

"It's a step in that direction."

"Yes, but I feel like we, I, could do more."

"Tara, you have done more than anybody could have asked, and I am thankful for it. It's our turn now, mine and the other officers that needed your help. You worked long and hard to give us information that years of investigation failed to uncover, and I promise we will give it the same effort."

Tara sighed, "If Sartin accepts my story."

"He will. He has to, for everyone's sake."

She stretched her lithe body and gathered her knees in a fetal pose. "How about holding me before you take me home? I could use the sheriff's strong arms right about now," she said wearily.

"At your service, ma'am," he said as he embraced her. "At your service."

She rested there for a heavenly few minutes until they knew it was time to go.

Chapter 31

The Shawnee County Sheriff's Department was a crowded sea of people when Ran and Tara arrived. When they located Tony Sartin, he explained that a group of officer trainees had descended on the offices for the day, and with the latest murder and an uncharacteristic string of convenience store holdups the previous night, the place would be controlled chaos for most of the day. The lieutenant appeared frustrated and on edge, which did not bode well for the two of them when they finally joined him in his office. After he requested that all his calls be held for the next hour and made sure his guests were comfortable, Sartin sat down across from them behind his large metal desk and stared over it gravely.

"Do you two have any idea the position you have put me in?" he started.

Ran shared a concerned look with Tara. "Just hear us out, Tony. That's all we ask."

Sartin remained stern. "I have a criminal investigation division to run here, do you not understand that?" he barked. "That means I have to have the cooperation of the Medical Examiner and local departments. *You.* But instead I am kept out of the loop while a rogue sheriff and his pretty pathologist take it upon themselves to fight crime like a couple of caped crusaders."

"Tony."

"Let me finish," he growled, and Ran thought for the first time that they may not come out of the meeting unscathed.

"You," he pointed at Ran, "I should shut out permanently. No free reign of my department. No assistance beyond what is mandatory. My people at your disposal.

"And you, young lady, are in a world of trouble."

He spoke frankly in deference to her gender, but the fire still burned in his expression. "I have heard a lot of good things about you since you showed up, quite the training history. Are you telling me in all that time you failed to learn the proper procedures involving the dispensation of information? Sheriff Price had no authority in the Stanton matter; it was completely out of his jurisdiction and totally in mine. Any details that he receives are through my release. *Mine.* You have seriously undermined me and this department, and I can't begin to tell you how this will make me look with my captain. If I can't control the actions of the two of you, how can I be trusted to operate an entire division? Damn your self-interests," and he pounded his fist on the fragile desk in anger. "Damn it."

He pushed back into his chair with a finality that spoke volumes. Tara was frozen, her job in serious jeopardy. Ran took advantage of the break in Sartin's speech and leaned in.

"Tony, I think I speak for the both of us when I say we know we were way out of line on this and we apologize."

"It's too late for apologies, Ran. You know, I thought we were friends."

Ran spoke honestly. "We are, and I know my actions don't support that, but I felt like I had a valid reason to keep you in the dark."

Sartin was shaking his head. "Hear me out, please. You wouldn't have called us here if you didn't want to get an explanation. You know me well enough to know that this wasn't some wild goose chase I went on, and until the preliminary report on Stanton's autopsy, what we discussed was investigative hypothesis only. I hadn't withheld anything from you, and Dr. Phillips was only helping me understand the possibility that a string of cases, some that she had encountered during her residency, could be linked. Please, just hear us out and then tell me you wouldn't have kept this to yourself until you were absolutely sure.

"You've been an investigator almost as long as I have, Tony. You know from experience that sometimes you feel a certain way about a case, and you chase down leads on your own time to see where they lead you, to see if they have legs to stand on because you don't want to look like a fool. All the while the need to solve the case is pushing you, keeping you awake at night. The victims are screaming your name, and sometimes you are willing to do whatever it takes to stop the voices.

"Yes, we are guilty of procedural mistakes, and you have every right to be angry, and neither of us would hold it against you to bring us down, but listen first, and see if all the time and risks we took were not for the right reasons. We never thought we could finish this alone, and now that we have solid evidence in support of our hunch, it's time that you consider it and determine whether Shawnee County is ready to go in our direction."

Ran's words rang with a deep passion, and the long pause prior to Sartin's response gave the impression that they had struck a nerve and earned them an opportunity to present their findings. The lieutenant appeared reluctant, almost unwilling to comply with their request. He shook his head in a show of denial, and Tara's heart sank.

"I can't believe I'm doing this, but all right, let's see what you've got."

Ran relaxed slightly. They still had some work to do. Sartin saw the hope in his friend's face. "But if I'm not convinced that what you have found is worthy of the actions you have taken to undermine this office and my authority, I will proceed with the proper disciplinary measures, are we clear on that?"

He looked at both of them for understanding. Tara nodded meekly; Ran sat up in anticipation of his chance at redemption. "Whatever you say, Tony, but believe me, it won't be necessary."

"I hope not, Ran. I really do."

For the next three hours, Ran and Tara presented their case, and aside from a few phone calls and knocks at the office door, Sartin provided them what seemed to be his full attention. As was his way in Ran's experience, the lieutenant was an attentive audience, jotting down his thoughts on a legal pad instead of halting the flow of a speaker's words with misdirecting comments and abrupt questions. Though he possessed many of the same rational, by-the-book beliefs that had proven obstacles in Ran's acceptance, Sartin appeared receptive but maintained a poker face for the majority of the lecture.

Tara lost her early nervousness, and because it was really the second time she had given the lecture, her words and the general flow of the ideas were more coherent and logical than Ran had remembered them. Maybe it was because he had been through it before, but the science and its terminology were more listener-friendly, and Ran was able to put an investigative spin on the facts in support of the doctor's statements. He thought their combined efforts, unpracticed and on display in the less than hospitable venue, showed their shared fervor. In the end, to their surprise, Sartin appeared genuinely willing to entertain their hypothesis. Whatever the reason, either the forensic anomalies or the evidence he had witnessed himself in the Shawnee County killings, the head of the Criminal Investigation Division was quite possibly moving to join their team. When they had finished, he had only a few final questions before tipping his hand, and he directed the first of those to Tara.

"The fingerprinting technique you used—the use of X-ray and infrared to analyze chemical residue—why have I never heard of it before, and why wasn't it used in the previous cases?" Sartin began.

"It's fairly new, Lieutenant, at least in the public sector, and the expense is so great right now that very few state agencies are employing it, relying on standard fingerprinting that has been accepted for years," Tara said. "It started with some scientists at Los Alamos under military contract, as all things seem to, and has had some practical use in Scotland Yard."

She seemed to blush slightly. "I'm kind of a forensics nerd--reading all the latest materials, trying new methods of evidentiary detection when it's practical. When you look at these cases and evaluate the fingerprinting that took place, it's obvious to me that traditional contrast enhancement with powder and liquids were erasing valuable forensic clues. I made a few calls, got the right equipment, and intact prints with chemical markers were the result. Simple really."

"Yeah, simple," Sartin said, and he looked back to his notes.

"Is there any precedence to support this?" he asked. "I mean, does science have any proof that an organism can so rapidly mutate? I know creatures change—caterpillars become moths and butterflies—but that is part of their DNA structure, isn't it, not a mutation? But for a human to change at such drastic levels, and so quickly? It's so unreasonable."

Tara saw where he was going. Like Ran, he was rational and stood on the ground of logic. Blindfolded as he was, he would be willing to take a precarious step forward if he could be assured his foot would touch solid ground. He needed a little scientific faith.

"I want to be careful when I say that a complex organism has evolved within its lifetime, because we know that it takes multiple generations for a genetic change to become evident. Let's start with the understanding that mutations are necessary for diversity and evolution. Without them, the only life on earth would be the same as it was millions of years ago-- single-celled organisms. It is through eons of reproduction and natural selection that the human species has arrived where it is today.

"If a mutation helps an organism survive, it is considered beneficial and it will most likely reoccur in future generations. But like the name suggests, most mutations are detrimental to an organism. Physical abnormalities and hereditary diseases are the results of genetic mutation, and these have survived in the gene pool for thousands of years. It's almost like nature is telling us, 'Sure, go ahead and get smarter and stronger. Learn to adapt to your environment, but always be ready to pay the price.' Some of us are obligated to suffer for man's advancement, and it is as if we were being reminded of our mortality. 'Move forward, but remember that life is fragile.'"

Ran marveled at Tara's way with words.

"Getting back to your question," she said to Sartin, "no, we have no evidence that both rapid and advanced genetic metamorphosis has ever occurred in a higher level organism, unless you consider environmental mutagens, like radiation, or naturally-occurring ones such as viruses, but even these do not affect the change that we have seen with our man. These cause damage and disease in the organism's lifetime, but could not account for the physical and chemical aberrations that our evidence has demonstrated. Mutations are heritable for the most part. The genetic materials for mutation are passed to the offspring where they can either reveal themselves or lie dormant until successive generations to emerge.

"What we do have proof of, and what I think you need to hear, is what is called spontaneous mutation—mutations that occur as a natural process within the cell and are not induced with some outside agent, as in the example of mutagens. These mutations are point specific and a good example of one is a DNA replication error. Due to chemical misplacement, a DNA strand can sometimes fail to replicate properly, so we know mutation can be rapid. The question is: Can it directly affect the organism and not await reproduction to make itself evident?

"Are you with me so far?"

Sartin looked impressed. "So far. I am interested in how you are now going to make the leap to host DNA transmogrification," he said to the surprise of his two guests.

Ran piped up, "You're interested in what?"

Tara smiled, "I believe the lieutenant has been playing dumb. If you knew where I was going with this, why didn't you just ask me how I thought the mutation could be occurring?"

"I wanted to see just how far you have thought this through," admitted Sartin. "Forgive me. Pre-med. Considered being a forensic pathologist at one time myself, but the lure of law enforcement never quite got out of my system, so I reinvented my career direction and here I am—in homicide. The love for the science of it, though, is something I brought with me."

"You never told me about that," Ran said.

"You never asked, and you probably wouldn't have wanted to listen either," Sartin smiled. "It is always police work with you."

Ran was happy to see his good friend had softened significantly, but he didn't take for granted that they had sold him.

"Dr. Sartin. I like it."

"Shut up," and then to Tara, "but you may continue. The previous cases, the autopsies and lab results. They all give ample support to your claim, and I am impressed with the direction you have taken on this. I understand your theory that a dormant gene has become dominant, but the chemistry of it escapes me. Are you suggesting he is new man?"

Tara said, "Not a new man. A reinvented one really. By not abandoning the basic premise that his genetic code was in place at birth and that all organisms are constantly in a state of genetic repair, it is not farfetched to make the jump to the idea that a recessed primitive gene, in response to some physical or psychological stimulus, replaced a weakening, inferior gene, and by doing so caused vast cellular reconstruction, affecting tissues and entire organ systems. Chemical changes cannot be considered voluntary, so it follows that the process was a biological response to either internal or external factors that moved the organism to redefine its existence. Factor in the primitive, barbaric nature of the resulting specimen, and it follows that the design has its roots in man's earliest forms, possibly as far back as life's emergence. I realize it is the subject of folklore, but the pieces are all in place. We are not talking about evolution in the general sense. My assertion is that the organism, the man, has devolved, reverted to a simple state of animal existence where only the most primal of behaviors and needs are revealed. He eats, he sleeps, and something I haven't shared with Ran— he seeks dominion. A place to call his own. I think that place is here."

"Do you mean the delivery truck?" asked Ran. "How does that show he is setting up housekeeping?"

"That, and the Sherwood murder," said Tara.

"Delivery truck? Wait a minute. You're getting ahead of me. What does that have to do with all this? said Sartin.

Ran took a few minutes to describe the robbery behind Dalton's Restaurant while Tara in turn validated her advancing theory. Sartin looked intrigued.

"There is every indication that the mutation is complete. Every killing shows a heightened destructiveness, and the circle is closing on their locations. The increased biting, clawing, and tearing, the evisceration of the internal organs, and the first eyewitness sighting. It all points to growing aggression and territorial instinct. He is exhibiting all the characteristics of a predatory animal."

"But why here, and why all the killing?" asked Ran. Sartin looked to

Tara with equal question in his expression.

"That is the one thing I haven't been able to nail down," said Tara with an almost defeated look in her soft face. She had regained the confidence that had led them this far within the first ten minutes of her oratory, and for the first time since pleading her case to Sartin, she balked with doubt.

"Alpha male performance was my first guess, but that is always in conjunction with gender roles and a desire to control the female population of the herd, but we have seen no indication of sexual motivation. We know that within the animal kingdom males will fight for the privilege of reproduction. In accordance with natural selection, it ensures that the next generation will be the best of the best. There is no reason to believe it is for procreation," Tara conjectured.

"Unless killing is what turns him on," offered Ran.

"Possibly," Sartin said, becoming an active theorist for the first time, a happening not lost on Ran or Tara, "but animals don't kill for sex unless there is a female to win. If we continue with the premise that he has regressed to pure animal instinct, we need to keep him there. How about a simple territorial response to perceived threats?"

Tara was obviously thoroughly enjoying the exchange with Sartin at that moment, something Ran had been unable to provide with his limited knowledge. He was glad to see her ideas being given a learned credence.

"I considered that, but why in stealth mode? Wouldn't he benefit from a powerful display of force and strength, strutting around and daring a challenge? No, it's something more…personal I think?"

Ran said, "Personal? Sounds human to me."

"Exactly," Tara said. "Ran, you mentioned that your eyewitness saw this thing smile, right? A clearly human act. What about this: if we work off the belief that he spent more years, formative ones, as a normal man than he has as this monster he has become, I think it is fair to assume that some of his human qualities remain, suppressed but retrievable should they come in handy. Wrecking a meat truck for dinner, for example."

"OK, so let's go with that. Say it was a familiarity with human habitations that led him to the truck and not animal qualities, like an increased sense of smell. What human factor would justify the killings?" Sartin asked for he and the sheriff.

Tara said, "Why do people kill? You guys are the authorities there."

"Greed, jealousy, hatred," said Ran.

"Lust," added Sartin.

"I think we can dismiss greed and lust," said Tara, "and jealousy implies that he covets. I have seen nothing in the records to indicate he gains something from the deaths, unless he is collecting body parts, which just doesn't fit the mold for the DNA reconstruction. The stimulus has to be so psychologically crippling that it affects him at the very core of his being—the genetic level."

"I like anger. Anger is good," said Ran, though he felt his contributions were becoming less helpful.

Sartin said, "Yes, and anger can be that agent, but something made him angry, so much so that he is methodically destroying at a serial pace, and enough to cause a mutation that renders him bigger and stronger, thereby more capable than ever to crush his victims. We are missing something here."

The three of them sat in silence momentarily. Nothing seemed to fit.

"What emotion is unique to humans that causes an anger and rage of this magnitude?

It was good to have their secret out, and Ran and Tara could see that Tony Sartin had accepted their speculation. For whatever reason, his love of medical science, his friendship with Ran, an appreciation for the investigative efforts they had put forth, or simply because every state and federal agency from here to the Atlantic seaboard had come up empty, Shawnee County's criminal investigations head was on board. Once again, Ran had Tara to thank for her commitment to their work.

"What if it is altruism?" Tara said with a lowering of her voice.

Ran hated to show his ignorance since he had already demonstrated a scientific deficiency over the last few weeks, but he needed to know and figured he would just go ahead and fail the entire report card.

"Altruism?"

"Revenge," said Sartin. "Interesting."

"Revenge," said Tara at almost the same time.

"It would answer the need for a catalyst to trigger the genetic recoding," said Sartin.

For Ran it didn't fit, and he needed explanation. "Excuse me. Revenge?" he interjected. "I feel like I just got dumped on the side of the road and you two sped away. Why would he be seeking revenge across half the country, only to settle on northeast Kansas to claim his kingdom? Don't you usually take revenge on people you know?"

Tara and Sartin were, as Ran had observed, leaving him behind, though it was purely unintentional. It was amazing how quickly Sartin had adopted the theory as his own, and now he was sharing postulates and supposition. If Ran had not been so relieved that his friend was a teammate, he might have been a hair jealous yet again.

"It is clearly evident that he has been stalking his prey for all these years. Consider all the case files," said Tara. "Victims are attacked in isolated situations, removed from the scene for further destruction, and then discarded in remote areas. We know predatory animals take their kills to places where they won't be bothered."

Ran had suddenly reverted to doubtful mode. Whether it was this morning's second look or his investigative side refusing to consider the farfetched, he was challenging the very assumptions he had come to get Sartin to consider.

"Yes, but that is for a quiet dinner. You said the computer showed no signs that he was actually eating them—only biting."

Sartin fielded this one. "A tiger stalks, attacks, drags its kill to a private spot, and eats its fill. The motivation is hunger. The animal meets its needs with instinctual, violent, and productive results. The idea that our man is driven not by hunger but by some deep, primitive human emotion, like revenge, fits the theory perfectly."

Tara nodded her agreement while Ran still appeared confused.

"Look, Ran, you guys came in here to tell me a fanciful tale of a mutating killer that has been hunting this country's residents for years in hopes that I would buy into your theory and not subject you to legal action. You took a huge chance given the circumstances, and though I was skeptical at first, I gave it a chance and can see in its merits. The science is the selling point, and you have Dr. Phillips here to thank for that."

He gestured to Tara and repositioned himself behind his desk. "God knows this stuff wouldn't have come from your stubborn head," he smiled. "And with all this, and the lengths you have gone to entertain the possibilities, you are challenging the idea that he is fulfilling a vengeful wrath that was instilled within him years ago. You accept that he is the Wolf Man, but you can't allow for him to be settling an old score."

"Ran stuttered, "Well, I just don't see…"

"Beyond your nose sometimes," Sartin finished for him. "I'm not saying that everything I've heard today is written in stone. The uniqueness of the biology is a problem. What I am sold on though is that a crazed sociopath, fashioned from environmental and hereditary contributors, has ravaged the countryside as a serial killer while playing the part of Average Joe all the while. He has been able to remain undetected due to a primal behavior that apparently has manifested itself in measurable, physical alterations. Call it revenge. Call it a sick, twisted aphrodisiac. Either way, he is killing, and he has come here to roost.

"Which brings me to my next question, Sheriff. How do you propose we find him?"

They spent their remaining time outlining a preliminary plan, acknowledging the fact that this was to be a game of hide-and-seek, with Shawnee County as their playground and a crazed Goliath as their objective.

Sartin was the source of manpower, so he would have to convince his superiors that a large number of county investigators and officers, in conjunction with state patrols, would be required to blanket the area in and around the Sherwood Lake vicinity in search of their suspect and widen it gradually. He felt he could get the assistance they needed for at least a week before a new approach would be demanded.

It was obvious that the biological conclusions they had drawn should remain among them, though they did have an eyewitness description that could be distributed through the departments. If they worked under the assumption that their suspect was either in hiding or leading a normal life in obscurity, they could get cooperating departments to avoid looking for an outsider that was simply coming to the area in search of his victims. They would spin him as a new resident, which, if their theory was right, he had been for over a month.

This would mean tying all three murders together, and the forensics, Tara suggested, would support a serial killer. She would have to give the latest victim a cursory exam to be sure, but her experience in the cases beyond her office and the brief description of the body Sartin provided her told the young pathologist that they clearly had another in the series.

Tara also reminded them that it was highly likely that he was responsible for other killings and that the bodies remained undiscovered while friends and family reported them as missing persons. The high temperatures of northeast Kansas and the large population of night scavengers that accounted for most of the state's animal life could probably guarantee that proof of any further victims was improbable.

Ran believed the geographical profile he was expecting might give them some solid leads, and he promised to forward that information to Sartin upon its arrival.

It all sounded so simple, and Ran voiced his concern over the logistics. The area they were considering to cover was over 550 square miles, with heavy wooded areas throughout, mainly along rivers and creeks, and large patches of prairie land with little to no vehicular access. He would be more than a needle in a haystack; he could avoid them indefinitely. He admitted their only hope was a chance sighting or, and he paused for a moment, another killing that might narrow their boundaries. If Tara was right and he was acting with a territorial objective while satisfying his emotional thirst, they might be able to reduce their search area considerably if they could chart his movement, but for now, the entire county was viable.

"We have a fair idea what we are looking for," Sartin concluded. "The key will be stopping it once we find it. You've heard the expression *cornered animal* I'm sure? Well, if this thing is what the good doctor and poor Mr. Daniels described, we may be in for a fight."

"I think you can count on it," Tara said gravely. "He's come too far to back down now."

Ran let out a deep breath.

Chapter 32

With Tara back at the medical examiner's office determining whether the body of George Stanhope was a legitimate candidate for the serial killer argument that Sartin was preparing to pitch to the county sheriff, Ran gathered his deputies for a quick late afternoon meeting before dispersing them throughout Auburn. His contribution to the search would be miniscule since he had only three men at his disposal, and two of those were part-timers whom he had overused the last few days, a situation begging for complaint from the mayor. Combined with the small area that they could claim as legal jurisdiction, the Auburn Sheriff's Department would be of little help. They could protect their own, but the real investigation needed to extend far beyond their boundary, and Ran cursed the small town authority that he had adopted years previous. Sartin would have undoubtedly granted Ran and his men greater access to areas outside the city, but Ran was hesitant to make the request, not because he feared he would be in the way but rather he felt a strong commitment to the people he lived among. He could never forgive himself if something happened in Auburn while he was stretching his boundaries and doing so with just enough men to give proper protection to those that warranted their service. *No*, he reasoned, *he had to guard the home front and trust that his fellow officers, especially Tony Sartin, could do the jobs he knew they were competent to perform.*

Once again, he felt his contributions were insufficient.

The expectant faces that hung across his desk completed Ran's feelings of helplessness. They bore the expressions of inexperienced boys who were excited about the prospects of confronting danger without the slightest idea of what awaited them. The three were as far from battle ready as they could be, and Ran was getting ready to cast them on the waters to locate a catch that was more terrifying and lethal than any of their worst nightmares. He couldn't help but conclude they were sheep being sent to the slaughter and that the Lilliputian dimensions of their town was the one thing working in their favor. Safety was their duty, but who would protect them? Ran had no other options.

After he had sent them on their individual assignments, putting more emphasis on the nighttime hours since the killings had seemingly been confined to darkness, Ran planned his own midnight surveillance. A familiar face recently to members of Sartin's staff, the sheriff believed he could scout the areas in and around Sherwood Lake without reproach for being outside his jurisdiction. It was the most recent kill site, and the terrain and dense wooded areas provided the perfect conditions for a man wanting to hide out. If Tara's conclusions were genuine, and there was every reason to believe they were, the killer had now left behind his conforming lifestyle, most likely a home in any of the countless neighborhoods that dotted the eastern upper quarter of the state, and was living as a wild animal as his ancestors had done millions of years ago. At least it was a starting point, and of all the things they believed they did know, his origins and most recent living quarters among them remained a mystery.

As if on cue, Polly transferred two successive calls to his office that would turn the situation to their advantage. The first was from Tom Avery, and Ran realized he had completely forgotten the profiler's report. Since the realization that the suspect had most likely abandoned most of his human existence, the geographic profile had seemed of secondary importance and of little help. But with still more questions than answers, nothing could be discarded.

"Tom, how's my favorite Canadian?'

"I'm probably the only person in Canada you know, so I'm not sure how to take that."

Ran said, "You are, but I still meant what I said. Have you had any luck figuring out where my boy takes his mail?"

"Well, I am going to forward you the jeopardy surface map, but I can tell you with confidence where he isn't," Avery said. "I didn't have the chance to follow the normal operational procedure, but we knew that going in."

"Don't beat yourself down, Tom. I'll still consider you the best around even if you fell short."

"Falling short is not part of my vocabulary. I got more for you than a month's worth of investigation could have revealed, and all from my Canadian outpost. How's that for delivery?"

"It's why I turned to you," said Ran.

Avery brought to the table years of profiling experience and a background in crime scene investigation. The procedure he had been denied involved an inspection of the crime scene or scenes and lengthy meetings with lead investigators. He had only been given the paperwork that constituted a mere third of the profiler's determining processes. It was a testament to his skills that he had gotten anywhere at all, but a summary of local crime statistics, demographic data, and a study of street, zoning, and rapid transit maps had provided enough information for Avery to draw an informed conclusion. Ran was sure the profiler's pride and reputation were factors in his efforts and guarantees that the findings were accurate.

"The map will reiterate what I tell you, but basically you can expect your boy to be living in seclusion, a place off the beaten path. He is a very private person. I'm sure you figured that from his attention to removal of the bodies from visible areas to more intimate settings."

Ran agreed, "Makes sense."

"If he works in the public sector, which is highly improbable, look to jobs where he can maintain that insular world, like a machine operator or welder. Little human interaction is the key. My bet is that he is self-employed, even so far as working out of his home, where he can remain aloof. You have to think along the lines of an esoteric lifestyle. It would follow that something involving the Internet or computers in general would give him the sterile environment he needs."

Ran said, "Sterile, as in…?"

"As in free of human contact. His killing methods reek of a man who loathes society and people specifically."

"A real social butterfly, huh?"

Avery acted like he missed the joke. He was in his zone, and his confidence in himself and his techniques made everything superficial in comparison. "All of this is reinforced by his nomadic tendencies. What he does for a living must be feasible in the confines of his terminal relocations. Self-employment and the ease of computer access would allow for the constant movement. I can't see him in any other activity because they would require human interaction, which he undoubtedly avoids like the plague, unless, that is, he has the itch to kill."

"It all makes perfect sense," Ran said.

"Of course it does," Avery remarked. "What else did you expect?"

Ran admired people that oozed with confidence to the point of arrogance. As long as the bragging pride was justified, he saw no reason why someone shouldn't revel in his or her talents.

"As you will see from the jeopardy surface, and I spent more time with his present residence than those previous, he is most likely within a ten to twenty-mile drive of grocery stores and retail locations. If he could get food or business supplies delivered to his home without human contact, even these would not need to be nearby, but I am sure he avoids bringing people to his home when possible. Stands to reason he has a post office box as well."

"Fantastic, Tom. You came through as always," said Ran.

"Oh, and one more thing, check with relocation services and realty companies that specialize in finding homes for businessmen. Homes to buy. Wouldn't want an owner or leasing agent making unwanted visits. I would imagine he has a place set up ahead of time and transacts all his needs over computer. Damn things are making it so that we may never have to converse again face-to-face."

Ran looked up from the conversation and saw Polly waving at him, her index and middle fingers splayed to signal that he had another call on line two. "Tom, I really appreciate this as always, and I will watch for the maps, but I have another call coming in. I hate to break this off so quickly, but we have a real situation here. Thanks, really."

"Understood, and, hey, thanks for the opportunity. Real challenge, this one. First serial killer I have profiled that removed so much of the human element from his existence."

"You have no idea."

Ran depressed the button at the receiver's cradle and answered the other call. It was Tony Sartin. It seemed too early for an approval from the county's sheriff since the request called for a large expenditure of funds for additional man hours. There were political considerations, especially in law enforcement, and for all the passion he had for his profession, Ran hated that stumbling block above all else. Forget the low pay, long hours, and lack of public support, he could deal with that and accepted it as part of the job when he had come on the force decades ago. What he would never understand was why they had to jump through hoops and kiss the appropriate backsides to protect and serve the public. It just didn't make sense.

"Ran, glad I caught you. There is a situation up in Jackson County that may interest us."

"Jackson County? Another murder?"

Sartin said, "No, thank God. It just came in over the state system. I have been monitoring it since the Stanton murder in case our boy was crossing county lines. It may be something or nothing at all."

The sheriff was impressed with the Shawnee lieutenant's tenacity but at the same time not surprised that he had gone above and beyond his duties as head of his division. Checking state and federal crime reports was a job for rookies, and in the chain of command, high-ranking officers regularly delegated tasks of a tedious nature, but Sartin, like Ran, had never forsaken his love for honest police work.

"Just a minute. What about the county sweep? Did you already get a go-ahead on that?" redirected Ran.

Sartin said, "I made my pitch, and I feel pretty good about our chances. The resources we have here are far from stretched thin, so it's not a matter of availability as it is marketability."

Ran knew what his friend was implying, and he didn't need further explanation. Sartin would wait for county officials to determine the cost-effectiveness of such a manhunt in relation to public perception and media coverage. It wasn't so much whether the plan could be successful but how the sheriff's department would look in the process. If it looked like the county was sending its white knights to defend the castle walls and not throwing tax dollars at another wasteful program, they would get the green light.

"Of course, the medical examiner's opinion will help, and I guess Maxwell won't be back until tomorrow," added Sartin.

Ran said, "I can promise you, Tara will be in his office first thing to make her appeal. You know, she can be very persuasive."

"No argument here."

Tara had made a solid impression on Sartin, which seemed to be standard for her.

"So what's up in Jackson County?"

Sartin explained, "I noticed on the Monday report that there was a case of property damage at a home in Hoyt. Are you familiar with the area?"

"Just by name," Ran said. "I can't say that I have ever been through there. Small town, right?"

"Maybe 500 folks. I called the county undersheriff, Jeff Harvey. We worked patrol together in Denison before he got a sergeant's position in Jackson. He gave me some interesting details on the case and agreed to meet with us this evening at the location."

"Well what makes you think it is tied to our cases?" Ran asked. "And how did you sell it?"

"Word travels fast on the plains of Kansas, good buddy. He already knew the particulars about the murders here and the Leavenworth disappearance, so I told him we were making inquiries regarding any abandoned dwellings that might suggest violence or unexplainable conditions. This one just seemed to fit."

Ran was now interested. "What did the preliminary report indicate?"

"The house is on a lonely stretch of road just off 75," said Sartin. "A water meter reader put in the call. Noticed the front door was lying in pieces in the front yard and a truck sitting in the driveway. No one answered his calls from the porch, so he reported it immediately.

"Two Jackson County uniformed deputies responded and found some wild stuff inside. Nothing Charles Manson, but just out of place for a country home surrounded by Kansas wheat fields."

Ran asked, "Sounds like a typical B and E. You guys get that a lot in the rural settings where there is a house every quarter mile. What caught your attention on this one?"

"It was a combination of things, and after talking to Jeff, it fit that much more. Even though there was very little furniture, there were thousands of dollars of technical equipment that you would think would be taken if it were a robbery."

"Technical equipment?" Ran said, and his heart leapt as he recalled his previous conversation with Tom Avery.

"Computers. Monitors, hard drives, all the latest stuff, and it was set up right in the living room. No couch, no dining area, nothing."

Ran interjected, but only as a devil's advocate, "Still, some things could have been taken."

"Agreed, but why not take the money items? And the refrigerator...stocked full of meat. Top to bottom. Nothing but packaged meats."

"That would definitely tie into our man."

Sartin continued, "I thought you'd like that, and how about this one? Right in the middle of the wood floor—a huge indention, like a meteor crashed through the roof. No other damage except for a few random holes in the wall, about the size of a large fist."

Ran liked the possibilities of this being a starting point in their search. When they had separated at lunchtime, the one thing they had not agreed upon was where to begin. An umbrella approach to the whole area was the only option since the entire county had been the subject of murders, body disposals, and in the case of the delivery truck, occurrences that were likely related to the others. But if this was the house where their serial killer had temporarily settled on his circuitous route through the eastern United States, then they could label it the epicenter from which all investigation could fan. Ran glanced at his detailed map of Shawnee County and its bordering brothers, then thought of the surface map he would be receiving from Avery tomorrow. *Maybe, just maybe,* he thought, *we know where the breadcrumbs start.*

"There were some other things," Sartin said as he pulled Ran back into the discussion, "but the real kicker was the front door."

Ran said, "Yeah, sounds like our delivery truck. Those metal doors looked like they had been through a grinder."

"Right, but there was one thing different about it."

"What?"

"The door was shattered *from the inside out.*"

"Inside out?"

Sartin seemed happy with the results of calling Ran. "I knew that would get you. Hinges. Door frame. Parts of the brick wall surrounding it. Jeff said it looked like a tank fired a round from under the roof. Pretty promising, huh?"

Ran said, "Very. What time are heading up?"

"I told Jeff we would meet him there at 7:30 so that we have a good hour of daylight left. Can you be here in thirty minutes?"

"Definitely, and by the way, I heard from Avery in Canada."

"The profiler? Any help there?" Sartin asked.

"Plenty," Ran acknowledged. "I just got off the phone with him when you called, and you're not going to believe this, but if I didn't know any better, I would swear you just described the type of house he promised would match our boy. It's amazing. Everything down to the computer gear. Is it possible that it's the place?"

Sartin reflected, "After years of no evidence, I think it was time law enforcement finally got a little taste. I can't believe that hours ago I was ready to throw the two of you to the dogs, and now here I am working with you on crimes that have gone cold for years, *and* we have some footing."

"It's the nature of the profession, Tony. It's what I love about it," said Ran. "A surprise at every corner."

For Ran it was more than that, though, the thing that drew him out of bed every day to don a policeman's uniform and fight the never-ending battle. He didn't live for the successes or the job-well-done satisfaction that many looked for. It was simple really: He needed closure, for himself and the victims. Every beginning required an end, and each ending welcomed a new start. He could never rest until he had helped close the tragic chapters that affected people's lives, chapters that became a part of his personal story as well. Removing the bookmarks and reaching the back cover was his reward, and his life's bookshelf was full of completions. That was what drove him.

He left a message on Tara's home phone, informed the evening dispatcher of his schedule, and left Auburn for Topeka, his hopes mounting in anticipation of the capture and his unspoken fear of what they were truly dealing with increasing in unison.

Chapter 33

Not long after Ran Price and Tony Sartin had left the vacated house in Hoyt and concluded it was worthy of lab teams and computer forensics for the following morning, Jason Bradley was walking back home from an unsuccessful night of fishing, his pole and small tackle box swaying rhythmically in each hand. An Auburn resident for all of his thirty-two years, Bradley lived off Southwest 85th on the northwest end of town and regularly traversed the 500-foot distance from his farmhouse to a large pond where he attempted a moment of escape from his less-than-appealing life. The body of water, the property of an abiding neighbor and mainly used for livestock, was a good source of average-sized catfish if the time was right. It was on the far side of two tree lines separated by a short open field, and it was in this cropped pasture that he crossed, headed toward the second stand of trees that created a wall of dark growth at the back of his place.

Bradley was the quintessential tough-luck guy. Divorced, friendless, and unemployed, he barely managed to drag himself out of bed everyday to repeat a routine he embraced with a strong self-pity. He was a prisoner of lost hope, the lone inhabitant of a concrete tomb of endless failures and forgotten dreams where he wasted away in a downward spiral of depression. The self-imposed damnation that greeted him each morning was a combination of fate and lethargy—when things went bad, and he had had more than his fair share of rough times, he consistently failed to respond with anything remotely resembling determination. Instead of picking himself up and rolling the dice for better results, he stumbled away beaten and forlorn; the desire to turn things around was never in him.

His wife of six years, a high school recluse like himself, awakened one day to the realization that there was more to life than nursing a man's ego and left with his children for Wichita and a fresh start. She had pleaded with him to make some changes, if not for her then for the twin girls, but he had answered her appeals with only a blank stare. Her requests soon became demands, and within a few months she had gathered her few belongings and the blue-eyed babies and fled south, the tears of regret streaming down her face as she made one final attempt to pull her sinking husband from his wakeful coma.

From the front door, she looked at him sullen and unresponsive across the room. "Jason, we're leaving now," she said with swollen eyes.

The kitchen clock marked the passing seconds with soft clicks that interrupted the silence.

"Jason, for God's sake, say something," she screamed, a show of emotion unseen in her until recently.

He looked up at her slowly with a face that lacked animation, but nothing escaped his lips.

She gathered in a deep, halting breath, hurting for herself and the man she had once loved. The shell that sat in stagnation before her was only an illusion of that man, a carbon copy on the outside but hollow and empty within. She couldn't follow him down his destructive path, wouldn't drag the children along to witness the decay of their father, and hadn't been able to bring him back.

"You..." she said shaking. "You never gave yourself a chance...or us."

The door had closed softly behind her, and when he could no longer hear the hum of the car engine that carried the only family he had left away, a single tear fell on the front of his shirt, the last drop of feeling left in him.

That had been five years previous, and in the interim he had turned away from concerned friends and recently lost his job due to a poor attendance record. A monthly visit to the bank to deposit an unemployment check and an occasional trip to the grocery store were the only things that drew him out of the house, that and his evening fishing excursions.

The littered house had been his parents, bought and paid for prior to their deaths, and they had left him a small inheritance that was near depletion and would soon be gone. Becky was still expecting child support, and an attorney had started calling him constantly to remind him of his obligation. Something had to give, and if history was any indication, it was not going to be Jason Bradley. He had stepped over the edge of caring.

A bright summer moon cast its nocturnal light on the field and revealed the enclosed area with a blanket of hazy luminance. Bradley could have made the trip back to his house blindfolded and was familiar with every rut and rise that occupied his direction. He visited the pond not for the sport of fishing, sometimes he never got his line wet, but for the simple act of communing with something other than his television, which he mindlessly stared at most of his unproductive days. Regardless of his detachment from all things social, he still found the urge to occasionally connect with nature, not because he found it peaceful or refreshing as most people, but for the reminder that there still remained something free of the destruction he associated with human intervention. Everything in his life had crumpled; his communion with the still waters that echoed with the calls of frogs and insects was a brief respite. Without it as an outlet, he most surely would have failed to perform the most elementary of life's daily tasks and sunk into a state of apathetic oblivion.

The aging trees that marked the shared property line loomed majestically before him as he approached, their crooked branches meshed in a show of mutual support as their trunks anchored a wall of defiance. Though there appeared to be no accessible entrance into the stand, Bradley confidently moved to a slim gap in the otherwise solid structure and disappeared into its depths. The line was no more than twenty feet in width at its thickest, but to the casual observer it would have seemed that the hiker might never emerge on the other side given its density, but after a few experienced seconds of sharp turns and twists, he surfaced unscathed into his own backyard, the largest part of a square acre of land his parents had maintained for many years. The outline of the white two-story lay dozens of paces ahead, and Bradley continued his return with a slightly elevated state of mind, though seemingly nothing could return him to anything resembling alive.

The blow was swift and devastating, lifting him off his feet and sending him twenty feet parallel to the tree line where he landed with a dull thud and skidded to a pain-filled stop. Disoriented and struggling to recapture the air that had been violently ejected from his collapsed lungs, Bradley lay splayed on his back, the right side of his torso alive with searing agony. His eyes were immersed in pools of burning tears, adding to his confusion. He had been taken completely unaware, and for the first time in years, his heart was beating with emotion he had been either unable or unwilling to provide his desperate Becky so long ago. But what surged through his veins was not compassion or regret but a genuine fear, and after such a lengthy time of walking death, it was surprising that Bradley still had the ability to care about living, that he was concerned at all whether death was fast approaching.

But he had no time to consider his future, to weigh his options and make a choice, because Death was here, now, and in the sky that was quickly becoming clear above him with each rapid blink of his eyes, a figure loomed, large and menacing.

Bradley winced as his ravaged body rebelled against the damage done to it, and the crouching shape that stood over him stayed transfixed. A warm fluid ran from the corner of his mouth as he tried to speak, but the lack of air made the formation of words impossible, and he fought to capture the slightest of breaths, but to know avail. The impact had crushed his ribs, driving shards of bone like projectiles into his delicate lungs and making them of no use. He tried to move his legs and arms but was greeted with a resistance that refused to budge.

He was helpless and racing to unconsciousness, his brain demanding oxygen his body couldn't deliver. A vice-like grip soon closed on his bare neck, and Bradley could feel it tighten with each slowing beat of his fading heart. He had wished for an end to his misery many times previous, lying in bed in a position very similar to the one he was in now, so distraught over the emptiness that filled him but incapable of effecting his own deliverance.

A deliverer had finally been sent, though now that the moment of release was imminent, now that escape was fast approaching, Bradley screamed in his mind for another chance. He wanted a reprieve. He would give life another go, fight off the depression and loneliness and make a change. A little help and he could start over, salvaging what remained and making the most of the days ahead, but he needed that help. He searched the silhouetted frame surrounded by a blanket of stars and tried to discern a face of forgiveness. Surely this person would offer him the opportunity to make things right.

The grip around his throat increased and teetered on a compression that would cast him into a darkness not unlike the black water that had enveloped his fishing bait only minutes ago. His mind fought against the inevitable, and in a final moment, he heard her again, clearly this time.

You never gave yourself a chance...

"*I will, Becky. I promise. I want to try.*"

The spinal column that rushed life-giving blood to his brain, the home to Bradley's thoughts of what could be, collapsed and severed under the incredible force that circled it.

In the pond across the tree lines a small fish flashed on the surface in retreat from a larger predator, escaping to live yet another day.

Chapter 34

Armed with forensic lab results from the Sonny Melton and Mitch Stanton cases and a summary of both the Stanhope autopsy (conveniently performed by Clifford Weyland the afternoon before as a matter of what he called "authority") and reports previously filed as cold cases as far east as the Carolinas and south to Louisiana, Dr. Tara Phillips had marched into the office of a weary Ron Maxwell and outlined her position with such determination that he agreed with her as much for the logic behind the argument as he did for a moment's peace.

With the chief medical examiner's confirmation that they were probably dealing with a serial killer, Tony Sartin was then able to push through his plan for extra patrols throughout the Shawnee County area and a coordinated sweep of what he and Ran thought were ideal locations for their man to hide. The KSBI and KHP were soon enlisted for their help as well, and federal offices in Kansas City were alerted to the real possibility that a suspect was crossing state lines during a multi-year murder spree, a guaranteed way of bringing the full support of all departments into play.

The discoveries at the house in Hoyt and the records search that followed reinforced Tara's conclusions and the experienced summation of profiler Tom Avery. In the end, law enforcement was in agreement that their suspect, now identified as Sebastian Caine, had moved at least a dozen times and over 3000 miles in the course of four years, carrying with him the hardware for a small but trusted remote computer repair service and a lust for blood. With Sheriff Ran Price's lengthy list of potential crime locations, cold case files were re-examined and forensic evidence re-considered. It was suggested that Caine had eluded capture through a combination of intelligence, luck, and poor police and forensic work, making his identity unknown to over twenty-two investigative agencies, but privately, the failure degenerated to childish finger-pointing and placed blame. Based on the many horrific crime scenes and eyewitness testimony, regardless of the reason he was able to practice his murderous ways uninhibited, it was accepted that Caine was a formidable sociopath with crazed intentions who must be respected as an extremely dangerous individual.

All that was left was the matter of finding him, and doing so immediately.

Three more murders had occurred in the course of five days—one in Auburn, just half a mile from the school, and the other two just outside the city proper, a stranded motorist along Highway 335 and another Sherwood Lake resident, this time a middle-aged woman apparently out watering her flowers in the tolerable temperatures prior to dawn. Each victim suffered the same ghastly fate, and though there had been no further witnesses to the acts, several sightings of what could be Caine (a large vague figure seen in dense areas from the roadside) had been reported within the twenty-five mile square strip of Shawnee where authorities were concentrating their efforts, a narrow band of pasture and small groups of homes from Auburn north to the lake area. Search dogs, helicopters, and horseback patrols were used for the thick, wooded locations, while units such as Ran's oversaw the more populated sites. Robberies had also continued—back porch freezers, a number of convenience stops and restaurants, and one home invasion that had left the house relatively untouched except for an imploded back door and decimated refrigerator.

For those involved, everything had happened so quickly.

Enforcement teams were being coordinated through Tony Sartin at Shawnee County, and they were asked to step up their sweeps at a rate proportional to Caine's attacks. All the while Ran savored the increased activity while at the same time fearing for his town. He took personal responsibility for the loss of another of his sheep—he had only met Bradley once during a town hall meeting over the volunteer fire department—and had had a hard time shaking the guilt. Assurances that he couldn't have foreseen the attack on the man did little to ease his self-blame.

His first step to avoid a repeat offense was to send each of his deputies to designated homes where they were instructed to warn the owners of the potential threat stalking their town and ways they could protect themselves. Ran had joined in the door-to-door contact, asking those he served to lock their doors and avoid stepping outside after dark. Auburn was effectively under martial law as businesses and services such as newspaper delivery were ordered to delay their activities until sun up, and even then residents were encouraged to limit their movement and never be alone if at all possible. The added coverage by his old friend at the *Topeka Tribune*, Glen Dobbs, reminded the doubters that a suspected serial killer was loose in northeast Kansas and that citizens were advised to take extra precautions while the police attempted his apprehension.

From his command post at the SCSD, Sartin, assisted by multiple agencies, was coordinating a massive manhunt, the largest in Kansas since the BTK serial killer and as challenging as the Richard Grissom murders of 1990. They were taking a huge chance concentrating their efforts in such a small area, but the recent murders and robberies pointed to the belief that their suspect was more than comfortable lurking in the shadows of the rural area while striking at will. The contention that road blocks would help lock down the perimeter was enacted by Sartin, though he had only done this to appease department heads who, unaware of the monster they were looking for, believed it quite likely the killer would attempt to flee the area. They were still not privy to the medical information developed through Dr. Phillips from the medical examiner's office, and Sartin, like Ran previously, believed their actions would only be hindered by the incredible story. In the lieutenant's experienced judgment, Caine would be hunted whether he was a common man or a supernatural freak of science. Either way, there was a killer in need of apprehension.

As for Tara, she was quick to gather forensic samples from the latest victims to verify her DNA postulate and see whether any further change had taken place in the chemical restructuring that had created the animal that walked among them. A thorough genetic workup was overdue, and though she wanted confirmation immediately, Tara knew that a definitive report through the lab was necessary and at least a week away. Now that their suspect had been identified, she could suffer the wait without the pressing need for answers that had weighed her down since their chase had begun.

She had sat down recently in the hectic examiner's offices with the Caine file Ran had presented her in the hopes she could "identify just what when wrong," though she doubted any general records could reveal the dark mysteries that surrounded his metamorphosis. The only child of a hard-working New England father, Sebastian Caine had grown up in an environment and followed a course of study worthy of someone of his financial background. He had performed with average success through high school, and following the death of both parents within less than a year of each other, Caine had taken a surprisingly sizable inheritance and

studied at Boston University. Upon graduation he had simply
disappeared, showing up in southern Texas later where he soon began a
modest life as a computer programmer. Though only in his mid-twenties,
the young man had started his own business and then began an unnatural
nomadic journey across the South and up the Atlantic coast before
shooting across the middle of the country, which had most recently
ended with a stay in Hoyt, Kansas. His business traveled with him, and
his dependability and skills kept him afloat the entire time, though a
sudden drop in performance over his last few weeks in Kansas had left
his clientele on the decline and his future in flux.

Other than the strange inability to stay in one place, which was now
completely explainable, the biographical history spoke of nothing out of
the ordinary, at least nothing that might explain the genetic transfer that
had abruptly changed his life permanently. There was no documented
history of violent tendencies. No episodes of childhood illness that may
have affected his physical development. No massive injuries requiring
blood transfusions or records of psychiatric care. The man's life was
unremarkable.

Tara daydreamed about what it must have been like for him when he
realized his world was turning upside down. Had he been confused?
Most certainly. Afraid? A normal reaction to something so foreign. Why,
then, hadn't he sought a doctor's attention? Had he been concerned about
the response he would receive trying to explain his affliction or did he
lack any faith that the medical community could help him? *Or was it
possible that he didn't want to be helped?* The change must have been
exciting, invigorating, a shot of pure adrenaline. It was conceivable to
her that in a moment of great decision, he had chosen to hide his new
identity, to protect the thing that he was becoming. His movement across
the country demonstrated this, and the very fact that he isolated himself
from society supported the idea. Given the unique and utter fictitious
nature of the entire storyline, this preternatural response actually seemed
to fit the best.

Her role in the investigation had come to a crossroads, as had her
relationship with Ran. It had only been a matter of weeks since she had
entertained the thought of helping the Auburn sheriff, a man with whom
she had found an instant attraction and divulged an unbelievable tale.
They had hit it off instantly, a miraculous occurrence considering the
conditions under which they had come together. Their commitment to
their professions had led to a bond to each other, and Tara cherished the
memory of her directness with Ran in that regard and his awkward yet

gentle response.

They had agreed to put their newfound bond on hold while giving the case that had brought them together first priority. It had seemed the right thing to do at the time, but now that Tara's scientific insights were not in demand and Ran's skills as an investigator were being called into action, she was beginning to look at the covenant as completely unfair. True, relationships deserved the full attention of both parties, and they had recognized that if they wanted to give themselves an honest chance, it would have to come later. A mature choice, but she regretted the decision all the same now that her time was not wholly occupied by thoughts of forensic study and genetic mutations. She was in love, and the emotion that filled her didn't want to hear about duty and service. It only wanted fulfillment.

It was during these unforeseen moments that Tara chastised her pettiness and reminded herself of the job that remained, namely the capturing of a man who had killed dozens over the course of a few years. If she was determined to begin again with Randall Price, it could only happen with a positive outlook. She would shelve her selfishness, look for ways to further assist the man she saw as her future, and pray he stayed safe. An evil had descended upon them, and it was only continued support and encouragement that would see them through it.

Chapter 35

Ran had spent most of the afternoon in a crowded conference room in Topeka with a dozen police officers. It had been a meeting of frustrations and argued courses of action, and Ran, now headed over to the medical examiner's to touch base with Tara, believed they had too many chiefs. Tony Sartin was showing signs of fatigue trying to keep all the involved departments working together, and Ran felt empathy for his good friend. He had run up against similar problems while heading task forces in Los Angeles and had come to the conclusion that there was no good way to do it. Egos were always a problem, often a greater hindrance to an investigative manhunt than bureaucratic red tape or uncooperative citizenry. Everyone wanted to have a hand in the methodology and credit for the catch; consequently, the goal became that much harder to attain. Ran figured it was that way everywhere, whether in the corporate world or in the blue-collar efforts of the average work force—recognition was the dangling carrot

With almost a week under their belts, the group assembled to locate and detain serial killer Sebastian Caine was having zero success. Though state and federal agencies were asked to only assist in the pursuit for now, Sartin was getting pressure from his superiors to bring things to an end or relinquish his command to federal authorities whose interest had peaked with the discovery of Caine's multi-state murder spree. Ran knew from experience that the feds would descend upon Shawnee County soon, bringing with them an authority that would supercede the present chain of command and leave Sartin in charge of little more than bagels and coffee. It was emasculating and, as Ran had seen on occasion, left a mark on men's careers that they never quite erased.

Tony Sartin had been there for Ran time and again; he was determined to see this through for him, for all of them, even if it meant doing it alone.

The meeting had started with reports from the various unit

commanders regarding their operations the previous day. Patrols, horseback and canine units, and infrared aerial groups reported nothing significant, though the dogs had seemed highly agitated during a sweep of the wooded area just north of Auburn, a narration not lost on Ran. It was understood that they were not looking for just any man, but an evasive, cunning killer who could cover his tracks and remain hidden for long periods of time to avoid detection. Still, it was felt some signs would be discovered, whether it was a place of rest or a feeding area, and it was perplexing to the group that nothing substantial had been revealed. In the meantime, deaths were continuing, culminating in the cat and mouse game that was leaving everyone involved exasperated and ready for some alternate means of capture, everything from the ridiculous to the sublime. A member of the state patrol suggested a line sweep, but it would require volunteers to effectively cover the square mileage they were considering, and public involvement was out of the question. One of Sartin's sergeant's outlined a scenario in which one of his men could act as bait in an open field surrounded by armed officers—a reasonable plan if they were hunting the average four-legged predator, but it was thought that Caine killed with the patience of a saint, and he wouldn't attack without carefully evaluating his surroundings. It was agreed that conventional means were out of the question, and though everyone acted as if Sartin was spinning his wheels, no one could come up with a better approach when pressed. It soon became anger fueled with helplessness, and Ran chose to observe the melee silently than add to the problems.

Sartin refused to cave in during the commotion, reasserting his authority and faith in his conservative though thorough procedure, and Ran expected nothing less from the veteran police officer.

"We will continue with the same plan until I am told otherwise," Sartin had said with a firm voice to show his displeasure with their squabbling. "If you have exhausted every grid in your designated area, start over, and when you're done, do it again. He's not just going to march out into the open with his hands in the air yelling that he's had enough. I don't think he's impressed or intimidated one bit with our efforts, and until you realize and your men realize that this isn't just another B and E suspect hiding out in mom's attic, we'll never get him."

Sartin was fired up. "He's out there, and he knows we're on to him. Let's blanket the area and make him think twice about another murder. Tomlinson, I'd suggest you go back to the location where the dogs hit last night and work out from there. Corporal Wellman?"

"Sir?"

"Let's move aerial patrols along the outskirts of neighborhoods, especially Auburn and the Sherwood areas. Fence lines. Storage units. Anything that might provide cover. Alert ground units to anything suspicious."

"Sir."

"Sheriff Price, would you object to three additional patrol units in Auburn?"

"Not at all. The more the merrier."

Sartin said, "I will have the officers on your front porch at dusk for instructions."

He had been leaning on the desk with balled fists, but now stood erect to make his final point. "Gentlemen, you have your orders. Let's make him nervous. Good luck."

The assembly rose with renewed purpose, but it was likely their doubt would return with another unsuccessful night. All Sartin could do was hope for success as he gathered his paperwork before the retreating group. Ran stayed behind to talk with his friend.

"So, how do you think it went?" Ran asked.

Sartin shook his head. "I'm as disappointed as they are. What baffles me is that they know we are doing this by the book, but they still want to act like there's a better way," Sartin said. "Failure breeds anger and doubt and that can lead to apathy. I just hope to God they're ready if we get Caine backed into a corner."

Ran agreed with the lieutenant's assessment. The biggest problem with extended surveillance and lengthy patrol was what veteran police referred to as the Hyp Effect, a word derived from the Greek god of sleep Hypnos suggesting that the dulling consequences of a stakeout or some repetitive activity can lead to a hypnotic state, causing even the most seasoned officer to miss the obvious. Sartin was clearly concerned his men may have already been lulled into an attitude that could prove detrimental to their objective.

The two men walked to Sartin's office, reflecting on the lieutenant's holy appeal.

"Why the added patrols? Something you're not telling me?" asked Ran. "Don't get me wrong...I appreciate the help."

Sartin was reflective. "You know why I did that," he said. "Like it or not, Auburn is slowly becoming the eye of our not-so-little storm. Tell me you don't see that."

They reached Sartin's office and settled into chairs across from each other.

"It's been my biggest fear since the first Sherwood Lake killing and the delivery truck break-in," Ran acknowledged, "but you don't think the city limits needs added security, do you? Don't you think we should be concentrating our manpower in the wooded areas bordering? He's out there, lurking, but I don't think we're going to see him on anyone's front porch."

"No, then explain to me the home and business invasions. What about the Gunther lady near Sherwood? In all your cold case studies did you find a single instance of a victim attacked in her own backyard?"

Sartin was clear in his conviction. The only person he and Tara had to convince of their beliefs was now the theory's greatest advocate.

"He's starting to show his feelings of invulnerability—getting braver with each passing day. If he enjoys anymore success, we're going to see him walking straight down Main Street in the light of day, and why shouldn't he? We've posed about zero threat."

Ran took issue with the final assessment. "I think the reason he isn't marching through town right now beating his chest is *because of* our increased presence," Ran said. "Bolder? Yes, but he's still using the darkness, still sneaking around and surprising his prey. And the fact that he continues to attack a lone individual reinforces the thought that his basic approach remains unchanged. I'll take the extra men, I welcome them, but I still think our search is on the perimeter. Tara keeps reminding me he's responded like an animal since this all started. We can't treat him like the typical serial killer."

Sartin agreed, "Typical he isn't, but I think we need to tighten our security anyway to ensure the public's protection. What good is our search if we keep getting people picked off? Better we sacrifice losing him than another one of our citizens."

"I see your point, Tony, and if it means anything, you couldn't be handling this any better."

"Thanks, and it does mean something. Are you headed over to the fair doctor's?"

Ran nodded, "Thought I would touch base with her before tonight's activities. See what new insights she may have."

"She's pretty amazing."

"Amazing only begins to describe her."

With less than an hour before he needed to be back in Auburn to discuss patrol strategies with his deputies and the new officers joining his charge, Ran pulled into a visitor's space in the ME's lot and walked directly to Tara's office. She wasn't there.

A meandering search of the facility that lead to numerous inquiries about his needs finally led him to the small lab the department had on site. Tara was focused on a glass slide through the eyepiece of a large microscope, her right hand scribbling away without any apparent visual support as she adjusted the device with her free hand. He stood there quietly for a moment, in respect of her concentrated work as much as his desire to just take in the sight of her.

And then, "Isn't there some law against sheriff's loitering in medical buildings?"

She had probably known of his presence since the time he had stopped at the door.

"If you would like to press charges, I'll see what I can do," he said, stepping into the sparse lab.

Tara looked up from her work and pinched the bridge of her nose. "No, I think I'll just let him hang around," she said. "He may prove good for something."

They both smiled as he closed the distance on her, though he stopped at the table she sat before to continue their conversation. It was an unspoken understanding that they maintain a professional distance on the job, and they had begrudgingly honored it.

She closed the file she had been writing in, crossed her hands on her lap, and stared at him contentedly.

"Well, Sheriff, what's on tap for tonight?"

"The same," Ran said with a hint of his own frustration, though he would have never shown Sartin. "I really feel like we are chasing our tails."

"In a manner of speaking, you are," she said standing. "Come on. Buy me a pop and I'll tell you what I think."

Ran joked, "Tell me what you think? When did you start expressing your opinions?"

"Follow me and leave the sarcasm here," she smiled. "You never know what I might be able to help you with."

"There is no denying I keep coming back to the mountain top for some insights."

They walked side by side down the hallway to the break room. Ran filled the machine with enough change for both of them, but he knew he would need a heavy dose of caffeine at some point for the night ahead. They spoke of simple things as they returned to the lab—their workdays, their need for more sleep—the comfortable topics that allowed them to put Caine and the murderers aside for a brief period. Once back Tara returned to her tall chair while Ran chose to stand. He would be sitting a great deal until morning.

"So you're planning to continue the search in the same area?"

Ran folded his arms. "It seems our only option right now. A heavy dose of ground and air assault to keep him on the move and leery of seeking another victim. We have to be a presence or he's just going to do what he wants with immunity."

He spoke as if he was trying to convince himself they were doing the right thing.

"And the dogs?" she asked.

"Oh, they sometimes act like something interests them. Their posture changes. They look excited, but the trail is always empty."

"Could be they're confused."

"No, these are seasoned trackers," Ran argued. "We found more than enough of his scent at the Hoyt house. He's just staying a step ahead."

"Or his scent has changed just enough to make the dogs useless."

"Is that possible?"

Tara opened the file folder in which she had been writing. "Very possible. Even likely. He has been altered at a chemical level, the very substance the dogs use to trace a source."

She thumbed through the handwritten pages.

"I threw together some probability tables this morning."

"Just *threw* some together, huh?" Ran offered in light mockery.

"Well, instead of sitting on my hands waiting for further lab data, I thought it would be wise to lay out scenarios based on potential biological factors. Remember when I told you he could either die from the altered DNA or be totally absorbed by the new cellular structures, two becoming one? I felt I should now play out the next round of possibilities."

"Let me guess—he could split in two at a geometric rate and become an army," Ran said. "World War III."

"Very doubtful, but the idea of mitosis at the multi-cellular level? That would be a trick, and after what I have witnessed, I wouldn't be surprised. But no, he isn't going to divide and conquer.

"No, what I have formulated are more rational explanations for his potential state both now and in the future. Some are advantageous to us; some are good for him."

"Great."

Tara said, "I could be wrong."

"You haven't been yet."

"Biological processes are predictable but can be undependable. Ultimately, anything could happen."

Ran said, "I'll take curtain number three, Monty."

"Let's start with number one."

"You're the boss."

"And don't ever forget that."

Tara had arrived at her conclusions after a painstaking process of measuring a variety of biological factors, including scientifically-known DNA functions and explanations of mutation. Caine had changed, evolved, mutated, regressed—it was all the same to Ran. He was not the man he used to be, though Tara had previously argued that he was always the monster that was now roaming eastern Kansas. It had just been a matter of time for the right conditions and effects to take place.

The first potentiality was familiar. Caine's engine could still throw a gear, and he would burn out like a match. Ran had learned to expect the worst, so he let the chance pass without giving it much interest. The next two prospects that Tara detailed left him empty and yet angry.

"He may have reached the end of the cellular cycle. What you see is what you get, so to speak. It is the most likely, and if I were asked to put money on it, the odds would be the best here. Not to devalue the third alternative, which is the least probable, but must be mentioned due to the molecular changes we have seen. I looked at this a hundred different ways, used the latest though admittedly preliminary forensic samples I obtained, and it can't be ignored: There is the slim chance that he will, how can I best put it, *reconfigure*."

Ran signaled his ignorance with splayed hands and narrowed brows.

"Reconfigure. Changing his composition, his structure, even his intellectual patterns."

"Like a complete alteration?"

Tara nodded, "Nothing left that is recognizable."

"Into what?"

"Whatever the genome dictates. Definably organic, comparable to his present size, but a marked change is not out of the realm of what could be. I don't fully understand what is happening to his genetic sequencing, but I have proof that it is changing. How far the information extends is anybody's guess."

"So give me some particulars," Ran requested. "Are we talking a third arm or another pair of eyes?"

Tara said, "Anything that is encoded in his hereditary information can show up, but I would think what appears will be adaptive qualities, as we have seen with his altered jaws and increased hormonal output. If it benefits his existence and is available, it could rapidly appear, but I can't predict particulars. The human genome is an enormous data bank. If it were a book, it would be 1.5 million pages long and over a billion words. No one could foresee his changes other than to say they could occur. I don't think your third arm is practical, but larger eyes for greater vision, duplication of muscle layers for increased strength, a lengthening of the olfactory chambers for a better sense of smell. I could name dozens of ways he could improve himself, *if* he has the ability."

Ran said, "Let's go back to the first theory."

"Again, I could be wrong. I am lacking in time and equipment, and I could certainly use a few advanced courses in genetic science. I'm just trying to arm you with all the information you may need."

"And you know," Ran said, "how much I value it. I may act apprehensive, but trust me, I take every bit of it seriously."

She looked at her watch. "Don't you have a meeting to go to?"

Ran looked at his own watch and jumped up from his chair. "Yes, ma'am. See, everything you say is important."

"What's most important to me is that you're safe out there."

Ran wanted to take her in his arms, but it wasn't the place. "I will be," he said. "I don't like leaving behind unfinished business, and Doctor, we have quite a lot."

"I'll say."

Chapter 36

Caine had to feed before the hunt now, supercharging his internal furnace to prepare his body for the massive amounts of energy he would expel. The aftermath continued to involve rest, but nothing close to the recovery time his former self had required. Sleep for Caine was not carried out in the traditional sense any longer; he had abandoned the deeper levels of suspended consciousness that most organisms relied on and was instead finding physical strength through short periods of dormancy in which he was completely alert. His mind, having left behind its dependency as well, was no longer tied to the inferior qualities of its weak counterpart, the human brain. With the change had come a realignment of the wiring that operated his systems, the same processes occurring in the fields of robotics and computer technology, and the similarities were not lost on him. He was the next generation of earth's dominant species, and he was assuming his role in rapid stages. Some of his human concerns, though, still lingered.

The fear of discovery remained, an inconvenience that he tolerated while he grew accustomed to what he was becoming. He was completely aware of the increased activity in and around the area he had chosen to occupy while the changes persisted, and as long as nourishment and prey were accessible, he would stay and deal with the attempts to stop him.

He respected their efforts without viewing them as threats, especially the actions of one he had monitored since his arrival, choosing to avoid contact but not to the point of complete isolation. He enjoyed their frightened eyes, shared their stares but not their flights of terror, and he relished the satisfaction and superiority those moments provided; consequently his movements were guarded yet relaxed.

Their dogs and helicopters offered little in the way of concern as he left ambiguous scent trails and used cover with ease. It was in many ways a territorial behavior he was exhibiting, but to him it was only a matter of dominance and control. When the change was complete and his surroundings were still conducive to success, he would stay until he either tired of the situation or felt the urge to move on. Nothing but his desires would dictate his actions.

Auburn and its surroundings were the perfect locations for him to cut his teeth on the position he was preparing to take in the new world. An ample food supply and a revolving door of defenseless, cowardly beings to appease his primary needs were the allure, and after determining that his changing body would not tolerate a lengthy journey of relocation, he had settled on the area with complete confidence. It was here that he would leave the final vestiges of his former existence and realize his full potential.

With the sun set and the cooling breeze of night lightly brushing his nearly-naked frame, the Caine that now was crossed pitch black fields of dry grass, easily passing over the aging barbed-wire fences that separated properties and contained the occasional herds of livestock, and moved into the town unnoticed, his mouth beginning to salivate in anticipation of his day's meal. He looked for fresh, uncooked meats whenever available but was willing to eat cooked or frozen. He had developed a taste for red meats, savoring the thick juices that his cavernous mouth released. In moments of great hunger when animal flesh was unavailable, he had resorted to other means of protein consumption like thick wedges of cheese and cartons of eggs, which he popped into his mouth like pieces of candy, shell and all. His prior experiences had taught him that some foods provided sustaining energy while others were only immediate sources that would fail him in short time.

At no time in his scavenging for meals had he ever killed and consumed one of the many animals, wild or domestic, that he encountered in his movements, though he was not disgusted by the idea. Their capture and rending would be quick and effortless, but for now it was unnecessary. The thought of devouring his kills, though, was abhorrent. The very idea of putting their filthy, putrid flesh into his temple made his stomach turn. He repeatedly spit from his mouth the vulgar taste that accompanied his attacks, yet the feel of his jaws clamping down on their soft flesh while torrents of blood cascaded down his chest was something he refused to sacrifice.

He moved within the confines of deep shadows and structures large enough to hide his massive body. Though large, he was lithe and quick, feline in his motion. A visual blur of step and gesture, Caine was the peripheral action that turned heads without concrete revelation. Seen and unseen, he went with determination and assurance, always vigilant to the odors that traveled along the wind's current as his heightened senses worked in natural harmony with his environment. It was in this manner that he would locate both food and prey. Superior to any species now or before him and with each day furthering the distance that lay between them, he was a combination of every predatory animal that had ever lived, the ultimate killing machine, borrowing the finest features the kingdom had to offer in nature's creation of a perfect weapon.

It was his perception, but it would soon belong to the masses.

Beyond the back door of a large, brick building on the north end of town, deeper in the heart of the community then he had previously gone, Caine detected the succulent scent of beef. As the end of summer was fast approaching and children were preparing for their return to study, the local school had begun its own preparation, stocking its large, walk-in freezers with supplies of ground beef and sliced turkey for the compartmentalized hot meals that would be served within a week. He noted the lingering smells of diesel, canned foods, and other products that had obviously been a part of the delivery process that afternoon. Caine licked his lips with eager expectation, his heart rate increasing with the promise of the delicious choices that awaited him.

After a brief confirmation of his obscurity, he traversed the broad parking lot and came to the door, grasping the silver handle that sat locked in defiance of him. With a quick yank that called for little effort, the handle gave way and the door buckled slightly, creating a gap between itself and the frame, but remained in position. Slightly irritated, Caine thrust his hand into the gap, curled his fingers back toward the door, and pulled it away from its deadbolt and hinges. He absentmindedly tossed it aside, its metal surface skipping across the asphalt in loud reverberation, but he was unconcerned. A meal waited, and he was single-minded now in his purpose.

His nose and its accompanying internal structures, new to the body that had once been Sebastian Caine's, led him across a sea of stainless steel cabinets, drawers, counters and sinks to a large freezer door. Refrigeration units hummed in the otherwise silent kitchen. The door gave way to a rectangular space and tight walkway, surrounded on each side by tall wire shelves where large stores of frozen vegetables, meats, and other products sat invitingly. He was led unerringly to the source of his whetted appetite, and within seconds was devouring large containers of ground beef, poultry, and breaded fish fillets. The blocks of meat offered little resistance to his forceful bite, and he swallowed with satisfying contentment until his hunger was appeased.

As was now his ritual, he moved from this daily meal to venture out into the world that he claimed as his own, where he was free to roam and frequently kill if the conditions were favorable. Boundaries were not forced upon him, but he traveled within the confines of an area that he had predetermined, a territory whose every square inch was familiar to him. He would cruise its interior as both owner and resident, occasionally chancing upon a stray in the herd that shared it with him. What followed was violent and gratifying.

It was not his practice to raid their homes; conversely, he staggered his movements and lay in wait. Death was his to exact, but fate brought the lowly to him. He was only an instrument of removal, to empty them of their life source for their careless and submissive natures. They were inferior, meek, and most importantly, common. He recognized the need for the systematic elimination of all things inferior, and it had started with him. Now reborn and risen from the ashes of a pathetic life, he was the destructor, sent to sterilize and wipe clean. It was his destiny.

This night would be different in one respect, though, as he moved stealthily under the partly cloudy skies to the open grounds beyond the buildings. He sensed a challenge to his reign, had felt the winds of defiance gathering, and his superiority called for him to meet it head on.

It was a perfect night for the hunt, and he growled deeply in response to its prospects.

Chapter 37

Ran had outlined his plans for patrol responsibilities with his deputies and the three additional officers Tony Sartin had assigned him, and with Ran behind the wheel of his own cruiser, the units left the Auburn Sheriff's Department around ten o'clock to begin their watch of the town and its perimeter. The sheriff had ordered that they remain in constant radio contact, checking in with him every 30 minutes, before reassembling at dawn.

It would be another long night. Everyone needed sleep, and a good meal had not been had by anyone since the patrols began. Ran feared their physical and mental conditions may prove detrimental to their efforts, but there was little he could do about it.

After leaving Tara that evening, he had been overcome by the familiar feeling that things were getting ready to erupt. During lengthy investigations in Los Angeles when hundreds of pieces of information had been gathered through phone calls and interviews and lab results, Ran would instinctually see a conclusion approaching like a runaway freight train. What he could never foresee, though, was whether his efforts meant gratifying success or cold failure.

Detailed planning and thorough research and inquiry had always been his weapons of choice as Ran carefully focused his efforts and narrowed his field of investigation. It had been a time-tested approach allowing for little oversight or misinformation. He had forever believed that the means to an arrest were available regardless of the circumstances; it required patience and determination, and he had never been lacking in the latter. An answer lie waiting, and it would most often fall naturally into his lap after he had cleared a path to it.

The dead ends were out there, and all the sleepless hours of work couldn't deter a detective from running head long into them. Even with the best tools at his disposal, the truth could avoid detection. Stubborn men like Ran required repeated impacts with the inevitable before accepting the fate of their cases, but even so, it was never fully embraced. A cold case was like a miscarriage; they had nurtured it along toward a rewarding conviction only to have it removed from their care and boxed away in abandoned limbo. These were never forgotten, and Ran often returned to them occasionally in the hope of a fresh approach yielding better results. It was rare, but sometimes a clue emerged that led down a different track, and from there, the answer he was looking for.

The case of Sebastian Caine struck him in a unique way. Maybe it was the forensic complexity of the case coupled with Tara's singular DNA theory or possibly the geographic and serial profiles that found no equal to other cases. Whatever the disturbing qualities, Caine had presented Ran with a challenge that, for the first time in his career, was unlike anything he had encountered previously, and that alone made his feelings of finality suspect. He couldn't deny them, but could he trust them given the foreign territory he had entered? Either way, Ran was uncomfortable with the direction things were going. Walking through Caine's house and studying his file had only complicated his intuitive skills.

Compiled within twenty-four hours after the discovery of a shattered door at a residence in the small farming community of Hoyt, the file on Caine had been unremarkable, lacking in any life-altering events that would explain such murderous behavior. An only child in an average, middle-class home, Sebastian Caine had seemingly embraced mediocrity during his developmental years, receiving average grades while avoiding any activities that might involve him athletically or socially.

A middle school counselor remarked: "Student is pleasant to talk to but remains unenthusiastic about school life and the interactive experiences it offers."

He was a loner in every respect, and though he had no record of disciplinary actions, he was on a few occasions the object of student harassment, most likely because of his special physical qualities. Large for his age, Caine was evidently the object of verbal abuse on occasion, though Ran knew that most children suffered some kind of assault from fellow classmates along their scholastic journeys. It was the unfortunate part of the pre-teen and high school environment, and few psychologists blamed peer teasing and ridicule as the definitive factor in the construction of a killer's mind. There was no denying its contribution to the troubled psyche, but for the Caine who now threatened the very streets Ran policed to have been the creation of a hostile society, the jabs of a few obnoxious bullies could only have been a small part of a greater picture.

The death of his parents prior to college was probably difficult, but his adult mind had already developed the ability to deal with the loss and the subsequent orphaned condition he found himself occupying. His stellar collegiate performance followed by a drastic move from the New England states to the Gulf Coast supported the belief that he had handled their deaths well and sought a fresh start upon graduation.

With a computer degree in hand, he had proven a capable programmer, and though his solitary lifestyle persisted, he was considered by employers and colleagues to be efficient and dependable. Eccentric, segregated adults are often the subjects of passing comments designed to belittle, but there was no evidence that Caine's personality would have conjured break room discussions about his potential to murder dozens of people. Those questioned used words like *unassuming, quiet*, and *pleasant when spoken to.*

His had not been a past shrouded in any glaring trauma or emotional shock that would explain his transformation from meek computer operator to the creature that lurked among them. Tara had argued that something triggered the genetic transfer, that an event had awakened the dormant gene like a survival response and led Caine down the path of rebirth. Whatever it may have been, it wasn't showing up in any of his records.

Nor did the house he so violently vacated offer much in the way of clues to his darker side. When he and Sartin arrived and began their initial search of the residence, they shared the belief of some of the first officers on the scene—surely some thieves had discovered the open door prior to notification of law enforcement. The place was basically empty, and the thought that it had either been broken into or robbed after the fact was dismissed considering the tens of thousands of dollars of computer equipment that sat undisturbed in the front living area. It was the first thing visible upon entrance and would not have been missed by the dumbest of criminals. Since the door was blown outward and no other sign of forced entry was observed, it was concluded that Caine had been the last person in the house.

He had lived the dull, unattractive life of his childhood within the confines of the house, which offered him the basic necessities and little else. He apparently spent all his time in front of his computers; the only other room with furnishings was a bedroom featuring a twin bed and a scarred dresser filled with the requisite socks and underwear. The clothes closet was comparable to the room, sparse and uninviting. The kitchen did have a half-stocked refrigerator with out-of-date meats and spoiled dairy products, but there were no dishes, pots, or silverware. His life was void of accessories, and the only extravagance he afforded himself was the state-of-the-art equipment from which he earned a living. Even his vehicle was old and ordinary.

What was telling was the large crater in the wood floor of the living room, its edges splintered from some great impact, though the ceiling did not betray the source of the projectile. An old burn barrel was the only occupant of an overgrown front and back yard, and police were still trying to determine who had kept the grounds for Caine since there was no sign of yard equipment. The barrel was recently used, and early examination had found bits of charred clothing that had been collected for forensic analysis. The computer hard drives were gathered as well, and Ran was curious to learn what secrets Caine might be hiding there.

The proof that Caine was their man had been found in the bottom of a computer cabinet in an old, worn album. Pressed between the pages had not been the traditional memories of the past—family portraits, letters, and vacation memorabilia. Neatly cut and pasted on the first 57 pages of the album had been newspaper articles, each detailing the circumstances surrounding either the disappearance or murder of individuals along the route previously pinpointed by Ran in his investigation. There, in the well-worn pages, were cases the sheriff himself had pulled from the federal crime bank as potential ties to the murders both in Kansas and those encountered by Tara during her pathological training. There were, of course, many more, some that had fallen through the missing persons cracks of understaffed departments, and others that had been attributed to factors outside of Caine's methodology (The body of a vagrant in South Carolina had been found beside a heavily-traveled overpass, his body a mangled mess. His cause of death, regrettably because of his homeless history, was listed as an accidental vehicular event.) They were in perfect chronological order, slightly yellowed but pristine otherwise. A little over four years of history, carefully catalogued for future reference. And at the bottom right corner of ever page, in sharp contrast to the even lines and clear lettering that formed the article, was a dark red streak that trailed off the edge.

A streak of blood.

A tag of death and apparent symbolic trophy of the night.

Forensics was already at work on the album, trying to match each smear with the page's victim, but authorities didn't need lab results to confirm what they knew.

With overwhelming evidence that Caine was their man, it had taken little time to put together search teams that had now narrowed their efforts to the relatively small stretch of land of which Auburn was featured. Regrettably, they had come up empty night after night while Caine had continued his murderous rampage, and there was dwindling hope that the man would be found before fleeing the area for safer hunting grounds.

The evening air felt refreshing as it bellowed through the open window of Ran's cruiser, and he let it wash over him in a moment of retreat. He had become consumed by this case, more so than those he had given more investigative time, and wondered if his intuitive sense that everything was reaching an end was simply his desire for the madness to stop and for peace to return to his life and the little town he now called home. He had seen far worse during the first twenty years of his career—crimes involving children ranked at the very top—and in every situation, he was able to detach himself emotionally in order to effectively perform his duties. This was far different. Maybe it was his rank within the Auburn department or possibly the intimate nature of the town's small population. There was Tara to consider. Her willingness to put her job and reputation on the line for him added to the pressure. Whatever the reason, he knew his life could never return to anything resembling normal until he had freed himself and the rest of those around him from the threat of Sebastian Caine.

His thoughts were interrupted by a voice on the two-way radio. "Sheriff Price, come in please."

It was Polly Sheridan. She had agreed to switch her shift to the night so that Ran could have her available should something come up in their patrols. She seemed to welcome the temporary change and had shown a different side during the events of the past weeks, a fire always simmering just under the surface had been erupting in effortless activity. The new shift was unprecedented since she had virtually owned the daytime since her hiring decades ago. Ran did not shower her with his thanks knowing her as he now did, and she did not wait expectantly for his undying appreciation. Like all good relationships, they just knew.

"Polly. Holding down the fort?"

"All quiet here. Just checking in. I hadn't heard anything from any of you."

Ran smiled, "I was just expecting some radio checks. Let me know immediately if something comes through from Shawnee County or any of the field units."

"You got it, Sheriff."

Dependable. Efficient. It was what he needed from his people more than ever. And as if to answer his appeal, he was soon inundated with reports from his six patrols. Bobby Helms and Chuck Forrester expressed their disappointment in an uneventful night so far, as did the three Shawnee County officers. Monk had observed some activity behind Whit Morgan's place on the south end of town, but it had only been the owner wrestling with a stray goat that had caught itself in some fencing. Ran feared the night would be another washout.

As he negotiated a slow turn off 11th Street on to North Hanover at the northeast part of town, Ran glanced at the photo clipped to his console, a blown-up driver's license mug shot of their suspect. He recalled the first time he had laid eyes on the man who had grown to mythological proportions during Tara's ongoing research and later eyewitness testimony. His first impression had been disappointment.

Caine was striking in appearance, but the object of legend he was not. Ran acknowledged his overall features as statuesque--a square jaw, Roman nose, and thick, black hair—but these stood in sharp contrast to what was an empty, almost childlike expression. His eyes were deep-set caverns of dark lifelessness that stared out hauntingly, and the thin lips peeled back reluctantly to reveal stark white rows of teeth.

The photo had been taken within days of his arrival in Kansas along with his vehicle registration, and it was noted that Caine conducted all of his other business via computer when possible, everything from banking to utility deposits. Even home sales and purchases were negotiated on-line, requiring him to make but only one or two face-to-face meetings in the process. These were quick and uneventful as his credit was exemplary and his desire to banter dollars and cents nonexistent. Few recalled any particulars in their meetings with him other than remembering him to be a large though unassuming man.

Forgettable, just like he wanted, Ran thought.

He sought anonymity and captured it with consistent success.

Ran brought the cruiser to a full stop on the shoulder of 14th Street from where he could observe SW Auburn Road enter the north side of town. Here it became Washington Street, which divided Auburn in two as it moved due south in a straight line and finally resumed its former name until running into Highway 335. Residents could then head northeast to Topeka or southwest to Wichita.

For forty-five minutes not a single car crossed into the community, and other than the slow, passing police car of officer John Thomas from Shawnee County crossing east to west on 14th, Ran saw nothing move in the still of the Kansas night. The gentle breeze that circulated through his open windows added to the otherwise pleasant atmosphere, and Ran imagined how relaxing a night like this could be with Tara at his side. He often reveled in thoughts of their future time together and what it must be like to spend long, tranquil evenings in each other's arms, the troubles they now faced miles away. It would be special, and it would be right.

In the distance the intermittent hum of highway traffic added to Ran's calming surroundings, and with the next radio check twenty minutes away, he let the moment of stillness wash over him in soothing waves. He embraced the pause.

"Sheriff Price, this is Unit 2. Come in. Over."

Excited. Words running together.

"This is Sheriff Price. What is it, Monk?"

"Sheriff, we got a possible B and E over here behind the school. Back door to the cafeteria looks clean gone. Advise. Over."

Ran had told his deputies to not proceed without backup during the night patrols, and Monk, regardless of his gung-ho approach to law enforcement, had followed that order.

"I'm a minute away," Ran responded. "Remain in your vehicle. Out. Units 3 through 7, maintain radio contact but continue your surveillance. I'll call you if I need you."

He was already halfway to the school before completing his last transmission, wanting to be sure they didn't drop their guard while he and Monk dealt with the break-in. It sounded like Caine was scavenging again in Auburn, so it was important that they be extra vigilant.

When he arrived at the back of the two-year old extension to the school, a dining and food preparation building that fed the district's 233 students, levels kindergarten through eighth grade, Monk was sitting obediently in the asphalt lot, his headlights and side high beam trained on the gapping rectangular hole that stood in contrast to the beige brick wall. This was the first potential Caine-related occurrence to be discovered during their nightly patrols. All the others had been reported in the morning hours. It was a good catch, and Ran let Monk know it. They stood between their cars as Ran outlined their approach.

"I'll go in first. Stay behind me and watch your back. Weapons holstered, but at the ready. I don't expect to find anyone here, but let's be ready. Standard procedure."

Monk looked completely wound up, his eyes darting.

"Monk, were you listening? Standard entry."

He nodded, though his face continued to hold an expression of high anxiety. "Sir. Standard entry. I'm ready."

"*Deputy?* Monk, I need you right now," Ran said with conviction. "Are you okay?"

"Yes, sir, Sheriff."

He took a deep breath. "Ready."

The two officers walked in a staggered line to the entrance, and as they closed the distance Ran could see the violence the door frame had been subjected to. It was Caine, all right, and he had wasted no time gaining entry.

"Sheriff. To your right."

Ran squinted through the glaring light in his periphery and saw what Monk had referenced—the metal door that had earlier sealed the back of the building. It lay some fifty feet away, its original plane bent to form a V-shape.

They continued to the threshold, and Ran, bent low with his right hand on his revolver and his left holding a large police flashlight, hesitated briefly then crept warily into the kitchen area. Monk was some eight feet behind, his posture mimicking Ran's, though he had forgotten his flashlight.

Ran swept the room with his beam, letting it creep into the dark recesses, and then moved toward what looked like the freezer area. A large metal door stood partially open further in and to his left, and from behind it came light plumbs of what looked to be smoke in rolling billows. It was as Ran had suspected. Caine had raided the school's kitchen freezer, stocked full in preparation for the returning children, and when he passed into its formerly cold interior he found it less than frigid, its shelves a jumble of torn and empty packages.

Monk had remained at the buildings back door, and Ran called to him that it was all clear. The deputy hurried in and joined Ran while awaiting further instructions.

"Looks like our boy got hungry again," Ran said, gesturing to he decimated freezer. "Call the command post. Have Lieutenant Sartin informed of our situation. Let him know we will stay here until his arrival."

"Yes, sir," Monk said, and he started off to fulfill Ran's order.

"Monk."

The deputy stopped and spun on a dime.

"Nice work."

"Yes, sir," he said, a slight smile peaking at the corner of his mouth. He was quick to draw his mouth back to stern, though, as he turned and exited the kitchen.

There was little they could conclude from the crime scene, but Ran was bound to follow procedure and inform lead investigators of it so the area could be properly processed. Meanwhile, it would pull a portion of their team off the streets, including some of the Auburn patrols, and that could spell missed opportunities. It was difficult to tell just when Caine had broken in and made his escape, but it was most likely within the last two hours, so a slim chance existed that he was still in the vicinity, but there were no guarantees. His movement had proven unpredictable, and his ability to place miles of separation between his locations was troublesome. He was definitely prone to fleeing his initial crime sites to enjoy what Tom Avery had described as "solitary fulfillment," a time of delayed gratification.

Avery had contacted Ran days after processing the geographic profile to touch base with him on the possible psychological make-up of his killer. Though he was not an expert in personality disorders, he had enough experience compiled over his career to provide Ran with some useful insights. He explained to Ran that Caine was not a psychopath in the traditional sense. Studies found these individuals to be manipulative and impulsive risk takers. Caine's practice had been to exercise patience, to carefully plan his movements and avoid notoriety. Tara, upon hearing this later from Ran, observed that the early Caine may not have demonstrated irregular mental behaviors out of necessity--he had to protect the creature within him. Now, fully emerged, the new Caine was showing signs more fitting to Avery's description. He was exhibiting a great pride in his work and was willing to be noticed while apparently lacking the self-restraint that had kept officials confused as to his whereabouts and identity. The new Caine, as Tara explained, brought with him not only a physical change but also a mental alteration as well. A personality profile of Sebastian Caine, the computer technician, was no longer viable.

When Monk returned to report that Sartin had been updated, Ran led him back outside where they waited for the swarm of detectives, officers, and lab technicians to descend. Auburn's watchful eyes were now cut by a third, and Ran hoped they would complete their work quickly.

There were still many hours of darkness left.

Chapter 38

When the teams from Shawnee County had completed their work at Auburn Public School, it was already four in the morning, and there was little time left to count on successful patrols. Sartin had informed Ran that units working the tree lines, lakes, ponds, and pasture land had reported nothing of significance. The men shared discouragement but agreed that the best thing they hadn't heard was the report of a missing person or dead body, so it was possible their efforts had not been totally unproductive.

The scene proved similar to prior incidents and no new information was gathered. A school official was notified, forensics was ordered to provide Dr. Tara Phillips with samples for analysis, and within a few hours, a temporary door was placed inside the slightly bent frame as those concerned slowly made their way out of the area.

Auburn returned to its state of slumber.

The rest of the town patrol was anticlimactic, and as the rising sun began to tint the night horizon with a touch of liquid gold ahead of its arrival, Ran and his deputies came together at the sheriff's office for a debriefing. Sartin's men were absent, having been told to retreat to Topeka for further orders after the break-in was discovered. Polly was clearing the dispatcher's desk of her personal effects as she readied to leave.

The three men that had gathered in front of Ran's desk were a contrast in energy and attitude. Bobby looked completely exhausted as he slumped in a corner chair with an expression that revealed his disappointment. Chuck was pressed against the bulletin board, joining the city and state maps that hung there, and he looked as creased and used as they did. His cowboy hat dangled limply from his hands as he sighed with an audible rush of air from his lips. None of them had adjusted to the change in their sleep patterns, and the added pressure of an alert watch only compounded the problem. Monk, though, was a different matter entirely.

Looking as if he just came off a deputy assembly line, Monk stood at rigid attention, his posture one of charged readiness. Whether it was the excitement at the school or his commitment to his duty as a law enforcement officer, the deputy was a model of loyal service and carried on him no signs of a long night of work.

Ran knew they had given him their best, but he was unable to come up with any words of inspiration after another fruitless night.

"Gentlemen, it may seem we are spinning our wheels out there, but I think it is only a matter of time before we or one of the other groups makes contact with our suspect. It's the nature of the business and we have to keep after it."

Ran tried to mask the discontent in his voice with little success.

"Shawnee County tells me we can expect continued assistance here until the matter is resolved, especially during the daylight hours when we are low on help. I think the additional night patrols are going to help. Try to stay positive. I don't have anything else for you other than to get some rest. We will be back at it again tonight."

Bobby and Chuck got their feet underneath them and waved their heavy hands to signal their leaving. Monk waited until they were gone.

"Sheriff Price, are we going about this the right way?"

"What do you mean, Deputy?"

"Well, sir, no disrespect intended, but I just feel like there is something more we could be doing. These patrols are getting us no where."

Ran exploded at his deputy. "We're doing exactly what we have been told to do, Monk. Damn, you sound just like those glory hounds at County."

He had never raised his voice to Monk before. "If you knew half as much about the procedures of police work as you do how to dress, I think that would be obvious. We are following orders, Monk, *proven police surveillance*, and it's time you and half of Kansas's law enforcement realize that. This isn't about shootouts, high-speed chases, and all the other crap the media throws at you and everyone else. This is reality, and of all people, you should know that by now having policed this backwater town. If you're looking for thrills, well then, you're in the wrong profession."

He stood with a file in hand and slammed it on his desk. Monk was transfixed in uncomfortable fear, and Ran leaned forward to let loose with another barrage. "What is it with you people? Do you think there is some miracle formula to suspect apprehension? Thank God we're in the sticks; you wouldn't last five minutes in the inner city."

He paced the floor in rage. It was a long time coming, years really. Ran had been kidding himself, thinking he was at home in Auburn, away from the pressures of LA crime. They hadn't needed him; he could do without them. It had all been a huge lie. Ran was built for investigative pursuit, and he had lived for the daily grind of success and imminent failure. Kansas had been a huge mistake because he wasn't Andy Taylor, content to fine jaywalkers and jail the town drunk on occasion. It had boiled behind a mask of acceptance, and now, he was letting it spill over. Monk just happened to be caught in the explosion.

"Let me remind you we are not up against your average criminal here. This guy didn't litter or pass out drunk in his neighbor's lawn. He's *killing* people. Tearing them to pieces. He is intelligent and resourceful, and we can't expect him to come walking in here and apologize and promise he'll never let it happen again. Face it, Monk. This is a whole new ballgame, and the country folk approach isn't going to cut it this time."

"I...I know how dangerous..."

"No, Monk," Ran said, "you don't know. No one here realizes what they're up against. *No one*. That's what is so disappointing about it. Everyone thinks there is a horse out of its fence, but this one is a murderer, and he's going to keep killing until he is tired of us. Then he's going to move on like he has always done and start all over again, and there is nothing any of you can do about it until you realize that."

Ran stopped, his passion released, and let his last words hang in the air. He had never intended on unleashing on Monk. The deputy didn't deserve being berated, but for the moment, Ran was past caring about his feelings. Monk represented everyone that thought they had a handle on what was happening, and they were sorely wrong. *If they only knew*, Ran thought. He exhaled heavily and stood at the window.

After a time, Monk said, "I'm sorry, Sheriff. I didn't mean anything by it. I'm just trying to understand."

Ran's anger immediately turned to regret. Monk hadn't deserved any of it, and he chastised himself for bringing his frustrations down on the one man in Auburn he had been able to depend on. He was loyal and held Ran in high regard. The tirade had probably cut deep.

"Look, Monk, I shouldn't have unloaded on you," he apologized, turning back to him. "We're all under a lot of stress right now. Forget what I said."

"No, Sheriff. You're right. We don't really have any idea what we're dealing with. We're ignorant about a lot of things, and sometimes we forget about the bad that's outside. That's why we are hoping you can help us. Sheriff," he appealed, and in the same breath became very animated, "you have to know what we can do."

"Monk."

"We're good people, Sheriff. Good people, and we don't take it lightly when there is bad among us," Monk explained. "We're just not used to it. You won't find a better group of people. Harder-working than most, but this isn't what we know. We don't act this way. We don't do these things to each other."

Ran felt terrible. "I want this as much as anybody. Really. I'm doing all I can."

Monk went on, looking hard into Ran's eyes. "I guess what I'm asking is, since you have been down this road before, is this the best way to go about it? What more can we do?"

"Like I said, we are following proper police methods. There is no quick fix," Ran admitted.

It was Monk's turn to look out the office window at the growing light. He stood reflectively. His shoulders visibly relaxed. "I don't believe that, Sheriff," he said quietly. "You have so much experience at this. There has to be another answer."

Ran wasn't sure what Monk wanted from him. The deputy had put him on a pedestal again, and Ran was expected to make things right. What he couldn't see was that they were doing everything short of lifting their search area at the corners like a blanket and shaking Caine out of it.

"These things take time. We have to be patient."

He spun on Ran, but his voice remained even. "We've been patient, Sheriff. We've been patient while our people die, while our stores and schools are vandalized. We've been patient."

He was adopting some of Ran's anger, and the fire that leapt from his eyes was impressive for the mild-mannered deputy. The sheriff shared his frustration, but they would have to wait it out.

"Monk, I don't like it anymore than you do, but trust me, we'll get him."

The deputy lowered his head and walked slowly to the office door. The straight-backed officer from the start of their meeting now looked tired and beaten. Auburn was his home, too, and he desperately wanted to protect it. If he thought Ran would be able to recharge him with an aggressive plan of action to spare its citizens, he had been mistaken.

"I'll call you this afternoon," Ran said, "and we can talk about this some more. For now, get some sleep."

Monk stopped at the door and looked over his shoulder at Ran. "Patient hasn't worked, Sheriff. It's time someone got mad," he offered. "I figured you already knew that."

He was out the door and gone.

He doesn't understand, Ran thought. *He just doesn't understand.*

Before he too could head home and get some sleep, Ran spent half an hour putting the finishing touches on his evening report. Finally, he crossed the room to put it away in one of the two file cabinets he had inherited as sheriff. The drawer barked with a high-pitched squeal of metal as he forced it open and again as it closed. Suddenly, he kicked it and brought his open hand down on it for good measure.

What more do they want from me?

He held his throbbing hand and paced around in disgust. The office, like the whole department, was incomplete, and still they expected him to deliver Caine. He had done all he could, and more, but what they wanted was a miracle, a bonafide water-into-wine from their willing but limited savior. None of them knew what he was up against.

As if on cue, Monk's words resounded in the air and mocked him. The deputy was concerned about his friends and family; his reaction had been born of emotion and not learned reason. Ran, Tara, and Sartin had gone the extra mile to bring justice to the citizens of Shawnee County, using tried and proven techniques in the search for their killer. Police procedures with a history of success, forensic inquiry utilizing the latest in medical and chemical breakthroughs, and their determined efforts. They had made great strides, even though Caine's identity had been chanced upon. They had solved the riddles of the physical clues left at the numerous scenes. Together, they had defined their serial killer.

And we aren't any closer to catching him.

In reality, they had answered their own questions, but not the immediate needs of the people they were working to protect. There was no call for pats on the back, and no reason to gloat in their combined solutions.

They had gone nowhere.

He had come from the big city with the skills and experience a small town like Auburn would never test, and he had failed. Failed, and it had taken a green deputy to make him see it. Ran had only thought he was doing the right thing for Monk, for Polly, for the people he called neighbors.

Monk was right. It was time to get mad.

Ran left his office and headed to his car. He would go home and force himself to get a few hours sleep. When he awoke, it would be with a whole new game plan.

Chapter 39

Auburn was gathering itself from another fitful night of sleep as Ran made his way home through the increasing daylight. A sporadic flow of cars, trucks, and SUVs was heading south to the highway and jobs in Topeka while neighbors remained behind to collect their newspapers, water their drying plants, or prepare to deal with children in the final days of school's summer break. Business owners swept sidewalks and lifted shades to mark the new day. Stray dogs followed familiar paths of foraging.

A killer was loose, but routines continued.

Ran provided the obligatory waves from his cruiser as his charges sought reassurance that all was well in their little hometown. His presence may have instilled comfort, but if his heart had been exposed on the sleeve that hung out the driver's window, those who hailed him would have seen his doubt and concern. The night's work had been unrewarding, and they were no closer to catching their man. The only satisfaction that could be taken, and it was temporary at best, was that the rising of the sun signaled a reprieve for the wary, a collection of hours during which they could exhale and regroup in preparation for the darkness and potential death that was to come.

Talk in the media had degenerated to exploitative conclusions that "a vampire" or "night crawler" had settled in Kansas, fearing the daylight during its nocturnal siege on readers and viewers. Observations surrounding Caine's nightly activities stretched from the bizarre to the idiotic, and most were unprofessional and disruptive to the investigation. As a result, calls were flooding the Shawnee County phone lines as a mass hysteria overtook the otherwise levelheaded members of the Midwestern community. Suddenly, everyone was seeing monsters, implicating neighbors, and basically turning the case into a sideshow. The added coverage had only fueled the federal authorities' interest in taking control of the case and relieving Sartin and Kansas officials of further responsibility. It was only a matter of days, possibly hours, before an entire shift in command would be implemented.

Ran drew the police car into his driveway and dragged himself up to the door, fumbling for the house key as he went. He would allow himself no more than four hours after a lengthy shower, eat, and then get back at it. Nothing could be gained with him sleeping, but he was wise enough to know that a rested mind would be more beneficial.

The door gave way to the cool, dark interior and shards of dull light scrambled around his frame to make their way in ahead of him. Ran purposely left curtains drawn and shades turned down in his absence, allowing the house to retain its conditioned air during the hot summer months. It was economical in appearance, but he preferred the feeling of seclusion when his days ended, and the quiet, sealed house offered the perfect escape.

He closed the door and walked straight to the kitchen in the blackness, his mind's eye tracing the familiar path, laid his gun belt on the counter, and flipped up the light switch.

Nothing.

Ran snapped it up and down repeatedly but got the same answer.

Bulb's out, he concluded, and retraced his steps to the living room and its wall switch.

Again, nothing.

"What the..."

He considered that the electricity was out, but if that were the case, it must have happened recently as the house stood in a pleasant cool. Contemplating a visit to his bedroom closet and the breaker box, he stood in limbo over his odd predicament, his eyes beginning to acclimate to the dark shades of grey that dominated the house.

I'll need a flashlight, he thought, and then simultaneously his body convulsed with a heavy blow to his now-constricted throat as he went up and back in suspended flight. His feet kicked above the distant floor as he dangled helplessly before an immense shadow, his hands automatically clawing at the vise that hung him there.

Disoriented and unable to breath, Ran squirmed like a fish on a hook for what seemed like an eternity. His eyes, pointed to the ceiling, teared with the pain and his lungs fought for some small channel through which to extract air. He continued to pull and tear at the source that held him, and he could now discern the strong hand and sinuous forearm of his captor.

He would pass out soon, and in the few seconds afforded him, he identified the source of his agony.

It was Caine.

The world swam into oblivion, and Ran was unconscious.

When he awoke, he was seated in his recliner. The room was still submerged in dark hues, and Ran's vision, already hindered, took time to adjust to his surroundings. He could discern a faint sliver of light prying its way into the room, and as his head cleared from the grogginess, Ran could see it was coming from the drawn curtains. Whether it was from the morning or afternoon he couldn't tell, but he had the impression that only a brief period of time had passed.

He performed a quick mental inventory of himself physically and determined that other than a sore neck and difficulty swallowing, he would be all right. Almost instantly Ran was struck with the memory of his attack and sat straight up in his seat in charged defense, scanning the room for his assailant. Only now had he come fully alert.

From the depths of shadows Ran was unaware of came movement, high and to his right, from somewhere in the recesses of the house, and a figure soon loomed above him in dramatic fashion, a colossal blotting out of the few rays of sunlight that had worked so hard to make entrance.

Ran's first reaction was to stand, but he quickly thought better of it. If this was in fact Caine, recollection of the deadly encounters others had had with him kept Ran seated. Something told him it would be stupid to make any sudden movements, and that something was the first real fear he had felt since joining the force so many years ago. He had experienced discomfort, anger, empathy, and gratitude, but controlled terror was a nerve that had never been pricked. Ran knew the taste would be unforgettable.

As if to confirm his identity, the unbelievable shape drifted backward effortlessly and spoke. Ran noted its surprising fluidity and grace; it was an immense ship in a minute harbor, and it navigated with remarkable precision. Within the dark form, Ran was able to distinguish the muscular contours and mythical mass that the thing before him possessed. There were signs of human composition, but the shear size of various muscle groups put the shape in a class by itself.

It had to be Caine, and Tara had only grazed the surface of his potential transformation.

"Price." Deep. Resonating.

"*Sheriff* Price," Ran said with an emphasis that only made his predicament that much more bizarre. He was obviously holding no authority in this court.

"Price, you fascinate me."

I *fascinate* you? Ran thought. *Try sitting on my side of the room.*

He began forcing aside his fear in an attempt to appear calm and in charge of himself, though the effort was difficult. He had never been more intimidated; Caine's commanding presence was undeniable. Most striking was the tone of the voice that thundered from the silhouette; it was as if a bear had learned to speak. The words seemed caught in a trailing growl.

"How so?"

As Ran's eyes grew accustomed to the fain light, Caine's appearance became more apparent. The taunt skin glistened with a heavy sweat, and Ran could now see that not a single thread of clothing had survived its owner's recreation. Thick locks of matted hair flowed away from his face and disappeared behind his incredible shoulders. His hands flexed slowly as if in time with some silent pulse. The vision was all too real, and Ran knew he was a false move or a condemning voice from his last breath.

"Your persistence," Caine rumbled. "Most gave up early, but you...you refused."

"Let's just say I was curious," Ran replied, and he could hear the terror in his voice no matter how hard he was trying to calm it. It cracked and weakened under Caine's gaze.

The mountainous figure shifted its weight and the floor barked in protest. "Yes. Curious...but foolish. You're wasting your time."

Ran marveled at the conversational quality of his words, regardless of the creature that spoke them. It was difficult to separate the two. "I figured saving people's life was worth my time."

"*Wasting...,*" Caine howled with what appeared to be a flash of anger, but he was immediately back in control. "...time. I'm advising you to walk away, Price. Consider it a courtesy."

What Caine evidently viewed as a gift was awkward and out of place. But the entire case had been otherworldly, so in some bizarre way it seemed to fit.

"You're telling me to let you continue killing innocent people and do nothing? You seem to know a lot about me, so I would think you would know I can't do that."

"Then you'll die like the rest."

Clear and direct. There was no reason to doubt Caine's words; Ran had seen the results of his aggression, but he was never one to accept things at face value, however convincing. The detective inside him had to have answers.

"You seem to know a lot about me," Ran said.

"I have found it beneficial to know my prey, both the weak and strong among you. You present an interesting...challenge, Price. Senseless, but admirable."

Ran said, "Well, I am glad I have provided you some entertainment, and let me say you have been quite the challenge too, sneaking around and butchering unsuspecting people."

He had crossed the line. Caine moved toward him in menacing strides, his hands clenching and unclenching in rapid succession. "I could just as easily walk the streets of your precious Auburn in broad daylight, but for now, this suits me. Your fear. The apprehension. It's very satisfying."

His manner was steeped in self-assurance.

"Can you tell me why? Why all the bloodshed? Surely you can afford me that."

Caine stepped even closer, and now Ran could smell the musk of a wild animal. His eyes looked red in the growing light, and he partially crouched in a stance of both defiance and strength. If there had ever been any doubt who was the superior being, Caine was making it obvious now. Ran felt renewed waves of fear wash over him, and he involuntarily lowered his head slightly in deference to Caine's sheer dominance.

"From the moment I came into this world, my destiny was put into motion. Since the dawn of man, I've watched and waited, observing the rise of your species as it claimed dominance over lesser creatures, only to corrupt and destroy what it should have never been allowed to possess.

"You are inherently weak, an arrogant, self-righteous being that prides itself on intimidation and threat, allowing your false superiority to cloud your intelligence. You persecute, oppress, and victimize and have always demonstrated a willingness to sacrifice others for self. Man has failed, and the world must now be wiped clean of its imperfections. Those that survive will curse their mistakes and recall the days of judgment, but in time the species will forget of its former place and accept what will be.

"The time for a greater king has arrived, and there is nothing that can stand in my way. I was centuries in the making, a machine of evolutionary perfection passed down through the ages to awaken when man had proven unworthy. You and those like you had your chance, but your weaknesses have destroyed you. With my emergence nearly complete, the cleansing has started."

Ran had been in awe from the moment he had awakened, but Caine's words had truly left him speechless. What the hybrid before him was suggesting was biblical in its magnitude – a purging of the earth in the wake of a new order. Man's history was filled with stories of great floods and fires that sterilized an evil world, and science had proof of cataclysmic events that brought nature to an abrupt halt, marking a genesis and the ushering in of the next dynasty. It was the stuff of myth and archeological deduction, of oral traditions and primitive reactions to a hostile environment, of spiritual reminders and respect for nature's unpredictability, and it was standing in a heaving mass of muscle and sinew in Ran's living room.

What he was also struck with was the familiar chords of his professional voice, and this time he would listen to it.

There were two clear possibilities within Caine's oratory, and in light of everything he had heard and accepted from the sharp mind of Tara Phillips and the forensic evidence that supported her claims, Ran knew either was feasible but only one likely. Caine could be the most demented of serial killers in history or the link to a new race of men, an adaptive, ultra-primate with designs on the highest rung on the evolutionary ladder. If, though, he was the Adam of a new species, the task before him, like his new body, was monumental. What he was detailing would require the work of hundreds, if not thousands, of supermen like him to displace mankind and claim their prize. Unless he could self-duplicate, and Tara had never mentioned any such replicating feat at his cellular level, the idea was pure insanity. And what of the power of one mutation against the strength of an entire species, the most highly intellectually-evolved group ever to rule the earth? Did he believe he could pick us off one by one like we were toy ducks in a glorified arcade shooting game? Sure, he was having his way with the small-time law enforcement of rural Kansas, but what success would he enjoy in the face of an advanced military assault, complete with high-tech equipment and weaponry? The magnitude of the endeavor, coupled with the primitive methods he had employed in his search for victims and food, made the former the safest bet.

Caine, the subject of strange, genetic alterations unprecedented in the annals of scientific history, was more the subject for biological and psychological study than mythical reality. Whether it was the chemical changes occurring within him or the fault of a base and cruel society, Caine was completely insane. Homicidal, psychopathic, and a real threat to the lives of those around him, including himself. Ran was simply looking upon a physically unique version of the countless crazies he had tracked down and brought to justice in his twenty-odd years of law enforcement. He needed no more convincing, and he would accept nothing else.

This was what he was more accustomed to dealing with – a bold, brash, and dangerous killer, but vulnerable. It was this quality he would use against the man Sebastian Caine. Putting aside the anomalies and forensic puzzles, Ran recognized a criminal when confronted with one. He would treat him as such from that moment on.

Ran chose his words carefully. He had concluded that outward signs of weakness could end his plans dead in their tracks. The only reason he was still alive was because he had demonstrated characteristics that Caine respected; anything less could prove costly. He was walking a precarious tightrope.

"You offer me little in the way of choice, Caine. Do I call you Caine?"

"If that suits you, but the Caine you refer to is no longer."

"You say man has run his course, that his time has expired. I can think of a lot of people, including myself, that may not be ready to hand things over so quickly without a fight."

Caine growled. "I expected as much, and as long as you and the better among your kind remain in opposition, you only delay the inevitable."

"I guess it's just our stubborn nature," Ran voiced. "You said it yourself – we are a proud bunch."

"Pride kills."

"Seems like there is a lot of killing going on...and for too long."

Caine warned, "As I said, you will die like the rest."

"I guess I'll just have to take that chance," Ran said, his serious tone undeniable.

"You *are* fascinating, Price."

"*Sheriff* Price, as *I* said."

Caine hovered above him momentarily, his eyes drawing a slow course over Ran's face as if he was seeking some visible explanation for the sheriff's brave words. His expression, clearly discernable in the growing light, was marked with bitter hatred. Ran knew he had taken a huge chance, but Monk's words continued to haunt him.

"You are a stupid little man after all. I came to you with a favor, and you spit it back at me? I had hope for you, Price, but I see you are all the same."

He stood to his full height, and Ran imagined his head pushing at the ceiling in protest of the accommodations. "Regrettable, really, but not surprising," Caine said with casual indifference, and he turned to the door. Ran felt the need to return a volley of defense, but he let it pass with tempered reign.

Caine's hand fell on the doorknob, and then he looked back over his enormous shoulder. "Prepare yourself for vengeance. You will reap what you have sown."

A burst of light exploded in the room and he was gone.

Ran remained in his chair. His hands had been locked in a death-grip with its arms, and only now did he relax his hold. Caine's departure also signaled the surfacing of intense pain in his neck, and he drew his chin toward his chest in an attempt to stretch the fire from it, but it was no use. He had obviously suffered some deep bruising and would be impaired for many days, but thankfulness to be alive was the best treatment for what afflicted him.

The event was short-lived, and yet it burned in his mind as an epic journey, a lengthy trek that had ended in the vast recesses of a hell on earth. He had been granted permission to gaze into its mouth, look upon its fiery lakes and dark caverns of suffering, and the site had left him empty, and in ironic contrast, bitterly cold. Behind the eyes that had floated above him and had burned like red coals, Ran had seen a presence of immeasurable evil and calculated intent. Caine believed everything he said, was driven by a passionate desire to correct untold wrongs, and stood on the precipice of delivering a judgment reserved until now for the immortals. He was a fallen angel with designs on retribution.

Ran needed time to consider his options, but the recent meeting had shown him there was very little of it left, and he had to act immediately.

He struggled to stand and was greeted with a vertigo that pushed him back down like a rag doll. Caine had debilitated him with one hand; it spoke volumes of the condition of those victims who had not been so fortunate. Ran squeezed his eyes tightly and took a deep breath, willing the vitality to return, which it did in halting stages. In time he was in the kitchen, splashing cold water on his face and recapturing his wits. His mind was a blur of potential actions, but nothing seemed more important than recovering from the encounter, so he gave himself a few more minutes to strengthen.

With his first lucid action, he crossed the living room and stepped out on his porch in a vain attempt to follow Caine should he see him, and with it he recognized he still didn't quite have it all together. He was being irrational, and this was no time for poor planning. Instead, he would make some phone calls, meet with the very people that could relate to his encounter with Caine, and help him reach a decision.

Things were getting ready to move into overdrive. They would have to do something quickly.

Chapter 40

Within an hour of his encounter with Caine, Ran was sitting in the familiar conference room of the Shawnee County Medical Examiner's Office recounting his story to an exhausted Tony Sartin and Tara Phillips. They each cradled a cup of hot coffee as if it were a lifeline. None of them had been sleeping well, the two men especially, who were normally tossing and turning at this early hour since the night patrols had begun. Ran had called them and arranged the meeting, briefly explaining his morning and promising further details at his arrival.

Though tired, the two were highly alert as Ran told his tale. There was real conviction in his expressive voice, and though he looked ragged with his baggy eyes, he was recalling the entire event with Caine with remarkable clarity. They could feel Caine's presence among them after he finished.

"Whoa," said Sartin.

Tara agreed, "Remarkable. He has a definite sense of self even after all that has happened to him."

She scribbled some notes on a pad she had brought.

Ran pressed, "The question is: Is he the psychopath that I think he is or do we continue to treat him like some immortal out of a Dungeons and Dragons video game?"

Sartin was inclined to agree with Ran. "He's crazy. Classic nut case...and dangerous. I don't know if it's a result of the biological changes he has gone through or not, but we need to treat him with kid gloves. He sounds delusional," he said.

Ran went on, "I don't know how you want to handle this, Tony, but I think I have the best answer."

"He has definitely raised the stakes. What's your idea?"

The two men were leaning into each other plotting their advance while Tara remained reflective, listening to the officers argue their point until she finally interjected her position.

"Let me stop both of you right here before you make an uninformed decision," she said with an air of condensation unlike her. "I think you're missing some of the obvious implications here."

Ran countered, "He's out of his mind, Tara. You should have heard him. *Watched and waited since the dawn of man. Centuries in the making.* I'm telling you, his brain is fried and he needs to be stopped."

He looked back to Sartin. "What I think we need to do is..."

"*No, it's more than that.*"

Loud. Commanding.

The detectives snapped their necks with involuntary surprise at her words, their lips slightly parted in muted shock. The vibrant though soft-spoken doctor had let loose a previously unfired cannon. She had their attention.

"Hear me out."

There was no doubt that they would. Younger, comparatively newer to the law enforcement business than her veteran associates, Tara had still earned their respect from the beginning. Whether it was her self-confidence or the knowledge of a pathologist with twice her experience, she had never carried less weight in their private trifecta. Her importance was beyond argument.

"If you haven't noticed, the gung ho, armed presence hasn't worked to this point, and after hearing your story, I think I understand why," she started, gesturing to Ran.

"Some of the things he said were very telling," Tara went on while referring to her notes. "He implied he has been waiting to emerge, years in the making, you said."

Ran nodded, "Those were his words."

"Since the dawn of man?"

"I know. Crazy."

"He also indicated that he has a pre-ordained purpose. For whatever reason, he believes he is here to punish mankind for its actions, Zeus' lightning bolt or God's Great Flood, if you will. As if it is some holy function he is performing."

"Like I said, out of his mind," repeated Ran.

Tara looked at him hard. "Out of his mind...and into someone else's."

"What?" the two men said together.

"Don't you see it? He *is* someone else, a persona that was years in the making. The man that was Sebastian Caine would never have ranted like this. Caine is gone, mentally and physically," she explained.

"So he's just Sybil in a Hercules suit?" said Ran.

"No, no. Sybil had multiple personalities that each took control over a short period of time. Caine's new self has displaced his former self, permanently by all indications. It is clear that the new personality is a manifestation of the DNA mutations we discovered earlier. The years of confusing forensics and cross country serial killing were a testing ground for the new Caine, a time of knowledge-gathering and...practice, before the final assumption of the body.

"He is someone else entirely, using the information he gained while leaching off the first Caine. He was a parasite, don't you see it? A parasitic, evolutionary evil that is now seeking to complete what it believes is its reason for existence—destroying man."

"But where would it get that kind of agenda?"

"If we work through the logic that he is not a singular being but the manifestation of Caine's life experiences, then we would have to conclude that some event or sequence of events in Caine's life triggered the change, such a profound event that the reaction caused genetic alterations."

"Is that possible?" Sartin asked.

"I think the proof was standing in Ran's living room this morning."

"That or a hairless Bigfoot," said Ran.

Tara, who had learned to deflect Ran's humor when she found it ill-timed, looked at him with her now perpetual straight face.

"He indicated that you were an interesting challenge, Ran. That he made it a point to know the strong and the weak among us. That he was extending you a, what?...*courtesy*, to warn you off the chase?"

"Right."

"That supports the idea that he used the computer technician to further his understanding of the world before permanent entrance into it. He lurked in the shadows of Caine's subconscious, choosing his moments of test-drives until he was ready to take ownership."

"And you believe this was all the result of some life-changing scar on his psyche? A complete biological change because his father spanked him too hard or his girlfriend cheated on him?"

"I would venture to say it was something much more significant than that, and not a single occurrence but years of compounded damage."

Sartin interjected, "Is there any science to support this?"

Tara reveled, "To this degree? No. But we have volumes of examples of patients who have shown measurable signs of mental and physical change due to catastrophic event or illness. I think this whole mess has given you a few gray hairs, Sheriff, if you need an example."

"I think Tony was referring to something substantial," Ran said, though he unconsciously dragged his hand through his short cut hair. "We all know you can give yourself an ulcer worrying over things, but this? This is a two-foot crater through your gut."

"Any psychiatrist, even your profiler, would be able to give you dozens of examples of complete mental breakdown and personality disorder resulting from severe emotional trauma. Disassociation and hyperarousal are prime examples of threat and adaptive response. As for physical responses, these are not as common but not unheard of. Chronic pain is most prevalent. Headaches. Body aches. Some studies have linked tumorous growths to high stress levels. Nothing like Caine, but then again, I don't think there is anything to this point like Caine. He is an anomaly."

"Anomaly is putting it mildly," voiced Ran.

"Whatever he is, whatever forces are at play here that caused his disease--and don't think it is anything other than that, a disease--he must be handled in a way different from what you two gentlemen are used to."

"How so?"

"Let's go back to his statements about Ran being fascinating to him and an interesting challenge. What did you take that to mean?" Tara asked him.

Ran considered the question for a few seconds. "It made me uncomfortable for one thing. Here's this monster with what may be my entire background in his back pocket," Ran started, and then with a crooked smile, "If he had had a back pocket."

No one was amused.

"I don't know. It's strange. You'll think I'm ridiculous."

"What?" said Sartin.

"It's like he saw me as his equal, better than the rest. A worthy adversary, I guess."

Sartin snickered.

"I know. I know."

Tara said, "I think you hit the nail on the head."

Silence, but two sets of eyes were on her in need of clarification. Tara was quick to deliver.

"For some reason he respects you, Ran. Not as a lawman but as a human he believes superior to others."

"We'll now I know the guy's insane," said Sartin.

"Shut up," Ran smiled.

"It's not funny, gentlemen, and it especially shouldn't be to you, Ran.

He may see you as a superior male, but he also views you as his greatest threat to success."

"What have I done to deserve that honor?" Ran asked seriously.

"Somehow he has deduced, either through the computer capabilities of his original self or just an intuitive side that came with his condition, that you stand between him and the resumption of his duty, his self-proclaimed destiny. Out of respect for you as an alpha male, he gave you a chance to walk away, to vacate the territory. It's a very natural, primal impulse. Remember, I told you the forensic evidence was pointing to an animalistic behavior. This morning was a warning. It's like a male lion growling at all potential pretenders to the throne. *Back off. This is mine.*"

"So he wants to fight me? Hell, he could have snapped me in two when he had the chance."

"No, that would not follow the role-play. He would prefer not to fight you, though he will if he has no other choice. Today was an opportunity for you to avoid a physical confrontation."

"I wouldn't call what I had this morning a choice."

"He expects the future to dictate the choice you made, I'm sure. The next patrol, the next surveillance, will mean you have made your decision. The next move would then be his."

Ran looked at her with understanding. Her sudden hostility in the beginning was justified.

"He would come looking for me."

"As well as he seems to know you, I would say he could take you at any moment."

Her words hung in the air with an incredible weight.

"This morning only reinforces that. It is more reason than ever to choose your direction carefully."

Ran and Sartin had jumped into a discussion of possible responses to Caine's morning revelations, failing to take into consideration the true nature of his twisted dialogue. The serial killer had fixated on Ran as the lead officer in the search for him, apparently for the entire time law enforcement had sought his whereabouts, and was giving the Auburn sheriff the opportunity to walk away without fatal consequence. It was the consideration extended between dominant males in the animal kingdom, whether for territory or females. Any actions taken from here on out, positive or negative, would reflect on Ran. Decisions would have to be carefully weighed.

"Well, I think it is safe to say that any aggressive moves will be viewed as hostile and worthy of attack," Sartin said. "That eliminates all the night patrols."

"Then how are we going to stop the guy if hunting him down is going to only make things worse, especially for me," Ran said.

Tara reflected, "It is clear he has his eyes and ears on everything, apparently always has. Your patrols would have continued to be unproductive while he kept killing. I don't think anything conventional is your answer."

"What then?" Ran said.

Tara shook her head, "I don't know...I don't know."

The three sat in silence yet again.

"Damn," Ran stood in frustration and began to pace the room. "Everything I think of calls for deploying officers, and he is bound to see that."

"See it, hear it, smell it. His mutation has reverted him to the most basic of sensual reliance while he has retained the evolved intellect. He exhibits the best of all characteristics, human and non-human," Tara said. "I think the best approach is to treat him like an animal with advanced survival capabilities. Only the sky's the limit on what he can do."

Sartin interjected, "Maybe we should look at this from the other side—what are his weaknesses?"

"He's not a very snappy dresser."

Tara said, "If you qualify him as a psychopath, then he is an emotionless predator, detached from the world and the victims he pulls from it. They tend to be fearless and exhibit self-control issues. I read that they can be like a high-speed car with poor brakes. There are four types, and I think we can eliminate some of them immediately. For example, he is not vulnerable to stress, uncommunicative, or charming, which actually narrows him down to what is called a distempered psychopath."

"What's that?"

"Quick to anger. Gets a rush from his kills, almost a sexual pleasure. Finds satisfaction in taking from others, as if with a sense of entitlement. The monster of our society—literally," Tara explained, and then she referenced Ran. "He described himself as a tool of vengeance, didn't he?"

"Something like that. Yeah," said Ran, "like he was punishing us."

"I thought earlier he had a motivation for all of this. I think revenge is it."

"Revenge for...?"

"Who knows?" Tara said. "It's his agenda, and we may never know how it all began, but he is out to right a great deal of wrong in his former life, that's for sure."

Sartin regressed, "So how do the weaknesses help us?"

"Let me turn that question right back at you. How do you guys normally deal with a psychopath?" Tara asked.

Sartin quieted, "To be honest with you, we've never had a full-blown psycho in Shawnee County since I've been here. Every murder I've ever investigated was a crime of passion or a premeditated death. This is out of my experience."

They both looked at Ran.

The former Los Angeles detective spread his arms. "Don't you think I've considered that? I trained among some of the chief investigators of the Zodiac Killer and Hillside Strangler murders," Ran said. "We have been following standard procedure. Tony has done this in textbook fashion, and I can't think of a better way to handle it."

He sounded as frustrated as he looked, and his defensive tone was understandable. Caine presented a unique situation, one that would probably test the most seasoned profiler. Ran fell back into his chair defeated.

They were lost. It seemed Caine would be free to fulfill his destiny, killing at will and leaving an unbroken path of destruction through the plains of Kansas. Victims would be the weak and the unworthy, those deemed inferior in the fiery eyes of Sebastian Caine, or what remained of him, judge and jury forever more. That was, unless, someone could figure out a way to stop him.

The answer evaded the combined experience of the two lawmen that sat puzzled in the medical examiner's conference room. A show of force or continued patrol meant death, for more than just Ran in all likelihood. They shrugged in helplessness.

As she had done countless times before, Tara provided the clear, almost elementary answer.

"No way," Sartin barked. "Too dangerous. He'd kill him for sure."

Ran stopped him. "Now wait a minute, Tony, I think she's right. It's the only option we have."

Sartin look at his friend and appealed to his reason, knowing full well the choice had already been made. "Ran, you're as crazy as he is if you do this."

"You know it's all we've got."

Tara said, "He's just hardheaded enough to make it work, Lieutenant."

She looked at Ran seriously. "This isn't a game, Ran, and if you make one false step, he's going to have a hard time getting to you because I will already have kicked your butt."

Her voice cracked slightly. It had been a hard thing for her to suggest given her feelings for Ran. Everyone in the room knew it, especially Ran. Her eyes had glazed slightly.

"Don't worry, Doctor," he said, reaching for her hands. "You're going to have me to boss around soon enough. I promise."

Tara looked away to gather herself, uncomfortable in the vulnerable moment.

Sartin said, "Ran, are you sure?"

He stood up from her and turned. "Let's put the wheels in motion. How much time will you need?"

Sartin paused in thought, checked his watch, and rose from his chair. "At least the rest of the day. I don't think anything of this magnitude has ever been considered. The logistics are mind-boggling."

Tara joined them. "That's the whole idea."

Chapter 41

Summer was nearing the end of its yearly assault on the plains of the central states, mercifully yielding to the short reprieve of the seasonal cycle and heralding the arrival of its bitter alter-ego whose frigid temperatures and sweeping snowfall would lessen the uncomfortable memories of the dog days. Evenings were beginning to provide cool contrast to the day's heat, a sure signal of fall's approach and one of many signs of change ready to befall the region. Children were already lamenting the start of their nine-month imprisonment while parents privately celebrated. Storefronts sported makeovers in line with changing needs, and companies recovered their full workforce as last-minute vacations drew to a close. Farmers were completing the final harvest of what had been average production, readying the soil for its dormancy in some areas while taking advantage of those crops that thrived in the last possible weeks of bounty. It was a time-tested and all-too-familiar segue.

The visible nuances of nature's changing landscape stood as the greatest indicator of alteration. Grasses, their roots lengthening in search of life-giving moisture as their tips browned from sporadic rains, welcomed the dew-laced mornings with green relief. Their larger cousins were beginning the slow process of drawing back from their outer extremities and ceasing growth, taking with them what water was becoming available as they readied for another period of simulated death. The air filled with the blooming aroma of colorful perennials that thrived on the comfortable degrees offered with the setting sun. Foraging animals were busy in instinctual preparation for the pains of decreased supply while demand remained a constant.

The world was in flux, and those that called it home prepared themselves for its pending death and glorious rebirth. It was a vibrant phoenix, but once exhausted, would seek repose until it was called forth yet again. The circle was closing, and nothing could stop the strong tide of change.

For Ran and his friends, it marked a pivotal time as they prepared to try and bring another critical cycle to an end; this one, though, was far from natural. Sebastian Caine was a force spawned not from a circle of life but of surging death, a torrent of dark evil and sinister elements that was gaining momentum in an unchecked fury of human destruction. There would be no renewal, no growth from the path he left behind, only misery and emptiness. The land Caine would ravage would never again spark growth. In his unfertile clutches, cold fear alone would survive. He was the antithesis of life, and unlike Mother Nature, he followed a perpetual line into an eternal winter.

While Tony had headed what was believed to be the first use of martial law in Shawnee County, Ran had initially coordinated Auburn's response to their plan and then spent the last few hours prior to its enactment in what could best be described as a crash course of scientific study with Tara. As Tony had suggested, the logistics of their idea had proven a major stumbling block, and it was still not clear whether they had received full cooperation, but little could be done in this late hour to ensure the absolute safety of the stubborn few who had chosen to ignore the requests of their local police. If things went as they predicted, no one would be in immediate danger, but it was discomforting to know that any unforeseen problems would potentially jeopardize the well-being of citizens. It was a huge risk, and the military equivalent of collateral damage was an outside possibility. Only a select few were made aware of the potential setbacks.

The administrative leaders of the cities and counties had been the hardest sell, and in some cases, had washed their hands of any future wrongdoing in typical Pontius Pilate fashion. It would be Lieutenant Sartin's final act as head of the overall operation to capture the serial killer, and federal agents waited expectantly for his removal and the implementation of their own high-level operation. The only thing standing in their way to this point was the fed's long-standing tradition to allow local law enforcement to recognize their own incompetence and shortcomings. Faced with failure, they would bow to the true professionals whose secretive society would provide state-of-the-art, time-tested results.

They had scoffed at the threesome's plan, citing numerous examples of profiling that argued against its success. But federal authorities, like other agencies involved, remained ignorant of the true nature of the killer. To them he was just another psycho murderer.

The scope of their idea comprised hundreds of personnel--police officers, administrative assistants, special operations units, medical staff, and state and county authorities--and had taken the entire day to put in place. It had been rushed and loosely organized, and their fear was that they had missed an obvious loophole. Sartin had put his reputation and potentially his job in question with its mere suggestion, and it was viewed as the last act of a desperate man. There were lives on the line, too, mainly Ran's, and this reality only heightened their anxieties.

Once started, the plan was irreversible. Should it fail, they could very well accelerate Caine's psychopathic obsession. The reward was worth the danger, but the cost could be unimaginable.

This and more circulated through Ran's mind as he took his position, the setting sun a fitting backdrop to the pending confrontation.

Sartin resumed his location at a temporary command post having fulfilled the first phase of the scheme contrived in the medical examiner's offices that morning and revised prior to initiation. His role would be superficial from here on out as he could only sit by and listen to the events unfold. Should the situation become volatile, he could order an immediate withdrawal and end to all operations, but it was agreed that most of the men deployed would be on their own while inside the perimeters of the designated zone. It was all so unpredictable, and Sartin sat nervously in anticipation of what he could no longer control.

Tara, too, felt helpless. For the last few months, she had been the driving force behind the search and scientific explanation for the killer that had confused and avoided authorities for years. It was during this time that she had met and fallen in love with the Auburn sheriff, a man she had done her best to prepare for the apocalyptic sequence of events that were about to unfold. He had placed his trust, his very life, in her hands, and like Sartin, she had no further stake in what would be. She tried to busy her thoughts with the medical frenzy that would follow her discovery, but her mind was ceaselessly called back to Ran and his safety. The beginning of his part in what had originally been her macabre playscript could start at any time, and it could last anywhere from seconds to hours. Nothing was in her hands, especially the fate of her future with Ran Price. She could only count on his skill and judgment.

Tony was to call her when it was over, regardless of the outcome.

Caine had not shown himself the entire day, though it was clear he could come and go with little chance of detection. What was not reported, too, were instances of forced entry anywhere within the perimeter he was believed to occupy. Businesses and homes stood unmolested by all accounts. This was not the first time Caine had left the communities alone, and it only added to his mystery and compounded his unpredictability. In some ways it was a positive sign for Ran and his crew as their plan counted on Caine's nocturnal tendencies, more likely if he had in fact chosen to remain isolated during the daylight hours.

The night was crystal clear and a gentle north breeze cooled the parched earth. The moon, in its three-quarter phase, spread its reflected light in diffused revelation, exposing a landscape of rolling fields, clutches of thick, entangled brush, and peaceful pockets of dwellings. It was in the latter that a preternatural silence hung eerily over the yards and connecting streets, normally alive with activity marking the end of another day. Among the homes were no outward indications of life, yet soft yellow hues burned in windows, suggesting habitation. Dogs failed to break the calm with their demanding barks, and the occasional passing car or vibrant sound of children at play was missing from the equation. The hum of florescent lights provided a hypnotic ease and familiar tone though failed to appease the unsettling nature of the moment. The peace that had fallen with the sun upon Auburn and its outlying sisters was out of place, even in this rural stretch of countryside. It was like a calm before a storm, tranquility dipped in preparedness. Nothing appeared wrong, but everything was wrong. The heart beat, but the body failed to show animation.

Something huge was about to unfold.

Centered in this picture of profound slumber stood the solitary frame of Ran Price, striking in the backdrop of emptiness that surrounded him. It was in many ways symbolic of the path that had brought him here and the new man he had become. Prior to his involvement in the policing of this quaint patch of Kansas pasture land, one that he now called home, Ran had been a detective of single-minded purpose and self-reliance. He had practiced his trade alone for many years, counting on his own brand of investigative justice. Rabid Randall, the relentless badger. It was only in the last few months of his epic journey that he had leaned on others, drawn strength from their support, and discovered the value of shared effort. It was during this, his own transformation, that he had found the meaning of friendship, the worth of colleagues interested in a shared goal, and the importance of love. It had been through Tony, Tara, Polly, and Monk, the skills and commitment of men like Tom Avery, and even his deputies Bobby and Chuck, that Ran had been given a fresh start and new perspective of himself. He had found that he could lean on others, that dependency was not a sin but a tribute to humanity. They were all in this together, and for the first time in Ran's previously empty life, he couldn't dream of it any other way.

Standing on a slight hill just northeast of Auburn in a wide field of recently plowed soy, the wind caressing his back with invisible support, Ran looked like a classic Greek sculpture—transfixed, rigid, purposeful. His arrival had been timed with the sun's complete departure, and he felt like an intruder on the quiet so painstakingly planned during the hours previous. Though similar to an actor making his appearance on an elaborate stage, Ran's entrance on foot was neither dramatic nor applauded. His costume was uninspired--his regular sheriff's uniform minus gun belt, and though the air offered a comforting cool, beads of sweat poured from his face in heavy streams and his shirt darkened with patches of anxiety. The only connection he had to the outside world was a tiny one-way microphone at his collar. A thin wire joined it to a concealed transmitter pack taped to the small of his back, and though its location was already proving uncomfortable, he fought the compulsion to reach back and tear it off. The next stage was underway, and he was isolated and vulnerable.

Ran surveyed the scene from his simple perch and found his eyes working well with he natural light afforded them. Acre upon acre of tilled and harvested soil rolled in steady waves in all directions, temporarily broken by solid tree lines of oak and maple and county roads flanked by barbed wire fencing. Off to his right was Auburn, frozen in illuminated repose. His eyes could make out the dancing flicker of headlights on the highway to his left, but it was the only movement he could discern from the landscape. Behind him lay a vast stretch of open pasture where his cruiser sat some two hundred yards away on an old dirt road.

With everything in place, Ran balled his fists in anticipation and allowed the imaginary curtain to rise on his performance.

"CAINE! CAINE!"

He repeated the name in long, deep shouts, his throat burning with the force as the syllables flowed across his tongue and out to their intended receiver. Ran turned his head side to side with the vocalization and tensed with every exertion. The herald's cry was piercing and strong, and in the vacuum of silence that the area had become, its effect was far-reaching.

Ran was calling him out (an *alpha male's challenge* in Tara's words), and it would be Caine's decision to either accept it or turn away. If what he had told Ran was true and he was acting with territorial aggression, he would defend his claim and honor Ran as a perceived threat. It was a primitive, instinctual response they were relying on. The rest would hinge on pure luck.

The call went out for ten minutes in Sartin's estimation, who listened with heightened concern. His friend sounded determined, his deep voice spiking the receiver's meter with its commanding tone, but the helpless lieutenant feared for his safety nonetheless. In fantastical terms, Ran was a modern-day exorcist, calling the name of his enemy to join him on a spiritual battlefield, but practically speaking, there was nothing ethereal about the vocal battle line being drawn now.

Caine was of substance, born of the real original sin, murderous and wholly evil. This was the true Armageddon.

When it seemed the repetitive summons would go on forever, there came an abrupt silence. For the longest, excruciating time, a painful void filled the previously thunderous broadcast. From Ran came nothing...then:

"He's here."

For Auburn's sheriff the next few seconds were surreal and captured as a frozen image of time eternal. From a clearing directly in front of him at a distance immeasurable in the hazy light came liquid movement, and from it a form emerged in distinct shape and purpose. The lunar glow provided to the landscape revealed the steady gait of what approached, a manlike structure of mythical proportion. Denied his earthly name, this advancing creature could be confused with the ancient Prometheus for his sheer size and appearance. As he closed the distance on Ran, it was obvious he had gone through another biological change, possibly the final transformations he had alluded to that morning.

From what Ran perceived to be seventy-five yards, he could clearly see that Caine had increased in height and weight, his musculature distinct and impressive. His bare feet met the ground in rhythmic thuds, and his arms kept time with the effortless stride. His dark mane trailed with unkempt abandon, and for a brief second, Ran wondered if his power rested in those Samson locks. His expression failed to reveal his intent, but his eyes were fixed forward, presumably on his challenger. He was fast and brutish and three of Ran, rolling toward him like an oiled machine.

Ran questioned himself a final time but remained fixed in his position, standing on the tracks as a human locomotive bore down on him. He had to exude confidence and his own measure of strength. Any show of fear, according to Tara, would be met with unmerciful regard.

Caine visibly slowed within thirty feet. He showed no fear or caution once he had broken stride, and his confidence was obvious. A ghastly smile parted his lips as he came to a full stop. His breathing was smooth and untaxed. Ran felt his own lungs constrict with Caine's presence. His clothes were soaked in unchecked sweat, and the device on his back seemed to be hanging to his skin precariously. Caine, in contrast, was bathed only in self-confidence.

Though Ran's feet rested on a plane well above his adversary's, Caine looked down on his opponent with mocking pride. "Price. I see you decided not to take my advice."

"Well, you really didn't leave me much choice."

"To live or die? I think your options were quite clear."

He'll measure you. Feel you out. It's part of the dance.

Ran filled his chest in mock defiance. "I think you underestimated me, Caine. I expected more from a man of your...talents."

Caine laughed. A hearty, unsettling sound. He turned his face to the stars sprinkled across the blackened sky and sent his amusement to the heavens. Ran shuttered uncontrollably, for just a split second, but was able to recapture his stalwart posture.

"And what do you hope to accomplish with this...this display?" he spit out as his arms gestured toward Ran's place on the earthen rise.

"Accomplish? Just making a point, Caine, like you did this morning. You understand that, don't you?"

He took a full step toward Ran. "You just don't get it, do you, Price? This may have been yours at one time, with your guns and your dogs, but this is mine now," he said evenly, his powerful arm sweeping the landscape.

He's going to know instantly whether you are telling the truth or just making empty threats. Don't threaten him; just tell him how things will be.

Ran held out his arms in a show of confusion. "Guns? Dogs? Do you see any of those things here?" Ran questioned, and then took his own step forward, lowering his voice in the process. "I told everyone to stay inside until I was done with you. It's what a man in charge can do."

He laughed pretentiously, a genuine effect, and surprised himself with its authenticity. "I didn't want there to be any doubts."

Caine looked him over with cautious regard for the very first time. This was a pivotal moment. If time were to be on their side, Ran's challenge would have to ensure the precious minutes that were required.

Tara had condensed her knowledge of psychopathic behavior in a sixty-minute session of disjointed facts and medical opinions with Ran, but it had all run together in a hurried attempt to prepare him for the night's encounter. Among other things, Tara had emphasized that Caine would follow no rules, that his actions were unpredictable, and that his state of mind would be highly volatile. He would most likely view their meeting in the dark fields of Kansas as a high-stakes drama, a game of mortality on which he thrived.

Psychopaths play the game in three stages, though there was no guarantee that Caine would do anything by the book. Phase One was nearing closer, as Ran was being assessed for his value. Caine would simply decide whether the sheriff was a benefit or threat to his environment, but all the while he would hold him in the highest contempt. Ran could never expect to win honor from the crazed killer because he saw himself far superior to everyone else.

Ran could expect manipulation to follow if Caine saw things unfolding toward new opportunities, the second step in the contest. The killer may try to seduce Ran, making him vulnerable to exploitation and deception. If Caine thought Ran might prove useful, he could pursue this path, and it would mean Ran would have to dance and deflect the subtle temptations. Tara thought this would be the best scenario and a timely exchange. She hoped the final stage would remain out of reach, as it was the least definable. Caine could tire of the game or believe his advantage exposed; either could prove life-threatening.

Ultimately, Tara reinforced her contention that Caine was unique. He could kill without warning, and if Ran was alive for longer than three minutes from the moment of contact, it was only because murdering him did not appeal to Caine at the time of opportunity.

"Make no mistake, Ran. Killing you would be like swatting a fly," she had said with serious description. "It all depends on the mood that strikes him. You've seen killer whales toss seals in the air over and over before devouring them? Remember: it's a game to him and he decides when it's over. He'll toy with you, and you have to respect him. He's not human, Ran. Far from it. He'll do whatever he wants, without reason, without regard for himself or others. He's fulfilling some twisted plan of dominance and destruction."

She had finished their lesson with an emotional discharge unlike her normal collected self. The long nights, the heartfelt expressions of care and hopes and dreams to come from it all, had tested her greatly. "Nothing you say or do can stop him. Don't try to be a hero. Just buy Tony a few extra seconds."

She had started to cry, and he had held her in the time that was left them. It was her idea to cast him as the bait, and she was feeling the weight of her suggestion in its full force. He had promised her he would be fine. It offered little in the way of solace.

The seconds were dragging, even in the gaze of the monstrous mutation whose thoughts were not belied in his expression. Had Ran sold his story, the tale the three of them had conceived and staked his life on, or would Caine decide this once-fascinating human was a minor inconvenience that required immediate elimination? The next few moments might determine the fate of all of them.

Caine gave him a final, cursory glance and then looked across the open field at slumbering Auburn.

"They do what you say because they are weak. They don't deserve to live, yet you allow it."

He spoke with a candor Ran had not expected, his attention lost in memories of long ago. "They are detestable. Inferior, pathetic, vile creatures that ravage each other for no other reason than to feel better about themselves," he said with rising voice. "They serve no purpose. What value could you possibly find in them? Vessels of disgust. Shells holding hatred and jealousies, and you choose to support their existence."

His entire body was tensing with the oratory, and he turned back to Ran with a look of accusation. "Why would you perpetuate them?"

"I am one of them. *You*...you are one of them."

Caine's face contorted. "I am nothing like them."

Ran trusted his instincts. "You may be superior to them, but we're all men. We're all human. Inside us are the same evils, the same faults. You are only elevated by that knowledge."

"*No. I share nothing*," he yelled, beating his chest in a primitive show of force. "You've proven your unworthiness with your submissions. I am the new order. I have waited to rid the world of its imperfections. It is my destiny to break them, to break you, and spill the bitterness that rests within. Man's time is up. The cleansing has already begun."

He had guessed wrong. The volcano of raw fury in Caine was spiraling out of control, and the impending explosion was evident. Ran's mask of deception had been a fleeting dream, a foolish charade that was ending all too quickly. Their time was up, *his* time was up, and there was nothing left to do but retreat.

"You'll never finish what you've started," Ran said, his feet moving backward with short, involuntary strides. "You can't go on with this forever. There are more like me who won't be so easily eliminated."

"If the others are like you, my task is already complete," he said with venomous delight. "You will all know that I am invincible."

With a speed born of primal reaction, Caine grasped Ran below the shoulders in his two crushing hands and lifted him from his hilltop. He held him as a fragile prize, a gift to the gods for their amusement.

"Here, see your great man now," Caine barked to the sky. "Behold your failed evolution and prepare for the revenge earned through your trespass."

He was like a mighty thunder, pounding the air with his inhuman voice and shaking Ran with whip lashing emphasis.

Caine lifted him even higher, and with a force unlike anything Ran had ever felt, the self-proclaimed exterminator of mankind slowly drew his huge paws together, compressing Ran's lungs as his ribcage gave way to the pressure. His head throbbed with blood red fire from the constriction, and his eyes filled with burning tears of searing pain. In his years as an officer, Ran had given every waking minute in service, ignoring a life of his own while ensuring that of others. Suspended here, above the swimming lights of the town he had made a home, he was about to make the ultimate sacrifice.

The first gunshot echoed through the still night, breaking the silence and opening a large hole in Caine's back just below his shoulder blade. He dropped Ran in startled response and groaned with more anger than pain, spinning in defiance. Ran lay a crumpled pile on the ground at his feet.

From somewhere deep among the trees where he had listened to Ran call his name, a second shot was delivered with equal accuracy, this one catching Caine above his sternum. The killer of dozens staggered with the heavy blow. A third round followed a heartbeat later, emerging from a short brush pile three hundred yards southeast, impacting his left shoulder with shredding purpose, penetrating his chest cavity at the end of its path.

The marksmen, three snipers on loan from Kansas S.W.A.T., had covered two miles on foot while downwind from the contact location and undetectable to the greatest of sensory organs. They had completed the distance in less than fifteen minutes and stayed well concealed with their stealthy maneuvering and battle fatigues. With them they carried long-range rifles with high-powered scopes. Their headsets delivered orders from the command post, and they had been given clearance to take out their target no more than thirty seconds after establishing their dispersed positions.

Roadblocks miles outside the established perimeter in all directions and the tireless door-to-door law enforcement demands for citizens in Auburn and surrounding neighborhoods to stay within their homes during the one-night curfew had ensured that residents in the area would be out of harm's way. The overall effect of the stagnant environment was to impress Caine with Ran's superior position in the territory he laid claim to while giving Sartin's men unbridled room to operate in a public-free venue.

Tara's directions had been implicit, based on her examination of the ritual behaviors seen in the animal kingdom. Territorial males defended their concerns with a great tenacity, challenging all pretenders to the throne with little doubt of their intent. Vocalizations, shows of strength, and submissive displays from their charges were primitive signs of superiority, and Ran had needed to appear equal to Caine for their unstable plan to have a chance. Rarely did these confrontations escalate to physical attacks, but when neither proved the victor, a fight, sometimes to the death though not normally requiring completion, was necessary to crown the true leader. Based on Caine's violent history, they feared he would rush to the final level with little regard for primitive etiquette.

With a muted Ran lying unmoving on the battlefield, it was unclear whether they had been too late to stop it.

The bolt-action rifles continued to deliver their deadly payloads, and with a headshot that drove shards of shattered bone deep into his brain, Caine dropped to his knees with a heavy thud. His arms reached southward toward his afflicters, and a growl issued from his bloodstained lips. The death cry was long and agonizing, and it seemed to beckon to a greater power to answer his appeal.

He had come full circle, from victim to predator to victim once more, a casualty of the world that created him. Here, kneeling in supplication on the bare earth, his mutated life force ebbing from a dozen different wounds, there was nothing left to fear.

Born into a lonely world, he left it in much the same way.

Chapter 42

The autopsy of Sebastian Caine sparked little in the way of medical or investigative interest. Dr. Tara Phillips' findings revealed some biological anomalies, but too few to provide answers to his psychopathic behaviors. The brain showed indications of hemispherical separation, which was standard in the criminally insane. An enlarged heart, overactive glandular production, and a skeletal structure demonstrating advanced growth were not unprecedented and could be found in numerous pathological studies. DNA and other chemical analysis failed to uncover the genetic mutations that Phillips had tracked during Caine's killing spree. Without definitive proof that previous samples matched those acquired at autopsy, the killer's completed cellular transfer was undetectable. The primitive gene that had traversed thousands of years of human evolution and was released by some unknown emotional trigger had escaped responsibility.

Local, state, and national media were provided superficial information in connection with the serial killer's demise. Linked to a string of murders along the East Coast and most recently in the Midwest, Caine had been pursued vigorously for years, always a step ahead of law enforcement, until his identity was determined thanks to the efforts of the Shawnee County Sheriff's Department and Lieutenant Tony Sartin, who, under the close supervision of federal authorities, brought the killer to justice. Caine was tied to dozens of brutal murders, and it was believed that number would increase as forensic investigators and criminal profilers evaluated the hundreds of unsolved crimes still on the books in the same path of his crazed destruction. Questions as to the motives for his actions were debated on every major news network and talk show, though in time, Caine was enthusiastically placed in the historical archives of famous mass murders along side the twisted minds of men like John Gacy, David Berkowitz, and Charles Manson. Whether he deserved a special place in the annals of criminal history was inconsequential; the police had wrapped a tidy package of explanation, tied it with a bow of believability, and placed it in the hands of a gullible public.

Justice had been served.

Tony Sartin was uncomfortable with the attention he received for spearheading the successful operation, knowing it was the concerted efforts of Ran and Tara that had brought the horror to an end. He had reluctantly agreed to keep their involvement secret so as not to muddy the waters of the final reports and keep the truth under the radar. If asked to discuss their findings, it was believed a scientific frenzy of disbelief and reprimand would result, jeopardizing Tara's position and uncovering some of Ran's old wounds.

"Bask in the sunshine, Tony. You earned it," Ran had said to him that afternoon with a pat on the back before heading back to Auburn.

Sartin had feared it would be the last time he would see his friend alive, and when he had heard the groans of Ran and triumphant screams of his assailant, he had been sure of it.

They had been ordered to approach the area slowly, unsure of Caine's condition and unwilling to expose anyone else to potential harm. Once the first of the sniper's had confirmed the kill, medical units were immediately dispatched, along with teams from the sheriff's department to cordon off the location. Since they had removed all signs of a police presence within the perimeter to give credence to Ran's claims of supreme rule, it took an agonizing five minutes for help to arrive for the fallen sheriff. He was found unconscious and in shock, his breathing dangerously shallow. Paramedics were able to get him stable before transporting him to Topeka Medical, but it was touch and go the first few hours. Tony and Tara waited impatiently for word of his condition, pacing nervously in the waiting area and regretting their decision.

It was a few hours later that they were allowed to see him.

Ran's injuries were extensive. Both of lungs had collapsed, one due to a perforation from five broken ribs. His left arm was crushed above the elbow and required numerous pins to bring the bone together; the other arm had fractured. He had also suffered a concussion in his fall from Caine's grasp along with cuts and abrasions. Doctors had promised a full recovery, though the healing process would be lengthy.

Tara took time off to stay at the hospital with him, where he drifted in and out of a fitful sleep for three days. His pain was extreme and drugs kept him groggy and confused for an additional week. Finally, after a stressful period of reassurances from the hospital staff and the agony of seeing Ran so helpless, he began to show signs of healthy recovery, and within a month he was on his feet and at home, a walking ball of energy wrapped in plaster and slings.

Sartin had been able to deflect the majority of questions that circulated in the private and public communities regarding Ran's role in bringing Caine's years of killing to an end, and with the help of a few close friends, he was able to fabricate a believable story placing Ran at the scene by coincidence. Auburn's town council recommended a citation of bravery, and soon everything was back at his gradual, easy pace.

Subsequent visits from Polly and Monk during his convalescence assured him that the sheriff's office was running smoothly, though it was the time spent with Tara and his friend Tony Sartin that kept his spirits alive. To him, they were the reward he had been granted.

After two more months of rejuvenation, Ran was back at work. His left arm hurt with the changing temperatures and was to become a frequent reminder of the past, but he considered himself fortunate nonetheless.

"Do you still think about it a lot?" Sartin had asked him one evening as they sat on the back porch of Shawnee County's newest captain, drinking a beer as the kids played whiffleball in the setting sun. "Do you ever relive it?"

"No so much any more," Ran reflected. "But sometimes I'll wake up at night, sit straight up in bed, and it's like I can hear his voice. Distant. Accusing. That usually puts an end to my sleep."

"I'll bet. Man. I'm so sorry, Ran. How do you get away from that?"

"Just like this, my friend," Ran replied. "Just like this."

He watched the boys in the yard and smiled along with them.

The relationship between Ran and Tara grew as quickly as his body healed, and though they had resumed their busy schedules, they always found time for each other. Tara's reputation in the medical examiner's office advanced with the seasons, and she soon became the go-to pathologist in a five-state area when it came to tough explanations of death. She loved her job, and Ran's pride in her was only surpassed by his love.

They rarely spoke of the summer that brought them together, except in reference to their first meeting or Ran's uncomfortable reactions to her extroverted nature. What mattered was that they had found each other. In a world frequented by pain and darkness, a measure of goodness and light had been shed upon them.

One night, after a relaxing dinner at Dalton's, a memory they encouraged, Ran suggested they take a short walk down Auburn's lonely main street. He had been quiet most of the evening, and Tara could tell he was troubled somehow. After a few minutes of silence, Ran squeezed the hand he was holding.

"Do you ever wonder if there's more like him?"

Tara wasn't sure what he wanted to hear. He rubbed his arm absently with his free hand.

"I mean, could he have been the only one?"

Tara said, "Scientifically speaking? I guess there is always the chance that nature will repeat itself."

He was lost in thought.

"But the odds are astronomical," she added.

They walked half a block further.

"When I was standing in that field, and Caine was coming for me, I've never been so afraid in my life."

"You had every reason to be."

"I didn't think I was going to make it. To never see you again. And then I thought, '*I'll be damned if I let it end this way.*'"

"It must have been terrible," she said in a comforting whisper.

Ran nodded, "It was. You still owed me for your half of that first dinner."

She snapped her head to see his smiling face and then feigned a blow to his chest.

He jerked back in laughter. "No, not in the ribs."

She put on her best pouting lips, and he gathered her into his arms on the tranquil sidewalk of his hometown. He looked down into her eyes.

"Doctor, I love you."

"And I love you, Sheriff."

They huddled for a moment in the cold air before continuing their walk.

Everything would be right in their world.